Red Hawk Books

Certificate of Publication

First Edition. First Printing.

Title:	Uteless
Subtitle:	A Coming of Age Story
ISBN:	978-1-9160843-0-8
First Edition	2020
Dedicated on:	20th December, 2020
Dedication:	Steve Banister
Signed by:	Oscar Fovarge
(a.k.a.)	
Date:	20th December, 2020

MORE REVIEWS FOR "UTELESS"

"I'm surprised that names have not been changed to protect identities. As this is not a fair representation of our school, I am passing the matter to our solicitors." *Hamish Mackie B.A. (Hons), MA (DL), Head Teacher, Stonefield School*

"Haven't had time to read it all, but it's probably not bad. I hope you haven't ~~exajerated~~ ~~exxajerated~~ ~~exxaggerated~~ exaggerated your rugby-playing abilities though. You were never THAT good'." *David Jones*

"I've checked your spelling and added a glossary. Was I really that horrible back then?
This is not the quote to include. That's coming in a later email." *Bel xx*

"There's hardly any maths in it." *Yasmin Abbasi*

"Who cares? I was Head Boy and you weren't." *Matt Collier*

"This has made me furious with my husband." *Sonia Partington*

"How dare you! My lawyers will be in touch." *Rawley Partington*

"Watch it, kid. OK?" *Your dad*

"Let me know if you have any trouble with anyone mentioned in your book. I'll sort them out." *Grandad*

ALSO BY OSCAR FOVARGE

Novels

This must be earth

Poles Apart

Plays

We'll meet again, Lili Marlene

The Pygmalion Effect

OSCAR FOVARGE

UTELESS

Red Hawk

Red Hawk Books
London and Swansea

Red Hawk
Books

Red Hawk Books is an imprint of Red Hawk Media Ltd
whose addresses can be found at
www.redhawkmedia.co.uk

First published by Red Hawk Books in 2020

A catalogue record for this book is available from the British library
978-1-9160843-0-8

Cover design and layout by Adam Evans

For Ron and Laura
with heartfelt gratitude

If you can look into the seeds of time
And say which grain will grow and which will not,
Speak, then, unto me …

William Shakespeare

CONTENTS

Part One

Down Under

The unanswered question

'Life is what happens when we're busy making other plans.'

The Reverend Love teaches English but spends a lot of his time trying to make us think. 'What do you think about that quotation? Anybody?'

Nobody.

'Rawiri?'

'Um..., is this going the way you planned, sir?'

'Ah, very good. Turning the question back on me with another question. Chris. Any thoughts?'

'I'm too young to know.'

'Why do you think that?'

'Right now I'm living my life according to other people's plans.'

'What other people?'

'My parents and ... um... my parents.'

'That's a rather pessimistic view, isn't it?'

'It's my reality.'

'OK. Bran, what do you think?'

Chris turns his head to watch me. I know if I say something stupid he'll be on it as soon as we leave the classroom. He's a good mate, but he thinks I'm sentimental and naïve. Right now I've got a cracker that'll keep him quiet.

'My dad says that if you fail to plan, you're planning to fail.'

'Yes, good. I think you'll find that Benjamin Franklin was the first person to say that. OK, here's another one. "Everybody you meet is fighting a private battle that you know nothing about." Now, there is one more sentence in this famous quotation. I've left it out. Can you guess what it is? I'll give you a clue. It's three words. Anybody? Michael?'

'Leave them alone?'

'Not a bad guess. Rakesh?'

'So don't ask.'

'No. Yesse?'

'So shut up.'

'No, you're getting colder, so I'll ...'

He's interrupted by a loud, insistent bell ringing in the corridor.

'Start a fire?' says Rawiri.

The Reverend laughs. 'Very good. Right, it's probably a false alarm, but let's behave as if it's the real thing.'

Once all the kids have trooped outside and the 'all clear' is given, it's time for lunch. There's rhubarb crumble with custard for dessert and everybody's trying to wangle a second helping. It's no surprise that most of us have forgotten the Reverend Love's question, or the need for an answer.

Haka boys

You can't help liking the Reverend Love. He has a smile for everybody. Rawiri calls it 'nominative determination'.

'What's that?'

'It's like when people are determined to live up to their names.'

'You mean, Mr Love has to show that he loves everybody?'

'That's it.'

'Nom what?'

'Nominative determination.'

Chris doesn't take anybody's word for granted. 'How do you know that, Ra?'

'My sis told me.'

It makes sense to me.

'So it's the same with Mr Savage,' I say.

'How's that?'

'He teaches the *haka*.'

Rawiri laughs, but Chris looks severe. 'What's savage about that?'

OK, I'd better not go there, but it gets me thinking.

Does the Reverend Love live up to his name because he's such a box of budgies? He never gets angry, even if a boy's disrupting choir practice. Does he teach through kindness because that's the best way? Does everybody like him right back because they sense a genuine goodness? He sort of makes you think about what it means to be a good person.

Or is he called the Reverend Love because he's rubbish at tennis – and I mean seriously, eye-rollingly *bad* – even though he's head coach for all the school teams? 'Fifteen-love, thirty-love, forty-love, game, set and match', to whichever opponent the Reverend Love is playing, 'six-love, six love'. At least that's what happens when he plays me, and it's been happening ever since I turned thirteen. The captain of the First Six told me that the Rev does sometimes win matches at his local tennis club, but only because lots of members are even worse than he is. In fact, most only go there for the cucumber sandwiches, cream cakes and cosy chats on a

Sunday afternoon. But I sometimes doubt if the Reverend has ever held his serve against a Greystone College boy.

Mr Savage, on the other hand, knows everything there is to know about the *haka*. He's taken Greystone Seniors from Division Five in the Polynesian Festival all the way to the top half of Division Two. Promoted every year. If the senior *haka* team gets into the Premier Division any time soon, it'll be up to us juniors to keep the flame alive in years to come. So we practise Wednesdays and Saturdays, and always go to the senior sessions to see how it's done.

'*Ringa pakia!*' (Slap the hands against the thighs.)

'*Uma tiraha!*' (Puff out the chest.)

'Let me hear that big breath out!' calls Mr Savage. 'The louder the sound, the bigger the breath. Remember, you're drawing in the *hauora*, the breath of life. Again!'

'*Uma tiraha!*'

'Good!'

'*Turi whati!?*' (Bend the knees.)

This is where we cross our arms over our chests and shake our hands, getting ready for the big moment.

'*Hope whai ake!*' (Let the hips follow.)

'*Warwae takahia kia kino!*' (Stamp your feet as hard as you can.)

And we're off, pounding the floor with the soles of our trainers. Rawiri's got the lingo and a big voice, so he's our leader, shouting out the questions.

'*No nga hau e wha o Aotearoa…*! We are the four winds of New Zealand. We have arrived from Greystone College to obtain the knowledge.'

'What is the knowledge?'

'The loyalty, the friendship, the confidence together, the support of your comrades, these are the treasures of our journey.'

'Do you expect struggles before you?'

'There will be struggles, there will be battles. But we will follow our treasured aspiration. If we bow our heads, let it be only to a mighty mountain.'

'Are you willing?'

'We are willing!'

'Are you ready?'

'We are ready! We are strong!'

'Stop! Stop!'

Mr Savage gives us a patient smile. 'OK, I know you really want to be the rugby All Blacks doing the *Ka Mate…*'

He's right about that.

Ka mate! Ka mate! Ki oru! Ki ora! It's death, it's death! It's life, it's life!

Some of us have come straight from a rugby match. Greystone's Under 15s 36 St Mary's 9. We're still in our grubby kit. Chris has a graze on his knee and Ra has dust in his hair from the dry pitch. We all know the dream. Play for the College First XV, get picked for the All Black under-16s, the under-18s, and then… the dream.

Represent the All Blacks. Play in the Four Nations, followed by the World Cup. Beat the French in the semis, even if the ref's on their side and doesn't give you a single penalty in the second half. Then beat England in the final, 'cos revenge is sweet.

'Are you still with us, Bran?'

'Yes, Mr Savage.'

In fact, I haven't heard a word he's said and everybody else is grinning. Did he ask me twice?

'As I was saying, you have to show that you understand the words. "The loyalty, the friendship, the confidence together, the support of your comrades, *these* are the treasures of our journey." Don't just pound it out. Build it up. You want your audience to *feel* the meaning. Let's try it one more time.'

Before we can begin, someone behind me hums out a code we all know. It's the first bar of a song. 'Love is in the air!'

More sniggering, and I look around. Sure enough, there he is striding towards us from the direction of the chapel. Behind him trails Jinks, captain of the Second Six. We all know what they're after. They're carrying rackets, tennis bags, towels and plastic bottles.

Mr Savage has also noticed. 'Yes, Reverend Love. Which one do you want?'

'Young Kelleher.'

You'd think my mates would help me out, but they're grinning at my bad luck.

'But we've just played a rugby match, sir.'

'Then you'll be nicely warmed up.'

That's Mr Savage selling me down the river.

'Right, then, give it some jandal for the Reverend's benefit, but with the phrasing I asked for. One more time. After three...'

The other lads give it the works, but I have to admit I slack off. In a few minutes Chris and Ra will be back in the dorm eating Anzac and Afghan cookies and slurping L&Ps, while I'm out on court hitting balls with Jinks. Why can't they give me a break? We won our rugby match, smashed St Mary's, we're nailing this *haka* and tennis matches against the other schools are a doddle. The guys who choose tennis do it because they have to do something. They don't get picked for rugby, cricket, athletics, swimming or soccer, so they play tennis. Or their version of it: moonball kicked off with donkey-drop serves. I only got picked for the tennis team because the Reverend saw me thwacking a ball around on court after scrum practice one day.

'It's all right for you,' I say when we finish stamping out the "two steps upwards and the sun now shines".

'We'll wait for you, mate.'

They do, lounging on a grassy bank behind Jinks and the Reverend Love as they double up against me. Ra tries to put me off by imitating the Reverend's pat-a-cake overhead and weird little skips when he volleys.

'Come on, Bran, concentrate!'

It's not so easy when my mates are cracking me up. But then the Reverend surprises us all.

'I know it's not easy when the crowd is trying to put you off, but it's all part of the game.'

My mates look pretty shocked, especially Chris. He doesn't like to hurt people. The Rev must have eyes in the back of his head.

'Right, that's half an hour. Let's call it a day. Thank you, Jinks. Let's collect up all the balls.'

I can't help having a whinge as we toss the balls into a bag.

'Why do I have to do tennis practice, sir?'

'Because you're talented, Bran.'

'But I much prefer rugby, sir.'

'I know. But at this school we encourage and develop all your talents.'

'But we'll win anyway, sir.'

'That's not the point. I want to see you get better every time you play. And there are one or two sides we haven't played yet who've got a few decent players. You don't want them springing a surprise, do you?'

He has a point. The worst thing at Greystone's is to get beaten by King's or Lindisfarne.

I join Ra and Chris on the bank.

'You were putting me off.'

'But you look so funny waiting for one of the Rev's dollies to bounce.'

'Funny how?'

'Like all serious.'

'Tongue between teeth. You'll bite it off one day.'

'It's no joke trying decide on smash, volley or let it bounce.'

'It's the dread parabola of uncertainty,' says Chris.

'The uncertainty of what game the Reverend thinks he's playing.'

'But you are getting better.'

'I am?'

'Yeah, better and bitter.'

'It's all right for you. The Rev's got me doing everything. Choir practice, tennis, reading the lesson.'

'That's 'cos you're so good at it.'

'Anyway, stop whinging,' says Ra. 'If you kept your head down and weren't such a show-off, you wouldn't get noticed.'

They have a point. There are some kids who bottle it and lead a cosier existence. But what's the point of that?

We sit on the bank and listen to the silence before sunset. Even Ra keeps quiet when we do this. It's my favourite time and I think the other guys feel the same way. Behind us the school is quiet, as most kids are getting ready for the evening meal. We can hear a few guys beyond the treeline still out there doing hockey practice. *Pock, pock, slap.* Swallows skim the open green of the cricket and rugby fields. One evening last week a pair of black swans flew low over our heads then wheeled away towards the sea. Their wings took them past on gentle breaths and I heard Ra take a gulp of air. For once he said nothing, just stared. The things I remember most are their red beaks and the little creaks and grunts as if they were having a natter on the wing.

'That's freedom,' said Chris.

He's always saying stuff like that.

Back at Hillary House I run into Myers. For once he doesn't want me to make my bed properly.

'Bran. Your dad called and left a message with the Housemaster.'

Why didn't he just leave a message on my cellphone?

'He can't make it this Sunday, but you can go out as a guest of one of the other boys.'

'I'll ask Rawiri.'

'Make sure he asks his parents first.'

Ra says 'no problem'. Chris is coming, as usual. His parents live on South Island and only come up twice a term. But his mum sends fantastic parcels of Danish food once a week. We sit on his bed and chomp our way through the goodies, but I can't match Chris for eating hot dried chillies. He's the dorm's hot-food-no-drink champ. But the competitions do give him the hiccups.

I try Dad's phone, then Mum's. No-answer-leave-a-message on his. Mum's says 'out of range'.

Haka girls

Rawiri's family live out by the coast, north of Auckland. The house is near a cliff with steps down to the beach. Out back is a field divided into a pony paddock for his sisters and a mown area with a set of posts for rugby practice. Sundays at Ra's are all about rugby, swimming, eating and tongue-wrestling with his sisters.

They're a bit jealous that their only brother gets to go to a school like Greystone's. They call us posh and stuck up. If we brag about winning a rugby match, one of them points out that we only play against the other major private schools and a couple of state schools with a rugby tradition. It's no use arguing that these schools probably have the best teams. It's not our fault if the other schools don't take sport seriously.

Chris and I keep cool and never react, but Ra can lose it big-time. We're used to being shouted at and called names by kids from state schools. They use words a Greystone's boy would never repeat in public. But, for some reason, Ra gets riled up whenever his sisters start cutting him down to size.

'Don't rise to the bait,' says Chris. 'That's what they want.'

'But it's unfair!' blurts Ra.

'So? Life is unfair,' says Chris.

But, on this Sunday, the sisters are like different people. Their mum has gone off to visit her parents and Airini, the oldest daughter, is in charge. There's no Ra-baiting today. The mood is subdued and everybody's trying to be kind. Maybe one of the grandparents is ill.

'Have another pancake, Bran.'

'Thanks.'

Around midday Mr Kimura arrives in his ute, churning up a cloud of dust in the driveway, and bursts into the kitchen. He's big and treats most things like a comical emergency.

'Right! Shark and tatties. Who's coming with me to get 'em?'

We all want to go.

'In that case, we might as well eat in the restaurant.'

So we pile into the shiny new ute that my dad sold to Mr Kimura, and he treats us to fish and chips in the best beachside restaurant on North Island. There's a table waiting for us on a packed verandah overlooking the beach.

Airini doesn't want all her chips so she offers them to me.

'You need your strength if you're gonna play rugby.'

'So do Ra and Chris.'

'Yeah, but you're a bit skinny for your height.'

'My dad says I'll put on weight later.'

'Might as well start now. How do you cope anyway? Ra tells me you're a forward.'

'Yeah, number eight. I catch the ball at the lineouts.'

'That makes sense. Tell me, is he any good?'

She means Ra.

'He's quick and brave.'

'And him?'

She means Chris.

'Not so quick, but he's always there when you need him.'

'And are you boys really as good as Ra says you are?'

Mr Kimura butts in. 'Mr Greeff calls them his three musketeers.'

'Why's that?'

'When the ball's out of the scrum, it's their job to win it back or make sure they keep it. They're marauders!'

He puts his great big arms around us and ruffles our hair. We like that word. It makes us sound hard. Marauders. I like it better than musketeers, which – let's face it – is a bit French.

We're so full after lunch we get into swimming togs and jandals, go down to the beach and flop. Mr Kimura falls asleep and snores. He looks like a beached walrus. By the time he wakes up there are only two hours left before we have to be back at school. Being late for Evensong means big trouble, even when it's a parent's fault. For some strange reason, all the girls want to come with us, so we shower, get back into our school uniforms and climb into the ute.

Girls, I've discovered, like to sing when they travel. My mum used to sing all the time when she drove. I think it was because I was a small kid. Now I'm older she's stopped. Maybe she thinks I'm embarrassed, but I quite like it. My dad would sing too sometimes. But he's a quarter Irish, a quarter-Maori and half-Italian, so it comes naturally. Mr Kimura's a full Maori and he gets going as soon as he's in the car.

'You are my sunshines, my only sunshines! You make me happy when skies are grey…'

He's the only man I've seen singing a happy song with tears streaming down his cheeks. Even the girls are embarrassed.

'Dad!'

'There's nothing wrong with a few tears. Some of the greatest men in history were famous for crying.'

'Like who?'

'Abraham Lincoln.'

'That was a long time ago.'

'Winston Churchill.'

'Really?'

'John Kirwin,' offers Rawiri.

Silence. John Kirwin played rugby for New Zealand and became famous for cracking up.

Mr Kimura frowns. 'Be fair. He was ill. It wasn't his fault. But what about Brad Thorne when the All Blacks won the World Cup?'

'He wasn't crying, Dad.'

''Course he was.'

'Tears of joy.'

'Well, there you go then.'

When we get closer to school the girls start singing 'Po Atarau'. They must be doing it to see how much they can make their dad cry. They must know he can't deal with a farewell song. Which is a bit mischievous. Or maybe one of their grandparents really is sick. They almost get me misting up as well. Chris doesn't say a word. He gets like that when he's on the edge, like at Sunday evensong when we sing 'Abide With Me'. He goes quiet and his eyes well up. I guess he's missing his folks.

The school grounds look magical in the evening light with the rugby posts outlined against the pohutukawa trees.

Big hugs from all the girls when we reach the dorm. They've never done that before. Airini really hangs in there for a few seconds and gives me a kinda wet kiss on the cheek. Whoa! Too touchy-feely for me. It's not as if she's my mum, and even she knows where the line is.

Mr Kimura shakes my hand.

'Good luck, son.'

'Thanks for today, Mr Kimura. Really appreciate it.'

But I'm thinking, what the heck? It's not as if I'm going away.

Po Atarau

Chris sees it first. We're out practising kicks and catches, and Rawiri has just fumbled his second out of nine. If he drops a third he has to do twenty push-ups.

'Don't make it tumble end over end!'

He's seriously irritated.

'But that's what the kicker makes it do. Keep your eye on it and take it against your chest. You've got to smother it.'

'Isn't that your dad?'

Chris is gazing past me towards the avenue of maple and horse chestnut trees that skirt the practice pitches. A white and yellow vintage Holden is cruising the track. My dad imports brand new 4x4s, SUVs and utes from all over the world, but he's really a vintage car freak who just loves those 1960s station wagons from Australia. This one's got the windscreen sun visor and white-wall tyres. The chrome gleams and I can tell from the thrum of the engine that it's a recon job as clean as its two-tone upholstery with all the little stars in the fabric.

What I don't get is why Dr Manley, the head teacher, is in the car with Dad.

'Hi, son.'

'Hi, Dad.'

'Hi, lads.'

'Hi, Mr Kelleher.'

Chris and Ra are doing that for the Head's benefit. Otherwise, they know my dad as Bill.

'Bill Kelleher, ten percent down and utes on the road!'

That's what the ad says, and that's why most of the prefects never give me a hard time just for the sake of it. They'll be wanting their first motors in a year or two.

'Rawiri, Chris, I need a word,' says the Head. He's drawing them away.

'Not great news, Bran.'

'Mum?'

'Yeah, but don't get worried.'

'Is she ill?'

'No, well, yeah. It's nothing physical, not really. She's just tired. She needs a long rest. The thing is...'

I don't like it when he says 'the thing is'. I've seen and heard him do that with customers. The thing is, your cheque bounced. The thing is, I can only give you two thousand dollars in part exchange, because the thing is, I think you've been running this car too long without a service.

I've noticed that sometimes the 'thing' is a roll of bull's wool. As in: 'See how he fell for that? Most people don't keep up with their service schedules, so they feel guilty. I was just taking a flyer. I can re-sell those wheels for six thousand bucks, I reckon.'

'The things is,' he says, 'Mum's gone back to her parents.'

'In England?'

'Yeah.'

Why'd she do that? And not tell me? Nobody said a word.

'She didn't want you to worry, and I promise there's nothing to worry about. I mean, not like that.'

It's better when he promises, because he always keeps a promise. But I don't like the sound of 'like that'. Like what?

'And the thing is, she wants you to be with her.'

'How long?'

'Just for a bit.'

'What's a bit?'

'It's hard to say. But just long enough to get her strength back. She's staying with your grandad and grandma. Just resting up. That's why I couldn't come on Sunday. I was taking her to the airport.'

'Why didn't you phone?'

'We didn't want you to be upset, 'cos there's nothing to be upset about. Mum'll be OK in a while, and you'll get a nice trip to England.'

'What about school?'

'Dr Manley says you can come back at any time. If you have to stay a bit longer, we can fix you up with a school in England – temporarily – and you won't fall behind. And they're pretty nifty at rugby over there as well, so you won't miss out.'

'They're not that hot.'

'No, but it'll be an experience. Not many kids your age get a chance to travel the world like that.'

Sometimes you eat and drink a mixture of stuff that really should be kept separate, and you get that churning feeling in the stomach. That's what my head felt like.

'You all right?'

'Just a bit of a shock, I guess. I'll miss my mates.'

'Yeah, that's the worst thing. But look ahead. Your mum will really appreciate this. She needs you. And I can't be there because of the business. You understand that, right?'

'Yeah.'

'So I need you to do this for your mum and for me. I know it's a big ask, but sometimes these things happen and we need to deal with it.'

'Like a high ball we have to catch?'

'Exactly like that. Taking responsibility. None of us can always be strong. We need each other. Your mum and I need you now.'

'OK.'

'OK. We'll go back to the dorm and get your stuff, and I've booked you on a flight for tomorrow evening. First Class. You'll stay with the Harrises in Sydney for a couple of days. He's the guy who runs the Holden parts company. He's a good man. Then on to Singapore. You'll stay with Mr and Mrs Megat for a day. Then on to London. OK?'

'Why can't I go direct?'

'Because you'll be jetlagged and gaga if you try that. Much better to do it in stages.'

My dad's good at stuff like that. Really organised.

'The thing is, you'll probably be back by Christmas.'

Part Two

Up Over

England

Fly boy

Dad says I met my grandad when I was four years old, but I don't remember much about it. He says Grandad asked me if I liked ice cream, but he had a different accent and I couldn't understand what he was saying.

My gear comes through on the belt, including my extra bag with the skate- and ski-boards. Dad says I won't be able to skate on roads in the UK and there's hardly any snow. But I checked online and it said there are loads of parks and good beaches for surfing. At worst there are dry slopes for skiing. You never know, I said, there could be some good spots, so Dad forked out for the extra baggage, but he refused point blank to let me take the surfie.

'Too big. Hire one if you really need it.'

I start through customs in the 'nothing to declare' channel – nothing to declare except my brilliance at rugby. Should I really say that if they stop me? Maybe not. Right, left, left again. The sliding doors open and it's pretty weird, like being on the red carpet, or running out onto a sports field, except there's no cheering. Everybody checks you out, but nobody wants you except for one person.

I skim the hand-held signs. There's no Bran Kelleher. Look for an older bloke with grey hair. There's a sign for Bran Cooke. That must be it. He's got my surname wrong. How'd he manage that?

'Grandad?'

'Bran?'

'Yes, Bran Kelleher from Down Under, and my mum's Catherine.'

He looks me up and down, taking in my replica All Black shirt. There's more surprise than smile.

'Of course you are. Much taller than I expected. I'll meet you down the end.'

I get there first by a long way. Grandad Cooke is heavy and moves pretty slow, like the old rugby forwards who come to watch the matches at Greystone's.

'Have a good flight, did you?'

'Yes, really good. Apart from the delay. I travelled Air New Zealand to Sydney and Dad's friends took me to see a rugby match the day after. Australia Schools against Tonga.'

'Australia won, I suppose.'

'Yes, easy. Then Qantas to Singapore and London.'

'Feeling tired, are you?'

'Not really. Slept on the plane.'

'Right, then. It's a bit of a hike to where I'm parked. Can you push that by yourself?'

'Yes, no problem.'

I lean into the trolley and trundle it through the crowds.

'How's Mum?'

'Not too bad. Did Bill tell you how it was?'

I take a second or two wondering why he doesn't call him my dad.

'Yes, he said Mum's tired and needs a long rest.'

'That's about it. We're taking a left here.'

The noise of planes and buses hits us as a door slides open and I get my first look at England from ground level. It's grey and damp with puddles everywhere, exhaust fumes from the bus station and the metal-shearing scream of jet engines.

'Hungry?'

'Not much. They served us a big breakfast over Germany.'

'Lucky young man. I left home at four o'clock and I'm looking forward to my breakfast, or should I say lunch? We'll stop at a service station.'

I'm not sure all my luggage will fit into Grandad's car. You couldn't even see it when we came down the line of parked vehicles. I check out the make. You see them in New Zealand, but they're just not very practical. Dad calls 'em 'tinnies'. 'Use once, refill, use again, chuck away.'

'Right, then. Let's see how we do this. Luckily, I cleared all my tools out.'

It's not too bad in the end. He folds down the back seats and the big case just fits. The other one goes on top and my hand luggage slots down between the backs of the front seats. The prezzies I brought have to go on the floor between my feet. The front seat really is a bucket. It's like the recovery position, but in a chair. I've never travelled this close to the road before, except in a go-kart. Any closer and I'll be scorching my backside. I hope the floor doesn't collapse.

'You drive on the left,' I say.

'Surprised?'

'I thought you drove on the right in Europe.'

'Good point, but we're not European enough to drive on the wrong side of the road.'

I think he's joshing with me, but it's hard to tell.

'How far is it?'

'To home? Not far. About fifty miles. To the service station and breakfast, about ten.'

I seriously wonder if this tinnie will make it. We're in the middle lane and a black cab comes up the inside. Should I tell Grandad that the driver is waving his hand across his face, as if our car is letting out smelly farts?

I look over my shoulder. The air out back is definitely smokey.

'Anything wrong?'

'No, just wondering where I put my phone. I ought to text Dad and let him know I've landed.'

'That'll cost you a bundle.'

'He told me to. Or I could facetime him later. Will the service station have wifi?'

'I've never asked, but it probably will.'

The phone's in my bag, so I txt. *Landed. Grandad's picked me up. In a tinnie on the motorway.*

'Shall I add a message from you, Grandad?'

'Say you send him Steve's usual.'

Txt: *Steve sends usual.*

I hit send. 'OK. Done.'

We're still sitting in a traffic jam when Dad txts back. *Great, Bran.*

Hope you don't have to push. Give Steve my usual in return. Speak l8r.

'Dad sends his usual in return.'

Grandad looks a bit grim at this, but maybe he's annoyed by the traffic. We move about ten yards every minute. The traffic the other side is hurtling by.

'What's the speed limit here, Grandad?'

'Seventy. But a lot of people do eighty or more.'

'It's sixty back home.'

'That's plenty.' He looks across the motorway. 'They don't get there any quicker.'

'I've never gone faster than fifty.'

He turns his head.

'You drive?'

'Just on the farm. Dad gave me an old ute.'

'A what?'

'A ute. A utility vehicle. A pick-up truck.'

'Oh, right.'

'I got it for my last birthday. It's a Ford F1, with the V8 engine and three-seat cab. Dad had it re-built ground up.'

'Really? And you drive it at fifty?'

'Well, I'm not supposed to. Dad said I should never drive it at more than thirty, but I got a bit carried away one day, you know, on the long stretch by the lake.'

'You're fourteen, right?'

'Yes, last month.'

'Still a bit young to be driving.'

'We start when we're twelve usually.'

'Twelve?'

'Yes, if you've got the space. Most of my mates get their first driving lessons on farm roads. I taught my friend Chris to drive.'

'You taught him?'

'Sure.'

'What did his parents think about that?'

'No idea.' It's a good point. What did they think? They certainly never thanked me. 'They never mentioned it.'

'Maybe your friend never mentioned it.'

'Why wouldn't he?'

'Time for brunch.' Grandad pulls across to his left and heads up the inside lane.

'Dad said to buy you a meal.'

'He did?'

'Yes. Can I treat you?'

'Treating me, eh? Maybe you'd like to pay for the petrol an' all.'

'How much is that?'

'About thirty quid.'

'I've got that.'

'You have?'

'Yes, dad gave me some UK currency.'

'He thinks of everything.'

'Yes, he's pretty organised.'

'Seems so. But put your money away, son. You'll be needing that.'

He says it in a tired voice, a bit like my mum when she's overdone things. Unlike Mum he seems a bit of a misery guts. And I have to say his English is a tad ropey. What's with all the dropped 'h's and glottal stops? Mr Maddox, our English teacher, would look at you over the top of his glasses and say, 'Sic'. In your written work he'd put it in brackets – (sic) – beside your mistakes. Which meant you had to work out what was wrong. And that's why we talk about a bad test result as 'a bit sic'. It's one of our in-jokes. But you'd have to be a Greystone's scholar to appreciate that.

'I was hoping to get home in time for the match. England – Australia today. Autumn internationals. We play New Zealand in two weeks. Two wins and we'll be number one team in the world.'

'No chance, Grandad.'

He looks shocked. 'And why not? We've won the World Cup before now.'

'I have the same conversation with Mum all the time. Northern hemisphere teams don't really get rugby, Grandad. It's not just about brute strength. It's about power and flow.'

He looks at me so long the ketchup drips out of his burger onto his plate.

Wake up

I wake up when Grandad says, 'Want a first look at Berkshire?'

We're still on the motorway. On the right is a single giant windmill towering over a modern office block.

'Was I asleep for long?'

'About ten minutes. It's the jet lag.' He points. 'That's the local stadium.'

'Who plays there?'

'Reading.'

'Soccer?'

'Yeah, well, we call it football.'

'It looks ...smallish.'

'Yeah, well. We do what we can in Berkshire. Berkshire born and Berkshire bred. Strong in the arm an' thick in the 'ead.'

He smiles. It seems a bit harsh.

'Were you born in Berkshire, Grandad?'

'Me? Nah. Wiltshire. Just down the road. But your Grandma was born here.' He grins. 'Wodja reckon? Berks and Wilts. Two lamest county names in England, eh?'

I grin back, guessing this is a Pommie thing where you joke about yourself. Self-depredation, Chris calls it.

When I next wake up we're slowing towards the back of a very long queue.

'Not another one.'

Grandad raises his eyebrows in resignation. 'We'll miss the beginning of the match at this rate.'

'You like rugby that much?'

'One of my mates had tickets for it.'

'At Twickenham?'

He nods. 'It's all right. He found someone else to go with him.'

Maybe that's why he seems so grumpy.

'But I wouldn't wanna miss picking up my grandson.' He gives me a weary smile but I reckon he means it.

'Does Grandma like rugby?'

'Grandma hates all sport. And I mean all.'

'What even, like ...' I tried to think of an inoffensive game.

'Whatever you're thinking, the answer's yes.'

A stunner. I don't think I've met anyone who hates all sport.

Next time I wake up, we're in the countryside, sort of. There are narrow lanes and fields on either side. A big country house, a small, straggly sort of village on either side of a wider road, then a dodgy-looking housing estate opposite a line of terraced cottages. The one on the end is in a terrible state, with the wreck of a car in an overgrown front garden.

'Whoah!'

Grandad laughs. 'Yeah. You wouldn't want to live next door to that.'

There's a pavement, but I can't see a reason to walk there. It's the spooky end of the village.

The view changes over the next rise. More fields, edged by suburbs. Detached houses on one side and a few blocks of flats on the other.

'Almost there,' says Grandad.

We turn left and head uphill to the bigger houses with gardens front and back and garages almost as big as bungalows.

Grandad's car has trouble on the gradient. He slips it into first gear and gives the world outside a blast of black exhaust. The car swings into a steep driveway and grumbles to a stop. I worry the handbrake won't hold. Looming over us is a shiny new Freelander. It's from the lower end of the Land Rover price range, but it puts Grandad's chugger in the shade.

'Just take your valuables for the minute,' he says.

A small ranch-style house with a low outbuilding to one side and a double garage fronting the roadside. Behind and at the side a few ponies grazing a paddock. Through the front gates a view over the countryside. It could almost be a boring bit of New Zealand, except the light is very dull and the mist keeps drawing curtains across the landscape.

Grandma is waiting in the hallway.

To me. 'Hello, dear.' To Grandad. 'What took so long?'

'Traffic.'

'I've had lunch ready for ages.'

'Plane delayed. I had to wait two hours, then we hit traffic jams on the motorway. You got my texts?'

Grandma doesn't answer and goes to the kitchen. She has tight white lips.

I look around. It's all incredibly neat. Soft white carpets, cream-coloured furnishings and curtains. A village of miniature ceramic houses on the long window sill in the living room. Spotless.

'Where's Mum?'

'Yes,' says Grandad. 'Where is Catherine?'

'She's in the granny flat.'

'Is she coming for lunch?'

Grandma gives him a strange look. 'I doubt it somehow. But you'd better have yours before it gets cold.'

'I think the boy had better see his mother first.'

'Then I'll just leave the food on the plates and you can pop them in the microwave. I should have been at the salon ages ago.'

She looks business-like and sounds annoyed, but gives me a hug before she leaves.

'Nice to have you home safe and sound, Bran.'

What does she mean by that? This is not home.

Cuddle

Dad and I joke that Mum is the cuddle champ of the southern hemisphere.

'Do you want a cuddle, love?'

'Let me give you a cuddle.'

'Don't worry, my love. I'll have a cuddle waiting when you get home.'

It just means a hug, and now she's hanging on and swaying me back and forth.

'I think you've grown since I saw you last.'

'How long is it?' says Grandad.

'A month at least.'

'Oh, he'll have grown in that time. Boys do. Once they start shooting up, there's no stopping 'em.'

I'm glad there's no-one else to see. My mum gets emotional over the smallest thing.

I don't want to say that she's changed, but she has. Her face is rounder, puffier, and her eyes look more like the local sky, greyer, less blue. She's smiling through the tears, but there's no sign of her usual laughter. She's generally bright as a bell, as Dad likes to say.

I point at the bandages on her forearms. 'What happened?'

'Sprained my wrists. So, this is the granny flat. Sit down with me on the couch.'

A cuddle on the couch. I want to say that I'm fourteen and this is strictly inappropriate, but as Dad says there are times when my mother is vulnerable. She's the one who needs the cuddle.

'I'll leave you then,' says Grandad.

'No, turn the telly on and watch the rugby with us.'

'You sure?'

'Yes. Bran never passes up the chance to watch thirty grown men chasing a lump of mud.' She ruffles my hair.

'OK. I'll bring the food across. But the boy's got me worried, mind. He's told me England have no chance. Not even against Australia.'

Grandad heads for the main house and Mum hangs on to me.

'How was Bill when you left?'

'Dad? Not happy, but all right. Said to give you a kiss.'

'Well, where is it then?'

I kiss her on the cheek, which doesn't count as soppy as it's not from me in any case.

'Did he tell you why I'm here?'

'Said you were tired. Needed a rest.'

'That's all?'

'Yes.'

She stares across the room. 'Is that all?'

'Yes, that's all.'

'Everybody needs a rest from time to time, even if they don't know it. But I didn't want to have a rest without you. Do you mind?'

'No, it's OK. All my mates were jealous. They'd love to get a holiday in Europe, especially during school term.'

'I'll bet.'

Grandad comes back with a tray of steaming pie, chips and beans.

'Haven't you got the telly on yet? We'll miss the anthems.'

Hugs

The anthems are good – God Save the Queen and all that, what a dirge - but it's downhill from there. England scrap to a win by 20 – 13, but I don't think Grandad appreciates my match analysis. Sure, you've got to win your scrums, but it's all too static and not enough options given to the player with the ball. It helps if you can pass the ball out of the tackle without spilling it. All the arts that Mr Greeff instilled in us from day one. If the Aussies hadn't wussed it and missed an easy penalty when they were 13 nil ahead, it could have been a different story.

'Well, in my book a win's a win,' says Grandad. ' 'Specially as we now have a you-know-what.'

I don't know what, but Mum does. She normally tells me what 'what' is, but today she doesn't even want to discuss it.

'What's what?'

'What what?'

'The what what you mentioned.'

'*Which* I mentioned.'

'OK, which what, whatever.'

'Can't, 'cos this is in the way.' She taps the end of my nose to say I'm being nosey and she knows she's getting a tickle. There's nobody more ticklish than my Mum.

'Are you coming? It's getting cold.'

Grandma's standing in the tiny hall like a schoolteacher watching kids misbehave, so we all troop across to the main house, where the table is perfectly laid for dinner. She must have come back from her salon – whatever that is – and prepared a meal instead of joining us. The first thing I do is get orange juice on the tablecloth.

'Sorry.'

Grandad gets his own back, but with a grin. 'It helps if you can pass the juice out of the carton without spilling it.'

Grandma has no idea what we're laughing about.

By the time we get to dessert we're in family meeting mode with

Grandma in the Chair. Judging from Grandad and Mum's expressions, I reckon this is what they meant by a you-know-what.

'Now, first thing,' she says, 'we have to decide if Bran starts school on Monday or Tuesday.'

School? What school? I've got a school already.

Grandad explains. 'You may be here for a while. So you shouldn't miss out on your studies. Besides, you'll have the chance to make new friends and plays sports.'

'And I have to go into a clinic for a week or two, so you'd be all on your own,' says Mum.

But what about school uniform and stuff like that?

'You packed your Greystone's blazer?'

'Yes.'

Dad persuaded me to pack it. ('Always be an ambassador for Greystone's when you get the chance.')

'So you can wear that for a few days and we'll get you the uniform,' says Grandma. 'It's a very good school.'

'Is it an independent school or…?'

'It's a state school. A comprehensive. And a very good one.' She seems annoyed.

'In my experience all state schools have rubbish rugby teams.'

Shouldn't have said that. Sounded a bit up myself. The dining room goes dead quiet for a few seconds.

'It's a decent school,' says Mum, 'and the important thing is to make friends and carry on learning.'

'Yes. Sorry. OK.'

'Good, that's settled then,' says Grandma. 'And if you can start on Monday, Grandad and I can get back to running our businesses.'

Sounds as if Mum and I have been costing them money. I wish Dad were here. He'd sort it out in a flash.

I glance at Mum. She's looking at her plate, unsmiling, sad, almost crushed.

'So the next question is, where Bran's going to live? Grandad and I have discussed it, and you can have your own space here. There's a nice big loft area with dormer windows that we don't use very much. Or you can stay in the granny flat with your Mum. The trouble with that is there are only two rooms out there.'

I'm torn. The idea of a big space to myself is appealing. The granny flat 'out there' is tiny. I didn't see the other room, but it can't be more than a box. On the other hand, I'm wondering if Mum would be sad with me in the big house, separated from her, even if I'm only a few steps away. But I'll be living in Grandma's space. Although she seems nice enough, there's something not quite right about the vibe between her and Mum.

'I'll stay in the granny flat.'

Mum looks up from her plate and smiles.

'I guessed as much,' says Grandma.

What does that mean? That I'm some kind of mummy's boy? That doesn't bother me. Sticks and stones.

'And we should call it "the mummy flat",' I suggest.

'You'll make me sound like a dead Egyptian,' says Mum.

'But you've got the bandages and, like Dad says, you are very well preserved.'

Mum starts to laugh, but then her eyes fill with tears. Grandad looks shocked, Grandma stands stock still with a coffee pot poised in one hand. Then Mum recovers and carries on laughing, but Grandma's not amused.

What is it with adults? I can usually banter all day with Mum, but sometimes she gets these moods which go from one extreme to the other. And people look at me as if it's my fault. I wish Chris was here to give me some advice.

'Fine, so you'll live in the …with your Mum,' says Grandma. 'And then we have to discuss the Saturday job.'

The what?

'Now, the thing is,' says Grandad, 'I'd be happy for you to come and work with me on the gardening, but I employ a young married man at the moment – they've just had their first baby – and I couldn't reduce his hours. It wouldn't be fair.'

'But you're the boss and can do whatever you like,' says Grandma.

'True enough, and I also like to do what I think is right.'

Grandma clearly thinks it's wrong.

'In that case, Bran can come and work in the salon on Saturdays. There's one girl I'd happily let go.' She turns to me. 'You can sweep a floor, can't you, Bran?'

'Sure.'

'Can you make tea and coffee?'

'Sure.'

'And you can hang up coats and answer the phone?'

'Sure, but why do I have to work?'

'Because we all have to pay our way. Times are hard…'

'Hard*er*,' Grandad corrects her.

'Times are harder, and we're trying to keep our businesses going in tough times. We've got lots of bills to pay and we all have to make a contribution, however small.' She turns to Mum. 'So, it'll help – when things have settled down – if you can lend a hand in the salon as well.'

Mum looks up quickly. Her voice is quiet but sharp.

'*That* will never happen.'

Mum's very quiet when we go back to the "mummy" flat. She shows me into the tiny bedroom.

'I made it up for you,' she says.

I'm glad I didn't bale on her and opt for the big house across the way.

'I don't get Grandma,' I say.

'How's that?'

'Well, she hugs everybody, but she's kinda… cold.'

'She can do a hug, but she can't do a cuddle. Do you know what I mean?'

I think about it for a few seconds and the shock sinks in.

'But… when you were a child…'

Mum shakes her head impatiently. 'She's not my mum, Bran, and she's not your Gran. She's your Grandad's second wife.'

This is what Chris calls 'the emotional turmoil of non-traditional family life'. I never really understood what he meant till now. It's like tectonic plates shifting in your head.

'You don't like Gran… what's her name?'

'Her name's Audrey. You can call her that. You *should* call her that. For my sake.'

She gives me a cuddle.

'It's a long story, Bran. I'll tell you sometime, but I'm really tired now and we both need some sleep. OK?'

'OK.'

Once Mum's in bed with the lights off, I send Dad a long email about the day's events, ending with:

Gonna need some cash, or Audrey's gonna make us work.

The bus

Grandad tells me to watch out for a yellow bus bound for 'Stonefield School'.

'It's the only yellow school bus in this area and it's driven by an Irishman called Callum. You can't miss it.'

I'm the only kid waiting on the corner by the main road. I try my phone again and there's a message from Dad. I'm hoping he'll say 'you don't need to go to school in England', but all I get is 'Good lad. You'd be in class in EnZed anyway this morning. Roll with the tackles. You'll be fine. Proud of you.'

A white bus full of school kids blows past through the morning mist. Pools of grinning kids at the side windows, some of them making weird gestures. I almost choke on the exhaust. Don't they service these buses?

Then comes the yellow bus. 'Stonefield School'. I put out my hand and it stops. The front door hisses open.

'New boy, are you?'

Definitely an Irish accent.

'Yes.'

'Hop on.'

I mount the steps.

'Oooooooh!'

'Hey! Stripey!'

'I say, has anyone seen my chauffeur?'

The driver motions me down the gangway with a jerk of the head.

'Don't mind them.'

I turn to face the gawping, grinning, tittering horde. Even the older boys are smiling.

What's their problem?

Callum urges me to take a seat. 'There's only one.'

The mob begins to chant and point to my front and left. 'Rehab! Rehab! Rehab!'

The empty seat is a few rows down, by the aisle. I sit next to a grimacing kid with a huge, close-shaven head who looks something like my own age, but is so large going sideways that one thigh overlaps onto my seat. He seems delighted at this unexpected company, which makes the kids all around snigger and hoot.

A girl sitting across the aisle gives me a sympathetic smile with a hint of apology.

'They'll get over it,' she says. 'Just give them time.'

'What's that about rehab?'

She indicates the four seats in our row spanning the aisle. 'They call this rehab. It's for social misfits.'

I can see how the large boy beside me would fall into that category, and the haunted, cowed-looking girl by the window who's hardly shifted her gaze from some spot beyond the glass. She's dark-skinned. Indian, maybe, or Pakistani. But why would this other girl be in rehab? Her clothes are a bit quirky – colourful, knitted gloves and an exotic beanie – but she seems perfectly normal.

'Why are you here?'

'I'm supposed to be your carer. According to them.'

'Who are "them"?'

'They're the jokers and bullyboys from Years 9 and 10.'

We're interrupted by a kid leaning forward.

'Hey, Stripey! Where're you from?'

'New Zealand.'

'What're you doing here?'

'My family's over here for a bit.'

'A bit of what?'

Snorts and squeals.

'A bit of time out.' But my questioner has fired off his punchline and doesn't care about my answer.

The girl is watching me with approval.

'Good for you. Don't let them get to you. They're not worth it.'

This was overheard.

'Watch it, Wilde!'

'Yeah, just do your job and look after those deviants.'

She ignores him.

'I'm Bel.'

'I'm Bran. Bran Kelleher.'

'Is Bran short for something?'

'Just Bran. And Bel, is that short for something?'

'Belinda. But only my mum and dad call me that.'

'B. Wilde. Is that nominative determination?'

'What?'

'Y'know. Be wild?'

She does a tiny frown, a little crease between the eyebrows. 'Do you mean nominative determinism?'

I'm gonna kill Rawiri by txt.

'Yes, that's what I said, didn't I?'

She does that little frown thing again, but gives me the benefit of the doubt.

The kid beside me has been listening to every word, leaning towards me, his large thigh pinching down on mine.

'D'you fancy each other, then?' he says with a ludicrous smirk and a weird accent.

I can feel my face locked in a grimace of disbelief.

Bel leans across. 'Not everything's a soap opera, David.' She sits back and lowers her voice. 'Too much TV.'

'You're very patient,' I say.

'That's my job, running rehab on Callum's school bus.'

Identity

'Bran Cooke, is it?'

'Bran Kelleher.'

The school secretary looks confused.

'I've got Cooke here.'

'It's Kelleher.'

'Well, your grandmother came in last week to enrol you...'

'That wasn't my grandmother. My name's Kelleher. I've got my passport here.'

I start digging around in my backpack.

The secretary rises.

'Just one moment.'

She knocks and goes through a connecting door.

The secretary's office has shelves of ring-binders from floor to ceiling and two computers running. The other, older secretary is looking at me over her reading glasses. I don't think she believes me. Good thing I brought my passport.

'Step in here a moment, please.'

Next door are four men and the secretary. They've all been joking about something.

'Hello, Bran. I'm Gordon Mackie, the head teacher. Mrs Creasey and Mr Carson are assistant heads and Mr Edwards teaches History. Mrs Jennings tells me we've got your name wrong.'

I hand over my passport.

Mr Carson butts in. 'Can I see that bag, folder, whatever it is?'

I don't see what it has to do with him, but I let him look.

'Looks like a new computer tablet… a new mobile phone…rather expensive by the look of it… a wallet… do you have any cash in here?'

'About fifty pounds, sir. I left the rest at home.'

'The rest?'

'My Dad gave me some UK cash.'

'What does your father do?'

'He imports selected car brands into New Zealand.'

This makes Mr Carson smile but I can't think why. He hands back my black leather gizmo case.

'In future, don't bring that into school. In fact, I suggest Mrs Jennings puts that and the cash in the school safe. You can collect it at the end of the day. I'd recommend a basic mobile phone for emergencies.'

'I'd like to hang on to the cash.'

The room goes quiet. Maybe they think that I, a whipper-snapper, don't trust them. And they'd be right. Dad has trained me not to trust anybody with money. The gear is one thing: it's easily identified. But cash is different. I'm about to suggest that I make a record of the serial numbers on the notes before I hand them over, but Mr Carson relents.

'Just keep it well hidden.'

The head teacher has been examining my passport.

'New Zealand. Bran Kelleher. Next of kin… Mr William Kelleher and Mrs Catherine Kelleher. Is your mother British?'

'English, sir.'

'What would you call yourself?'

'I'm a New Zealander with an English mother, sir.'

Mr Edwards intervenes. 'Do you play rugby?'

'Yes, sir.'

'What position?'

'No 7 or 8, sir.'

'A loose forward.' He nods his approval.

'Although,' says Mrs Creasey, 'we're not a sports academy. We do sport as recreation at this school.'

Mr Mackie hands the passport to Mrs Jennings. 'I should copy the details and keep it with the other items in the safe.'

I watch my personal possessions being taken from the room.

'Right, Bran. We just have to decide which year you should be in. Year 8 or 9.'

What the heck? I was starting Year 9 back home.

'I can tell you straightaway, Mr Mackie.'

Mr Carson is fixing me with a beady eye.

'Do you know what a simultaneous equation is?'

'Yes, sir.'

'Do you know what a quadratic equation is?'

'Yes, sir.'

'Have you done any calculus?'

'Yes, sir.'

He looks sceptical.

'How old are you?'

'Just turned fourteen, sir.'

'And you've done some calculus?'

'We started it last term, sir.'

He gave up, so Mr Edwards stepped in.

'What subjects did you study at your last school, Bran?'

'English, Maths, General Science, French, Spanish, Latin, Geography, History, Music, and Te Reo Maori, sir.'

'Te what?' demands Mr Carson.

'The Maori language,' says Edwards. He's looking at me like I'm some kind of interesting specimen in a jar. The others are looking at each other as if I'm a puzzle to be solved.

'Have you ever studied ICT?' asks Carson.

'No,' I say, 'but…'

'Year 8,' he declares triumphantly.

'But what?' asks Mr Edwards.

'But we did computer programming as part of our maths and science classes.'

'Fair enough,' says Mr Mackie. 'I suggest Year 9 and see how we go for a week or two.' He's looking at a computer screen. 'Year 9. They're having English in C12. I'll take you over.'

'They've got a supply teacher again,' warns Mr Carson.

Rehab extra

'Ooooh!'

'Haaah!'

I get it. It's the Greystone's blazer. They think I'm flash.

'All right, calm down, please. I'd like to introduce a new pupil to Stonefield School. This is Bran Kelleher. He's come to us all the way from New Zealand. I hope you'll give him a warm Stonefield welcome. I'll leave you with…,' Mr Mackie doesn't know her name.

'Miss Wright.'

'Right. With Miss Wright.'

I look around the class. Some of the same kids from the bus and the only empty seat is next to David, the outsized kid. He looks like he's just won a big fat cream bun as a prize. Across the aisle, in the seat nearest the gangway is Bel. Next to her is The Girl Who Stares Through Windows. I'm back in rehab.

'Now, then,' says Miss Wright. 'We were talking about families, which come in all shapes and sizes. Can somebody give me an example of a type of family?'

Bel has her hand up.

'Nuclear families.'

'Hurrrrgh!'

'Boom!'

'That's right. What is a typical nuclear family?'

'Two parents, with about one point eight children.'

'Haah!'

'Point eight children!'

'Where did you come across that statistic, Belinda?'

'On the radio, I guess.'

'Which programme?'

'Not sure. Radio 4, I suppose.'

'You listen to BBC Radio 4?'

'My mum does all the time.'

'They haven't got a TV, Miss.'

'Come on. Settle down.'

'They can't afford one.'

'You can't get TVs at Oxfam.'

'Thank you, Belinda. Good answer. Nuclear families, with married parents and, typically in this country, with one or two children. Any other kinds of families?'

'Ask Daffy Jones, Miss.'

'Who's Daffy?'

David raises his hand and stretches his daft grin even wider.

'Is your name Daffy?'

'It's David.'

Teacher to class. 'Then I suggest we use names, not nicknames. Now, why should I ask David?'

'Ask him how many brothers and sisters he's got, Miss.'

David's grinning like he's just won the lottery. He gives me a look of triumph, as if he's going to knock my socks off.

'I don't think we need…'

'Go on, Daffy, tell her.'

'I've got twenty-one brothers and sisters, Miss.'

We all watch Miss Wright trying to absorb this information. She looks about eighteen herself, small and blond and trying to be very serious and in control, but she's lost it.

'It's his accent, Miss. He's Welsh. At least his mum is.'

She recovers enough to say, 'I have no problem with a Welsh accent. I'm just not sure I heard the number.'

Almost the whole class answer as one, 'Twenty-one brothers and sisters!'

I look at Bel. Her anger shows itself as resentful boredom. She's doodling on her notepad. The page is a mass of intricate squiggles, figures and faces.

'Go on, Daffy!'

'They're all half brothers and sisters, Miss.'

'I see.'

''Cos my dad keeps getting women pregnant.'

'Does he?'

'And nobody can stop 'im.'

You can almost see the questions whizzing through her brain, but she can't say what she's thinking. Neither can I.

''Cos he refuses to use a condom, Miss.'

'Right. And why is that, David?'

'Wot, Miss?'

'Why does he refuse to use a condom, David?'

She's brave.

'Wodja mean, Miss?'

'Is he religious?'

'Haaah!'

The class erupts.

'I mean, is there a reason he won't use contraception?'

From the look on David's face, you can tell he's never thought about this. But others have plenty of answers.

'He's a horny git.'

'Selfish bastard.'

'Scrounger.'

Back in New Zealand, that was fighting talk, but David accepts all these insults as accolades. He's proud of having twenty-one half brothers and sisters. That's his shtick. He's a phenomenon. It's his claim to fame.

Miss Wright struggles to regain control.

'Right, we've just had two examples of families at opposite ends of a spectrum. Now let's try to fill in a few more examples in between. Belinda, can you give us another example?'

Bel is clearly her go-to girl in a crisis.

'Cohabiting couples with children... extended families... same-sex couples...'

At the end of class, I ask Bel where to next.

'Maths. But which set are you in?'

'No idea.'

'Are you any good at Maths?'

'Top three, usually.'

'Then you'd better follow me. There are only eight of us.'

'Is David one of them?'

'What do you think?'

Miss Wright has made the mistake of leaving class before anyone else. Suddenly I'm catching a bombardment of rubbish aimed at David. He grabs the back of my jacket, spreads it out and uses it as a shield. I wrench myself free.

'You there!'

It's Mr Carson, glowering from the doorway.

'You've only been here five minutes and you're already causing a riot. Don't they have school rules in New Zealand?'

I know I should just keep quiet, but there's something about Mr Carson that annoys me. He's the sort of guy my dad would sort out in two sentences.

'No, sir.'

'No what?'

'No, Greystone's College doesn't have rules, sir.'

Now everybody's watching me. Nobody moves.

'Explain.'

'My school in New Zealand doesn't have rules, because Greystonians are supposed to know how to behave.'

'And how is that?'

'Like gentlemen.'

'Haaah!'

'Hurrgh!'

'Waah!'

I know I couldn't have said a stupider thing, even if it was the truth. Greystonians know how to behave. There's only one unspoken rule. Behave like a Greystonian. It's a kind of circular thing, but it works. Greystonians make mistakes, but they don't behave like morons.

Mr Carson is enjoying the moment.

'Then I think we've all had an enlightening demonstration of what Kiwis call a gentleman.'

We all file out.

'Bran?' says Bel.

'Yes?'

'There's a big rip in the back of your blazer.'

School's out

'There's no black leather case here.'

'But I handed it in this morning. The other secretary put it in the safe.'

'Wait a minute.' She starts dialling on her mobile.

David appears at the door. 'Come on! You'll miss the bus. Callum's waiting.'

'I've got to get my stuff.'

'But we'll have to walk home.'

What does he mean *we*?

'You don't have to.'

The other secretary gives up. 'Sorry, I can't get anyone. Come back in the morning. I'm sure it'll be all right.'

'Come on!' says David.

There's nothing I can do. I have no idea where this school is in relation to my Grandad's house. All I know is that it took about twenty minutes to drive here. How far? Five miles? Ten? And it's starting to rain.

We run up the drive. The yellow bus is the only one there and there's a ruckus. They're shouting at me for being late and laughing at David's style of running. With each step he seems to go as far sideways as forwards, as if he's stamping on bugs either side.

'Why are we waiting?!'

'Move it, Stripey!'

There's a volley of screwed-up paper balls as I come through the door. Callum leaps from his seat. He's slender and wiry and not much taller than me. At first his voice is a gentle Irish lilt.

'In your seats.'

He waits for us to settle in, then his voice hardens.

'You!' He points to one of the paper chuckers. 'Get down here and pick it up.'

No movement.

'I've got all day and all night.'

Groans.

An older boy with a serious manner, more like the boys at Greystone's, addresses my 'Stripey' tormentor.

'Nash. You threw it, you pick it up.'

'But it wasn't only me.'

'Then get your mate to help you.'

'Who are you? Teacher's pet?'

'No,' says Callum, 'he's my mate. If you want a debate you can work out your arguments as you walk home.'

David leans across and makes a show of whispering in my ear.

'Callum's got a black belt in karate.'

This seems unlikely as Callum is skinny. But he also appears to be in total control.

Nash sneers his way forward to the steps and picks up the balls of paper.

He snaps at a first year. 'Get your feet out of the way!'

The kid lifts his legs like a submissive dog.

'And there's one that went in the gutter. Nobody chucks litter out of my bus.'

Nash steps down, retrieves the rubbish and climbs back up.

'Right. In your seat and let's get moving.'

Nash points his finger as he goes past.

'That was your fault, Stripey.'

It's a threat. I turn to look at his mates. They're all glaring at me as if there'll be trouble in some dark alley one night.

The gent

B.Wilde - Year 9A

I've met a gent
Who wears his stripes with pride,
Like a young zebra
Or yearling tiger,
I'm not sure which.
Predator or prey?
It's too early to say.

He says 'Yes' not 'Yeah',
Stands up straight,
And watches the world with care.
We stare back, eyes wide, claws sharp,
Waiting for a mark of innocence.
He wonders why we chatter and gorm
A world away from his norm.

Will he come down to us?
Shall we stretch up to him?
Will he run with a flash of hooves
And fear, or withdraw to a patch of shade
With a bored flick of the tail?
I'll wait and see
From my spotter's tree.

My apologies, Miss Wright,
For not writing that text
On 'Families' again.
I prefer poetry to prose
And the title you chose
Is such a familiar subject.*
I hope you don't object.

*See our last supply teacher's lesson plan.

The sultan of style

I'm staying in the big house while Mum's having her rest so there's no concealing the evidence.

'How did that happen?' asks Audrey.

'Some kid called David ripped it.'

'On purpose?'

'He was trying to hide behind me when other kids started throwing things.'

She looks resigned and glances at Grandad. 'I wonder why that doesn't surprise me.' Then she turns brisk. 'Luckily, it doesn't matter. One of my clients had a whole pile of Stonefield uniform leftovers, and she went all the way home, bless her, and brought them back.'

She points at two large plastic bags on the kitchen floor.

'Why would she do that?' asks Grandad. He's been very quiet till now, watching and waiting. That's his style.

'Barbara Nash. She's a lovely woman.'

'But what did you tell her?'

'That we needed a Stonefield uniform. Try them on.'

I take the clothes to the downstairs shower room and tip a bagful onto the white, deep-pile carpet. They look limp and washed-out against Audrey's luxurious interior. There's a dark-blue school blazer – far too big for me – and two maroon, v-neck pullovers with the Stonefield badge. Several white shirts, two pairs of charcoal grey trousers and, unbelievably, three pairs of worn, soiled-looking underpants. There's a ManU polo shirt, a pair of football shorts – can't tell if they were always dark-grey or started life as blue – and a pair of maroon sports socks with light blue tops. Wrapped in a shirt is a school tie which looks as though the owner spent serious class-time chewing both ends.

Finally, in the second bag is a sleeveless, black, down jacket. This is too small and makes me look like an armadillo with a human face. You've got to be kidding.

I try on a pullover. It's at least two sizes too big and one cuff is frayed.

The other is almost shredded.

I go back to the living room.

'It's all too big or too small.'

Audrey pulls a face and grabs my arm.

'So just roll up the cuffs.'

I'm so shocked I can hardly speak. She cannot be serious.

'Am I supposed to wear this stuff to school?'

'Well, since you tore your jacket...'

Her face is pink now, her eyes dark but flashing. Doesn't she get it? There are a couple of day kids at Greystone's who come to school in badly fitting clothes. But they're kids on special scholarships, sent there by church missions. Everyone is kind to them because we know they're orphans or come from families with special needs. But, otherwise, nobody at Greystone's would be seen dead in another boy's hand-me-downs.

I don't know how to explain this to Audrey.

'The shirt collars are too big. There'll be big gaps…'

'Just tighten your tie a bit more. You'll soon grow into them.'

'The tie's a mess.'

'Keep it tucked inside your pullover.'

'And the trousers are so long I'll just walk on the hems.'

'Pull them up. I'll find you a belt.'

I step back and look at her.

'Am I really supposed to turn up at school looking like this?'

Her cheeks turn a deeper red.

'Beggars can't be choosers.'

'Who's a beggar?'

She starts to say something but changes tack.

'There are plenty of kids wearing outsize clothes. It's a style.'

'It's not mine.'

'Oh, we are stuck-up, aren't we?'

'Would you wear a pullover that looks this big?'

'I did when I was your age. It was very fashionable back then.'

'I know, I've seen the old films.'

She turns away towards the sink.

'Just like your mother.' She starts shaking out some lettuce in the sink. 'Those are the clothes you've got and you have to go to school. Make the best of it.'

I have one last try.

'Does Mrs Nash have another son at Stonefield?'

'Yes, she's got three sons.'

'And I guess the Nash in Year 10 is the gabby one who tried to provoke me all day.'

'Mrs Nash is very nice!'

'Her son isn't. He'll know I'm wearing his brother's cast-offs and he'll let everybody know.'

'Then that's his problem, not yours.'

How is it some people listen but don't hear? Or is it the other way round? Nash looks like an expert at making life miserable for other people. If it didn't work, he wouldn't do it.

'I'll text Mum about this and ask her.'

'You can't do that. Rest means rest. She's not allowed phones or laptops.'

'Is it some sort of nunnery?'

'It's a sort of retreat. And don't go bothering her with this when she comes out. This is exactly the sort of thing she needs a rest from.'

What the heck does that mean? I've never had to pester Mum about stuff like this. It never happened.

Besides, I can't text or mail anybody without my gear. Let's hope I can get it back tomorrow. No point whinging about it now. Audrey will probably hit the roof, as if it was somehow my fault the stuff disappeared.

Although the house looks smart, the walls are cardboard-thin and I can hear Grandad and Audrey talking after I've gone to bed.

'You were hard with the boy.'

'Well, he needs to learn that you can't always get everything you want on a plate.'

'I think he knows that already.'

'Lots of people had it tough. My sisters and I had to live with our grandparents as well, and I was last in line for hand-me-downs.'

'But people accepted it back then. That's the way it was for most people.'

'Oh, no, it wasn't. I didn't know anybody else who had to put up with it.'

'Then if *you* didn't like it, why does *he* have to put up with it?'

'It won't do him any harm to learn the real value of things.'

'And you've mastered that, have you?'

'I think I have. Without people like me running businesses...'

'I know, we'd all be on jobseeker's allowance. But that is knowing the price of things, not their value.'

Why didn't Grandad say that when I was in the room? Why didn't he back me up? Now I have the choice of going to school looking like an upper class twit fallen on hard times in my ripped Greystone's jacket, or like a weird cross between 80s trailer trash and 90s grunge. There is no way either of those can be a style statement at Stonefield Comp.

Busted

I get off the bus at Reading station. Where to now? I need to ask directions.

'Excuse me…'

Then I see Grandad. He's hurrying along, the front of his trousers smeared with mud.

'Come on, I'm double parked.'

I follow him to the car. An express coach trying to leave the station has just pulled up behind, unable to pass. Black looks from driver and passengers.

'Get in!'

Grandad pulls away as fast as he can. I get ready for a blast. He looks as red in the face as Audrey last night. But his tone is strangely calm.

'What's the plan?'

'I just want to buy some proper clothes.'

He nods. 'I saw you on the bus. Luckily, we were working in a front garden. So I just got in the car and chased the bus down the Oxford Road. I thought you'd be heading for town.'

We're on a busy road going away from town through a business park and it doesn't look promising.

'Where are we headed?'

'We need the Stonefield superstore. As usual, they've got a monopoly on uniforms. Your head teacher arranged that.'

'I wouldn't have found anything in the town centre?'

'Only trouble. What were you thinking?'

'I was taking an initiative.'

This time he grins. 'Good answer. You'll need that one quite a lot around here. Here's the store.'

Inside are two levels.

'Got your list?'

'In my head.'

'What's on it?'

'Pullover, tie. I've got shirts back home. Maybe Dad could post them.'

'No, get 'em here. It'll be cheaper than posting from halfway around the world. You'll need a decent winter jacket and some sports kit.'

We go up the escalator to the clothes department. People are staring at Grandad's trousers.

'Did you fall over, Grandad?'

'Slipped getting out of the trench we were digging. When I saw you on the bus. And I don't care what people think. Just in case you were wondering.'

He waits patiently as I test clothes for size.

'Have a couple of blue shirts as well. You're allowed to wear light blue.'

'Not sure I've got enough money.'

'Don't be daft, lad. I'm paying for these. We'll talk about it in the car. And you'll need a new mobile.'

'But I've got one, Grandad.'

'That's debatable. You need something cheap as chips at that school. Trust me.'

When I had the basic uniform, he took me down the racks to the coats.

'Something quick and cheap here. We'll get you a proper waterproof online.'

As we went around the store, Grandad kept meeting people he knew. A minute here, two minutes there. Yakking, we call it in EnZed. I'm surprised. Didn't realise Grandad was a natural yakker. At one point he sends me away to buy a rugby ball in the sports section.

We meet another acquaintance at the checkout. Bloke in a suit. He comes up behind us with a basket containing expensive phones and stuff.

'Hello, Steve.'

Grandad stiffens and puts on a fake smile.

'Hello, Councillor Collier.'

'This one looks like he should be in school.'

'He will be, once we get him into this uniform.'

Councillor Collier looks distinguished and smart. Suntan, grey hair, expensive suit.

'One of yours is he?'

'One of ours.'

'Not splashing out on the phone, I see. Very sensible.'

He's looking at the cheapo on the basic deal Grandad has just bought me.

'Not at the rate phones get nicked in school these days. And what about you?' He nods at the Councillor's basket. 'You won't forget to put that lot on expenses, will you?'

They're grinning at each other now, teeth bared.

The total comes up on the till – almost £300 – and I just pray Grandad's plastic will cover it. By the look on his face Grandad's saying the same prayer.

'The gardening business must be doing all right,' says the Councillor.

'Good honest work is its own reward, Graham. As you well know.'

Grandad turns away without waiting for a response.

'Who's that?' I ask.

'Nobody. Come on. We need to get you into school by lunchtime.'

We drive back towards the Comp.

'Now, then. When Audrey asks who paid for this lot, we say it was you, using the cash Bill gave you. OK?'

'Sure.'

'Audrey's a good woman in many ways, but she's got a problem with money. You understand?'

'I think so.' In fact, I had no idea, but saying you do makes things easier.

'When we get back, hide the cash. All right?'

'OK.'

'I'll show you where. And don't flash it around when you spend some. At least not in front of Audrey.'

'OK.'

There's more to Grandad than meets the eye. Or maybe less. I dunno.

He turns off the main road towards the house.

'Can't turn up at your school looking like this.'

Grandad lets me into the 'mummy flat'. We go into my bedroom and he pulls up a length of flooring under the bed.

'This is where Audrey's mum used to stash her valuables.'

'Then Audrey knows about it.'

'No. Audrey was the one she was hiding it from.'

Wow. What a family.

'Right, then, five minutes.'

I climb out of the cruddy clothes and into my new gear. Not too bad. The colours are dull and the badge is lame, but it could be worse.

Grandad rolls up in a dark-grey suit, blue shirt and red tie. He scrubs up well. You'd never guess he'd just scrambled out of a ditch.

'Do you want any of those old clothes?'

'No.'

'Then let's put 'em back in the bags and shove 'em under the bed.'

As we drive towards school, I tell Grandad about my missing gizmos and passport.

'Didn't they say where they were?'

'The secretary said she didn't know.'

It felt good climbing out of the car and walking towards the secretary's office beside Grandad.

'Is Mary Jackson here?' he asks.

'Mrs Jackson retired last year.'

'I see. This is my grandson, Bran. We've been buying the uniform, so he's a bit late today.'

'Well, we'd normally expect a call...'

'I know. But he tells me his passport and some expensive electronic devices were placed in your care yesterday and they've disappeared.'

'Ah, yes. You'll have to speak to the Head about that.'

'Good, I'll wait.'

'Well, I don't think he's...'

'Not a problem. I'll wait. If you could sign my grandson in, I'll wait outside the Head's office.'

Part Three

A Kiwi Abroad

The rules

'Right, usual rules. B-team kicks off.'

I've never been in a B-team before and don't intend to stay here for long.

Mr Parker seems the kind of PE teacher who'll recognise talent. 'You play ball with me, and I'll play ball with you. But, remember, it's my ball.'

True, he was talking to kids – including David Jones - who were trying to skive off games, but he seems serious about rugby. This lot talk a good game – 'England are gonna thrash the All Blacks next week' – but most of them are hunched over against the cold or rubbing their hands together. One is even wearing gloves. That wouldn't be allowed back home.

The whistle blows and a kid drop-kicks the ball towards the left-hand touchline. It goes pretty flat and bounces a couple of times. This gives me a chance to get up there – though there's not much support from anyone else – and time my tackle to perfection.

I go whump!

He goes, 'Urrgh!', spills the ball backwards and collapses.

It must be the easiest try I've ever scored. Just pick it up and touch down under the posts.

When I turn back, Mr Parker is power-walking towards me and blowing his whistle like a kid trying to learn the trumpet, with beetroot cheeks and knotted brow.

'What was that!?'

What was what?

'What do you think you're doing?'

'Playing rugby, sir.'

'I said "usual rules". That means no tackling.'

'No tackling?'

'Usual rules!'

'But that's tag rugby, sir. I didn't know…'

'Look what you've done!'

I follow him back to the kid I tackled. He's moaning and struggling for breath.

'He's winded, sir.'

'I can see that!'

'Just stand him up and bend him forward.'

'I don't need your advice! Go and join the other lot!'

He means the shirkers who are supposed to be running around the playing fields.

'But I didn't know what your rules are, sir.'

He twigs that I've got a different accent.

'Where are you from?'

'New Zealand, sir.'

This cracks up the other kids.

'Well, I don't care where you're from. In any case, that was sheer thuggery. You took him in the air.'

'No, he didn't, sir.'

'Quiet! This boy could have broken ribs.'

Mr Greeff taught us what to do with a winded boy. Just bend them forward to un-spasm the diaphragm and get them breathing again.

'Put him down! Who told you to do that? He could get a punctured lung!'

I drop the kid who is now gasping in cold air.

'He was winded. That's all.'

You know when you've been sent off, so I turn and jog away to join David and the bunch of other losers who are loafing around on the far side of the playing fields.

'I want you outside the Head's office after school. Do you hear? What's your name?'

I hear the other kids telling him. It's a name he won't forget. I've left a real impression in my first game of rugby in Pomsville.

Conversations adults have about teenagers: No 1

'I'm afraid it hasn't been a good start, Mr Cooke. In his first week here, your grandson started a riot in class, assaulted a boy on the rugby field and the police are investigating ownership of some very expensive devices found in his possession.'

'It would have been better if you'd had time to see me a few days ago, before these stories got out of hand, but let's rewind this conversation and take the allegations one by one, shall we?'

Mr Mackie is familiar with parents who defend their children against each and every accusation. Steve Cooke seems little different, though his tight smile suggests he will use sarcasm rather than shouting to get his way.

'To begin with the so-called riot. I believe another boy ripped my grandson's jacket while using him as a human shield against other classmates.'

'That's not the report I received.'

'Perhaps you should ask the pupils. A teacher who steps into a classroom and jumps to conclusions in two seconds flat isn't a reliable witness.'

Mr Mackie does not accept the suggestion that Mr Carson is unfair. Mr Carson is his right-hand man.

'As to the second accusation. It would seem sensible to warn a new boy that this school plays tag rugby up to the age of sixteen, especially if the new boy comes from New Zealand.'

'What's so special about New Zealand?'

'The schools there play serious competitive rugby from a younger age.'

Mr Mackie doesn't accept that either. It was his idea to restrict proper rugby to the older age groups on grounds of health and safety. He doesn't want parents suing his school or, even worse, him. In his view, it's the New Zealanders who are getting it wrong.

'Finally, why did you think you had the right to confiscate the boy's possessions, then hand them over to police, including his passport?'

'We had grounds for thinking they could be stolen.'

'And what grounds were those?'

'The reputation of the boy's father.'

'You have suspicions about Bill Kelleher of Auckland, New Zealand?'

Mr Mackie is nonplussed. Who is Bill Kelleher of Auckland, New Zealand? And who, for that matter, is this Steve Cooke of Tynehurst near Stonefield?

'Here is Mr Kelleher's email address. You can write and ask if he can supply receipts for the items you confiscated. Once you've had a reply, I expect their immediate return.'

'That's out of my hands, I'm afraid.'

'Because you've handed the items to the police?'

'Yes.'

'Then I suggest you get them back.'

'The police will have to complete their enquiries first.'

'And we all know how long such a low-level matter is likely to take. I suggest you get the relevant information from Bill Kelleher, then send it on to the police admitting you made a mistake.'

'Mr Cooke, I'm trying to run a school of 1,200 pupils here…'

'Then I hope the other 1,199 haven't been subjected to three similar injustices in the space of a few days.'

'Mr Cooke, we do what we think is the right thing at the time.'

'Of course you do. When I was the elected head of the Education Department in this town, I thought it was the right thing to build this school. But I never imagined that fifteen years later its pupils would be playing an apology for rugby, or that staff would take pupils' possessions for no good reason. I look forward to your phone call telling me when my grandson will be getting his property back.'

In the opinion of Mr Mackie the man departs with a ridiculous amount of dignity. A quick glance through the window confirms that he drives a very small car. Even so, it would be worth getting a secretary to check on Steven Cooke of Tynehurst. Some old dinosaur of an ex-Councillor, no doubt. In fact, better to make a discreet call to the present Leader of the Council. Graham Collier knows everything and everybody in these parts.

The tramp

Less than ten days in England and my identity's been wiped out. No tablet or smartphone. Can't reach my dad. Can't speak to my mum. Her 'week or two of rest' is turning into 'two or three'. No idea what my real mates in EnZed are doing. Maybe they think I don't care. Maybe they think I'm some kind of 'here today, gone tomorrow' kind of mate.

Instead, I'm supposed to mix with a bunch of kids I just don't get. David Jones, for one, is always lurking. His shadow looms over my map.

'What are you doing?'

'I'm going on a tramp?'

'What's that?'

'Sounds disgusting,' jeers Nash.

'A walk, a trek,' I say, trying to ignore the sneery boys.

'What you wanna do that for?'

'I want to find out about the area.' I point to the green bit interlaced with the occasional narrow line. 'Ever been here?'

'I went to Newbury once.'

This sets up a mock horror riff with the other kids.

'Daffy went to Newbury!'

'I went to Basingstoke once, but *never again*.'

'I'm planning to go to Maidenhead one afternoon.'

'You nutter! You'll never survive.'

David's cheeks turn lobster red.

Matt Collier comes over. He's the kid I tackled when I should have tagged him. Once he realised it was a genuine mistake, he shook hands.

'Where're you going?'

Matt always has a couple of kids trailing in his wake. Wherever he goes, Greg Potts and Carl Jenkins won't be far behind. And their every move is followed by the glances of the three As - Alys, Alison and Alicia – Stonefield's girl band in the making. They're always giggling 'He's fit!' or moaning about how 'Love sucks', and falling out with each other every second day, then making up. At least that's what Bel says. I don't know if she's jealous of the Three As. They call her 'Oxfam', because she was once seen buying a pair of fingerless mittens in a second-hand clothes shop.

Do I care? Not much. We never had these problems at Greystone's. Simple. No girls, no probs.

'Where're you going?' asks Matt.

'Into the hills.'

'What's there?'

'Dunno. That's why I'm going. Wanna come?'

'When?'

'Sunday.'

'Yeah. Maybe.'

'I'm gonna take some food and a thermo.'

David is still hovering, even if Matt and his mates have blocked his view.

'Can I come?'

Matt rolls his eyes. Greg and Carl do the same.

'There's walking involved, Daffy.'

'So?'

'Proper walking. Like, miles.'

'So?'

'You can hardly walk to the shops and back.'

David doesn't have an answer to that. He knows it's true.

'And we're not gonna help you carry all the food you'll need.'

Greg Potts always goes over the top. He's expert at twisting the knife that Matt sticks into his victims. A real cheap shot. That's how he stays mates with Matt Collier. I don't want to go with any of them, but then again I wouldn't mind some company.

'You're going to the White Horse hills, right?' asks Carl. 'On the Ridgeway?'

I look at the map. 'Yes, near Uffington.'

Greg makes a face. 'My aunt says there are snakes.'

'Can't be very big ones.'

'Adders. Her friend's dog got bitten.'

'Did it die?'

'Almost.'

'Must have been small or old.'

'It was a Rottweiler, three years old.'

'You seen snakes in New Zealand?' asks David over their shoulders.

'There are no snakes in New Zealand.'

'Hurrghh!' says Carl, sneering at David.

'But I went tramping in Australia with my mum and dad and we saw plenty.'

'Poisonous ones?'

'Yeah. We saw two tiger snakes and a King Brown. They're deadly.'

'Weren't you scared?'

'No, they were OK. My dad says you just have to keep away from the sharp end.'

'What if you don't see it first?'

'Bad news. You have to stay alert, especially the second person in line. The first wakes the snake up and the second gets bitten.'

'Anyway,' says Matt, pointing at the map, 'there's not much there. What's the point?'

'I like trekking. You get to know the country.'

'Yeah,' says David, as if he knows exactly what I mean.

'How you gonna get there?'

'Bus and walk.'

'Bus?' says Matt, like he doesn't know what it is.

'How would you do it?' I ask.

'I'd get my mum or dad to drop me off.'

'And pick you up later?'

'Yeah.'

'That's not tramping. That's cheating,' says David, as if he's suddenly an expert.

'Shut it, Daffy, you Welsh windbag.'

'So, you're not coming?' I ask Matt.

The Three As are listening and watching.

'I didn't say that.'

On the bus home there's a spare seat across the aisle from Matt and behind the Three As. They point it out. Do I take it, or stick with 'rehab'? I know Bel's watching me decide and switches her gaze to the window as I pass by. She's deep, but David's all on the surface. He packs a sad, looking betrayed, disgusted and hurt all at once. What can I do? These guys are gonna be my trek mates. I need to know them. I don't see David lasting more than a mile, if that.

The Three As whip around and kneel on their seats to lean over the backs. Suddenly it's a q-fest about EnZed.

'What's it like?'

'Can you do the haka?'

'Have you got a girlfriend?' This was Alison's question.

'What does your dad do?' That's Matt.

'Why are you here?'

My answer about the haka gets a mixed reception.

'England are gonna stuff you at the weekend.'

Luckily, my Dad taught me the right answer to that sort of comment.

'Then somebody needs to tell 'em it's rugby, not cookery.'

It's surprising how a little bit of humour can boost your street cred, but a lot of that depends on the right result on Saturday.

A couple of Year 11 lads in the seats behind are interested in the haka.

'Could you teach us?' This is the guy they all call J.B., the serious Year 11 kid who keeps Nash in his place.

'I guess.'

'But it's really just for Kiwis and Maoris, right?'

'No, you can make up a haka specially for your team or school. My school has its own words and moves. And girls can do the haka, too.'

'But how do we create the words?'

'I can help with that.'

'You know Maori?'

'Yeah, we studied the language at school, and I'm a quarter Maori anyway.'

'You are?'

'Yeah, my dad's part-Irish, Maori and Italian.'

'Whoah, what a mongrel!'

'Put a cork in it, Nash.'

'So you reckon you should have a school team haka?' I ask.

'No, I'm thinking about my rugby club. If you join, we'd have a good reason for doing a haka. And it seems to give a team an edge.'

'If you do it right. It's not about wasting your adrenaline. It's about concentration and focus.'

'That's what we need. Can you come and meet our coach tomorrow morning?'

'How do you know he's any good?' demands Nash.

J.B. smiles. 'I saw him tackle a guy on the playing field last week.'

All work no play

Audrey's got the grumps.

'No, you can't play rugby on Saturday. It's time you did some work. I had a Saturday job when I was your age, *and* I had to look after my brothers and sisters on Sundays. Sorry, but that's that.'

'So, if I work on Saturday, can I go on a tramp on Sunday?'

'Definitely not. You're too young.'

'Too young to go for a walk?'

'Not out there. People get lost in those hills.'

'But I've walked alone in the mountains in New Zealand. I've got a map and a phone.'

'Who gave you a phone?'

Whoops, shouldn't have said that. Grandad looks like he knew it would happen sometime. But who'd let a kid loose in the world without a cellphone?

'And who's paying for it?'

I've learnt my lesson. Where Audrey's concerned telling lies is allowed and necessary. It's a matter of self-preservation.

'I am.'

She doesn't look convinced.

'Phone or not, the answer's no. That's the end of it. When you're sixteen, fine. But not now.'

I'm wondering if Audrey's a few sammies short of a picnic. She's red in the face again, daft as a two-bob watch. But I keep quiet, in case she really spits the dummy.

Grandad keeps shtum, but we exchange glances. He knows. He knows I know he knows. I know he knows I know.

I'm up at seven in the morning. There's no change in Audrey's mood, so I txt J.B.. 'Sorry, can't make it. Have work.'

He txts back. 'No worries. CU Mon. JB.'

Breakfast with Audrey. Grandad's gone already. Some important gardening job in the Thames Valley. 'It's the one we all want,' he said. 'Plenty of work in one place all year round and with decent pay.'

Audrey shakes her head. 'He's been chasing a job like that for years.'

I make a mental note. Audrey lacks faith: in Grandad, in mum, in me.

'Now, there's something else really important about this job, Bran. Apart from making tea and sweeping up hair.'

Uh-oh.

'The fact is, I'm sure… I *know* my staff are stealing from me.'

'How?'

'I think they give their friends free haircuts. And I think they steal my customers. You know, give them private appointments at home, instead of booking them into my salon.'

She's watching for my reaction. She's gonna ask me to be a snitch.

'So, that's why I need you there to answer the phone. You take all the bookings.'

'OK.' That's not snitching exactly.

'And I'm sure they take time off. You know, leave early. Take turns covering for each other.'

'Yeah, my dad has to deal with that stuff.'

Audrey shakes her head. 'You can't trust anybody.'

'That's what Dad says.'

I can sympathise with Dad, but it's a lot harder with Audrey.

'So I need you to report anything fishy.'

That's a cinch. Anything to do with cod, haddock, tuna or shark. But I'm not a snitch and I won't do it. Unless it's something clearly criminal.

'OK,' I say.

We drive into town. Fair play to Audrey, she has a private parking spot right outside her shop.

SHEAR DELIGHT – 6 DAYS A WEEK – BY APPOINTMENT ONLY.

'I like the name,' I say.

'I don't, but I'm stuck with it.'

Inside are two young women and a young man with the blondest hair I've ever seen. It's almost silver and sort of combed down and across one eye. I sense glitter on his eyelids. The powerful whiffs of perfume, soap and all sorts of hair gunk make me want to leave the door open. Next time, I'll bring my own gas mask.

'I'm Wesley. This is Gwen and Melanie. And you must be Brandon.'

'Bran.'

'But we've decided Brandon's a much better professional name, haven't we, girls?'

I haven't seen that much lipstick since Rawiri's cousin's wedding, and the bouncy waves of hair are enough to make you seasick.

'Brandon!' says Melanie. 'We love that name!'

I'm about to say, 'It's not my name', but Audrey stamps on the atmosphere.

'Never mind that. Is Stacey here?'

'No, she had a late night looking after her …'

Audrey's not listening. 'Give her a call, will you, and find out what time's she's coming in?'

Squelch.

'Right, Bran. You can start by making tea and coffee. I'll show you where everything is.'

It's a big place. Two shop fronts with a connecting door and two smaller rooms behind.

'This side is the teaching salon. We train students from the local college. They do their practical training with us. The ones who can be bothered to turn up, that is.'

The tiny kitchen is behind this area. Teabags, mugs, instant coffee.

'Your first job is to go two shops down and buy four pints of milk. No more. It has to last the whole day. Two pints for customers and two for staff. If anyone wants more than four cups of anything they'll have to buy their own milk. Next, turn on the background music. Use these CDs here. I only allow popular classics in here. Nothing rowdy. This is a quality establishment. Now let me show you how to answer the phone.'

Audrey boots up the old desktop. The appointments diary pops up onscreen.

'It's really easy. Answer the phone with "Good morning or good afternoon, Shear Delight". OK? Keep your voice nice and breezy. These times are booked, these aren't. Offer clients a time. If they accept, just type their names in the green square and it'll turn pink. You can let people re-book or cancel, no problem. OK?'

'OK.'

'No private phone calls on this phone. OK?'

'OK.'

'Stacey operates the till and deals with credit cards, but you have to enter the amounts taken next to each client's name. OK?'

'OK.'

I can see the staff giving each other knowing looks behind Audrey's back. They need to be careful; there are huge mirrors everywhere.

'You can book people in without an appointment if there's a gap in the schedule. OK?'

'OK.'

'Right, here's some cash. Pop out and get the milk. Four pints. Semi-skimmed. And here's some money for a ready meal at lunchtime. Something you can pop in the microwave.'

Past the bus stop, step over the Friday night pizza, past the pub advertising England versus Samoa on the big screen later in the day - sorry, but I have to support the Samoans – and swing into the newsagent's with the small refrigerator cabinet at the back.

By the time I return, Stacey's arrived.

'Hello, love! Nice to meet you.'

She's like my mum. Same age, big smile, but bigger in all directions.

'Right,' says Audrey. 'I've got an appointment in Goring. I'll be back before closing.'

We watch her pull away from the parking space and turn into the traffic heading north.

There's a lull. We're all watching each other.

'An important appointment… with *shopping*!' whoops Wesley.

'An important appointment… with *ladies who lunch*!' purrs Melanie.

'An appointment with… a *cream bun and a hot chocolate*!'

It looks like a repeat performance.

Wesley fixes me with a mischievous sideways glance. 'And we're stuck in the shop with Auntie Audrey's very own… *spy*!'

'Don't make the boy blush,' says Stacey.

Too late, even if they mean to be kind.

'Ah, bless 'im. How's your mum, darlin'?'

'Do you know my mum?'

' 'Course I do, love. I was at school with her.'

'She's having a rest.'

'I know. Bless. I'll pop over to see her next week.'

'I'm not sure anybody's allowed to see her. She's supposed to be getting a complete break.'

' 'Course she is. I'll see her when she comes home then.'

The bell on the front door pings and we have our first customers. I take their coats and offer them cups of tea.

'We'd love one, we're that parched.'

'You're Cath's boy?'

'So tall!'

'Heartbreaker, just like his mother.'

'I know some ladies who'll be coming back just to look at the view.'

What view? There's only the road and the traffic.

'What is it today, Eileen?'

'Less grey, more blond.' She shivers melodramatically. 'Brr, let's turn off the funeral music, can't we?'

Is this where I say "classical only"? Or is the customer always right?

I don't get a chance, because Wesley slides a CD into the player and a blast of ABBA speeds up everybody's movements by twenty per cent. That's got to be good for business. I just hope Audrey doesn't come back for something she's forgotten or a sneak inspection. Does this place have CCTV? I check the corners for cameras. Unless they're fiendishly well hidden, I reckon I'm in the clear. In any case, I get the impression Audrey's staff do whatever they like when she's out on a shopping spree.

'Watch and learn' my dad says, so I sit behind the desk waiting for calls and trying to get online.

'No chance,' says Wesley. 'We have to use our own phones.'

He considers me with pursed lips and head on one side.

'What do you think, girls? Do we need a makeover?'

'Definitely,' says Melanie.

'If I've still got a slot at 11.15, I'll give you a Wesley special.'

Now I'm praying for new clients. There is no way I can turn up at Stonefield Comp looking anything like Wesley. On the other hand, I could convince him to give me a cut my mum has never allowed.

By 10 o'clock the salon is full. Smocks, curlers, hairdryers, women's magazines. Boiling kettles, steaming cups of tea and coffee. Gossip.

'She looked so beautiful on the day.'

'I heard!'

'Such a beautiful dress.'

'I know. I saw a photo. Smashing it was.'

'And you made a super job of her hair.'

'Well, I thought I'd gather it back a little, because she has lovely cheekbones.'

'She has!'

'A pity to cover them up. I said to her, you should wear it like this more often.'

'Well, I know Mike really appreciated it. His best man – y'now, Kevin...'

'Oh, I know Kev. He was in the year above me at school...'

''Course, you were. Well, he said the first sight of her absolutely took Mike's breath away.'

'Bless!'

'And he's not just a hunk, either. He's a lovely man.'

'Oh, you don't have to tell me about hunk. All the girls at school were in love with Mike.'

'Ooh, if I was thirty years younger...'

'What was he like at school?'

'Dishy and cheeky with it.'

'He hasn't changed.'

'Yeah, but he's nice cheeky, isn't he?'

'Ooh, yes. Not a mean bone in his body.'

'He'll be a lovely dad, he will.'

'Definitely. Are they going to try right away?'

'If their texts from Kingston are anything to go by.'

Screams of laughter. I'm watching the clock. No sign of more clients. By ten fifty-five there are only two seats taken.

'Take a seat, Bran.'

Here goes. When you go into the ruck you have to be fully committed.

'Now, then, who do you want to be?'

'Richie McCaw.'

'Richie McWho?'

'Richie McCaw. Former captain of the All Blacks.'

'You know something, you're speaking a foreign language.'

'He's talking about a rugby player.'

Wesley shivers. 'Oh, not one of those big brutes. Why do you want to look like one of them?'

'Richie McCaw's brill. He's a legend.'

'But what does his hair look like?'

'It's like a stiff sticky-up brush on top.'

'Sticky-up's one thing, but I'm not sure your Grandma would like that.'

'Audrey's not my Grandma.'

'Isn't she?'

Wesley's out of his depth now and Stacey's shaking her head at him. Touchy subject. I see it all in the mirror.

'Now, you see, what I would suggest, given the shape of your head… see, you've got a lovely straight nose… perfect size and these great big green eyes are to die for… and lovely ears, see?'

All the time he's pulling strands of hair down and across my forehead and stroking the hair forward past my ears. Crikes! He wants to make me look like a girl.

'I think a few highlights to bring out the green even more. Don't you think, girls?'

The sound of a door opening.

'Ah, just in time.'

I flick my gaze left and see Grandad reflected in the mirror.

'Haven't started anything, have you?'

Wesley almost recoils from Grandad's gravelly voice.

'No, we were just thinking…'

'You don't really need the lad, do you? Because there are some people I want him to meet.'

'Oh, no… if Audrey doesn't mind.'

'She will and she won't. Come on, Bran. I brought your kit. There's a rugby practice at a local club. I've got you a trial. Hurry up. We've only got fifteen minutes.'

Freedom

Grandad gives me fifteen pounds towards my trek.

'In case anything happens. And whatever happens, don't be late. Five o'clock. Orright?'

'OK, Grandad.'

I have my rucksack with the food, water, phone, map, guide books, compass and waterproof. Travelling light, just as Dad taught me.

I walk down to the bus stop on the main road. It's grey and overcast, but the forecast is for sunny spells later.

David Jones is waiting at the bus stop. He's wearing a T-shirt, baggy jeans and cheap, black trainers.

'Aren't you freezing?'

'Wha'?'

I guess not. But he's the last person I need on a trek. I glance at my watch. The others have got three minutes, assuming the bus is on time.

'There they are,' says David. He's disappointed.

A Range Rover slows and stops in the space reserved for the bus.

'Call me and I'll come and get you! Don't go into any streams or rivers! And don't go near any cliff edges. Have you got your sandwiches?'

David giggles. I don't know why. He's not carrying anything. One light shower and he'll be miserable.

Only two lads climb out of the Rangie: Matt Collier and Greg Potts. They're pretty well tooled up. Nice all-weather gear. Two smart ski beanies. Decent walking boots, tightly laced. Matt's mother gives David and me an anxious once-over as she pulls away.

'Is Carl coming?' I ask.

'Nah, something came up,' says Matt.

'Good. We don't have to wait. Here's the bus.'

Which, apart from the driver, we have all to ourselves. So far, so good, but there's a twenty-five minute wait in Didcot for the connecting service to Wantage.

'Let's get a taxi,' says Matt.

'Why?'

'I don't wanna waste my life hanging around.'

'Who's gonna pay?' asks David.

'Why? Got no money?'

'Not for taxis.'

'Well, either we get there fast or I go home,' says Matt. 'Waste of time, this.'

So three of us agree to split the fare.

'You owe us, Daffy.'

'It's all right,' I say. 'I've got his. And his name's David.'

'Don't be daft. His name's Daffy. Always will be,' insists Greg.

I wonder why Greg is so aggressive.

'What did David ever do to you?'

'Exactly what he does to everybody.'

'What's that?'

'Exists,' murmurs Matt.

I can't tell with Matt if he means it, or if he just enjoys making clever remarks.

'An' then there's that whinging Welsh accent that drives everybody nuts.'

I know Greg means that.

I want the taxi to stop in Wantage so we can walk from there and see a bit of the town. But Matt wants to get going on the walk, so we scoot through the little market town and head for the high ground two miles south.

'See? We'd have had to walk all this way, just to get here.'

What is it with Poms? They accuse everyone else of moaning but never stop whinging themselves.

The driver drops us off where the road crosses the Ridgeway.

Matt doesn't like what he sees.

'It's just a track,' he says.

'What did you expect?' I reply. 'A moving walkway?'

'No.'

I'm just annoyed at this point. There was stuff to see in Wantage. I'd checked it all out in a guidebook. But these guys couldn't be bothered.

'So,' I say. 'You're not too posh to walk then?'

' 'Course not.'

I turn west and hope no one notices we're walking away from home. We'll have to walk back the same way, and I'll probably take some flak, but I want to see the White Horse.

'Keep up, Daffy!' Greg's on his case like a terrier snapping at a roly-poly labrador. David's doing his best, but he's already ten yards behind.

A path worn into rough grass falls and rises over the gentle hills, making for an easy walk. The landscape folds and unfolds under a changing sky, opening out or closing in as we progress. Clouds seem to be chasing their shadows, which accelerate up the hillsides and away over the tops in a vain attempt to escape.

'It's gonna dump on us,' says Greg, eyeing some darker clouds away to the north.

'It'll miss us,' I say.

Matt halts and looks anxiously around. 'How do you know?'

'I checked the forecast. That cloud's a long way off.'

'Wodja mean?' shouts David as he lumbers up. 'What's gonna crap on us?'

'If your legs worked as well as your ears, you wouldn't have to ask stupid questions, Daffy.'

I decide to drop back and walk with David. It must be agony walking in those cheap trainers. Matt and Greg don't think much of my decision and stride out ahead. After another forty minutes they're behind us and I sense a mutiny.

'Does this actually go anywhere?'

Luckily we're just about where we need to be.

'Can you tell what it is yet?'

'What?'

'That line on the hill.'

'What is it?'

'Just a bit further. You'll see.'

They're not happy, but they don't want to miss out.

The white line on the hillside lengthens and shortens relative to our position. Sometimes it disappears. Just as Greg starts talking about going back, we reach the top of a slope and there it is across the valley.

'Whoah! Who put that there?'

'What is it?'

'The White Horse of Uffington.'

'Why... ? Wot...? Who...?'

David is baffled, his forehead creased in wonder.

'Stop babbling Daffy. It's just a load of white paint.'

David turns to me. 'Is it?'

'It's chalk. It's everywhere round here.' I kick at the turf with my heel. 'If you dig down an inch or two, you get white chalk.'

'So, it's landscape art. I did some of that at summer camp last year.'

'Yeah, but this could be three thousand years old.'

'Who did it?' asks David.

'Nobody knows. That's the beauty of it. People all over the world have copied it, but this is the original.'

'OK,' says Matt. 'it's a mystery. Is there anything else to see round here?'

I nod across the valley. 'Do you want to climb up to it?'

They scan the distance in between and I can tell they don't fancy it.

'Let's have a rest first.'

We find a stretch of level grass facing the White Horse and crack open the rucksacks. A road winds from left to right just ahead and then drops away towards a village in the valley. David slumps down full-length on his back. There's a V-shaped stain of sweat on his tee-shirt below the neckline.

'You look awful, Daffy.' To Matt's credit he looks worried.

'Come on, Daffy. Don't leak all over the grass,' says Greg. 'I hope you're not gonna croak. I don't fancy carrying you down again.'

David's makes an effort and hoiks himself up on one elbow.

'Seen any snakes?' he wheezes.

'Don't be…' Matt begins.

'There's one!'

David leaps up and points into a tussock of taller grass, inches from where Greg is sitting.

Before I can put him right, Greg is off down the hill. We watch him go. It looks as if his head is bobbing on green-blue waves as he plummets downwards in leaps and bounds. We stand up to get a better view. David is gurgling away beside me, enjoying the sight of his tormentor retreating in a blind panic.

'Reckon he's headed for the road.'

Greg's halfway down already. It's surprising how much further things appear in a hilly landscape. We watch him stumble, fall, keep going on all fours until he regains an upright stance.

'Greg! Greg!!' Matt calls hopelessly, but there's no hint that Greg can hear.

'He ain't coming back, I don't reckon,' says David triumphantly.

In no time at all Greg is floundering across flatter land just a hundred yards or so from the lane. He disappears into a ditch then reappears on the road, walking now, as if relieved to be back on a man-made surface.

Matt appeals for understanding. 'I'd better go with him.'

'Why?' demands David.

'Y'know,' shrugs Matt.

I don't know, but there's no point making him feel bad.

'I think he's dropped something.'

There's a speck of black halfway down the steepest slope.

'Yeah,' says Matt. 'Looks like his beanie. I'd better get it.'

'See yah.'

'Yeah, see yah.'

I'm left with David and take a look inside and behind that clump of grass. 'Where's this snake?'

He hangs back. 'There.'

'You mean this plant?'

He comes closer and looks at the mottled, shrinking leaves of some weed on its last legs.

'Is this what you mean?'

'Well, it kinda looks like... No, there!'

A couple of feet away is what looks like a dead snake on its back. I poke it gently with a stick looking for zigzag patterns, but instead find two yellows marks just behind the head.

'It's a grass snake.'

'Is that poison?'

'You mean poisonous? No.'

'Looks dead.'

'Yeah, but maybe not. Grass snakes are brilliant at playing dead. But I wonder why this one is out and about in this weather. It should be in somebody's compost heap, in the warm.'

'Well, I reckon him's dead.'

'We'll see. Let's leave it alone and come back later.'

I push the stick into the dead leaves to mark the spot.

David is hyped up, delighted to have gotten rid of the other two.

'Where shall we go?'

I point across the valley. No reason why he shouldn't suffer a bit for being a lousy mate.

'Let's head for the top. We can eat up there.'

There's nothing like a run downhill then a climb up the other side. The closer you get, the more you want it.

David's only just started the upward slope by the time I reach the carved chalk. Fair play to the lad, he doesn't bottle it.

'Want a sandwich?'

This time he slumps face forward on the grass.

'Mind the rabbit poo.'

I can see he's bothered but also breathing too hard to really care.

While he lies face down, head on forearm, I take a few pics with the rubbish camera in my rubbish phone. A pity I still don't have my smartcell. But I might be able to send these to Dad, as soon as I can get to a half-decent computer.

We split my sandwiches when David has the strength to sit up.

'How we gonna get back?'

'Same way we came, walking.'

'Have we gotta go back the same way?'

'We could chicken out and follow Matt and Greg.'

'Yeah, those two losers.' He looks away to the north-east, the direction the deserters took, though they're now well out of sight.

'How far is it?'

'I'm walking back to Didcot to catch the train.'

'How far?'

'Twelve miles.'

'Twelve *mile*? How long'll that take?'

'Depends how fast you can walk? But I reckon about three hours.'

'Three *hour*?' He makes it sound like the worst insult.

'It's about twice as far as we've walked till now. You can do that. Easily.'

In fact, I doubt it very much. The problem with Matt and Greg taking off is that David is now my problem. What happens if he can't actually walk that far?

'Can't we get a bus?'

'No buses on Sunday afternoons.'

''Ow bowt taxis?'

'Expensive, and we've taken one already. Anyway, we still have to walk back to Wantage to find one, and we may not.'

'May not? God, you talk posh.'

'I'm not God.'

'God, you think you're clever.'

'He or she probably is.'

'She? 'Ow can God be a she?'

'How can you be sure she isn't?'

'You need a good punch, you do.'

'Would that be God's work or your own?'

'Shut it.' He ponders the sky. 'That's rain, that is.'

It is. In fact, we can see it raining in four or five places far away, with the light bursting through clouds somewhere near Oxford.

'So, how we gonna get home?'

'We're going to walk.'

'That's what you said five minutes ago.'

'Just put one foot in front of the other. We go over the hillocks just like before but in reverse order.'

'And why do you call thems 'illocks?' He pronounces this like zillocks.

' 'Cos most are small. Not big enough to call hills.'

'Why don't you just call 'em small hills?'

' 'Cos I don't have to.'

'Wodja mean?'

'I mean I've a large enough vocabulary to call them what they are.'

'And them's hillocks, is it?' He emphasises the 'h' in a fake posh voice.

'The small ones are, yes.'

' 'Illocks pillocks!'

'Don't start. You're not five years old.'

'Wodja mean?'

I wonder if this is what having a younger brother is like, with the constant nagging and whining? I'm pretty sure my parents couldn't produce a kid like David, but if brotherhood's anything like this, I'm glad I'm an only child.

He takes off a shoe, then a sock and wrings it out, but not without spattering filthy water all over the open sandwich box.

'How did you manage a wet sock?'

'Puddle.' He points. 'Down by there. Anyway, clean dirt,' he says. 'That's what my mum says.'

'Mine too.'

'You won't mind eating the soggy sarnie, then?'

'You sure? Can I have another one?'

' 'Course.'

'You sure?'

'I'm not gonna let you go hungry, am I?'

He settles down and takes a socking bite.

'How's that? Gritty?'

'Yeah, but good.' He takes in the scene, his short hair pinned back by a sudden gust of wind. 'We should do this again.'

'Yes, and next time you can bring some food.'

He chews a large mouthful and swallows about half of it, spitting specks of ham and bread when he speaks. 'Only had cash for the bus.'

'Why didn't you ask your parents for food and cash?'

'Parents?' He says it as though it's a ridiculous idea. 'I asked me mam. But she only 'ad bus money. Usually she doesn't 'ave that.'

I want to say 'next time, I'll bring food for two', but my dad has warned me about that. 'You can't solve the world's problems. You can only solve your own.' That's what he says and I guess he's right. If I do it once, this kid'll be all over me.

'Have some water,' I say.

' 'Aven't you got Coke or summat?'

'No, water. It's what you drink on a proper trek. Sweet drinks are for wussies.'

'Sounds hoity-bloody-toity that does.'

'Does your mam say that?'

'Yeah, how'd you know?'

'Just a lucky guess.'

The permanent grin shifts to a frown.

'Taking the piss, you?'

'Just a bit.'

The grin comes back. 'Thought so.'

The sun suddenly breaks free of cloud and we lie back on the grass.

Even so, there's a breeze and David starts to shiver.

'Have my waterproof.'

He takes it and makes the arms look like tight sausage skins as he pulls it on. A red kite plays the wind currents directly above, angling its tail, its wing tips splayed.

'Wazzat?'

'A red kite.'

'That's not a fucking kite. That's a fucking bird.'

'Will you stop swearing!'

'Wot?'

I think he honestly doesn't know what words come out of his mouth.

'Stop swearing.'

'I'll stop swearing if you stop talking rubbish.'

'It's a bird of prey called a red kite.'

'Oh, yeah? Owjoo know that?'

'I read it in a book.'

'It's all fucking books with you, in'tit?'

I don't say a word.

'Woz wrong?'

'I told you, stop swearing.'

'Yeah, well… It's not even red.'

'It's reddish.'

'Radish?'

Before I can crack a proper grin, my rubbish new phone gives out a rubbish chirp. It's a text from Grandad.

'Where r u? Don't be late.'

I text back. 'In hills. Loadsatime.'

When we wake up it's almost two o'clock.

David panics. 'We're gonna be late!'

I look at the map and the railway timetable.

'Me mam'll kill me.'

'Why would she do that?'

'She gets worried if I miss me dinner.'

It takes two minutes of chat back and forth before I realise that he means 'lunch'.

'Yeah, dinner.'

'You thought you'd be back for lunch?'

'Yeah, 'course.'

'How can you go on a trek and be back for lunch? That's a stroll down the street, not a trek.'

'How'd I know you're nuts, you?'

'Call her.'

'With what?' He's holding his arms out from his sides as if to say 'search me'.

It's true. No food, no dosh, no phone. I offer him mine.

'What am I gonna tell her?'

'Tell her the truth.'

He looks at me as if that is a completely alien concept.

'No, *you* tell her the truth.'

'If you like.'

'Then she'll kill *you.*'

'Calm down. Just take my phone and call her.'

'Don't wanna.'

'OK, tell me the number and I'll call her.'

'Can't.'

'Why not?'

He broods darkly for several seconds, his frustration building like water behind a dam. But instead of a torrent bursting through a wall, his anger collapses and he flops backwards like a barely dripping water hose.

'She 'aven't paid the phone bill.'

'OK. Not your fault. We'll just have to walk back the way we came, then join up with the sustrans route and walk to Didcot. Three hours. Catch the train to Reading, the bus to Stonefield and you'll be home for dinner.'

He looks at me as if I've lost it. 'I've missed me dinner!'

'What do you call the meal you eat at seven o'clock?'

'Seven? Nobody eats at seven. We eat at six.'

'What do you call it?'

'Tea.'

'Then you'll be home for tea.'

'Me mam'll be so mad I won't get no tea.'

There's no point talking to this lad.

'Come on. You can whinge as we walk.'

At the bottom of the hill, we find our marker stick still erect among the leaves. There's no sign of the snake, which David finds impressive.

'I shoulda stamped on its 'ead when I 'ad the chance.'

'Why? They're harmless. Anyway it's against the law to kill reptiles in the UK.'

'Owjoo know that?'

'I read it.'

'Nose in a book. That's all you are.'

'Whatever. But now you need to be shoes on track.'

If truth be told, it's a lot further than it looks on the map and it's hard yakka. David's soon tailed off.

'Come on, Dave. Give it heaps.'

'What?'

'You've got to go faster.'

He moves his arms quicker but the legs fail to keep up, so it looks a bit comical. I want to let him catch up and walk together, but have the feeling we'd go even slower.

We reach a ford that's no more than a row of large stepping stones. Water's pouring over the ones in the middle.

'Are we s'posed to cross that?' asks David.

' 'Course. What else can we do?'

I go first. Easy-peasy. I look back at David. He looks like a bush caught in a whirlwind, branches flailing.

'Relax, and take it slow. Copy me.'

I go back and point at his willy.

'There's your centre of gravity. Just move it gently across the stones. Ignore the water. Take small steps. It's just like walking in a straight line.'

He jumps off the last stone with a gawky grin, his trainers squishing water.

'That was easy.'

'Yeah, it's a cinch.'

'Who taught you that stuff?'

'My dad.' The next words are out of my mouth before I remember. 'Doesn't yours do stuff with you?'

'Don't see him, much. He's a busy man.'

Yeah. The man with twenty-plus kids.

We have to go uphill past a ruined cottage.

'Let's go in there next time,' says David, as if certain there's going to be a next time. 'And we should go down this side of the river, for a change, like.'

His tone is strangely chirpy now, while I'm starting to feel bushed.

The last stretch to the train station is a hard slog. We must have walked twenty miles, most of it over rough ground. My ankles are barking and I wonder how David is still on his feet at all. The tickets cost six pounds each, but by the time I hand over the money I'm only thinking about getting a seat for the next half hour.

My rubbish phone gives another rubbish chirp.

'R u OK?'

I txt back. 'On train. All OK.'

Leaving Reading station I try to get my bearings. Left or right?

'Where's the bus stop for Stonefield, David?'

'How do I know?'

'You live here.'

'Not *here*.' He gives a shrug as if this might as well be some place like Alice Springs, Australia, rather than a few miles from Stonefield.

I'm just looking around to ask a stranger when he shouts.

'It's that one!'

As I turn he almost knocks me over. I see the bus. It's just leaving its stop and heading up past the station.

'C'mon!' shouts David. 'Next stop!'

And he's off, chasing the bus. I look up the street but can't see if the post near the next crossroads is a bus stop or just a sign on a pole. But I do witness the amazing sight of David lumbering across the plaza outside the station, then dodging traffic across the roundabout on the station approach. The way his backside is going reminds me of a rhino charging away through the bush. We saw this once when my dad took us on safari in Tanzania. The only thing missing now is the dust cloud, but David is determined to catch this bus. I don't rate his chances, but I break into a jog. If he catches it, the driver might wait for me.

As the bus sweeps around the roundabout towards the town centre, David's beetroot face glances back over his heaving shoulder, his eyes widen to comedy cartoon proportions and he puts in another burst. I'm not sure how fast he's going, as so much of it goes sideways, but he's definitely a man on a mission.

The bus slows, the brake lights come on. David puts his head down and – would you believe it? – *sprints*. If it's a stop, there's no one else there. David reaches the door, says something to the driver and looks back for me.

'Come on! Shift yer arse!'

When I get there, he's apologising to the driver for the bad language and the lack of cash.

I pay the fares.

'Cripes, David. You've got stamina.'

'Eh?'

'Stamina. I thought you were bushed.'

'Wozzat?'

'Y'know. Tired.'

'Yeah, well I am. Completely knackered. But you don't know my mam.'

'You should play rugby, mate.' He looks as if I've just landed from another planet. 'Seriously.'

'Nah, me mam don't like me getting mucky.'

Mrs Jones

There's a moment's silence as we step through the back door. Just long enough for me to recognise the aroma that David brings with him to school. Kid's food, kid's sick, fried food, warm milk, used nappies.

Four pairs of eyes stare at David. Different eyes. One set is narrow and foxy, the other three great saucers of wonder, disbelief or innocence. But then the mouths engage and they all shout the same thing followed by something different and all jumbled up.

'Whaah-haaah!'

'Just you wait!'

'You're *so* gonna get it.'

'Mam! Look who's here!'

The baby in the high chair just points and gurgles through jam smeared lips. 'Davvy! Hurrrgh!'

Then a very loud voice starts somewhere on the floor above.

'Dafydd Jones! Where are you?'

There's a rumble across the floor, then a hammering on the stairs like heavy clogs on bare wood, then the half-closed kitchen door flies open.

'Where the hell've you… ?!'

She notices me. The fierce glint in her eyes and the tight cleft between them softens instantly.

'Who's this?'

'My friend.'

'Hello, Mrs Jones,' I say and hold out my hand.

'Aaaw,' she says, not believing the outstretched hand. I'm guessing from her expression that she means 'Ooooh', but her voice is too hoarse.

'Woss yer name, love?'

The origin of David's Welsh accent is clear.

'Bran. Bran Kelleher.'

'Aaaw, are you Cath's boy?'

'Catherine Kelleher?'

'As was Catherine Cooke. Who went t' New Zealand?'

'That's my mum.'

'Aaaw! Lovely! An' you're mates with my Dafydd?'

I am, as my dad would say, in no position to argue, so I say, 'Yes.'

'Aaaw! Me an' your mam go back years, we do.'

'Really?'

'Yeah, we do. At school together, we were. Same class an' all. How is she?'

'She's away at the moment. Having a rest.'

'Aaaw, 'course she is. Love 'er. Sit an' 'ave a cup of tea. Bronwen, put the kettle on. And Dafydd, give the baby 'er food.' She begins to bustle. 'I don't know. Have you been feeding 'er bread and jam again?'

One of the girls swoops.

'It was Mikey.'

Mrs Jones turns on the boy with the foxy eyes. 'What have I told you about feeding the baby your rubbish? Go on, Dafydd, good boy. Show 'im how it's done.'

Mikey finds the tables turned. He was looking forward to the anger aimed at his older brother, but now he's on the receiving end himself.

My phone is vibrating like an angry hornet in a jam jar and I know it's Grandad.

'I'm going to have to go, Mrs Jones. My Grandad's wondering where I am.'

'Don't you worry about him. I'll have a word. You brought my Dafydd home safe.'

I'm not sure Grandad'll buy that, but it seems impolite to leave when I've been offered tea.

'I'll give him a call if it's OK.'

'You don't have to ask me, love.'

I dial the number.

'Grandad, I'm at Mrs Jones's house… You know, David Jones's mum… She's invited me to have some tea. No, just a cup of tea. OK… OK… OK…'

'What did he say?'

'He's coming to pick me up.'

'Ah, love 'im. He can have a cup as well. Kiley, get the chocolate biscuits out of the tin and don't touch 'em with your fingers.'

She says words like 'bis-skits' and 'fin-guzz' with a slight pause in the middle and a musical lilt.

I watch David warming the little jar of baby food, then sitting beside his little sister to spoon it gently into her mouth.

'Little cow, she never lets us feed her.'

'Bronwen! Don't you ever call your sister names like that, yuh lettle betch.'

'Well, she just spits it out when we try to feed her.'

'That's because she wants Dafydd to do it. You know that.'

I'm glad the kids on the school bus can't see David cooing and doing the baby talk. He'd never live it down. But he's got the little ankle-biter loving every spoonful.

'So, does he behave himself in class, does he?' asks Mrs Jones.

Here comes the interrogation.

'Yes, he behaves.' Strictly speaking this is not a lie. I've said nothing about how he behaves.

'I'll believe that when I see it.'

So will the rest of us.

Grandad doesn't come in. He just honks the horn a couple of times.

'I think I've made him really late for something,' I say.

'See ya tomorra, pal,' says David.

'Yes, see you tomorrow.'

'Say hello to yer mam from me. And don't be a stranger,' calls Mrs Jones as I start to leave.

'I won't,' I reply, doing complicated sidesteps past all the toys and junk in the hallway.

I just have time to notice that there's not a single carpet on any of the floors, and David's schoolbag has been emptied out on the hall floor, the contents scattered and torn, including a couple of textbooks.

I wonder what excuses he'll have at school on Monday. I wouldn't snitch, but I'm not sure I want that bond of knowing the truth but keeping quiet. At least, not with David.

Ground rules

Grandad's trying not to lose it.

'You've dropped me right in it, Bran.'

'But I texted.'

'That's not how it works in our house. You can't text your way out of an agreement. We said no later than five. It's quarter to seven.'

'I'm sorry. I didn't know your rules.'

'Well, you've brought a Family Meeting down on our heads. Audrey's going to spell out the rules. Sorry, but there's not much I can do about it. I went out on a limb yesterday, but I can't fix this for you.' He glances sideways as he drives. 'And she does have a point.'

In the event, she has several.

1) Unless and until I can find myself another Saturday job I will work in the hairdresser's on Saturday mornings.
2) No sloping off to play rugby.
3) No roaming around the countryside.
4) Negotiate what times I intend to be home.
5) Half an hour of housework per day.
6) Help out by doing some supermarket shopping on Friday nights.
7) Make my own bed.
8) No floordrobe in my room.
9) Wash my own clothes and polish my shoes.
10) No socialising with David Jones and his family.

'Why not?'

'I will not have that woman in my salon and I don't want her, or her various children, having any influence on anybody I know.'

'What did she do?'

'It's not what she *does* that bothers me.'

'But Mrs Jones said that she and Mum were friends, at the same school.'

Audrey grimaces. '*Mrs* Jones?! I don't think so. And with friends like that... well... what can you expect?'

Grandad looks really uncomfortable, but keeps quiet.

'Anyway,' says Audrey. 'Are we agreed?'

I think about it, which irritates Audrey and makes Grandad nervous. But Greystone's boys are taught to think and respond in a measured way.

'This is your place. I'm a guest, so I'll do what you want.'

She turns puce again and the words come out of a human pressure cooker.

'That's just like your father!'

I know exactly what I want to say but, as Dad points out, sometimes it's better to bite your tongue. If I'm being like my dad, it's no bad thing. Anyway, what's the big deal about going on a trek for a day and getting back a bit late? What a bunch of wussies.

I guess Mum and I'll just have to get out of here as fast as we can. And I've got to find a way of making contact with Dad.

'Tomorrow, I'll be late because I have to go to the library.'

'What for?'

'I need some books for homework.'

'What's wrong with your schoolbooks?'

'There are better books in the library and more to choose from.'

She doesn't really accept this, but I reckon that's kind of check- mate.

'What time will you be back?'

'Six-thirty.'

'Six.'

'Six fifteen.'

'We eat at six-thirty. I want you here to help me peel vegetables.'

Grandad finally opens his mouth.

'I'll help with the cooking.'

'Fine, but I want Bran home by six. There'll be no rushing in and just sitting down at table. This is not a hotel.'

And that's the end of the conversation. I've no idea where the library is, but there must be one. And where there are books, there'll also be computers.

I don't plan to do any earwigging tonight, but the walls aren't any thicker than they were last week.

At first, all's quiet. But the pressure cooker has been on a low heat all evening. I go upstairs after dinner to tidy up my 'floordrobe' - a tiny pile of precisely four items – and 'do my homework'. Homework takes half an hour. I start re-reading Richie McCaw's autobiography and looking for my favourite quotes.

I can believe that better people make better All Blacks.

I know I should expect to be in tough situations, rather than hope I won't be.

I've played enough matches to know that it's not about wearing the jersey, it's about filling it.

But I'm starting to get a bad feeling that Richie's main mantra might also have to be mine, except nowhere near a rugby pitch.

Start again. Keep getting up.

I have to believe in the Real McCaw. If I do that, there's nothing anyone can say that will hurt me, not even one of Audrey's prize judgements.

'I expected a bit more support.'

'He's a good lad. He made one mistake.'

'He's arrogant.'

'He's led a different life. He's been taught to take the initiative.'

'Well, that's a recipe for disaster.'

'It could be his salvation.'

'The only thing that'll save him is hard work and self-discipline.'

'He's got that in spades. You should have seen him at rugby practice. He's got a lot of promise…'

'Why do you think rugby is the measure of everything? It's a stupid, macho game.'

'I know you think that.'

'Most people think that.'

'Not in my world.'

'Being mad on football would be bad enough, but rugby is brutal.'

'Everybody is entitled to their opinion.'

'Not when they're his age.'

'Audrey, the boy has grown up in New Zealand. They eat, sleep and breathe rugby down there. You might as well ask the boy to cut off an arm.'

'All I'm saying is, the sooner he deals with reality the better.'

'He could do a lot worse than hang out with friends who play rugby.'

'Such as?'

'Celebrity junkies, layabouts, TV addicts, junky junkies… do you want the list?'

'I just wish you'd support me for once.'

'I'm trying to support everybody, but you're making it hard.'

'I give up my house…'

'Our house.'

'This is my house.'

'And mine is over there? Is that what you're saying?'

If there is a reply, I don't hear it. But I do hear Grandad leaving the house a few minutes later. I look through the window and see him going across to the 'mummy flat'. Looks like he's sleeping alone tonight.

Cripes! I guess that's my fault. The sooner Mum and I get back to New Zealand the better.

Hooking up

'Morning, troublemaker,' says a smiling Callum as I climb aboard the school bus.

That's just the beginning of weird. It seems as if everybody's watching to see what I do. Matt, Greg and Carl are trying to look cool, but Nash is on his feet grinning. David looks hopeful but fears disappointment. The Three As are confused and ditzy, while Bel seems to be enjoying herself with a knowing smile.

I take my seat in rehab beside David.

Nash goes, 'Yaaahah!' and punches the air.

'What's going on?'

Bel turns her big blue eyes on me. She's wearing a dark-red knitted flower on her pullover.

'They've been having a massive argument about you.'

'Who?'

'Half the bus.'

'Why?'

'Don't ask me. I never understand these stupid arguments. Something about snakes and cowards.'

'Ah.'

'Does that make sense to you?'

David leans right across me. 'They ran away because they seen a snake. And we'd hardly started on our trek. Ran away to their mummies in their four-be-fours.'

I look at the back of David's head.

'Is that what you've been saying?'

He screws his head back towards me. 'Yeah, well it's true. Them's chicken.'

'And you're all over my lap.'

He sits up straight.

'Is that true?' Bel asks.

'Tell you later?'

'OK.'

'Do you know where the nearest library is? I need access to a computer.'

'You'll need to be a member.'

'Sure.'

'I mean, you'll need an adult to vouch for you.'

'Oh.'

'I could ask my mum.'

'You could?'

'Sure. She's a book freak. I'll let you know.'

Our first class is English and Mrs Hutchins is back and taking over from the supply teachers. She hands out our homework.

'David. When you're told to write about a family, you're not expected to make a list of your relatives. Matthew Collier? Nice, thank you. Bran Kelleher?' She sizes me up as the new boy in class. 'A group of boys at a posh school doesn't really make up a family.'

'But they can become a kind of stand-in family, Miss.'

'I don't think so.'

I look at the mark.

10/20 The subject is 'a family' not 'a group of friends'.

How unfair is that? Guys can become your brothers. In fact, they can become better at being 'family' than your blood brothers: supporting, covering, looking out for you. Why doesn't she get that?

'Yasmin... if you could stop looking through the window for a moment... Thank you...'

Why do people say 'thank you' when they don't mean it?

'There are no families to be found online, believe me.'

Yasmin's expression doesn't change for a split second. It's as if nothing Mrs Hutchins has to say could possibly be of interest. She doesn't even glance at the comments or marks, just puts the page straight into her bag.

'Belinda... you know you're not supposed to wear ornaments or decorations on your uniform.'

'It's for the poppy appeal.'

'That's not a traditional poppy.'

'I know it's different, but I got it by making a donation to the poppy appeal.'

'What's wrong with a normal poppy?'

'Nothing. I just prefer this one.'

There's a hint of challenge in Bel's eyes and voice.

'We'll see,' says Mrs Hutchins and hands over the work.

Bel doesn't do disbelief like the other girls. Her eyes don't bulge and her mouth doesn't fall open. She just goes quiet and sad.

'What'd you get?'

She shows me.

2/20 Do the tasks we set. It's our job to teach you, not the other way around.

Cripes! The Hutch is a hard nut.

David grimaces and mouths something at her back.

'Is there something you wish to share, David?'

The Hutch doesn't expect or wait for an answer. Eyes in the back of her head.

Bel sums it up as we leave class. 'She wants to be assistant head when Mrs Creasey retires.'

'What's wrong, Oxfam?' asks Alison.

'Got a rubbish mark, did you?' asks Alys.

'And she's right about the poppy,' says Alicia. 'It's cheap and floppy and it's the wrong colour.'

Sometimes you can only stand and stare.

Which is what I'm doing when J.B. and one of the Year 11 guys approach.

'Bran? I'm Mike O'Callaghan.' He's tall, broad and quietly spoken, with a manner that would fit right in at Greystone's.

'Yes, I've seen you on the bus.'

'That's right. And I saw you at the rugby trial on Saturday. I hope you're going to join the club.'

'I'm not sure. My grandparents need me to work on Saturdays.'

'I've got a similar problem, but I'm in the under-18s and we play matches on Sundays. Do you want to try out for us?'

'I'm a bit young, aren't I?'

'Yeah, but we'll look after you. Give it a go, if you want. We train at the club on Thursday nights, under the lights.'

'Lights?'

'Yeah, at the club's training ground.' He smiles. 'It's the big time.'

'I'd like to. But how do I get there?'

'My dad's the club physio and assistant coach. There'll always be somebody to give you a lift, no problem.'

'Sounds good.'

'Pick you up at five on Thursday?'

'Great, thanks.'

As we're swapping phone numbers, I get an idea.

'You know David Jones?'

'Yeah, who doesn't?'

I tell them about the kid who nobody thinks can run, let alone sprint.

'I promise, he was unstoppable after a long day, and I was bushed.'

Mike's sceptical. 'He's heavy. No question. But can he catch a ball, or pass? I doubt it somehow.'

'I'll find out.'

'OK. Let me know how it goes.'

Matt Collier and Carl Rogers are in the top group for Maths.

'I don't understand why you hang out with Daffy Jones,' says Matt.

'Yeah, being a chav is one thing, but he's Welsh with it,' adds Carl.

'Sure, he can be annoying… ,' I shrug.

Bel overhears and interrupts.

'The most annoying thing about David Jones …,' she pauses and we wait for her devastating assessment. ' …is the way other people treat him.'

They sneer, but there's no answer to that. I couldn't have put it better myself.

The Chin dynasty

There are only a few left on the bus as we travel through the villages, but Bel and I still get jeered when we get off together.

'They make a lovely couple.'

'Get in there, snake boy!'

'Keep away from the sharp end, Oxfam!'

We walk down a lane past a few houses.

'Are they always like that?' I ask Bel.

'Yeah.'

'You're used to it?'

'It's been like that from day one. People have their ideas and you can't shift them.'

'Back in New Zealand there'd be fights all the time.'

'Why?'

'You couldn't insult people like that and get away with it. Anyone who did that would get their head smacked.'

'Don't let them wind you up. As my mum says, we're strangers thrown together for a few years. It's totally random. We don't have to like each other.'

'Talking about liking each other…'

'What?'

'What's the deal with Yasmin?'

'What do you mean?'

'Well… she's really on her own planet.'

'Not surprising. Her mum died when she was six. She's like the rest of us in rehab. We're weird because we have messed-up families.'

That obviously doesn't apply to me, but I don't want to sound smug so I keep quiet.

She leads me through a gate and down a lane. The roadway turns into a track dipping down towards a copse with a cluster of buildings just visible through the trees.

'This place is awesome. You're way out in the country.'

'Not *way* out, but my mum needs the space.'

'Why's that?'

Before there's time to reply a woman appears from around the corner of a stone barn. She wearing a purple apron covered in white smears.

'Ah, there you are. Can you give me a hand?'

Bel rolls her eyes.

'Can I put my stuff down first?'

' 'Course you can. Do you want a cup of tea? I've made some madeira cake. Who are you?'

'I'm Bran.'

'I'm Zelda.'

Before Bel has time to warn me I'm shaking Zelda's hand and getting something sticky on my palm.

'He'll have to wipe that off.'

'Don't worry,' says Zelda airily, 'it's good stuff that.'

I raise my eyebrows at Bel.

'She means it's the world's most expensive porcelain. She's a potter.'

'Come on. Tea. Then I need your help.'

Her mother heads towards the house, brushing hair out of her eyes and smearing more white stuff on her brow.

The cottage is ancient with walls almost three feet thick. Just inside the back door is a golden retriever bouncing around with what looks like a huge grin on its face. It shoves its nose into my groin and tries to jump up.

'No, Oscar. Down!'

Bel goes down on her knees to play with him.

'Who's a lovely boy?'

'He hasn't had a walk,' says Zelda.

Bel looks up at me. 'Do you want to take him for a walk?'

'How long will it take?'

'Half an hour.'

'But if we go to the library…'

'Oh, I'm sorry, I'm firing a kiln.'

'Mum!' says Bel, exasperated. 'You promised!'

'I know. But Bran can use my computer here. Then we can meet in town tomorrow and we'll do the library thing. Bran, could you move those things?'

Zelda is standing over the table in the conservatory with a teapot in one hand and a cake on a plate in the other.

'Just put them on the sofa.'

I shift a dozen books and a pile of papers.

'I'm going to change.' Bel goes off through the living room and disappears upstairs.

'Plonk yourself down.'

I sit on the end of the settle and Oscar comes over to drop a ball in my lap then stares at it.

'You'll have to throw it for him.'

'Indoors?'

Zelda looks at me for a moment. 'It's a soft ball.'

I toss the ball gently through the conservatory arch and into the living room. Oscar scrabbles about on the tiles, trying to get some traction then bounds after it.

There's a crash that sounds like breaking crockery. I can feel my cheeks turning red.

'I'm really sorry,' I say as Oscar comes bouncing back with the ball in his mouth.

Zelda looks confused. 'I wonder what that was?' She goes and looks. 'Oh, that,' she says from the living room. 'I forgot I'd put that there. Don't worry, I didn't like it much. I can make a better one.'

'I'll pick up the bits,' I say.

'No, don't worry. We'll do that later.'

When Bel comes back, dressed in jeans and a thick woollen jumper, she gives me a teasing grin. 'Smashing the place up already?'

She pushes the books aside to make space on the sofa and I'm wondering what Audrey would make of this place. There's stuff everywhere, a bit higgledy-piggledy, but really nice stuff. Loads of books and paintings.

Dozens of ceramic and porcelain pots. Armchairs and sofas with saggy cushions, and exotic-looking carpets.

'Do you like the cake?' asks Zelda.

'Mmmsgreat,' I reply.

'Have another slice.'

'Mmm, thanks.'

'Did you have a good day?' she asks Bel.

That's usually a dud question from a parent, but Bel answers straight off.

'The Hutch gave me two out of twenty for my poem.'

'What? Why?'

'She said I should answer the question.'

'That's a bit mean. But I did say your last verse could be interpreted as a bit cheeky.'

'She's just a sad cow.'

'Now that *is* a bit mean, Belinda. But yes, you're right. She is a sad ruminant. Right, what I suggest is, Bran does whatever he has to do on the computer, then you help me lift a couple of things, then you walk the dog.'

'I have to be home by six at the latest,' I say.

'I'll drive you back.'

It takes a while to find Zelda's tablet, but Bel finally feels down the side of an armchair.

'Mum!'

'What's the problem? It's perfectly safe down there.'

I try to log in to my account but my user name and password are rejected multiple times.

"Anything wrong?" asks Bel.

I explain.

"You can send from mine."

She logs in and sets it up. I send Dad a brief update, then take care to delete the message in the sent folder.

Teachers confiscated my phone and tablet. Still haven't got them back. Am writing from a friend's computer. Looking forward to coming home. Mum coming back from rest soon. School is rubbish. Audrey's a nightmare. The rugby's not too bad. Might join a club for a few weeks to get some games. No messages from anybody. Something weird's going on with my account. Phone me at Grandad's. Miss you. High fives, Bran.

Zelda's workshop is filled with shelf after shelf of pots in different stages of creation. Two huge jars stand on potting wheels. They must be three feet high.

'I need to move these onto the shelf down there. Get your fingers under the wooden bat. That's it. And lift.'

It's heavier than I think and I'm off balance from the start. I try to squat and lower it gently onto the shelf, but it tips and I only stop it toppling over completely by sticking out my chin. Only then do I realise the clay is soft.

'Don't move,' says Zelda. She reaches round and pulls the jar upright.

There's a dent where it fell against my chin and another where it brushed my shoulder.

'I'm sorry.'

'Don't worry. That's easily repaired.' Zelda stands back and examines the pot. 'Mm, in fact I quite like that. I think I'll leave it. What shall we call it, Belinda?'

'How about a Bran jar from the Chin Dynasty?'

'Yes, I like that.'

I don't get it. 'My grandma… well, my grandad's wife, likes pottery,' I say.

'Really? Does she collect?'

'Yes, she's got about thirty miniature houses.'

'Ancient or modern?'

'Modern,' I say in her defence.

Bel and her mum exchange glances.

'I don't think she'd like what I do,' says Zelda.

'Pity,' says Bel. 'Mum's always looking for buyers.'

'How much are they?' I ask. I have visions of buying one for my mum, and maybe compensating for the ones I've damaged.

'That depends.'

'A small one, like that?' I point at a small ceramic box.

'That's about £75,' says Bel.

I feel the blood drain from my face.

Out on our walk with the dog, Bel says, 'Well, at least you didn't blurt out something like "Seventy-five quid? For that?!" Which is what most philistines do.'

'But it is a lot of money.'

'I know. But my mum's brilliant.'

'So, what do the big ones cost?'

'Thousands.'

'Does anyone round here buy them?'

'Rarely. She sells most in London. Or Paris. Or New York. But she gets less than half the galleries' selling price.'

I realise there's a lot more to Bel and her mother than I'd imagined.

'And it's really skilled work. My mum can throw a pot weighing 30 kilos.'

'I reckon I could do that.'

She stops walking and bursts out laughing.

'No, I mean she can take a lump of clay or porcelain weighing thirty kilos and throw it on her potter's wheel until it's a great big beautiful shape. There are lots of big men potters who can't do that.'

'But is she…? I mean, she's tall, but she doesn't look that strong.'

'It's not about strength. It's experience and technique.'

'And what does your dad do?'

'He's a travel writer.'

'Holiday mags?'

'Sometimes, but mostly books.'

'Is he travelling now?'

'He's always travelling. And my parents are divorced.'

'I'm sorry.'

'That's all right. He left when I was eight. I only see him once or twice a year.'

'That's tough. I'd feel really bad if my parents divorced.'

'Yeah, but that's because you're used to living with both.' She picks up the stick Oscar has brought back and launches it towards some undergrowth. 'I just hope I'm not like my dad.'

'Why's that?'

'He's had everything too easy. Y'know, inherited money and all that. I'd much prefer to be like my mum. Talented and brave enough to be poor.'

'Are you poor?'

'I asked my mum that question last week, and she said it depends. The thing is, we don't care that much about owning things.'

'But you've got lots of things.'

'Yes, books and stuff. But we don't care about the latest fashions and gizmos. That's why they call me Oxfam.'

We forget the time and it's a twenty to six by the time we get back to the house.

'I can't be late.'

'Really? Not another cup of tea?'

'My Grandad's wife is really strict.'

'Oh, right. Come on then.'

We cross to the garage.

'Oh, dear.'

'Mum!'

The seats in the back of their van are down in the back and the space filled with boxes and packaging materials. Even the passenger's footwell is crammed with assorted stuff.

'I'd forgotten about that. Just chuck it out. I'll deal with it later.'

When we're finally in the car, it's twelve minutes to six.

'Right. Here we go.'

It's one of the hairiest drives I've experienced. Zelda spends most of the ride trying to explain the difference between clay and porcelain.

'Mum, you were supposed to stop there.'

'There wasn't anything coming.'

'Luckily!'

'You see, porcelain from the East was so valuable in the early eighteenth century it was called 'white gold'. Some European alchemists thought they could quickly discover a formula for making porcelain, when in fact it had taken the Chinese centuries to perfect the process, and...'

'Mum! That was a roundabout.'

'I know. I just wanted it more than he did.'

We screech to a halt at my grandad's place with ten seconds to spare.

'There we are. Plenty of time.' Zelda smiles sweetly. 'Let me know when you want to join the library. Bye-ee.'

I think my mum would like Zelda.

Home

'Your mother's back,' says Audrey. 'She's across the way.'

I cross the drive to the 'mummy-flat'. Grandad meets me in the hall. He puts a finger to his lips.

'You all right?' he murmurs.

'Where's Mum?'

'In the big room. Take it easy. No fuss. She needs peace and quiet.'

'Sure.'

He points to a plastic bag on the hall floor. 'I got your things back from the police.'

'Great!'

'Steady. Go and say hello to your mum first.'

I go into the sitting room. Mum's in the armchair in the corner. She looks pale and small, but also softer and rounder, as if she's put on weight.

'Hi, Mum.'

She looks up and her eyes are sort of blank.

'How are you feeling?'

'Tired.'

'Still?'

I notice an impatient movement in the doorway. Grandad is shaking his head at me. Not the right thing to say.

'Great to see you.'

She looks at me again with those dead eyes. It's almost as if she can't hear me. Do I raise my voice? Grandad said to keep it down.

'I met a really nice person today. The mum of a girl in my class. Her name's Zelda. I mean, the mum's called Zelda. The daughter's called Belinda. And Zelda makes pots. Out of porcelain. Really big ones. And some small ones. And they cost a lot. Hundreds of pounds. She sells them in London and New York and places. And they've got a really nice place in the country. And they've got a dog called Oscar. 'Cos the family name is Wilde. So, Oscar Wilde, see?' She doesn't laugh or smile. 'Anyway, we went for a walk with the dog. And he's good fun. Chases sticks and tennis balls all day long.'

'What kind of dog?'

'A golden retriever.'

'I think… I think I like those… don't I?' She's looking at Grandad.

'You love retrievers. You used to play with Sian Jones's.'

'Did I?'

'It was called Sally.'

Silence. Grandad is watching Mum and I'm watching him. There's something strange going on. Mum's voice sounds feeble. It's as if her face and body have become puffier and her spirit smaller. She's wearing a fleece, but I can see the edge of some bandaging on both wrists. Did she fall again and sprain them?

'I'll ask if we can go and walk Oscar one day. It's only about twenty minutes from here. We can catch the bus. There's a river where we can throw sticks for the dog.'

Mum looks up at me with a blank expression.

For a moment I don't know what else to say, but then I remember my mum's magic word.

'Can I get a cuddle?'

She frowns slightly and her eyes frame a question. It's a long time coming but eventually the words emerge.

'Who are you?'

Blanked

Grandad beckons me into the hallway.

'You'd better stay in the big house tonight.'

'But what's wrong?'

'Now, then. Calm down. Your mum had some treatment. It can have side-effects. Some people lose their memory for a few hours… or days sometimes. She'll be fine in a while. She just needs a lot of rest.'

'I thought that's what…'

'These things aren't always simple, Bran. She needs time. She'll be right as rain in a while. And you can take her for that walk. She'll love that. OK?'

It doesn't feel anything like OK, but I guess Grandad knows what he's talking about.

'Go and do your homework and don't worry.' He points at the plastic bag. 'Go and play with your stuff.'

'Yeah, I'll email Dad.'

Across the way, Audrey's in the living room watching TV. The house is spotless as usual. Nothing out of place, everything squared up.

'How's your mum?'

'Not so good. Grandad thinks I should stay here tonight.'

Audrey has this way of nodding, as if that's exactly the answer she expected.

'Have you eaten?'

'No.'

'I made toad-in-the-hole for you and Grandad. Is that OK?'

'That's great.'

'About ten minutes?'

'Thanks.'

I go up to my room and take out the gadgets. They're so scratched and dusty I wonder if they're really mine, but at least I can contact Dad.

I connect them up to the mains and boot up. Nothing. They're completely dead, as if the operating systems are wiped.

Part Four

Life's a Scrum

Set piece

'See that? That's the way to do it. Well done, Bran. The player gets tackled and the loose forward is a split second behind to keep the move going. That's how the Kiwis do it. Watch them on Saturday. Right, then, let's finish off with some scrum practice.'

We split into two sets of forwards.

'We're one short, coach.'

'OK.' He turns to me. 'Can your mate push?'

'I guess.'

'Because he can't do anything else.'

I look over at David. He's been sitting on a bench outside the changing rooms ever since he tried to kick the ball forward but connected with someone's shin. Before that, he'd dropped the ball three or four times and missed a couple of tackles. The coach asked him to 'take a break' but was really telling him to go away.

'What's his name again?'

'David.'

'David! Come on!'

David waddles on to the pitch as if he's heading towards a place of execution.

'Take your time, but don't take mine,' mutters coach Probyn. He turns to me. 'He's second row. You're back row. Show him what to do. Right. Reds will put the ball in. When I say push, you move the pack one yard forward and drive over the ball. OK? I want one smooth movement.'

David and I are in the second choice blue team. Apart from anything else, we're years younger, cannon fodder for the under-18s.

'What do I do?' asks David.

'Put your head in there.' I point to the space between the backsides of two guys in the front row. 'And bind your arm over the guy next to you. Don't push forward, just try to hold them when they push us backwards.'

The eight guys in each team lock arms, crouch and face each other.

'Engage…ball coming in… Reds push!... Come on, push!... what's wrong with you? Push!... All right, stand up!'

Coach Probyn looks at the Red pack.

'Right, I want all eight of you pushing. Get ready! Crouch! Pause! Engage! Ball coming in! Reds push!'

The scrum does not move an inch from front to back. If anything it goes slightly sideways.

'Stand up! Right! Now then, stop mucking about. Otherwise it's four laps of the field. OK?'

Our hooker turns from the front row and whispers, 'When he shouts push, let's push. See what happens.'

'Get that David? *We* push this time.'

'Are we s'posed to?'

'It's a bit of fun.'

'Orright.'

'Get ready!... Crouch!... Pause!... Engage!... Ball coming in!... Reds push!... Hey! What?... Hey! Are you having a laugh? Stop that!'

By the time our pack stops pushing we've moved five yards forward and I have the ball under my feet at the back of our scrum. The three lads in their front row have been forced to stand up straight under our pressure, walk backwards and fall over the players behind them.

'Right, what's going on?'

I catch Coach Probyn's eye and point at David.

'Really?'

'We reckon.'

'Right, then. You. Swap places with him.'

David joins the other pack and a red-faced under-18 joins the Blues.

'Get ready!... Crouch!... Pause!... Engage!... Ball coming in!... Reds push!'

To understand what happens next, you have to imagine standing in the sea when a powerful wave sweeps you off your feet. There's nothing to hold on to as your team-mates are driven apart and the wave keeps coming. The Reds have done to the Blues what the Blues just did to them. And there's one common factor.

After the practice session, Coach Probyn drives us home. We drop David off.

'Well, Bran,' says Coach. 'I'm not sure what to say. Your friend can push, that's for sure. Never seen anything like it at his age. But apart from that, he's a total liability. No skills whatsoever.'

'I'll see if he wants to practise with me.'

'Work on kicking and passing. If he gets any better, bring him back. But I can't risk him breaking someone's leg, or worse. You understand that, don't you?'

'Sure, you don't want to get sued.'

Dinner time

I can tell there's something wrong from halfway down the road. It's a sunny day, but the weather over Grandad's house looks cloudy. The reason becomes clear as soon as I turn up the drive. Grey smoke drifts from every door and window of the 'mummy flat'.

I stand in the doorway and shout.

'Mum?!'

No answer.

I go across to the house.

'I'm sorry, Steve, but she's got to go.'

I stand stock-still in the hallway and listen.

'That's harsh, Audrey.'

'What? She's done nothing but turn our lives upside down since she got here, and now she's setting fire to the buildings. She's a danger to herself and everyone else.'

'I've got to think of the boy.'

'There are qualified people paid good money to handle this sort of thing, Steve. You don't have to take it on. You've done everything you can. More than you should.'

'It's just a rocky patch…'

'You always say that! But it's not just a passing phase. She's got a condition, and she'll probably always have it. You've got to recognise that.'

'Maybe. But she's my daughter and he's my grandson. I'm not walking away.'

'I never thought you would.'

There's a pause. Should I let them know I'm here?

Too late. Audrey's off again. Besides, I need to hear this.

'What's happening with the Council? Surely they can do something?'

'She doesn't qualify for much. Been abroad too long.'

'Can't you speak to Councillor Collier?'

'What, and ask if we can jump the queue?'

'He's not a bad man, Steve.'

'He's a crook.'

'He's successful.'

'If being a wheeler-dealer is being successful.'

'It can't hurt to ask. He might surprise you.'

'How can you even ask me to do that? After all the surprises that man sprung on me?'

'That's politics, Steve. You used to say it yourself. If you can't stand the heat, get out of the kitchen.'

'I did!' It's the first time I hear Grandad shout. 'And so did my daughter earlier today, but you blame us both! Nothing but blame, blame, blame. How about some compassion?'

I creep back out the front as Grandad stomps out the back door and gives it a proper slam.

Mum's coming up the drive with a shopping bag. She's wearing sunglasses and her hair's all over the place.

'What happened?'

'Hello, love. Had a little mishap with the cooker. But don't worry, I managed to get a nice steak for your tea.'

'I'm not sure we should go in there. It's really smokey.'

She tuts and tosses her head. 'It's just a little hot oil. I'll grill this and we can sit outside to eat. It's lovely weather.'

She means not cloudy, five degrees and getting dark.

While Mum cooks the steak I walk around the outside of the building and assess the damage through the open windows. There's nothing actually burnt, just a lot of smoke damage. The pale, bright yellow walls and white ceilings are now a dull, uniform grey.

Mum tells me what happened – sort of – as we sit in our jackets among shadows cast by the feeble patio lighting. The story goes something like this:

She wanted to fix my favourite meal. Goulash with dumplings. So she raided my underfloor savings.

'Everybody knows where Audrey's mother stashed her cash.'

'But that was *my* cash!'

'Don't you want to share with your mother?'

' 'Course I do.'

'Well, then …'

So she went to Tynehurst, bought some pork, got back, put on a CD and danced around the kitchen as she cooked. Somewhere in the process, she felt the need for a nap and burnt the onions. That would account for the sweet, caramelised smell. So she aired the mummy-flat and went back to the village for more onions. Unfortunately, she'd started simmering some carrot and coriander soup for lunch and forgot to turn it off. Lunch turned into something black and immovable in the bottom of a pan.

'You can't tell where the soup ends and the teflon begins. They do it on purpose, you know, so you have to throw the pan away and buy a new one. You can't just scrape those things. Anyway, I need to go on a diet, so it worked out fine in the end.'

But it wasn't the end of everything, just that part.

Having soaked the saucepan in the sink, she started over and had the pork simmering nicely in the sauce. There was just time for a twenty-minute nap. Which turned into an hour and a half. Not a problem. There was plenty of time to raid my cash again and nip back to the supermarket for some more pork, onions and tomatoes.

'Hang on. That was two lots of pork and we're eating beefsteak.'

Her eyes well up.

'You sound just like Bill when you use that tone of voice.'

'I didn't mean…'

'I tried my best.'

Brilliant. I've made my mother cry.

'Mum, I'm not complaining. I love my beefsteak. I'm just wondering what happened to the second lot of pork.'

'I started watching a DVD.'

'Which one?'

'Pride and Prejudice.'

'Which version?'

'The BBC series.'

'But that's, like, five hours.'

'Six.'

'Didn't you notice the smoke?'

'I fell asleep again.'

'But that's really dangerous.'

'Don't you start. I had Audrey shouting the place down, banging on doors and windows.'

'We need a smoke alarm.'

'We've got one.'

'It didn't work?'

'It did. But those pills I'm taking make me really sleepy.'

'You reckon?'

Maybe that sounds like Dad again, but this time she smiles.

'Where shall we sleep tonight?'

She looks surprised. 'I don't know about you, but I'm sleeping here. Nothing will make me sleep in that woman's house.'

'Sleeping in smokey places isn't good for you.'

'I've slept through worse.'

'Yes... you have.'

She laughs and cries at this, but mostly laughs. Then she starts with the hugging, which is a bit embarrassing as people can see us from the road.

I can't abandon her and sleep in the house, so we keep the windows open and share my bed under as much bedding as we can find. I wake up freezing in the early hours and put a rug on top, which adds more weight than warmth.

The drop kick of destiny

'Frack it!'

'Stop swearing!'

'That's not swearing.'

'It's an 'f' word.'

'Yeah, but not *the* 'f' word.'

David stoops to pick the ball off the road.

'Look, just let the ball come to you. Don't grab it. If the pass is any good, you just hold it to your chest or stomach.'

'*If* the pass is any good.'

'Are you saying my passing's rubbish?'

'It could be better.'

We set off jogging down the lane once more. David whips the ball at my midriff.

'Ha! See?'

'Well, if you're going to throw it at me…' I pick the ball out of the ditch. 'Just lob it gently my way. When you've mastered lobbing we can move on to spinning it, like proper rugby players.'

'I can spin it.'

'Yeah?'

'Yeah.'

I doubt it, but he is getting better.

'Good fun this. Never been down this lane. Wonder what's down here.'

'You know Bel lives back there. We just passed it.'

'You fancy 'er, you.'

'Give over, David. It's not a soap opera.'

'Yeah, sure. I knows.'

I whip a pass at him. 'Yeah? But does you catches?'

To my surprise he does, and we pass it back and forth, doing our best to make the other drop the ball in a sprint. David really does remind me of a rhino. You don't want to assume he'll give up on the chase just because he looks clumsy.

'Look at that!'

We stop dead before a pair of massive iron gates with a coat of arms on either side cut into the masonry. To our left, just outside an ancient wall, are two tennis courts surrounded by a high fence. Interesting. One is a grass court, the other an all-weather surface. In front of them is a wide expanse of closely cropped pasture.

'C'mon,' I say, 'we can practise kicking,' and I shimmy over the five-bar gate.

I met a few kids back at Greystone's who could barely kick a beach-ball, let alone any sort of sports ball, but they never tried for a team. Yet, compared to David, they were regular David Beckhams.

His default kick is a punt that cannons off the point of his toe-cap half the time, and slices randomly off either side for the rest. On a few occasions he misses the ball completely, then accidentally back-heels it.

'Don't kick it with your toe. Kick it with your laces.'

He tries… and kicks it into his own face.

'OK, do that again, but get your face out of the way.'

''Ow the frack am I s'posed to do that?'

'Lean back as you kick.'

After a few more slices, back-heels, air kicks and balls in the face, he loses his temper, boots it up in the air then ducks as it comes straight back down, missing him by a yard.

'How did you do that?'

'Wodja mean?'

'Are you left-footed?'

'Eh?'

'Are you left-handed?'

'Dunno.'

'You must know if you're left-handed. Which hand do you write with?'

'Dunno. Don't write much.'

"So how do you do your homework?'

'Me sister does me homework. Or me mam, if she's got time.'

'But your sister's younger than you.'

'Yeah, I keep telling her the answers are rubbish.'

'Who gets higher marks, your sister or your mum?'

He thinks about it. 'They're about the same. Both rubbish.'

'OK, then. Kick with your left. Use the laces, lean back a bit and kick to me.'

There's no question he's left-footed. The ball travels. Not accurately, and not very far, but it goes up and forward.

'See? I'll be as good as you soon.'

'Don't be daft. I can drop kick a ball further and higher than you can punt.'

I ought to know better.

'Oh yeah? Bet you can't drop kick it over that fence.'

He means the fence around the tennis courts.

'That's somebody's property.'

'Chicken.'

'I'm not chicken. It's stupid.'

He makes chicken-wing movements with his elbows. 'Baaw-wp-bwawp, bawp bawp!'

'OK, I'll kick it over if you fetch it.'

'You'll never get it over that.'

'I will, if you go and get it.'

'You'll never.'

'Now who's chicken?'

'Yeah, go on then. Drop kick, mind.'

The All Blacks don't rate drop goals. They're a wussy way to win a match, really scraping the bottom of the barrel. But sometimes a drop kick can change your destiny. Like Jonny Wilkinson's extra-time kick to win the World Cup for England in 2003. If you can't beat a team fair and square, then a drop kick is an acceptable way to put everyone out of their misery. At least that's what my dad said when he encouraged me to practise.

A fence around a tennis court? Piece of cake.

'Go on, then. Go and get it.'

The gate is locked so I squat and lean against a tree trunk to watch David heaving himself up the wire mesh.

'You're going to make a dent in the top of that.'

The only reply is his heavy breathing. It's like watching somebody out of their depth in water.

'What do you think you're doing?'

Uh-oh.

David hangs upside down, the top of the fence sagging under his weight as he tries to locate the voice.

'I said, what do you think you're doing?'

'Oh, 'ello.'

'What are you doing climbing up my fence?'

'We lost our ball, missus.'

It's clear he'll only make things worse, so I get up and walk out from under the tree.

'I'm sorry, I miskicked the ball and it went over the fence.'

'Then why aren't you fetching it?'

She's about my mum's age, red-headed, pretty and carrying a tennis bag.

'We drew straws and he lost.'

'Yes, well…' She looks me up and down. 'I'd much rather have you climbing the fence than him.' She turns to David. 'Look, will you get down? That's practically a new fence.'

David makes it to the ground, falling more than climbing.

The woman unlocks the gate. 'Go on.'

I trot onto the court to retrieve the ball.

'In other circumstances I'd be perfectly within my rights to prosecute for trespassing.'

I think I detect a repressed smile, but better not risk it.

'I'm really, really sorry.'

'Where are you from?'

'New Zealand.'

'Yes, I thought I recognised the accent. What are you doing here?'

'My mother's originally from Tynehurst. We're visiting for a few weeks.'

She looks thoughtful. 'Do you play tennis?'

'I play for my school back home.'

'Well, since you're here, you can knock up with me till my coach arrives. He's late.' She looks at David. 'You can be ball boy.'

'Wozzat?'

'On second thoughts, see that roller, over there in the corner? You can roll the grass court. But don't crash it into the net posts.'

David scowls. 'That's work, that is.'

'You damaged my fence while trespassing. It's a case of pay up or do a job.'

David looks at me for some sort of guidance. I make a face to say we've been caught bang to rights. He shrugs acceptance.

'Good. Start by rolling across, then go up and down. And try to make neat stripes.'

In the end her coach doesn't turn up for half an hour. We crack balls back and forth while David trundles about the neighbouring court with the roller in tow.

'Sorry I'm late. Did you get my text?'

Her coach is all smiles, as if being late is no big deal.

'No, we were playing.'

'So I see. Not bad.' He turns to me. 'You'll put me out of a job.'

There's that Pommie self-depredation again.

'Right, then. Thanks for the practice. You're free to go, but don't take liberties again.'

'We won't, I promise.'

She reaches into her tennis bag. 'If you want Saturday jobs, give me a call. I could do with some help around the garden. And with rolling the court.' She hands me a business card.

'Thanks. But I'll have to ask my mum first.'

'Of course. Off you go.'

David's tuckered out, so we walk back up the lane.

'Posh cow!'

'Shut up. She'll hear.'

'So? Making me roll her frackin' grass! I'll tell me mam, I will.'

'Pretend it was an interview.'

'Wot?'

'She's offered us weekend jobs.'

'I'm not gonna roll her grass. Not for any money.'

'OK, I'll find someone else.'

'Wot? You gonna work for a fancy cow like that?'

'Yeah, why not?'

'That's slave labour, that is. That roller's frackin' 'eavy.'

'I'd do it. Good training for a rugby player. And you'd get paid to do it. See? We're halfway to being professionals already.'

'You're bats, you.'

I spin the ball from one hand to the other. 'The drop kick of destiny.'

The thing

'The thing is...' Grandad begins.

No, please, not the thing! Better get my own thing in first.

'I've got a thing, too.'

'What thing?'

'I got a Saturday job.'

'Where?'

'At Buckston Manor.'

'Doing what?'

'Weeding, digging, pulling a roller.'

'How did you manage that?'

'David and I were passing by and we got chatting to Sonia.'

'Sonia Partington?'

'Yes.'

'I've been trying to get work at the Manor for years.'

'Shall I ask?'

'No... yes... no. Let's wait and see. How much is she paying you?'

'Four pounds fifty an hour.'

'That's more than minimum wage for someone your age. How did you manage that?'

'I told her what Audrey's paying me.'

'Audrey's paying you pocket money. A pound an hour, isn't it?'

'Yes, but the lady of the manor doesn't need to know that. I told her Audrey was paying me four pounds an hour.'

'So she thought she was gazumping Audrey?'

'Yes.'

'You cheeky lad!' Grandad looks 'officially' annoyed, but while his eyes frown his mouth smiles. 'I guess you'd better take it. It's better than being stuck in a hairdresser's for peanuts.'

'I will. What's your thing?'

'My thing?' He looks worried now. 'Three things. I've got tickets to London Irish against Bath tomorrow. Do you want to come?'

‘’Course!’

‘Good. The other thing’s... OK. Try not to get upset, but you and your mum have to move.’

‘Why? Where to?’

‘Not far. A little house on the outskirts of Tynehurst. It’s not in great shape, but it’s the only thing I can afford. And it’s bigger than the ‘mummy flat’.’

‘Audrey wants us out.’

‘These things happen, Bran. Sometimes two people just don’t get along. It’s better this way.’

‘Why can’t we just go back to New Zealand?’

‘Ah, well… that’s the other thing.’

The other thing

Do all adults cheat, bribe and lie? There's no chance I wanna watch rugby tomorrow. What did Grandad think? That he could buy me off with a Pommy version of the game in some crummy stadium? Pathetic!

But what the hell is Dad thinking? He lied to me. He knew he was sending me to Pomsville on a one-way ticket. He set me up and sold me out. So now I'm pulling up weeds in some posh person's garden for peanuts per hour. He must have known. He must have planned it. He must have cancelled my phone and internet services. He's changed his email addresses, everything. What's he playing at?

There's nothing to worry about, he said. You'll be away for a bit. Just long enough for Mum to get her strength back. She just needs a rest.

Liar!

There's nothing to be upset about. Mum'll be OK in a little while. You'll have a nice little holiday in Pommieland. You can come back any time.

Liar!

I need you to do this for me. It's about taking responsibility. These things happen and we have to deal with it.

You mean *I* have to deal with it.

Your mum and I need you now. You mean *she* needs me now and *you* don't.

Double liar!

Not many kids get a chance to travel the world. You'll be back before Christmas. Let's not say which year, 'cos *this* Christmas you'll be on your own, mate, with twenty quid left over after everybody's been lifting the floorboards and nicking your cash. Happy Christmas, son.

Liar! Liar! Liar!

'Are you all right, Bran?'

'What?'

Sonia's standing right behind me looking worried.

'I brought you some orange juice and a biscuit.'

'Thanks.'

She's looking at the piles of weeds. 'You seem to be going at it with a vengeance.'

'Just thought I'd get this bit done.'

'Yes, well, I think you might have taken out a few primroses and poppy plants.'

'Oh.'

She's right. I can see some of the leaves she said not to touch in one of my piles.

'I'm sorry. I'll go through the piles and save them.'

'But you've almost done your three hours.'

'No, I'll do it. It's my fault. I won't charge for the time.'

What am I doing? My Dad would always find a way to get paid.

'Well, just rescue what you can.'

Great! That'll be at least an extra hour.

The non-weeds look wilted and half dead as I sift through the piles. What's the point? Why should I care? They're only stupid flowers. Here today, gone tomorrow. But she did tell me not to pull them up, and I forgot. It's my responsibility.

See, Dad? I know what responsibility is. Unlike you. Cheat, swindler, liar!

Walking back along the lane I meet Bel and her dog.

'Hi. Down, Oscar! Bad boy!'

'It's all right. I'm muddy already.'

'Yes, you do look… grubby. What've you been doing?'

'A gardening job.'

'Where? At Sonia's place?'

'Yeah. Do you know her?'

'She's one of mum's best friends. And I clean for her twice a week. She's lovely. But her husband's a complete prat.'

'He is?'

'Sonia's his second wife. He was horrible to his first. Is he there now?'

'I didn't see him.'

'He doesn't like me letting Oscar loose on his land. He's so uptight. But Sonia's lovely.'

Do all Pommy kids talk like Bel? She seems very mature, judging everybody in a cheery sort of way, but you suspect it's all front.

'Are you all right, Bran?'

'What? Why?'

'You seem a bit down.'

I've promised myself not tell anyone. What do they care, anyway? What do they know? Kids are just junior adults. Selfish cheats and liars, all out for what they can get. She won't get me to spill the beans.

'I'm fine. What about you?'

'I'm OK. But my mum's having a hard time. The quality of the porcelain she's using has changed and her pots keep collapsing. But the supplier won't admit there's a problem. She's struggling to pay the bills, so she's been weepy since lunchtime.'

'It can't be that bad. Her pots cost a bomb.'

I know this sounds mean as soon as the words pass my lips, and a corner of Bel's mouth twitches in disappointment.

'They cost a lot because they're worth a lot.'

'How does that work?'

'Her pots are in museums. They're insured for ten times more than she got for them.'

'Yeah, but your dad's loaded.'

She looks at me the same way Sonia did just an hour ago. 'Are you sure you're all right?'

'Not really.'

And it all comes out. How does *that* work? I was determined to man up and keep it to myself. I know I shouldn't talk to these people. They're not my people. I'm a Kiwi. I should keep my mouth shut. It'll be all over that stupid Pommy kids' school bus on Monday morning.

But we perch on a stile and talk about it, while Oscar gambols around the field, nose to the ground, looking for rabbits.

'So my parents are officially separated.'

Bel grunts. 'I know that word. My parents were separated several times. It just meant my dad wanted to go off and do his thing. It was just a matter of time before they divorced.'

'I don't know how my dad could do it this way.'

'They can't stand the guilt, so they behave all weird. I wrecked my bedroom when my Dad finally left.'

'You did?'

'Yeah. Knocked everything off the walls. Ripped up my posters. Smashed my mirrors. Threw my books out the window. Tore down the curtains.'

Bel's usually so calm you can't imagine her doing anything like that.

'I just tore up Sonia's flower bed.'

Bel laughs. 'What did she say?'

'Not much. Just said I'd got some flowers along with the weeds.'

'She's a sweetie. Her husband would have fired you on the spot.'

'He sounds mean.'

'Totally self-centred.'

'They're all selfish, aren't they?'

'Who?'

'Parents.'

'Depends. After I wrecked my room, my mum didn't get upset with me. She walked about the garden picking my books and stuff out of puddles. She was crying harder than when Dad left. I was thinking about myself, but she was thinking about me. I did it to hurt Dad, but I hurt her even more. So I decided I'd never do anything like that again.'

Oscar comes up and tries to get us to walk. Bel pulls an old tennis ball out her pocket and throws it into the hedge.

'He likes a challenge.'

Should I tell her about my mum? About how she's in danger of burning down the house when she's not resting in some clinic? But it feels like a step too far. What would my mate Chris say? 'You've got to keep faith with at least one of your parents. It stops the other one renting out your room.'

My mate Chris. He's a world away and has probably forgotten me.
'Do you want to come home for some cake?'
'Will your mum mind?'
'Why should she?'
'Isn't she stressed out?'
'No, I cheered her up.'
'How did you do that?'
'I baked a cake.'

Lost and Found

We are here
waiting
not knowing
if wanted
unloved
inconvenient,
a memory
best forgotten
not found.

Children mislaid
in competing demands,
we can each be described
as a 'baggage',
sometimes undeclared,
more complex than luggage
since we change,
becoming
quite different from the item lost.

Longed for
regretted
dismissed
avoided
evaded
occasionally met
in a dream,
an unguarded, pixellated moment,
in an old photograph.

If you think of us
waiting
among the old feathers
in a pigeon hole
of your memory,
remember we are waiting to grow
out of sight
out of mind
beyond recognition.

B. Wilde (Class 9A)

10/20 Unnecessarily gloomy and far too vague. You must stick to the topic. It was 'On being a teenager' not 'Lost luggage'.

Part Five

Life's a collapsing scrum

Living the dream

I creep downstairs trying not to wake Mum. The carpetless wooden steps squawk as though they might crack and collapse at any time, but all I can hear is Mum's steady breathing.

She must have had another late night. Her bedroom door's open and a dressing gown lies on the landing.

I glance at the living room. Her armchair is the usual nest of blankets and glossy magazines. Glasses and teacups litter the low table. The TV screen announces the return of a shopping channel at 5pm. That's my mum's world now – screen shopping all night with no means of buying. When I come home from school, she tells me about some fantastic dress she's seen, or a piece of jewellery.

'I don't see why not. I used to be a model once. I could still wear that.'

But I won't be home tonight. Half-term begins and the County under - 16s are on tour. We're on our way to Bristol. It's Grandad's turn to be here and make sure Mum has what she needs.

There are three teabags in the tin and no new packet in the cupboard. Mum drinks several cups a day. If I use one now, she'll be out by lunchtime.

I search for a used bag. There's one attached to a teaspoon on the draining board. It'll have to do.

There's no bathroom in this place. Grandad's saving money so he can install one. In the meantime I just have to get used to lifting the washing-up bowl out of the sink, inserting the plug and running the cold tap. As I look in the mirror to shave using soap lather and a cheap disposable razor, I pretend I'm one of the first Kiwi settlers living rough but building a country.

It doesn't really work. In my case it's less about nation-building and more about removing all the bumfluff while missing the spots and pimples. Not easy in an old mirror Noah must have used in the Ark.

The club check-list demands one cabin-size hand-luggage case and a garment bag. I still have those from EnZed, but fewer clothes to go inside. I grew out of my Kiwi togs months ago.

1 club suit. No chance. David and I will be wearing our school uniforms. *1 pair pyjamas.* That'll have to be an old tee-shirt and a pair of boxer shorts. *1 light woollen V-neck sweater for evening wear, to be worn with tie at all times.* That'll be my one sweatshirt with tie-knot just visible. *£50 pocket money.* Fat chance. I've managed to save £24 towards this trip by doing eight tennis sessions with Sonia. Whatever she does, I just try to get the ball back. I'm a human wall at £4 an hour. I get less than for gardening because Sonia reckons it's partly recreation. Hardly, but I guess being paid sort of makes me a tennis pro. *1 mobile phone, to be switched on at all times for contact with management.* Maybe, maybe not. My crap phone is losing its chirp, so I keep it in 'vibrate' mode in a place where I can see it creeping across a surface like a big black beetle.

The most important item in my luggage this weekend is the roll of duct tape I got from Grandad to repair our rugby boots. If we tape them up from inside nobody will notice. Mine aren't too bad – just a couple of small holes at the insteps, but David's are falling apart.

I ease the key round in the lock on the back door. There isn't much that will wake Mum at this hour but she has a fear of burglars and an uncanny sense for any presence in the yard or garden.

The outside loo door has a latch which is easy to open without a sound. I don't flush and will be told off later for 'forgetting'.

I never wait for the school bus outside the house. It would wake Mum up, and I don't want those kids knowing where I live. Their comments as we pass the house are enough to seal my lips.

'What a dump!'

'Does anybody actually live in that place?'

'Maybe there's a body in an upstairs room.'

'Or a skeleton in a rocking chair.'

I beg Grandad to have the wreck of a car moved to a dump, but it costs to hire a removal truck and he's stretched as it is trying to pay the mortgage on this place. Luckily our neighbour is friendly and seems to understand our situation. She even called my Grandad once when Mum was having one of her turns.

Our line of houses is called 'The Dabs' because the houses were 'dabbed on' one at a time over two centuries. They were cottages for agricultural workers on the landed estate that used to give jobs to most of the local people. As the estate became poorer, the houses built for workers got smaller. Ours was the last to be built. Two small rooms downstairs and two tiny ones on the first floor. The last owner was too ill and too poor to do any work on it for the last twenty years of his life. His car rusted in the front drive, the brambles took over the garden, and the plaster crumbled from the walls inside and out.

A modern housing estate ends just opposite the posher end of 'The Dabs'. A gap-strewn wire fence protects a kiddies' playground from the main road. Three guys – they look no more than seventeen or eighteen – are sitting on the front step of a three-storey apartment block drinking from cans. It looks as though they've pulled an all-nighter.

'Oi! You!'

'Wanna buy a bike? Ten quid.'

They're pointing to a beaten up offroadie with no mudguards. At that price it has to be stolen.

'No, thanks.'

'Off on 'oliday, are we?'

'Movin' into school, are yuh?'

'Come an' 'ave a drink mate? Always start a holiday with a drink.'

I raise a hand briefly to show I get the joke. They stare, then burst out laughing as if I've done the stupidest thing in the world. They sound very drunk. The stuff in the cans must be strong brew and it's only eight-fifteen on a Friday morning. The patience of their neighbours must be powerful stuff to put up with that racket.

I stand at the bus stop just beyond the first 'Dab' with a stretch of hedge between me and the drinkers. Out of sight out of mind, with any luck. In the end it doesn't matter because Callum's bang on time.

'All right, Number Eight?'

That's his nickname for me ever since he read about us in the local paper. Luckily David's a number three. Being a number one or two would be a gift to the knockers.

'Two suitcases?!'

That, as usual, is Nash. He thinks the height of wit is to express the obvious in a pantomime voice.

'Yes, two. One, two. Very good.'

I slip the cases into the overhead rack and take my seat beside David. A quick glance at his bulging plastic bag tells me I was right to bring the second.

'I brought a spare, if you want it.'

'Thanks, mate. I've fixed a smart phone for you.'

'How'd you do that?'

'We'll have to skive off lunch to pick it up.'

My grandad's paying for my school lunches. I would normally qualify for free school meals – as Audrey takes pains to remind me, whenever she gets the chance – but it's a step too far for Grandad.

'That's one stigma we can spare the lad.'

Bunking off at midday would seem like a betrayal of his trust.

'I don't want to miss a meal.'

'You won't. My dad's buying us lunch.'

'Your dad?'

'Yeah. It's about time you met him.'

I'm not sure I want to, given his reputation.

'My Grandad got us a big roll of duct tape.'

David grins. 'Don't need it meself. See?'

He pulls a pair of brand new, bright yellow football boots out of his plastic bag.

'You can't wear those.'

'Why not?'

'They're soccer boots. A rugby player wouldn't be seen dead in those.'

Even worse, the sight of them sets Nash going again. 'Whoah, Daffy's got glow-in-the-dark boots!'

I try to explain that he's a forward and needs a boot with more support round the heel and mid-foot, but David's intent on besting Nash in a shouting match.

'So what are you doing this half-term, then Nash? Eh? While we're playing rugby for Berkshire? Eh?'

'I'm learning to drive.'

'How can you do that? You have to be seventeen.'

'Yeah, well there's a place where you can learn to drive off-road without a provisional licence. That's how much you know.'

'Don't talk daft!'

Sadly, it's David who's being daft. I've heard about those places.

'Yeah, well, we're all going together.' Nash means Matt, Greg and the Three As, Alys, Alison and Alicia.

'So, while you're rolling around in the mud like cavemen, getting your heads stamped on by Cornish kids, we'll be learning to drive in an ultra-safe environment.'

Alison tilts her head like a mean girl making a point. I know I shouldn't rise to the bait, but I do.

'Big deal. I had a ute in New Zealand.'

'But now you're uteless.'

I look around. Matt's staring at me with a look of distant yet utter contempt. His expression doesn't change for a second, even as the roars and shrieks of approval break out all around, as if their team has scored a goal. First the eye-bulging expectation, then the sheer shock and joy, followed by the celebration and the chant.

'Uteless! Uteless! Uteless!'

Bel glances across the aisle. 'At least we've got a new nickname. I was getting really tired of rehab.'

The Broken Glass

'Let's get outta here.'

I really don't like the look of this place. Any pub called The Broken Glass can't be a good sign.

David doesn't get it. 'Woz wrong?'

'We're not allowed in there without an adult, are we?'

'Nah, we go round the back. T' the garden.' David points at a poster on the outside noticeboard. 'Anyway, look. Callum works here.'

There's a photo of a familiar figure with a guitar. 'Irish Night with Callum O'Connor.'

Who knew our bus driver was multi-talented? But Callum is all right. If he plays here …

David's getting seriously irritated with my dithering.

'C'mon!'

People have very different ideas of what a garden should be. This one is just a grimy patio with a single table next to the drains and empty bottle storage.

'Orright, son?'

The greeting is from a tall skinny man sitting between a couple of beefy characters. He looks quite young until you get up close. His thick wavy hair is overlong, like one of those styles that was in fashion a long time ago. The lines in his face are masked by an apology for designer stubble and a tan, as if he's just come back from a holiday abroad. The watch on his wrist looks like a Rolex, but I'm guessing it's fake.

'What d'you want now, then?' He and his mates leer at David, then at me.

'You said you had a phone for us.'

'Did you make those deliveries?'

'Yeah.'

'Got the receipts?'

'Yeah.' David pulls a couple of grubby slips of paper from a pocket and hands them over.

He examines them. 'Yeah, they look all right. Get any hassle?'

'No.'

'Good.' The man stuffs the slips into one pocket then reaches into another to pull out a phone.

I can tell straightaway that it's used. You can see the wear and tear, but it's a recent model.

'Is this your mate, then?'

'Yeah, this is Bran.'

'So, you're the rugby star.'

'I'm all right.'

'And turning Dave into one as well.'

'He does that himself.'

'Left to himself he'd be a pizza-eating champ.'

'He can do both.'

This amuses the men.

'So, you need a phone?'

'I did yesterday, but my Grandad got me one.'

David swings around.

'Then why'd you come with me now?'

'I thought you said your Dad could get me some new boots, like the ones you got.'

The men laugh at this.

'Easy on, now. You've gotta earn stuff like that. Dave doesn't get stuff for nothing. Right, son?'

'Right.'

'So what do I have to do?'

'A few delivery jobs. Dead easy. But only if you're trustworthy. Are you?'

I want to say that he's the last man in the world *I* would trust.

'Yes, I am, but I've got a job already.'

'Yeah, but does it pay for new designer boots, eh?'

Designer boots! What's he talking about? You don't wear rugby boots to make you look good: you wear them to do a job.

'The thing is, I'm getting another job next week. So I won't have any spare time.'

The man's smile fades and the grey-green eyes harden like sapphire crystals. I've noticed that the two heavies on either side mirror their boss's body language and changes of mood, except that when his expression turns sharp, theirs turn blunt.

David's dad leans back in his chair and the knowing leer returns to his lips.

'Go on, get lost. And you,' he means David, 'don't bring me any more time-wasters. Orright?'

David gives me grief all the way back to school.

'Wot d'you do that for?'

'I don't care if he is your dad, I'm not accepting a phone from him.'

The whiteboard dancer

'The thing about history,' says Mr Edwards, 'is that it's not just about facts. It encourages us to challenge almost everything we think we know. For example, let's see... '

Mr Edwards, affectionately known as Ted, never uses the interactive whiteboard and instead has placed an old-fashioned board in front of it. He selects a red marker pen and writes BIG QUESTIONS in the middle at the top.

'Let's see... Jones.'

'...'

'Jones?'

'Wake up, Daffy!'

'Yeah?'

'Still with us, David?'

'Yeah.'

'Good. Now, you'd call yourself Welsh, wouldn't you?'

'Yeah.'

'Would you call yourself a Celt?'

David blinks.

' 'Course.'

'And how do you know that you are?'

'Me mam told me.'

'Your mother told you that you are Welsh and therefore you are Celtic?'

'Yeah.'

'But does the evidence support this? The question I'm asking is...,' he leaps towards the whiteboard and scribbles in blue: ARE/WERE THE WELSH CELTS? 'Are they descended... is David Jones... descended from the people known as Celts who originated about three thousand years ago in the area now known as Austria and Switzerland? Did those Celts invade this country? Or was it their art and culture that invaded this country?'

'How can art and culture invade a country?'

'Good question!' He leaps to the board again and writes the question in green on the right side of the board: CAN ART AND CULTURE INVADE A COUNTRY? 'That's your homework for next time. Think about it and write at least a page and give examples. Now then, next big question.'

WHEN DID THE LAST INVASION OF THIS COUNTRY OCCUR?

'Any answers?'

I raise my hand.

'1066.'

'Any advances on 1066?'

Bel raises her hand. Just the hint of a smile tells me she's got a killer answer. I'd hate her for that if I didn't like her so much.

'Belinda?'

'1688.'

Mr Edwards pretends he's surprised.

'1688? How could that be?'

'William of Orange was invited to replace James II.'

'But he was invited. That's not an invasion, is it?'

'Was the Spanish Armada an attempted invasion?' asks Bel.

'Most definitely.'

'But William's army and navy was three or four times the size of the Armada. So it looks like an invasion.'

'A good argument and another good question. If a foreign power arrives with a very large army, can it be anything other than an invasion?' He scribbles the question in green on the right.

'So which foreign power did William of Orange represent? Yasmin?'

'The Dutch.'

'Good. Where did you learn that?'

'I just read it from Bel's notebook.'

'Well spotted. Never miss an opportunity to learn.' Ted looks at the board. 'So, let's see. You've generated as many questions as I have so far.

Let's see if you can beat my number of questions by the end of ... '

There's a knock on the door and Mr Carson enters.

'Sorry to interrupt, Mr Edwards...'

'Not at all, Mr Carson.'

'I see the interactive whiteboard is out of action again.'

'I'm afraid it never has worked properly,' replies Mr Edwards.

'A pity, since it cost the best part of a thousand pounds.'

'Yes, imagine how many books we could have bought for that amount.'

They keep their eyes fixed on each other like two highly civilised cats skirting each other's territory, apparently relaxed but ready to strike and defend at any moment.

'How can I help, Mr Carson?'

'I need Jones and Kelleher outside the head's office immediately after final bell.'

Mr Edwards checks with us. 'Message received?'

'Yes.'

'Yeah.'

Mr Carson glares. 'That would be a 'Yes', Jones.'

'Yeah, yes.'

The class titters. You never know if David is cheeking a teacher or genuinely doesn't get it.

'I believe the pair of you brought luggage to school.'

'It's in my store cupboard,' says Ted. 'For safekeeping.'

'Good, I'll take it now. You'll find it waiting for you in the head's office.' He turns to Mr Edwards. 'I'll need you to accompany the boys as soon as the bell goes. It's imperative they don't go anywhere else. And no conferring or disposing of anything.'

Mr Carson turns to us while Mr Edwards retrieves our kit from the storeroom. 'Place your hands on the desk and keep them there till the end of the lesson.'

The two men nod at each other as Mr Carson leaves with the cases. Carson's nod means 'you have my instructions'. But what does Ted's mean?

The class have been oohing and ahhing, enjoying the trouble we're in, but now they're quiet and serious. This looks like big trouble and none of them would want to be in our shoes. Bel has turned pale. What does that little frown mean? That she's worried for us? That there are limits to friendship?

David is gurning as usual, as if he couldn't care less. I should have known he was trouble. Big trouble.

The interrogation

The contents of our bags are strewn across a side-table in the head's office. Mr Carson is feeling around the linings for any other hiding places, and Mrs Creasey enters from the secretaries' lair with a flourish. This is their sensation of the day, if not the week, and I get the feeling they're gunning for us.

'Have they passed anything to anyone else?'

'No,' replies Mr Edwards. 'As you advised, they had hands above the covers at all times.'

He seems to find the situation mildly amusing, but I can't be sure if he's tickled by the other teachers or our situation. Does he think we're just a pair of bad-egg halfwits, living out our tragi-comic teenage years?

'Thank you, Mr Edwards.'

He's dismissed. They don't want his lack of seriousness messing up their police-style investigation.

'Right, then,' says Mr Carson. 'Where is it?'

'Where's what?' snaps David.

I wish he wouldn't do that.

'You were seen going to a public house at lunchtime.'

'So?'

'Don't get fresh, Jones. You've broken several school rules. We're just trying to establish whether we need to call the police or not. You went to collect something from your father …'

'Owjoo know that?'

'Where is it?'

'Who told you?'

'It's our business to know where you are in school hours. Now what is it and where is it?'

I jump in before David can do any more damage.

'It was a used phone and his father still has it.'

'Why's that?'

'I didn't want it.'

'Why not?'

'Because I didn't know where it had come from.'

Mr Carson's stare is hard and disbelieving.

'Empty your pockets,' he says. 'All of them.'

The contents of David's pockets are more offensive to Mrs Creasey than if he'd suddenly pulled out half a dozen dodgy phones.

'Most of this is rubbish. Just throw it in the bin.'

'No, you can't. Thems coupons. And thems me brother's shoelaces.'

'I… Why… To begin with, I don't know where to start with your English, David Jones. *These are* coupons and those *are my* brother's shoelaces. And what are you doing with your brother's shoelaces in any case?'

'None of your business.'

Definitely the wrong choice of words. Mr Mackie has heard enough.

'Right, remove your jackets, shoes and ties.'

'What's this?' demands David. 'A strip search?'

'If we have to call the police, we shall.'

We're down to our shirts, trousers and socks and Mr Carson is feeling round my waistband, when Grandad is shown into the head's office.

'Mr Cooke. I wasn't aware we'd called you.'

'I'm here to drive the boys to a meeting point. They're playing rugby for the County this weekend.'

'I'm afraid they can't leave till we've established whether they're carrying stolen goods or not.'

Grandad doesn't seem surprised by the situation, as if somebody has brought him up to speed. He shoots me one of his honesty-seeking looks.

'Are you?'

'No. I was offered a phone but I didn't take it.'

'Good.' He turns to the teachers. 'Have you found anything?'

'Not yet.'

'Well, I can see you've had a thorough search. If you don't mind, the boys will miss their bus and then they'll miss the tournament.'

'I'm afraid that's too bad,' says Mrs Creasey.

Why do people say they're afraid when they're not in the slightest?

'They're representing this school and the County.'

'They may be representing the County, but I don't regard them as representing this school.'

'I see. Not a rugby fan.'

'I'm not a fan of criminals who hang out in pubs and supply their sons with stolen goods.'

'Neither am I, but punishing the sons wouldn't be my first thought.'

Mr Carson senses that Grandad's winning the argument and confronts David.

'These boots. Where did you get them?'

'From me da.'

'*From. My. Father.*' Mrs Creasey sounds like a pressure cooker about to pop its lid.

David stares at her bug-eyed, as if she's losing it. 'No. From *my* father.'

'Right,' Grandad suddenly takes control by turning on David. 'I've had enough of your backchat, and that's the last time you ever take my grandson to see your father. Do you understand?' He doesn't wait for an answer. 'My grandson didn't grow up round here, so he can't judge people like you. All right? And he's done nothing but encourage you to become a better person. Isn't that right?'

He gives David a split second to utter the beginning of a 'yes'.

'So don't reward him for raising you up by dragging him down. Got that?'

David's truly shocked by that and his eyes well up.

Grandad turns to Mr Mackie.

'Have you any reason to keep these boys any longer? Because I'm pretty sure they've missed their bus and I'll have to drive them there myself.'

'There is the question of breaking school rules.'

'Can you sort out detentions and so on after half-term?'

'We may have to conduct further enquiries.'

'There's the matter of these football shoes,' says Mrs Creasey.

David begins to gurn and say, 'Thems not footba shoes … '

'Shut up,' snaps Grandad. To Mr Mackie he says, 'I think you'll have to take up the matter of the boots with the boy's father. I'll certainly mention it to his mother.'

Mr Mackie ponders the situation. 'Fine. I'll see both you boys at lunchtime on Monday week. Make a note of that, please, Mr Carson.'

Grandad is already stuffing my gear back into the case. The teachers leave and Mr Mackie sends in a secretary to watch us re-pack, as if he thinks we might nick something from his office.

'Thanks, Grandad,' I say once we're out in the deserted lobby.

He grabs my shoulder and swings me round.

'Don't you ever... *ever*... put me in this position again. Do you understand?'

I do. And so does David. I think he's more shocked than I am by Grandad's anger.

By the time we get outside there are just two cars waiting: Grandad's and another I recognise.

Bel and Zelda Wilde are leaning on the bonnet of their old van. They stir themselves as we emerge from the building.

'How did it go? Are you all right?'

I start to make the introductions.

'We've met,' says Grandad. 'I'm sorry,' he continues, 'we can't hang about. I have to get these boys to Bristol somehow.'

'Is there anything I can do?' asks Zelda.

'I doubt it.'

'Are you sure?'

Zelda's keen persistence is beginning to irritate Grandad. He pauses and speaks slowly, trying to dampen her enthusiasm.

'These boys have to get to Bristol. I have to drive them. But I'm supposed to be looking after Bran's mother tonight and she shouldn't be left alone.'

'She could come and stay with us.'

'I'm not sure that will work.'

'We've got a spare bedroom. What could go wrong?'

Grandad and I glance at each other. He's wondering who this person is, poking her nose into our affairs. I really don't want anybody at school to meet my mum. I know it sounds disloyal, but I don't want anyone feeling sorry for us or, even worse, deciding we're a bunch of losers. If someone like Nash gets hold of this information I'll have to move to another school. On the other hand, I don't want to miss the rugby.

'The thing is, Catherine sleeps a lot,' says Grandad.

'Not a problem.'

'And… she forgets things.'

Zelda laughs. 'Join the club.'

'But she can forget a pan on the cooker, or leave a bath tap running.'

It's Bel's turn to laugh. 'That happens all the time at our house.'

'Not *all* the time,' Zelda protests.

'Mum! You left the hose running yesterday.'

'Only because I had a crisis in the studio.'

As usual, David can't resist getting involved.

'She might set fire to the place!'

I wonder how he knows that. Or is he just guessing?

'I'm a potter. We have smoke alarms, fire blankets and extinguishers.'

I can see Grandad worrying not so much about what his daughter might do to their living arrangements, but about whether she'd be safe in their care.

'It's just one night,' says Zelda. 'It'll be fine. We'll just be watching TV, or listening to music, or reading.'

'It's a very generous offer.'

'We don't want the boys to miss their weekend.'

'That's very kind.'

'Shall we just follow you?'

It's an offer Grandad can't refuse, so we head back to 'The Dabs' to hand Mum over to the Wilde side. I'm praying that Bel is truly discreet. That's the trouble with kids. Most of them are gabby and brain-dead like David. Most of all I'm praying that Zelda's fire extinguishers are in working order.

'If I find out who dobbed us up, I'll smash 'im to a pulp,' says David from the backseat.

Grandad stops the car right there in the middle of the street and Zelda brakes to a halt behind.

'And if you ever say or do anything like that, you'll never socialise with Bran or play rugby again. Do you understand?'

'Uh… whuh…'

'Do you want to play rugby this weekend?'

'Yeah.'

'Yes, please, Mr Cooke!'

'Yes… please… Mr Cooke.'

'Right, because if you have any doubts about behaving properly in future you can get out of this car right now. Now, do you want me to drive you to Bristol, or do you want to make your own way, if you can?'

'No… yes… I want…. Thanks… thank you… Mr Cooke.'

Schooled.

The egg

They long for these moments,
the protectors and carriers
of a single egg:
they put their bodies on the line.

They train for this,
the half-grown ruckers,
rehearsing scrums – crouch,
set, bind and push.

Coming in now -
'Brace yourself, mate!' –
these bullocks gingerly guard
the egg with cradling hand,

scrambling hoof and rutting head –
up and under, Gary Owen!
They stampede to repossess that falling,
tumbling focus of endeavour.

To cross that line,
Bisect the upper H -
'Straight through the middle!' -
brings pure joy.

All this sinew and muscle,
blood, sweat and bruise,
for egg preservation
and survival of the creed.
B. Wilde (Class 9A)

10/20 I have no idea what this is about. The subject was 'Tradition', not sport, if that is indeed your subject. Who is Gary Owen? And why the egg? What egg?

And another thing

"Stonefield Schoolboy Selected for England Training Camp."

Headlines are supposed to scream, but this one lied. The journalists couldn't get through on the phone. I was at school and Mum was over at Zelda's pottery most of the day, so a reporter and photographer turned up at the comp. Mr Mackie set up an interview in his office. His expression in greeting me was completely different from the last time we met.

'Ah, Bran. Have a seat.'

No mention of the two detentions Mr Carson gave me last week. I got off lightly. David got four, then an extra two for missing the first.

'Me mam needed me at home to feed the babby.'

The trouble with David is he thinks the whole world is against him. Just because he had one player trying to niggle him in the match against Dorset, he thought the entire population of south-west England was trying to nobble him.

'I gets me retaliation in first. Thems trying to do me.'

He was sin-binned in every match, though we lost only one in our mini-league and finished second overall. Our scrum went backwards and shipped penalties when David was in the bin, but made up the ground when he came back. Without him I wouldn't have been launching attacks from the base of the scrum, or nailing their halfbacks as they tried to deal with tricky ball going backwards. A marauding back row player looks good from the touchline, but it's built on the work done by the front five. Yet I'm the one being selected for training with the England under-16s.

The problem is, I'm not English.

'Sorry?'

The journalist can't believe what he's just heard.

'I'm a New Zealander. I'm not English.'

'But… isn't one of your parents English?'

'Yes, my mum. But my dad's a Kiwi and I was brought up there. That's where I learned my rugby and I've got a New Zealand passport.'

'Didn't you tell the selectors?'

'Nobody asked.'

Mr Mackie intervenes. 'Bran is eligible to play for Berkshire Schools whatever his nationality. In fact, all our County rugby players could be considered non-English.'

'How many are there?'

'Three. Of the under-16s, Bran here. And David Jones, who I think identifies as Welsh. And in the under-18s Michael O'Callaghan, who has an Irish father.'

It takes the pressure off me as the reporter can change the story. He wants all three of us in the photo.

'We'll go with something like "Local School Producing Elite Rugby Players".'

That pleases Mr Mackie, though he must know the school has barely lifted a finger to develop serious sports. I wonder what Mrs Creasey will make of that headline.

'All right, Number Eight?'

The old headline may have been wrong, but it's great for kudos on the bus. Callum gives me a huge grin. Matt and the Three As don't say another word about their new driving skills and Nash has to find another angle of attack. He leaves me alone and decides to bait David instead.

'Rugby's a game for thugs played by thugs. I prefer football.'

'Youse couldn't play any kind of ball, Nashie.'

'Look who's talking, Daffy-Two-Necks.'

It is true that David is developing a powerful neck which looks as wide as his head from the back. In fact, his muscles seem to be responding more than mine to our weightlifting regime.

For the first time ever, Bel turns round to face Nash.

'If you're going to quote something, at least get it right. Football is a gentleman's game played by ruffians, and rugby is a ruffian's game played by gentlemen.'

There are a few 'Oooh, ruffians!', but it settles the argument.

Grandad's waiting for me at home.

'Where's Mum?' I wonder.

'At the pottery.'

'Again?

'Zelda says she can help out. And she enjoys it, so it's no bad thing. It gets her moving and she earns some cash.'

'But she falls asleep all the time.'

'Zelda hasn't complained, so there must be something in it for her.'

Grandad seems anxious.

'I've had reporters on the phone all day.'

'About me?'

'Yep. And the Rugby Football Union.'

'Well, it wasn't my fault. I told everybody I'm an EnZedder.'

'Well, the thing is ...'

Not this again.

'What thing?'

'The thing is... strictly speaking... you're English.'

'How come?'

'Do you want a cup of tea?'

'No. How come I'm not a New Zealander?'

Grandad gets up and heads to the electric kettle. 'I need a cup of tea.'

Suddenly he seems older and smaller. I know he's been tendering for as much work as he can find without having to take on another worker. Sometimes I think he's come straight from a plastering job, but then I realise his hair's turning white. His forearms are still muscled, but his shoulders slump with fatigue. And now there's something on his mind that's sapping his strength even more.

He comes back to the table with two mugs of builder's tea.

'The thing is, Bran, I wanted to tell you this right away, when you came back from New Zealand. But... well... your mum didn't want me to tell you... and she wasn't well at the time... and I didn't know what to do.'

'What?'

'But now the papers are all over it, and you're telling them you're not English when you are...'

'What?!'

'The thing is… the fact is… Bill Kelleher's not your dad.'

'?!'

'Well, he was your dad for a while, but he's not your natural father.'

'Who is?'

Grandad is looking long and hard at the tea in his mug.

'Who is it?'

He looks up. One of his worst memories is stirring behind those grey-blue eyes.

'I don't know how to put this any other way, Bran, but David Jones is your half-brother.'

Go left, go right?

I stare into the jar for several minutes. It contains three ten-pound notes, cash Mum has earned at Zelda's place over the past week. Why shouldn't I take one? People have been bludging off me for months. It's just ten quid. Sonia owes me sixteen. I can pay back the jar next week when her la-di-daship finally gets around to paying me. Don't people realise that sixteen pounds isn't just pocket money to some people? It's a lifeline.

But it's Mum's money. She's earned it. On the other hand, she's told me nothing but lies since I could say 'Ma'.

Too bad. As Dad… as Bill used to say, 'Sometimes people have to pay for their mistakes.'

I'm a mistake. Therefore your ten pounds is mine.

I lift it out of the jar. Then take another to cover for emergencies. That's what we stateless people do. We nick stuff.

I slip out the back door and creep past the front windows to get a headstart on Grandad. Will he be worried? For sure. But I'm a consequence he must have seen coming. What does he expect me to do? Sit in the living room having a nice cup of tea and talking it through? I'm pretty much on my own now. I need strategies and tactics. In a time of crisis you have to keep a cool head and play the percentages. Focus. What is it I need now?

I stand on the pavement. If I go left, I head out of town towards Zelda's place. If I go right, I head back into town towards school. It'll take a while, but I need someone who won't say a word about this to anyone. Do I trust Zelda, Bel, my Mum? For some things, yes. But when it comes to gossip, I bet they're as good as anybody at blabbing.

So, Bill isn't my dad. To him I was just a pile of baggage he could get shot of by dropping me off at the airport. Same with Mum. She was just another barrier to a cosier future. When the going gets tough, Bill Kelleher wimps out.

Same with Audrey. Her cheap china miniatures mean more to her than live human beings.

Bill and Audrey would probably see eye to eye. Cash is king. If you don't hustle, you don't get. The thing is to be successful, never mind if you're no good at anything in particular. You can make a pile of money by being a middleman. Bill doesn't design or make cars. He doesn't build the roads or supply the fuel. He just talks his way to a dealership, then sells somebody else's creation. Then he buys it back for not very much and sells it again for more. He charges for new parts after ordering his mechanics to fit something used. It's all about what he can get away with.

As for Audrey, she runs a hairdresser's and spends most of her time shopping for tat. 'Making a home' she calls it. IMHO, making a private warehouse for crap.

And what about all the people stuck in car jams leading out of town? What are their lives like? Tailback, office, supermarket. Tailback, home, TV. A holiday once or twice a year in some foreign suburb made to look just like home. Pathetic. They stand still in traffic jams half their lives, their engines running, pouring crap into the atmosphere, and for what? They're not going anywhere. 'Cos they're scared. Scared of failing. So they sit in their living rooms – or their living rooms on wheels – and criticise anyone who wants to make a difference. If you spot a tall poppy, cut it down to size.

It's an hour's walk into town, but I seem to have got here in a few minutes, and I'm standing outside The Broken Glass. A song wafts out into the road.

'I would swim over the deepest ocean
The deepest ocean, my love to find,
But the sea is wide and I cannot swim over,
Neither have I the wings to fly.
If I could find me a handsome boatman
To ferry me over my love and I.'

An Irish lament, an Irish accent, a tale of exile. It sounds like

Callum. Now I just have to wait for someone who'll pass on a message and get me inside.

Who? Why? What? When?

They're waiting for me in the living room when I get back.

Mum, Grandad, Zelda. (What's *she* doing here?)

There's a pregnant silence. They've just stopped nattering about me. Natter, natter, silence. As if they expect me to explode right in front of their eyes. Or implode. And why not? I'm a walking, talking teenager, with 'shit for brains'. That's something my real-dad just told me down the pub.

'What's up?' It always pays to take the initiative. My non-dad taught me that.

'Where've you been?'

When Grandad's annoyed his face turns reddish-pink with a hint of grey, but right now it's grey-white, the colour of wholemeal flour. If I have to choose I prefer the pink with a hint.

'I needed something in town.'

'We heard a car. Did somebody just drop you off?'

'Yep.'

'Who?'

'A friend.'

'Who?'

Another silence.

'I'll be off,' says Zelda, sensing the tension and getting up from where's she's perched on one arm of a sofa.

'Is Bel home alone?' I ask.

Zelda smiles, in fact very nearly grins.

'Yes, but *she* can be trusted to be by herself.' She puts a hand on my shoulder. 'Anyway, good night. I'm glad you're safe.'

And she gives me a peck on the cheek.

Why? What does that *mean*?

I can tell Grandad's about to resume his interrogation once the front door closes. You have to get your questions in first.

'Why was Zelda here?'

'She was out looking for you! We all were.'

'Why?'

Now the grey-white *is* tinged with pink. Does the white mean fear and the pink anger? Or does white mean angry and the pink 'getting even angrier'. How does the body *do* that?

'What do you mean "why"? We were all crazy with worry.'

I turn to Mum. She hasn't said a word.

'Were you worried?'

Her voice is barely audible. 'Yes. Of course I was.'

'I'm sorry. But I got some bad news and had to fix a few things.'

'All right.'

'That's all very well … ,' Grandad begins.

Mum interrupts. 'Dad. Please. He's back. That's the most important thing.'

It's another surprise in a day of surprises. For the last few months my mother's been like a helpless child and this is the first decisive thing she's said in an adult manner for ages.

Grandad gives up and rises to leave, though I get the impression he'll return to this topic when he gets me alone.

'In future, call. That's why you've got a phone.'

It'll sound like cheek if I say the phone is useless without funds, so I say nothing.

Mum waits for the door to close behind him, then heads for the kitchen to make a cup of tea.

Why do the English need to pour something hot and wet down their throats before they can engage with anything tricky? My mate Chris had a phrase for it. OCTD. Obsessive Compulsive Tea Disorder.

Mum sits at the kitchen table. It's going to be a straight-backed, hard-chair discussion. She fiddles with a wristband. Since starting to work at Zelda's pottery, she's replaced her soft bandages and taken to wearing broad leather bands. To support her weak wrists better, she says.

'Half an hour then. You've got to be up for school.'

'I'm not going to school tomorrow.'

'Why not?'

'I've got a rusty bike to repair. I'm never going on the bus again.'

She looks at the surface of her beverage for some seconds.

'Are you ashamed?' she asks.

'No.'

'I mean ashamed of me. Of who we are.'

'A bit.'

'Because I'm ashamed of me. I've been ashamed my whole life. I don't want you to feel that way.'

'I'm starting to.'

I hate myself for saying this even as the words leave my lips. It's time to start from the beginning.

'Grandad didn't really explain what happened.'

She fiddles with the handle of her mug as though she might take a sip, but she doesn't.

'I had a thing with a bloke when I was at modelling school.'

'David's dad?'

'Yes.'

'He's dad to lots of kids.'

'He's not Dad to anybody. But, yes, he's a biological father to quite a few.'

'Why did you do it?'

'He was a con man.'

'He still is.'

'He was young and very charming. He drove us around in fast cars and made us feel special. For about five minutes.'

'Well, he doesn't impress me.'

'Have you seen him?'

'Yeah. David took me to a pub to meet him.'

She doesn't want to ask, but she really wants to know what he's like now.

'He's skinny and rat-faced and looks like a crook.'

She looks concerned by this.

'You don't care about him, do you?' I ask.

She looks bewildered for a moment. 'No. Not a bit. It's just that you don't usually talk about people like that.'

'Yeah, well, I do now.'

Her eyes well up. 'You're losing your accent.'

'What's that got to do with it?'

'When you said that … you sounded like a Berkshire lad.'

'Well, that's who I am, aren't I? I'm a Berkshire lout. A Berkshire yobbo. I've got no dad and we live in this shithole …'

'Don't!'

I know I'm being cruel, and I expect her to break down in tears. That's what she does these days. Sometimes I suspect her of crying just to get her way. When she wants to spend the day lounging in bed or propped up on the sofa watching pap on TV. But now there's a flash of anger in her eyes.

'But you haven't explained. Why were we in New Zealand and why are we here now? What happened? Why did Bill kick us out? What did *I* do?'

Now she does start crying and it's not fake. The tears run down her nose and drip into her tea. Do I say sorry? Never mind? Tell me another day?

Why do adults demand immediate answers from kids but postpone theirs till a time when we'll understand? That is, until they've forgotten the question and hope we have too?

'The thing is … '

Here we go.

'My mum died when I was twelve. And my dad got remarried two years later. To Audrey.'

That would explain a lot.

'She made me feel small and useless. Or maybe I just felt that way because of the way she is. She's not a bad person. She's just a bit cold and she couldn't have children herself.'

'But she had *you*.'

Mum looks at me with startled eyes that turn into a sad smile.

'But someone else's child is not the same as your own. That's just how it is.'

'A child is a child.'

She laughs through the snivelling. 'True. But you'll find out what I mean one day. If you have kids.'

Why do people think that 'you'll find out one day' wins any argument?

'Anyway. I fell in with the wrong people at school …'

'David's mum?'

'She was all right. But yes. She introduced me to her ex-boyfriend and … I got pregnant.'

'And she was pregnant too?'

'Yes. In a few weeks we were his ex-girlfriends and both pregnant.'

'How did you meet Bill?'

'He was over here on business and I was doing a modelling job in a car showroom. He was visiting and we got chatting.'

'How old was I?'

'Ten months.'

'Who was looking after me?'

'Sian Jones and her mum.'

'Not Audrey?'

'No, I'd never have let Audrey get involved. Anyway, she didn't want anything to do with me. I'd proved her right, you see.'

'So you met Bill.'

'Yes. He wanted me to move to New Zealand, and I took a chance.'

'And you both pretended he was my dad.'

'We would have told you when you were old enough. But we never got that far. He wanted to be your dad.'

'Why did he stop?'

'I got ill, Bran.'

'Are you going to get divorced?'

She leans back in her chair, looking slightly annoyed, running out of patience with my questions.

'Bill and I were never married.'

'But ... ' A hundred questions are racing through my brain. 'I have his name. I have a Kiwi passport.'

'He fixed all that. I don't know how. He just knew how to do it.'

'Do you speak to him at all? Are you in touch?'

'No.'

'Why not?'

'I don't think he wants to be in touch with me anymore.'

'Why not?'

'Grandad wasn't very nice to him. He blames Bill for everything. But that was unfair.'

'Why was it unfair?'

'Because I was ill. I wasn't very nice to Bill.'

'I didn't notice.'

'You were at school most of the time.'

'You weren't not nice to me.'

'You're my child. It's different.'

'Why?'

She gives me a piercing look through watery eyes and a messy fringe.

'I'm still ill, you know. I can start being not nice if you keep on with all these questions.'

I suddenly realise she's talking bull. She couldn't be nasty if she tried. That's her trouble. She never strikes back. Something stops her from being unkind. Why's that? Is she weak? Too sensitive? Is her depression the result of being pummelled by a vicious world?

'It's almost midnight, Bran. I have to be up early. Zelda needs me in the pottery.'

'OK, but I'm chucking a sickie. You have to phone the school.'

'All right. Just this once. But you have to stay indoors or we'll both be in trouble.'

'I have to de-rust my new bike.'

'Just tell me one thing, Bran. Where did you get the bike?'

'A bloke called Callum fixed it for me. The school bus driver.'

'That's the truth? Promise?'

' 'Course. Where do you think I got it?'

'I thought maybe…'

'From *him*? I'd never take anything from *him*.'

She's convinced. 'All right. We can take it to Zelda's. She's got loads of tools.'

'Won't she snitch?'

'Zelda lets you be who you need to be. She's the last person to snitch.'

'Yeah, but what about her daughter?'

'You don't trust Belinda?'

'I don't trust anybody. Why should I?'

'There's always somebody you can trust.'

'Who do you trust?'

'My dad.'

'OK. Anyone else?'

'You.'

'Yeah, I trust you and Grandad, too. By the way I borrowed twenty pounds.'

'I noticed.'

'I didn't need it in the end.' I release a tenner and a five from my pocket and put it on the table. 'But I spent some 'cos I was hungry.'

'Good. Are you hungry now?'

'I'm always hungry.'

'There's some chicken stew in the fridge.'

'Did you make it?'

'Belinda made it. She gave me some for you.'

What was that? Some form of charity? Make yourself feel better by feeding the poor kid?

In the end it's not bad. A bit spicy, but not bad. I'll keep the rest for lunch tomorrow, when I stay home and de-rust my new wheels. I won't go to Zelda's. Keep it discreet. The whole world doesn't have to know what I'm doing.

21st century skipping

The advantage of having a bike is you get to know the area fast and have a means of escape. I find a local map to guide me down narrow lanes, along canals, across main roads and zigzagging through the back streets and alleyways to school.

Grandad helps me construct panniers front and back to conceal my loot. He thinks sports kit and school books. I think food and cast-off junk.

The supermarkets on my route have areas out back where they keep the skips. During the day these fill with all sorts of nosh just past its 'sell by' date. But you have to be smart and you have to be quick. The staff don't allow 'skipping', so you have to watch and wait.

The best places are the smaller outlets, and the best time is after six when the night staff come on duty but the shop is still busy. Fewer staff to keep tabs on what's happening outside.

Park the bike on the blind side of the skip furthest from the back door. If it's a large skip, hook one end of knotted rope to the inside rear. Go round the front and check the skip for pizza, cheese, fruit and cake. Five a day and plenty of carbs is what the growing athlete needs. Check for larger items to hide behind. Hop in, drop down and go straight to the targets. If anyone comes out the back to chuck stuff in, duck down and hide. If seen, abandon loot and make towards the low side of the skip with a sheepish grin, then dodge to the back, climb the rope, drop to the ground and get on your bike. Under no circumstances try to retrieve the rope; you'll just have to get another.

Result after two or three raids a week? Balanced evening meals of pasta, pizza, fruit and veg. Plenty of processed bread, but forget breakfast cereals, tea, coffee, sweets and chocolate. These never reach their sell-by dates.

If the shop assistant's on his toes and doesn't like the look of feral kids, he'll have a go. But he needs to be fast and fit. They can zip down the side of the skip and grab the back of your bike, so you have to mount at the run. Having a sharpened broom handle attached to the back is a help. They have to run around it to grab your saddle. If they grab the stick, they're welcome to keep it.

Another result? Occasional questions from mother, depending on her mood. Deflecting strategies are needed.

'Where did you get that?'

'I went shopping?'

'Where'd you get the money?'

'I found some in my old jeans pocket.'

'I washed your old jeans.'

'That's why the notes were damp.'

'I went through your pockets.'

'You must have missed 'em. I'm thinking about getting my head shaved this summer. What do you think?'

That usually changes the subject. That or getting a tattoo of Richie McCaw on my bum.

I also persuade Grandad to help me make a two-wheeled trailer. He thinks tools I need for gardening jobs. I think bigger stuff from skips on industrial estates.

The problems turn up when you're competing for the stuff at a secure site. Especially if there's a gang. Especially if they're just having a laugh and don't really need the gear.

'There's some good stuff in there.'

'Yeah, but how are we gonna get it? The staff's out the back every two minutes having a smoke.'

That's when you take the lead.

'You can't rush it. They're bound to get one of us.'

You've watched the routines, and information is power. For best results you need two inside to grab the goodies and two outside to get them stashed. Always tell 'em they need their number, plus one: they can't do without you.

Hook rope over top of fence. Hoist two blokes over. Remove rope. Hop into skip and hide. Don't make a sound, morons.

Security guard strolls past.

While inside the skip you've identified the valuable stuff. Grab one each, head to fence, one hoists up the other, who hands the stuff over the top. Back to skip, back to hiding. No sniggering, morons.

Security guard strolls past.

Repeat until you've got all the gear you want, but don't get greedy. On the last run, attach the rope and climb over the fence. Retrieve the rope.

Security guard strolls past.

Split the goods and ride away home. Stop around a corner. Make sure the gang have departed with their loot. Check that the guard isn't in pursuit, then sneak back for a solo run to get that most valuable thing you hid from your mates while in the skip.

Think up a plausible excuse for when you get home.

'Have you got a TV in your room?'

'Yeah, somebody had thrown it out, so I took it. I never thought it would work.'

'But that's bigger than the one downstairs. You didn't take it from a skip, did you? Because I've heard that's stealing.'

'And they left a hairdryer beside it.'

'Ooh, that looks nice.'

But if they catch you red-handed you need an escape route, even if it's over the fence at the back, then over the garden fences at the back of terrace houses.

'Oi!'

If you're quick enough and lucky enough to avoid any big dogs or athletic occupiers with a mean streak, you'll reach a road eventually. Leave it some time, then slink back and recover your bike. Whatever you do, don't try again that night: the guard will be on heightened alert and feeling grumpy.

Once you've vaulted a few fences and dodged some big blokes' grasping hands, picking up a rugby ball and heading for the try-line becomes a cinch. Your mates lift you skywards to help you grab that oval ball out of the sky and you stuff it up your shirt and keep it. You shove the other lot backwards, smuggle the pill back to your little guys and set up another attack. It's a skipper's holiday.

You wouldn't take David on a skipping raid because he's too heavy and too loud. But on a rugby field he's there like a battering ram at the breakdown. I look over my shoulder these days and he's there. Sometimes I give him the ball twenty yards from the line just to see what damage he'll do. If some beefy boy in the other pack gets uppity, I wonder how he'll feel with a bit of weight bearing down, or a shoulder on the chin when he tries to tackle a bit high, or even a head-on smash to make sure he knows what's coming for the next eighty minutes.

'That was a bit rough today, Bran.'

'He started it.'

'Yes, but some of these guys are a lot bigger than you.'

'It's the size of the fight in the dog, isn't it? Not the size of the dog.' I don't like quoting Bill any more, but it comes in handy sometimes.

'Maybe. But I want you using your skills, not winding up the opposition.'

Has Coach forgotten this isn't the beautiful game? This is rugby, not soccer. It's all about sweat, nerve and being just that bit braver than the opposition.

I get the same at school. Mr Carson doesn't like the look of my bike.

'Where did you get that?'

'I got it from a friend and fixed it up.'

I've noticed that teachers don't trust kids who get things from friends not parents. They put inverted commas around 'friends'.

'There is something piratical about it,' says Mr Edwards with a mischievous smile.

I like that. Piratical. It's black all over because that was the only paint I could find, and a layer of paint keeps the rust at bay. What does Mr Carson expect? A bike in school uniform colours?

'I hear you've not been doing your homework.'

'I hurt my hand playing rugby.' I hold up a right hand with a grubby bandage disappearing up my jacket sleeve.

'Well, make sure you catch up.'

Why pick on me? There are loads of kids who never do any homework. Where am I to find the time, what with skipping and rugby? I do the minimum, calculate the angles, play the percentages. Provided I stay in the top half, what's his beef?

Riff raff

There's not much wrong with the hand and it doesn't prevent me working at Sonia's on the weekend. She may be posh, but she's my lifeline. Without the eighteen to twenty-seven quid a week she pays me, we'd be paupers.

I sprint the bike down the main road for a mile and a half, then turn down the lane. I catch sight of a head bouncing up and down in Zelda's garden. It must be Bel on a trampoline. I stop to watch and realise that it's Zelda bouncing and whooping while Bel's on the ground giving instructions.

It looks like fun and I get this sudden pang of jealousy. Why can't I be at home with my mum? I could teach her loads of stuff. But maybe she gets a go on Bel and Zelda's trampoline during the week. I'll have to ask. She never tells me anything about the pottery, except that she doesn't want to stop going there.

There's something fresh in the air as I speed down the lane. Farm machines are at work cutting and baling. A fox breaks from a hedge to cross the lane and crouches like a furry spring, working out what this new apparition on two wheels might mean. It decides I mean trouble and leaps the ditch into the hedge on the other side.

I hear the pock-pock of tennis balls as I approach Buckston Manor. Who's playing with Sonia? It's supposed to be my first job this morning. Swinging into the drive I see three men in tennis whites.

'Ah, good. Are you the gardening boy?'

'Yes, I'm Bran.'

'Good. You can make up a fourth.'

'Is Sonia not playing today?'

'You mean, Mrs Partington.' It's not a question, it's a statement and I get the message that I'm not to call her Sonia – at least not in his presence.

He hasn't introduced himself, but this has to be Rawley Partington, the infamous husband. He's tall, but heavy around the waistline. Bel's description of 'England's biggest overripe pear' seems spot-on. I don't see much prospect of him dancing along the baseline.

His partner is German. Slim, well-groomed, spiky grey hair, the sort you're sure drives a very expensive Audi or Mercedes. His playing arm and one knee are braced with professional-looking, logo'd supports.

'Falk, Eberhard,' he says with a swift bow of the head.

I recognise the manners. Bill has plenty of contacts like this.

'Kelleher, Bran,' I reply with an emphatic nod.

We prepare for battle.

My partner's manner is quite different. He looks to be in his mid-twenties, blond, gangling and with no expectations of winning this match.

'Hi? I'm Damian? I'm Sonia's cousin?'

Every statement is a plummy question mark.

'Right, I'm serving,' says Mr Partington, taking command.

'Don't I get a warm up?' I ask.

'It won't make any difference,' he snaps.

Damian grins and prepares to receive.

The charming thing about Mr Love was that he didn't make any show of knowing how to play the game, except in theory. Rawley Partington, on the other hand, goes through all the moves, as if he's doing a skit on a famous pro. He bounces the ball, leans back as if he's picking his spot, appears to toss the ball three feet in the air, and takes a terrific swipe in first-serve mode.

The only problem is that the ball barely leaves his throwing hand, so it's only just above his head as the racket comes through. The chances of hitting the service box on the other side of the net are minimal without lots of topspin.

'Bad luck,' grins Damian, though Partington's serve has bounced before going into the net, more like a failed table tennis shot.

They say that you judge a player's game by the quality of the second serve, and our host's is very much like himself: soft, lobbed and lucky. It bounces high and my partner pats it back to Partington's feet. Though his eyes watch the ball floating gently back, his feet fail to pick up any messages from the brain until too late. He leans to his right and stumbles, but the ball has already bounced and gone on to hit the fence.

'Out!' snaps Partington. 'Fifteen-love.'

Damian grins at me.

'That was in, wasn't it?'

'Yes,' I confirm.

Damian calls across the net. 'Are we playing Partington rules, Rawley?'

At first, he appears not to hear. 'What?'

'Partington rules, is it?'

'I don't know what you mean.'

He prepares to serve again.

'Play short,' Damian instructs me. 'Anything near the line will be out.'

Easily done, just add more top spin.

The next first serve is closer to my head than any line. I manage to angle away his second with a crisp, dipping shot to his flailing backhand.

Eberhard eyes me much like the fox did a few minutes earlier. He decides I'm the one that needs outfoxing.

We go at it for nine games. Rawley Partington and Damian lose their service games, while Eberhard and I win ours. When Rawley loses his third in a row, the score stands at 5-4 to Damian and me. We're the whipper-snappers giving the older men a run for their money.

Damian can't believe his luck. He imagined that his cousin's husband would bluster, thump and cheat his way to a convincing victory, but he now stands on the brink of a family upset. He has cheered my every winning shot. He has argued with Rawley Partington with increasing confidence over every disputed line call. He has even provoked his relative with some gloating commentary.

'Watch and learn, Rawley,' he says as one of my volleys arrows into the corner.

If Damian can hold his serve, we'll win the set.

His first serve is swept back by Eberhard for a clean winner. Love-fifteen. His next brings a framed lob backwards over the fence from Rawley. 15-all. Eberhard has decided to keep his returns away from me and thumps a clean winner down Damian's tramline. 15-30.

Rawley gets the next serve back, more by luck than design, but it loops towards me at the net for a simple put-away. 30-all.

Damian crows. Eberhard scowls. Rawley's cheeks flush a brighter shade of crimson.

Eberhard has had the measure of Damian's serve all set. His returns fizz with venom and top-spin. The only way to win the point is for me to anticipate, skip across the net and try to angle the volley towards Rawley.

The ball comes off the frame of my racket, turning an intended volley into an accidental dropshot. Eberhard tries to scoop it up but only succeeds in nudging it along the ground into the net.

I raise my hand in apology.

Damian punches the air and whoops.

I wish he'd shut up.

It's 40-30, set point.

Damian serves. Rawley returns.

It's another donkey-drop forehand, more like a lob than a drive. It's a simple smash at the net, but Eberhard tries a desperate forward rush. Maybe he thinks I'll take my eye off the ball and miscue. All he manages is to get in the way.

The ball cracks into his thigh and spins away towards the fence.

Again, I raise my hand.

'Sorry.'

But I'm drowned out by Damian's 'Yesss! First set to us.'

Rawley storms to the net.

'And the last one you'll ever play on this court.'

He snatches my racket away.

'Get off my property and never come back.'

'What did I do?'

I can see Eberhard frowning and probably wondering what's come over his host.

'If you don't know, then you certainly don't belong here. Go on. Off you go.'

'But I'm supposed to be gardening for Sonia.'

'I can assure you that *Mrs Partington* no longer requires your services.'

'Oh, for God's sake, Rawley…, ' says Damian, coming languidly to the net, still grinning.

'How dare you!' he hisses. 'I'm trying to do a deal here.'

He means with Eberhard.

'Well, if you want to keep it social just say so,' drawls Damian. 'But you never do, so why should we?'

He slaps me on the back by way of congratulation, but this just makes it worse.

Rawley leans towards me.

'In language you might understand… ,' he measures and emphasises each word. '*On. Your. Bike.*'

I turn to leave. Eberhard is zipping up his rackets. He casts me a sympathetic glance. The glance of respect for an equal on court. If anything, Rawley Partington's blatant cheating and his reaction to losing has done his deal more harm than my tennis. Was I supposed to throw the match? Are kids like me supposed to be ball boys and punch bags for rich men like Partington?

He's still berating Damian as I reach my bike.

'I can understand the behaviour of riff-raff like that, but you ought to know better.'

Crunch time

'They look like twins.'

Truck-tyre upper bodies, short stocky legs, short reddish-blond hair, gimlet eyes and thick, muscly, lobster pink necks.

'They *are* twins. The Crunch brothers. They do what it says in the name.'

More nominative determinism.

'Don't mix it with them. That's exactly what they want you to do. And don't wind them up. Let the referee deal with it. He knows all about the Crunchies.'

'But are they any good?'

'Their dad's trying to get them into the England under-18s.'

I can see them eyeing us up as well. That's what you do before a match. Try to figure out what their strengths and weaknesses are. The Crunch boys look heavy and strong. They obviously lift weights. But are they as strong as David? And are they as quick as I am? One on one I reckon they'll be easy to sidestep and outsprint.

David's swigging water from a bottle.

'Gone off the chocolate?'

'Nah, I'm keeping thems for afterwards.'

'Can I have one?'

'Sure.'

He lobs me a bar.

'How many have you got in there?'

'Half a dozen.'

'Can I have another?'

'You hungry?'

'I'm always hungry.'

'Yeah, I've noticed. Here.'

He lobs me a second. 'No breakfast?'

'Had some cornflakes.'

'Should 'ave a proper breakfast before a match.'

Imagine: I'm getting nutrition advice from David Jones.

'A'right? Had your sugar boost? Let's warm up.'

He's grabbed a ball and is heading out the door. There's no question he looks big and fit. He's also improved his skills so that passes hit their target and he can accurately kick a ball more than ten metres. I've created a machine: a souped-up version of a Crunch brother.

They go to work from the first whistle, working as a pair, hunting us down, trying to pick us off and take us out. When one of us goes down in a tackle they linger a second or two after the ball has gone, make sure the ref isn't looking and leave an impression on their victim. An accidental-on-purpose tread on a leg, a thumb in the eye, a pressure rub on the side of a head, a vice-like squeeze of a muscle on the back of a thigh.

The ref does notice one or two of these cheap-shot fouls, but he has trouble identifying which of them was responsible. Their twindom is their licence to cheat, and they obviously enjoy what they do.

I notice, though, that they avoid David. They got a sense of his power at the first scrum, when they pushed from the second row and not much happened. If anything they went slightly backwards.

When David lifts me at the lineout, they try to barge him away but discover he's more like a wall than a movable object.

Maybe they've never met this quality of opposition before and, after twenty minutes, they begin to run out of puff. We let the ball do the work, change direction, get the side-steps working or chip over their heads, and we have them trundling aimlessly about the field, arriving far too late and having to set off again for a new location, getting slower and slower each time.

By halftime we lead 36 – 10. They get a rest but are soon back to huffing and puffing with half an hour left in the match. We get the feeling that the Crunch brothers have never been substituted, but it's about to happen. Their dad is beside himself on the touchline. He can see his dream of free tickets to Twickenham dissolving as fast as his boys' athletic credentials. It's time for the coup de grace.

We get a penalty.

'Give me the ball,' I say. 'Watch this.'

Our opponents think we'll kick for the three points, but I tap and go, heading straight for where the Crunch boys are standing side by side, hands on hips looking like they wished they'd chosen a different sport.

Sidestep this way, sidestep that, then sprint between them. I do believe they collide in my slipstream before I offload to our wing, who goes over for a simple try. The Crunch brothers know they've been made to look slow and flat-footed.

'Enjoy that?' I ask them as I trot back to the halfway line.

The ref hears the question and doesn't like it. He thinks I'm showing a lack of respect.

'That's enough of that.'

I show him the red marks where they've been pinching me through my shirt.

'How about that? Is that enough for you?'

The ref knows what I'm saying, but I'm also breaking the rugby code. The ref rules and players never talk back.

As our No 10 lines up the conversion for another two points, I can hear their dad stoking revenge.

'All right, lads. You know what to do.'

Yeah, but can they do it?

'Leave it, now,' says David.

'What? I'm just showing them how rugby is really played.'

'They're thugs.'

'Sure. But they're also mugs.'

And some mugs just beg to be mugged over and over.

It's not long before the ball comes bouncing my way. Here we go again. Step left, step right. They've given up reacting to dummies. They just stand, fists clenched. One comes forward and completely misses me, the other steps backwards as I advance. He's big – bigger than David – but he's tired. I reckon I can hand him off and run right past him. But where's the other one? A quick look left and right. I can't see him.

David shouts. 'Pass! Pass!'

The brother backing away suddenly stops and stands his ground. Where *is* the other one? If you think about it for a split second, there is only one place he can be, and the hot breath on my neck can only belong to one person. One in front, one behind. A crunchie sandwich, in fact. And I'm the slender slice of something in between.

C-r-r-r-R-U-N-C-H!

Rest

'You need rest,' says the nurse as she fusses with the sheets at the end of the mattress.

But I've been resting for four days.

'What you do is not rest. You are a very angry young man.'

Now that really is far-fetched. I'm the coolest cucumber in my family.

'Cucumbers,' she replies, 'don't end up in plaster casts.'

No, just plastic wrappers in supermarkets. I don't see the difference. We, the lame and plastered, are stacked high in this place.

'But I just need to exercise a bit. Can't I have a small dumbbell to work my biceps?'

'No, you can't. You're supposed to be resting your whole body. Lifting weights won't do your broken ribs any good.'

The worst of it is not being recognised as having a respectable injury. Doctors and nurses think I've done something stupid, like come off my bike or fallen out of a tree. Even if I tell them I was wasted by a foul double-tackle in a rugby match, they're not impressed. The Crunch boys and their dad deny it, but I *know* I passed the ball a split second before they slammed into me. Strictly speaking, that's at least a yellow card each.

David refuses to tell me if they both got sin-binned.

'It didn't look like a pass. More like… you lost the ball in the tackle.'

That just adds insult to injury.

'You know I never lose the ball like that.'

He ums and ahs. 'I'm just saying. That's what the ref said he saw.'

'Is that what you saw?'

'I saw the ball pop up in the air.'

'Who caught it?'

'I did.'

'So it was a pass!'

'The ref gave it to them as a forward knock-on.'

'What!?'

'Yeah, well, it didn't matter. They abandoned the game 'cos it took ages to get you off the field into the chopper.'

David's getting better at rugby, but he's still useless at concentrating on the main points of an argument. It was a foul tackle and he needs to say so.

'Nobody's saying it wasn't a cheap shot,' he protests. 'But why are you pissed off at me? What happened wasn't *my* fault.'

Mum's here again. I can hear her talking to the doctors but I can only hear snatches of conversation.

'... clearly anaemic... long term consequences... overdoing the exercise... junk food...'

Hang on a mo'. I don't eat junk. Why doesn't she tell him? He'll think I'm some kind of bonzo from Woop Woop.

She wells up as soon as she steps around the curtain. Those red-rimmed eyes make me feel as if I – or both of us - have done something really stupid.

'How are you feeling?'

'Bored. How are you?'

I've got used to a mother who can't really face the world as it is. In this country, among her own people, she crumbles and flakes like pastry. But now there's a bit more steel, as if she's being endlessly patient with people, but doesn't want to tell them exactly what she thinks.

'I'm fine. I can't stay long. Zelda's coming to pick me up.'

'Why?'

'We're working.'

'At night?'

'She's firing her kiln, so somebody has to be there all the time.'

'Why can't she do it?'

'She does. We're sharing it, so we each get a break.'

'Is she paying you for this?'

'Of course she is.'

'So it's a proper job then?'

'Of course it is. Why all the questions?'

'Cos people take advantage.'

'It's nice of you to care, but you're the one we need to think about.'

'Yeah, that's true. Has Grandad found a lawyer yet?'

'I don't think he'll try.'

'Why not? Those kids tried to do me with dangerous play. Ask David.'

'Yes, all right, calm down. You don't need to shout.'

'Who's shouting?'

She gives me the endlessly patient look from the corner of one eye: deep breath in, head angled towards the view through the window, as if counting to ten.

Well, maybe I did raise my voice. Just a bit.

'You're so angry, Bran.'

'That's what the nurse said.'

'That's what *everybody* says.' Her eyes bulge as she emphasises the word.

That's new. Maybe my can-do, feisty attitude has cured her depression, even if it was clinical – whatever that means.

'The nurse told me you kept everybody awake last night.'

'How did I do that? I was asleep.'

'I told her it was probably the dreaming.'

'Well, they kept waking *me* up.'

'They were trying to stop the shouting.'

'I wasn't ... '

Well, maybe I was. A bit. It was all kind of mixed up in a dream.

As usual you can sense Zelda approaching from a distance. What's it called? Bonhomania? Something French.

The guy opposite with the whole arm in a cast starts to leer even more leerily than the way he leers at my mum. You'd think a man who fell sideways off a three-step ladder wouldn't be quite so full of himself.

She stops at the curtain and looks me over.

'You look better.'

'Better than what?'

'Bran... ,' warns Mum.

'Better than the last time I saw you.'

She pulls up a chair, and only then do I see Bel standing back and carrying a pile of books. She rolls her eyes for a second. Yeah, I know: embarrassing parents.

'How are you doing?'

'Bored.'

'I brought you some books.'

I nod at the dressing table. 'Add them to my collection.'

'Have you read these?'

'No.'

'Why not?'

'Like I said, I'm bored.'

'That's when you read.'

'I'd prefer a tablet.'

'I prefer to read from the page.'

What's she talking about? I wouldn't read books if I had a tablet. I'd be online doing interesting stuff.

'I have got a tablet,' I say, 'but there's a problem with it.'

'Give it to me.'

'Why?'

'I'll give it to Yasmin. I'll bet she can fix it.'

'Yasmin?'

'She does it for fun. Like some people solve Rubik's cubes. You should have asked before.'

'I didn't know ... I didn't think... '

'What?'

'I didn't know she can do that stuff.'

'That's unobservant of you.'

Unobservant?

'Does that mean stupid?'

'No. It means a smart person who doesn't notice something.'

'So what am I supposed to notice?'

'Well, who do you think gets the highest marks in maths and science?'

'I thought you did.'

She laughs. 'I wish. Yasmin thinks she's messed up if she gets 99%.'

If that's true, I never noticed.

'OK, I guess I am unobservant.'

'I'm not criticising. You were being ignorant, not stupid.'

Hang on. She's just called me ignorant as well as unobservant. Sometimes Bel's so cocky I just want to cut her down to size. Easier said than done. Even worse, there's now another girl better than me at my favourite subject.

'Anyway, your mum can give me the tablet …'

'That won't be easy. I hid it and can't remember where.'

'No problem,' says Mum, 'we'll find it.'

Great, they're gonna trawl through all my stuff. Memory scare. Is there anything I really don't want them to see?

'And you can read these books in the meantime,' says Bel.

'You're giving me homework now?'

'Not me. I thought you'd enjoy these. But Mr Edwards gave me this one for you.'

'It looks … dense.'

'It doesn't matter if the *book* looks dense provided the reader isn't.'

God, she's annoying. The others are suppressing smiles at her clever-clogs attitude. Even Three-Step Hero is chuckling in disbelief.

'But it is homework. Mr Edwards said to read chapter four at least. He's going to test you on it.'

I scan chapter four. Over twenty-five pages of closely spaced type and a few black and white photos.

'Are the rest of you doing this?'

'No, that's especially for you.'

'Why?'

'He thinks you'll enjoy it.'

'I'm supposed to learn all this stuff?'

'No, just read it.'

'That's not fair. We never get this much reading for History.'

'He thinks you can handle it.'

'What are you? His bitch?'

There's a stunned silence.

Then, 'You apologise right now, this second!'

Seeing Mum firm up like this is pretty alarming.

'Yeah, but… '

'Now!'

'Yeah, OK, I'm sorry … '

They can see I don't really mean it. But I didn't mean to upset anyone in the first place. Kids talk to each other like that all the time. Why aren't I allowed to do it?

Zelda rises, followed by Bel. Mum gathers her stuff together in a strop, but lingers until the others are out of the ward.

'I'll get Grandad to bring a card and you'll write her a proper apology.'

She kisses me even though she's upset and there's no escaping the smackerooney on the cheek. Can't move my head, can't move my arm.

'You want to be nicer to that girl,' says Three-Step after they've gone.

'Yeah, well, she's my friend.'

'Not for long if you keep that up. Cracking girl, that.'

How would he know?

'Is your Mum married?'

' 'Course.'

'Yeah? Where's yer dad, then?'

'Working abroad.'

'And what about the other one? She married?'

I was about to say yeah, he's abroad, too, but heard myself saying, 'I don't know any women called The Other One.'

Where did that come from? Maybe Bel's smart-Alec use of language is rubbing off.

Three-Step chuckles like a dying chainsaw. He likes me about as much as I like him. Not the sort of bloke you want lying opposite for weeks on end.

House of cards

Grandad brings me a batch of get well cards, and there's one that I've really been hoping for. The stamps remind me of a lost land, and the big, spidery handwriting is familiar.

'Aren't you going to open it?'

'Maybe.'

'It's from Bill.'

'I know.'

I read the others. There's one from Callum. 'All's well that mends well.' Sounds like a line from a new song he's writing. Another from a quiet, nerdy guy in my class I've hardly spoken to. 'Hope to see you back at school soon.' One from Audrey. 'Hoping you get plenty of well-earned rest.' What am I? An old age pensioner?

So far, almost all the kids in my class have sent cards. Maybe a teacher is telling them to do it. If so, 'Teach' isn't vetting them before they get sent out. Only a card from Nash would make me feel worse than the one from Matt and the Three As. 'All the best to the guy who may be uteless but knows how to send for a chopper.' 'No worries, mate! Paralympic rugby is a growing sport.' 'Chin up, no need to look down, 'cos it's all white down there.'

Yeah, all white plaster for my broken bones. I get it.

'Want me to put them with the others?'

'Yeah. But not that one. You can chuck that in the bin.'

Grandad's suddenly worried I mean the one from Audrey and is relieved when I hand him a different card. He takes it and reads.

'I see your point,' he says, tearing it in two. 'Not exactly sincere is it? Your mum wanted me to bring you one of these.' He hands over a new card in its cellophane wrapper. 'She said you'd know what to do with it.'

The first thing I'll have to do is apologise for its flowery pinkness.

'Can you write?'

'I'll try left-handed.'

'Good, because sometimes one has to make the best of things.'

He's wearing that 'why always me' expression.

'What?'

'I've been having a chat with the doctors, and they wanted me to have a chat with you first.'

You have to feel sorry for Grandad. Always the bearer of bad news. It's written in his face and stutters from his lips.

'The thing is… the doctors think you probably won't be able to play rugby again … that is, not top-class rugby … well, not contact rugby … tag rugby maybe … yes, probably tag rugby.'

'Why not? I'm not paralysed. *Am* I paralysed?'

'No, you're fine. Well, mostly. The thing is, you need the right physique for top-class rugby these days. I mean, look at them. When I was a kid I would have been one of the bigger ones on a rugby field. But now I wouldn't qualify. And you're tall, but you're not going to be heavy enough.'

'I'm fast.'

'Fast for your age. Fast for a forward your age. But will you be quick enough for a back? Even those are sixteen stone plus these days. You'll be lucky to be twelve stone, even if you're six feet two.'

'What about a player like Luke Charteris?'

'I thought you'd say that, so I looked him up. He might have looked skinny on TV, but he's six feet eleven and he weighed more than twenty stone as a player.'

'I could probably get up to sixteen stone.'

Three-Step sniggers. He's been earwigging the whole time. Grandad notices and gets up to pull the curtain around the end of the bed.

'You'll have to get used to the idea, Bran. You're terrific at rugby now, but top-level sport is a tough business, especially rugby. Only a small percentage get chosen. But there's no reason you shouldn't find another sport you can enjoy just as much.'

Yeah, like what? Tiddlywinks?

'I'll be in with your mum tomorrow when the doctors come to chat with you. OK?'

I nod.

'Do want me to draw the curtain back?'

'No, leave it like that.'

I don't want to see Three-Steps' gloating mug, though a drawn curtain doesn't prevent him trying some mimicry when Grandad's gone.

'*Am* I paralysed?' he asks in a falsetto voice. He answers the question in his own whiny growl. 'Just from the neck up, sunshine.'

If I had headphones I could block him out, but I have to use mental strength instead. He'll be out of my life at some point. This is only a temporary state.

I open Bill's card and two letters drop out. The first I open is from him. So I turn to the other. It's from the Reverend Love.

Dear Bran,

I was sorry to hear about your accident. …

(It wasn't an accident, for crying out loud!)

I understand from your father …

(Ask him if he still plays that role with me. You might be able to offer him a little sermon on that topic.)

… that you've had to give up playing rugby.

(Certainly for the time being, Rev.)

That is sad news for you, as I'm certain you would have been an asset to any team you chose to play for.

(Haven't you heard, Rev? I'm now a stateless, feral kid who nicks food out of skips.)

Whatever direction you decide to take in life, I hope you can continue playing tennis. You certainly have aptitude for the game, and it's a great way to make friends.

(Sure, if you can afford the kit, the travel and the club membership.)

Do keep in touch. Your friends here and the staff are keen to learn of your progress.

(What's the opposite of progress? *Con*gress? Doesn't sound right. Chris would know, or would hazard a guess. Bel would definitely know. But I don't suppose we're talking right now.)

Nice try, Rev, but your world ain't my world anymore. Time to see what the arch deceiver has to say.

Dear Bran,
I was so sorry to hear about your injury …
(Injuries. Plural!)
… and even sorrier that I can't be with you now.
(Eh?)
I was in Oz when I heard, and have to go to Japan next week. I'll probably be there when you get this.
I know how strong you are and I know you'll get through this. With any luck I'll be able to get over to the UK in a few weeks.
(What's luck got to do with it?)
I hope you'll be out of hospital by then and we can spend some quality time together.
(Yeah, well, should have thought about that earlier, shouldn't you?)
Until then, stay strong and do what you need to do to get well. I know you will.
Love,
Dad
(What the heck? You're not my dad! You *know* you're not my dad! Why keep up the pretence? You kicked me out of your life!)

In a flash, I know what to do. I take the new card that Grandad brought and open it up. I reach for the pen on the side-table and begin to write.

Dear Bill,

Writing left-handed, so a bit shaky. But I think you'll get the message.

Then I draw a mug of coffee. Beside it, I write in capitals and add arrows where needed.

NO FOAM
NO CAFFEINE
NO DAIRY
NO SUGAR
Then I sign off with just my name.
Yours sincerely,
Bran Cooke

It was a private joke we shared in a different life. We called this kind of coffee a 'Why Bother?' and smiled at the life-fearing folk who ordered it in cafés. He'll know exactly what I mean.

I address the card and prop it up by the books. Mum or Grandad can post it for me, and I'll have to write a letter to Bel. Quite what I'll say, I don't know. Being mean is easy. But what do you say to Bel, who puts people right but would never hurt them deliberately? I don't know if I have the words for that.

Hi Bel,

My grandad brought me a card with pinkish flowers on it so I could write you an apology for my crap behaviour. But I thought you would hate a cheesy card, so I've chosen this sheet from a notebook instead.

Thanks for bringing the books. I can't promise to read Ted's homework assignment, but I'll definitely read the ones you've chosen. I've just been told I'll never play top-flight rugby again, so I guess I should learn to read. It might come in handy.

I hate being stuck in bed. I hate being opposite a cynical guy who leers and sneers. I wish people like that would just watch their TV soaps and leave other people alone. I wish my bones would mend and I could be out of here tomorrow. I wish my left-handed writing didn't look like a four-year-old creating his first letters on paper.

On the other hand, the food ain't bad. One of my broken ribs perforated my lung, but missed my stomach. So I'll be able to eat the beef and mash we've been promised tonight.

Don't give up on me. Big hugs to you and your mum, and add one for my mum as well – since she's always at your place.

(How to sign off? Mmm. Tricky. Keep it solid, keep it simple.)

Your friend,

Bran

PS Big, big thanks to Yasmin if she tries to fix my tablet.

My left hand is aching by the time I finish. Mum once taught me how to make an origami envelope from a sheet of paper, so I have a go with my left hand and two fingers on my right. No chance. Can't even fold a sheet of paper.

What to do?

Three-Step is reading his creepy tabloid newspaper. I can hear him turning the pages and cackling softly at somebody else's public humiliation. If I could lens up this place I could make a video of a day in the life of Three-Step Hero and upload it to the Web. No such luck.

I pick up the tome Mr Edwards has sent.

Chapter 4. 'Albion from Above'.

What's Albion?

It kicks off with a poem. Not reading that.

1940. OK, not such ancient history. Bloke riding a motorbike. Doing 70mph. Another bloke driving a car in the opposite direction. I think I see where this is going. Yep. Head-on collision, a shower of sparks, a thirty-yard skid, gruesome injuries and the bloke on the motorbike carks it.

OK.

Might as well turn the page and keep reading.

Part Six

Summer Daze

Breaking up

Everybody wants me back at school for the final week of summer term.

'No point delaying. If you've come off yer bike, you have to get straight back on. Soon as you can.'

That's Grandad's philosophy in a nutshell. Pick yourself up, dust yourself off, and keep doing whatever you were doing.

Mum has reservations. 'Another week won't make any difference.'

'It's a week of his life, and life's short enough as it is.'

This could be a dig at Mum. Given a chance to stay in bed for an extra hour, she'll take it. The house is pretty messy when I get back and somebody (Mum) has been dumping stuff on my bedroom floor instead of tidying up properly.

'It's not a spare room,' I complain.

'I'm sorry. I was going to do it.'

'I'm the teenager. That's supposed to be my line.'

I spend most of my first day back home fixing my room and still feel dissatisfied. The floor's clear, the books are straightened, and the cards I want to keep from hospital are arranged on the bookshelves. But there's still something bugging me.

Grandad brings us fish and chips in the evening.

'Make a deal, Grandad?'

'What?'

'If I go back to school tomorrow can you give me a lift in the mornings?'

'*If* you go back. There's no if. And what's wrong with the bus?'

There's no good answer.

'I've got a job in Basingstoke. I have to get up early enough as it is.'

So it's back on the bus for me. Unless I walk. It's eight miles to school. Climbing the stairs leaves me puffed. I can't believe how white and skinny my legs are. Even so, my school blazer feels half a size too small. I may look thinner after months in hospital, but I've actually grown taller.

Before going to bed I stand against the wall in the kitchen where we keep a record of our heights. I was just shorter than Mum, who is two inches shorter than Grandad.

Mum puts a ruler across the top of my head.

'Yep! I thought so.'

'What?'

She runs a pencil along the end of the ruler touching the wall. I step forward and turn.

'See?' says Mum. 'You're taller than me now.'

That would be reason for satisfaction if I weren't going to look like a deadbeat in my too-small blazer.

'I phoned Zelda,' says Mum. 'She's giving us a lift tomorrow.'

'Why?'

'Because I phoned and asked her. Why do you think?'

Does Mum get stuff, even though she seems a million miles away sometimes? She's quiet, but she takes it all in. Is that what they mean by 'a woman's intimation'?

Lying in bed looking at Chris and Rawiri's card, I realise what's making me grumpy. It's not the wondering why they haven't replied to my long letters. (I probably shouldn't have gone on and on about the foul tackle and my wish to sue the Crunch boys and their dad.) It's not the aches in my side and hip. Or the itching beneath the cast where my arm had to be reset. It's the poster of Richie McCaw on the wall beside my bed.

He's bursting through the wall, head forward, knees pumping, headband bloodied, eyes focused on the future. He's concentrating a few seconds ahead to the try-line, but also years ahead to when people will look back and talk about one of the greatest captains in All Black sporting history.

This is the poster that got me up in the mornings, but now I feel like a fraud. I'll never be anything like Richie. I'm not even a Kiwi. Having this poster on the wall makes me feel like a pathetic wannabe. I'm glad I don't have to face Nash and the others on the bus this week.

Will Bel go on the bus, or come in the car? I haven't seen her for weeks. Not since she took my remark the wrong way and got upset in the hospital.

'Her father's in the country, so she's spending a lot of time with him.'

This was Zelda's excuse for her daughter.

'I thought she didn't like being around him.'

'Bran!' warned Mum.

What? What did I say? That's what Bel told me? Why don't grown-ups talk about stuff?

At least Zelda's not quite so uptight.

'Bel was a bit sniffy to her father's new girlfriend last time she was in New York, so now she's trying to be the understanding daughter and make it up to him.'

IMHO, that's the way to do it. Just say it like it is. Bel's got a short fuse and an attitude problem and she upsets people. Like she upset me.

If she's in the car, it could be a sign she's ready to make up.

And she is. Sitting in the passenger seat. Mum and I get past the dodgy sliding doors and sit in the back.

'Hi,' I say.

Bel half turns in my direction but doesn't actually look at me. 'Hi.'

She could be speaking to a complete stranger. Zelda throws her a brief, questioning look, as if to say that they'd discussed this scenario and come to some sort of agreement, of which a non-committal 'hi' was not part.

Then they talk about nothing at all. The weather. The state of the local fields after all the rain and the effect on farmers. The sky high price of porcelain imported from Australia. In other words, nothing of any importance.

Bel is all politeness, like a sales assistant feigning personal interest in a customer. Until she gets out of the car and we're alone together on the pavement.

'Did you get my note?' I ask.

'What note?' She has that little crease between the eyebrows when somebody says something dumb.

'I gave your mum a note to give you.'

'She never remembers to give me things.'

I can't tell if she's fibbing or not. With most people I can tell. With her I can't. Is this a good or a bad sign?

'I gave it to her while I was still in hospital.'

'I've been away a lot. It's probably in a pile somewhere. Or got chucked out with a pile.'

Isn't she going to ask me what was in the note?

'I wrote it to say sorry for what I said.'

The crease between her eyes deepens.

'I'm sorry you got hurt.' Her voice is restrained but cool. 'But some things can't be unsaid.'

Then she turns away and hurries off to join Yasmin, who's just got off the bus.

Mr Carson's walking out of the car park as I go down the drive.

'Ah, Kelleher,' he says. 'I haven't seen you for a while. Where have you been?'

'In hospital, sir.'

'Have you got a letter?'

'I got injured. It was reported in the local paper.'

'When was that?'

'Just before Easter.'

'Then we need a letter.'

I have more or less the same conversation with Mrs Hutchins.

'I thought you'd moved to another school. You're sure you weren't on holiday with your parents at any point?'

'No.'

'Because parents aren't allowed to take children on holiday during term time.'

I don't know what to say to this. I can feel my expression changing from disbelief to blank and on to mildly hostile. She seems to register the last and bends forward to scribble on a post-it note, which she attaches to the register. What does that say? 'Kelleher. Dumb insolence. Possibly criminal parents'? I wouldn't put it past her.

'Right. Settle down. This is not an examination year for most of you. On the other hand, it is time to start thinking of your future. Some of you may be put forward to take some GCSEs early in December this year. That will free you up to spend more time on subjects you may want to study for A-level starting in fifteen months' time. Now, who thinks they might want to do English at A-level?'

It's not my subject, really, but I raise my hand anyway and look around. Bel's hand is down and I'm not the only person to notice.

'Belinda. You don't want to study English?'

'No.'

'What are you planning to study?'

'Chemistry, Biology and Maths.'

Mrs Hutchins smiles. But it's more like a pained grimace and who can blame her? She's not the only one stunned by this announcement. The Hutch may be hard on B. Wilde, but she also knows that Bel is her prize-winning poet-in-the-making, a shoo-in grade-A star pupil, her goddess of limpid prose. (I learned this last phrase from the book Mr Edwards lent me.)

'Do you really think you can do as well in Maths or Chemistry as you would in English?'

Bel's answer is short and without emotion. 'Yes.'

No argument. The Hutch blenches at the sheer force and meaning of that single, quietly spoken word. It's not just a rejection of her subject: it's a rejection of her.

Mrs Hutchins takes down the names of those who are keen and willing, but the pleasure of anticipation is gone. An 'A-level star' has gone out of her life and left us poor, benighted planets orbiting a void.

I'm not that bothered. I want to do Maths, Chemistry, Physics and one other. It doesn't have to be English. I only raised my hand to be in one class with Bel, but now I'll be in two.

Mr Edwards takes us through a similar process. We're being lined up and readied for the exam treadmill, softened up for the mincing machine.

He at least remembers why I haven't been in school.

'Bran. Good to have you back. How are you feeling?'

'OK, thanks.'

'Good. Did you read that book I sent?'

'A bit of it.'

'Just a bit?'

'A chapter... or two.' I'm trying to be casual. You don't want to make teachers too keen. They'll only give you more work.

He seems amused by this and launches into a quick quiz just for me.

'What was George Allen's contribution to archaeology?'

'Erm, he took aerial photos.'

'Why was that important?'

'Before that, people used to dig to find things, but his photographs showed the bigger picture.'

'How do you mean?'

'The photos showed sites that nobody guessed were there. And they showed how the sites, like, related to each other.'

It's always good to chuck in a 'like', so people don't think you're showing off or talking posh.

If anything, Mr Edwards' smile is getting broader. Maybe I'm adding to his collection of howlers that'll make a good story in the staff room.

'Which word did not exist before William Buckland suggested it?'

'Um, prehistory.'

'What was the first archaeological site visited by Richard Morris.'

Easy-peasy. 'The Paviland Cave.'

'What is the argument of Morris's book? What does he say we underestimate?'

'Um...' That's a tough one. Why is he asking such difficult questions? And why are some people snickering? I don't think they know the answer. Unless they've just done a crash course in British prehistory. Which I doubt. Last time I was in this class, most of them were having trouble with the difference between Charles I and Charles II. Bel is giving me a weird, half-wondering, half-anxious look.

'We over-estimate ...'

Somebody whispers. 'Our speed of thought.'

Sounds like Matt being a smart-arse. Snickers turn to sniggers. But the comment throws me a lifeline.

'... um... no, we *under*-estimate the connections between things, um, between periods in history, er, and ideas, and erm, constit... , no *in*stitutions.'

Mr Edwards is grinning now. He nods. 'If you can answer those questions, it suggests to me that you've read the whole book. All 400 pages.'

I can't deny it. Anything to avoid chatting with Three-Step.

'Take a hundred per cent in your end of term exam. I hope you'll consider studying Medieval History for A-level.'

He leaves it at that, but he's pretty much sold me on the idea. History instead of English. A class not shared by Bel, but two out of four's not bad.

The downside is that Matt is also keen on History. Even worse, David has his hand up.

'Yes?'

'I wanna do 'Istry.'

'You do? Why?'

'To be with my bro'.'

He's looking at me with a scary, mates-forever expression. I'm only grateful he said bro', not brother. It could mean 'best friend', 'mate', a guy who'll die in a ditch with you, if need be. It doesn't have to mean that his waster of a father is also mine, genetically speaking.

'Well,' says Ted, considering this motivation. 'There are worse reasons for studying History. Not many, but the few there are tend to be notorious. So I look forward to your special insights from a Welsh perspective.'

'In a Welsh accent, at least,' murmurs Matt. The Three As giggle. He's got a following there, and – guess what? – they're all keen to study History as well. Relief only comes when they all, except for David, opt for

Modern History. David insists he's a medievalist like me, but there's not a kitten-in-a-blender's chance that he can even spell it. There's even less chance that he'll pass any GCSEs in twelve months' time. Without those, he'll not be welcomed back to study for A-levels in any case.

Mr Edwards must know this, yet shows no sign of discouraging him. But Matt and the Three-As can't resist a round of group smirking.

'Belinda?' says Mr Edwards. 'You're moving to another school, I believe. So none of this applies to you.'

'That's right.'

As Mr Edwards nods at this, to him, self-evident truth, shock waves rumble through the classroom. Heads turn. Eyes stare, glare and, in Yasmin's case, glisten in spite of her wry smile. The question of the day becomes, 'Where is Oxfam absconding to?'

To which Bel replies, 'Somewhere else.'

It feels like a judgement on us all. A punishment. How many of us are responsible for driving her away? There are at least a dozen prime suspects. But then a truth hits me like light flooding past a drawn curtain. Maybe it's me. I did this. What I did and said hurt her so badly, she's decided on a total change of scenery.

Suddenly the summer ahead looks even bleaker. There's no cash for a holiday. In any case, I can't do much more than loaf around 'regaining my strength' as the doctors put it. I can walk, but not run. Stretch but not cycle. Stand, but don't overdo it. Sit and lie down, but not for too long. I'm supposed to spend the summer 'listening to my body'. At the end of six weeks I may be able to cycle and jog. But not too much. Moderation in all things.

Meanwhile, my classmates are excited about their plans. Matt's off to the south of France. The Three As are distraught at being split up for the duration: one to the Greek islands, one to Norway and one to Martinique. They don't know how they'll survive without each other. Luckily, they have social media.

What can I look forward to? A summer being pestered by David. With any luck he's been invited to visit some long lost relative in the

South Wales Valleys.

'Got any plans this summer, David?'

' 'Aven't you 'eard? I been picked fer Wales youth rugby camp.'

'A rugby camp in Wales?'

'Not *a* camp. *The* camp. Wales under-17s.'

'A rugby training camp?'

'No. Proper rugby. Internationals an' all. We're playing a tournament. England, Scotland, Australia. You'll come and watch, won't you?'

Self-depredation

This going-to-school business is beginning to break up my weekends. What's the point? What's in it for me?

Chris once told me that kids almost never do better than their dads. Slave as much as you like, you won't rise above their level. Your parents can help you get to university, help you buy a car and a place to live, but you'll not be any better off than your dad was relative to everybody else. If you're a rich kid, you'll stay rich, unless you do something really stupid or give it away. If you're poor, your only chance of being rich and independent with as little effort is to win the lottery.

I thought my dad was pretty well off, but my real dad turns out to be a crook, small-time. He wears flash clothes but is probably on the run from just about everybody: the cops, social services and multiple single mums. With a dad like that, I've got no chance.

Uni? Forget it. Where do I get the money? Can I even afford to stay on at school? My body's so beaten up I won't be able to work through the summer holidays and save up. I can't even ride my bike, so I'm back on the bus and having to listen to everybody else nattering on about their wonderful lives. Bel's going to her father's in New York, then off to some fancy private school. I should have known she was basically a posh cow. Even David's 'on tour' with – would you believe it? – an international rugby team. I hate the way he says 'on too-er'.

I wish I could stay home this week. Even worse than nobody knowing what happened is the pity from those that do. I might as well get a tattoo on my forehead. 'This loser will never play rugby again'.

'Oi!'

It's the alkies over the road, sitting on their doorstep again after an all-nighter.

'Oi!'

'Mate!'

'Are you that rugby player what got injured?'

It seems impolite not to answer. At least they're showing interest.

'Yeah. That's me.'

'That's terrible, mate.'

'Come and have a swig.'

'Yeah, we've got a cold one fer yuh.'

One of them is waving a can.

'C'mon, end of term, innit?'

'Yeah, bunk off for once.'

Why not? Nobody missed me before, what's another few days?

The three of them cheer as I cross the road and duck through a gap in the fence.

'Yeah, get in 'ere!'

'Sit back there, mate. We'll hide you when the bus comes.'

They're much friendlier than I imagined and ask a lot of questions.

What's yer name? What year you in? How old are you? We've seen yer mum, where's yer dad?

'Is Carsick still there?'

'Who?'

'Carson? We called him Carsick.'

'I hated that guy.'

'Yeah,' I say. 'He's still there, still the same.'

'You wanna watch 'im. He doesn't like kids from our postcode.'

One them springs the tab on a tinnie and hands it over.

'Thanks.'

I take a swig. It's not very cold and has a foul after-taste. How can anyone drink this stuff first thing in the morning?

'Whatchoo gonna do when you quit school then?'

'No idea.'

'What, none? I thought you was one of them whiz kids.'

'I wanted to be a rugby player. But now … '

'What? Your injuries that bad?'

'Yeah. The doctors say that's it. No more rugby. So I don't know what I'll do.'

'You gonna leave school next year?'

'Might have to.'

'Yeah. We 'ad to quit.'

'I 'ad to quit. You got chucked out.'

'I got meself chucked out.'

This is clearly a sore point and they seem ready to row, but it soon turns back to banter.

'Yeah, well. Cheeking Carsick like that was sure to get you sacked.'

You can quickly see how this friendship works. Mick's the bitter one. He's more aggressive, but also more drunk, so he can't act on it. Sean's his best mate but likes an argument. Wayne's the sidekick to both. He tries to keep it cool and stop them going over the top.

' 'Ere's the bus,' says Mick. 'Get yer head down.'

I bend forward. The bus slows and stops. The guys are giggling and sneering. Callum hits the horn a couple of times, then pulls away. I hear the engine labouring under the weight, then gathering speed and going through the gears. The guys cheer. It's a clear victory. Alkies 1 School 0.

'Go on, get that down yer. The 'olidays start 'ere.'

'Yeah, there's more.' Mick turns to Wayne and hands him a latch key. 'Go 'n' get those six packs in me fridge. Time for some serious necking.'

I hope they don't expect me to drink the lot. I can barely manage this one.

It's weird how I felt a bit scared of these guys, but the more you get to know them the friendlier and funnier they become. I reckoned I was a serious sort of bloke, but these guys are helping me discover my inner comedian. I don't think anyone's ever laughed as much at my jokes. I must have been living in a zero-fun zone all my life. They think my stories about skipping, Three-Step and Rawley Partington are hilarious.

'I seen 'im in 'is four-be-four. Looks a right twat.'

'Yeah, but 'is missus is a bit of all right.'

'Stuck-up toffs, both of 'em.'

Why should I feel guilty about slagging off Rawley and Sonia? They fired me from my job – for being too good at tennis. The toffs'll never give kids like us a break. Their main task in life is to squeeze out the competition.

I'm on my fourth tinnie when a car swerves to a stop on the main road and two guys come busting through a gap in the fence. Is this a rival gang on a raid? Big mistake. There are four of us and just two of them. I'm ready to fight alongside my new mates.

The trouble is, they both go for me. It's hard to swing your arms when two heavies are lifting you off your feet.

''Ere leave 'im alone.'

'Shut yer trap, youse.'

I'm surprised my new mates don't put up more of a fight. They don't even stand up. At least I was on my feet ready to swing. Now I'm upside down being carried by an arm and a leg on each side. They push me through the gap in the wire.

'Ow! Watch it, you bastards!'

Then they lift me again, wait for a gap in the traffic and head for the parked car.

'Help! I'm being kidnapped!'

'Shut up!'

'You can't do this! You've got no right!'

'Shut up!'

'Scumbags! Creeps! Shitholes!'

Suddenly, I'm on the back seat with all the doors shut and a guy either side. One of them grabs the front of my shirt. He's really strong and shouting into my face.

'Stop swearing! I said, stop swearing!'

Then I see who it is.

It's David.

This cracks me up.

'What's wrong with you?'

'You? You?! You swear all the time.'

'No, I doesn't.'

When you think about it, maybe that's true. I haven't heard him swear for a while. David's getting serious. Ha! That's funny all by itself.

He looks like somebody's dad right now.

'C'mon, let's go.'

The driver turns the car around and we head off down the main road, away from school.

'Ahhhh. I get it. You want me to bunk off with you guys.'

'Yeah, sure, whatever.'

'Where's your sense o' humour, Daffy?'

'You call me that and I'll kick you out of the car.'

'Oooh!'

'And Carson'll be along any minute to pick you out of the gutter.'

'When those guys were at Stonefield, they called Carson 'Carsick'.'

'Yeah, well, I reckon you're the one'll be carsick any time now.'

It's not a bad point. We're going pretty fast and there are bends in the road and bouncy bits. Then it gets bumpier for a while. Then we stop.

'Why've you brought me here?'

There's no answer and they don't trust me to use my own legs. I'm hoisted down the slope towards Zelda's pottery. And there's my mum. Hi Mum! What's the matter with you? Always crying about something and letting everybody else boss you about. And the one being the bossy boots is Zelda, wouldn't you know it?

'Right, thank you, boys. Take him into the house. Put the kettle on, Cath.'

Who's calling my mum Cath? What a cheek! Ow! Easy lads. That's my knee. Hee-hee, and that tickles. Don't lift me under the armpits. It tickles, I said.

Daffy – oops – David, is *very* serious. He's even funnier like that. If David can be funny, Homer Simpson can be President, or ... Justin Bieber can be heavyweight champion of the world, or ... can't think of any more. Not when they're bouncing me off doorways.

'All right, never mind. We'll have to do it over the kitchen sink.'

What? Do what? Hey, whatcha doing?

They bend me towards the sink and Zelda takes the back of my head in one hand, turns my face towards her with the other and says 'open'.

Well, Zelda must have been as hot as Bel once upon a time, so it seems rude not to do as she says. I guess she means 'open your mouth'. Don't ask me why.

Then she quickly does something with her fingers at the back of my throat and my guts heave upwards.

Which is why they placed me near the sink.

What comes up is so disgusting it produces another heave. And another.

'Any more?'

I don't think so. Well, maybe just one mo-o-O-O-R-E.

Eughh. That's vile. There must be some law against this form of child abuse. I'll go all the way to the Court of Ruman Heights, if necessary. Mmm. Do I need to save any of this as evidence? In a plastic bag maybe. There must be a plastic bag somewhere…

'Right, let's take him to the spare bedroom. If anyone asks, we think he's had food poisoning and is in bed at his mother's place of work.'

I really don't want to lie down. On the other hand, maybe I do. Yeah, it's not so bad.

'There's a bucket by the bed, if you need it.'

Blimey, Zelda's a hard nut. That's where Bel gets it from. And my Mum at the back of the pack looking tearful. Cheer up, mother. It may never happen. Except it did. Well, something did. God, I feel rough.

'Are you all right?'

Zelda's staring.

'Headache.'

'Not surprised. We'll get you some toast, aspirin and a cup of tea. Remember, bucket.' She's pointing downwards, as if I might not hit the target.

The goons who kidnapped me are grinning now.

'Hang in there, mate.'

'You'll be all right.'

'Don't fall out of bed,' says David.

I grab his wrist.

'Don't tell.'

He leans towards me and mutters. 'That's the idea, so nobody else finds out… dimbo.'

Then they draw the curtains and go back down the stairs, laughing and chatting.

'Well done, boys! That was brilliant.'

'No problem.'

'Where did you learn that?' asks Mum.

'The finger down the throat trick?' says Zelda. 'I was married to a writer who drank. You learn things.'

It takes me a while to work out where I am. Then it all comes flooding back.

My mouth is dry. On the bedside table is a plate with a quarter-eaten slice of toast and a mug of cold tea. Next to that a tumbler of water. I don't remember eating anything. Did that evil Zelda shove it down my throat while I was sleeping?

Then I notice the open bedroom door. I'm being watched, or at least monitored. Bel is in the room across the landing. She's propped up on a bed reading a book. When I reach for the water she notices and gets up. I think she's about to come into the room, but she looks at me as if I'm some inconvenient stranger and heads downstairs.

A minute later, Zelda appears.

'How's your head?'

Good question. How *is* my head?

'OK. But I'm really thirsty.'

'I'll bring you some water, and more tea and toast. And you should actually eat it this time.'

'Is my mum still here?'

'Of course she is.' Zelda stops collecting the crockery and sits on the bed. I feel a lecture coming on.

'Try to help your mum, Bran. She needs help and she needs you.'

That's all she says before setting off down the stairs.

I know Zelda means well, but that is stating the flippin' obvious. My mum needs me. But kids need parents. We have no *choice* but to need them. It's all set up so we *have* to need them. But they need us more than they let on. They need us to need them. And we need them to need us to need … . My head hurts again.

The next hour sees a procession through the room. First, Zelda with the patient revival kit. Then mum with the quiet concern and awkward embarrassment for both of us. Then David Jones and Mike O'Callaghan looking pleased with themselves. They gleefully help me piece together what happened.

It turns out that my drinking mates didn't try to hide me when the bus turned up. While my head was down they caught the attention of kids on the bus and made vigorous pointing gestures at the back of my head.

It was clear who I was. What other kid gets on the bus just there? Even so, David, Bel and Yasmin denied it was me, or at least kept their views to themselves.

When my name was called in Mrs Creasey's class, there was a massive outbreak of smirking. Mrs Creasey demanded an explanation. When she got it, mostly from the Three As, she marched from the room. That's when David made a break. He'd seen Mike O'Callaghan parking his Mini in a side street. He was with Cheesy McGinty, bowling up late, as most Year 12s do when they have no classes. David intercepted O'Callaghan and Cheesy, broke the story and urged them to set off and rescue me from a life of booze and misery. Back at school, they insisted that David had persuaded Mike to drive him home for books and homework he'd forgotten, a story every teacher knew was a more than likely scenario. Cheesy had gone along, because he didn't think there was anything better to do. No teacher would find that hard to believe either. In fact, Mike had driven David home after delivering me to the pottery, and made him go into the house for books, so they wouldn't have to lie. They just didn't mention doing something else first.

According to Bel, Mrs Creasey had returned to the classroom a few minutes after David lit out and, a few minutes after that, Mr Carson was spotted striding purposefully from the main entrance to his car.

I don't learn this from Bel herself. She hasn't been upstairs since I woke up. Am I being sent to Coventry? For having a drink? For being a prat?

Mum brings me dinner. Chicken noodle soup. Food for convalescents.

'You *are* a convalescent. Alcohol is toxic. Your liver is trying to deal with it. Some teenagers get seriously ill or even die after doing what you've just done. You can be damaged for life.' She struggles to suppress the words, but she can't hold the lid on her feelings. 'Never do that again. Idiot!'

If I don't mumble 'OK' she'll be in tears again.

'And don't tell Grandad. *Ever.*'

'Orright.'

'And talk the way you used to.'

Cripes, talk about capturing the moral high ground by being a weepy mother.

'All right.'

'Zelda asked if you wanted to come downstairs and eat with us.'

'Yeah, I'd like that.'

Mum puts on her determined face. 'No, you wouldn't. And don't spill on the bedclothes.'

I blame Zelda. She's a bad influence. Mum was never this feisty.

Bel eventually turns up with dessert. Apple cobbler with ginger cream.

'We weren't sure if you could stomach this.'

'I could've. Before you mentioned the word "stomach".'

She tries not to smile at this and almost succeeds.

'Sorry I'm being a pain.'

The fledgling smile disappears and the frown is back. 'Yes, you are a bit.'

'How are things with you?'

She seems surprised by the question. 'All right. But if I wanted a little brother to look after, I'd ask my mum for one.'

'As if she'd give you one just for asking.'

'My mother's very resourceful.'

'Was there really a big fuss about it at school?'

'There would have been. But David saved your bacon.'

'Yeah, that was a surprise.'

'What?'

'David hatching a plan.'

'Why not? He's your brother, isn't he?'

So. She knows about that.

'Of course I know. Your mother works with mine.'

I notice she doesn't say *for* her mum. That's a point in her favour. But I don't like this idea that women talk about *everything*, as if it's the most natural thing in the world.

'Creasey and Carson were really fussed,' she says.

'Yeah. What is it with them?'

'They think your dad's a drug dealer and they like to nail people like that. Including their sons.'

'But I'm not his son… not in that way. I hardly know the man.'

'They don't know that. They just work with the information they have.'

'Bastards.'

'Don't swear, Bran. It doesn't suit you. Call them by their real names. My mum says they're hypocrites, 'cos they send their own kids to independent schools. They teach in a state school but they don't trust the product they're pushing.'

'Is that why you're leaving?'

'Not really. I've got parents who can home school me if they want. They sort of do that part-time anyway. So, I'd flourish anywhere…'

Now, is that arrogance or just straightforward honesty?

'… but my dad's been badgering me and my mum for years about my going to what he calls a proper school. I can't go to his old school because it's boys only.'

'Eton?'

'Yes. And he gets furious when I say the real reason is I can't bear toffs like him.'

'It's not only toffs who go to those places.'

'I know *that*,' she says impatiently, as if I'm some sort of halfwit. 'The trouble is, he's saying that he'll only fund uni for me if I go to Oxbridge.'

'Why?'

'He says the rest aren't worth attending if you're spending that sort of money.'

'That sounds a bit snobbish.'

'Du-uh!'

'Don't get upset with me. I can't judge. I've never met him.'

'Just take my word for it. The trouble is, if I don't get funding from him, I'll have to get a loan and Mum'll end up supporting me. And she can only just about cover her costs at the moment. She can barely afford to pay Cath… I mean your mum… but she can't do without her, either. It's really hard physical work and she's not getting any younger.'

'So he's sort of blackmailing you.'

'It's manipulation. He's very good at it.'

'And you gave in?'

'Not really. The real reason I want to change school is that there's no one at Stonefield who really cares about art or music. Not since Maggie Perkins left.'

'Mel Watkins cares.'

She gives me an inquiring look, like she's checking for signs of intelligence. 'Mel Watkins thinks that three chords on a guitar is musical genius.'

'I've never seen *you* perform.'

'I'm not saying I'm talented. I'm not. But I care about music, and I enjoy making music with other people. And that'll never happen with Mackie the Knife in charge, will it? He's only interested in school league tables.'

'So, anywhere but Stonefield.'

'Not anywhere. My dad kept saying I should try Rugby or Westminster. But that means leaving Mum on her own.'

'And she'd miss you, right?'

'I think that's what he secretly wants. To split us up. I know I'd miss her. So I did a deal with him. I'd go to an independent school *if* I could go to Langdon Park and *if* I could be a weekly boarder. It means I can come home at weekends, and the school's just the other side of town if Mum needs me.'

I'm trying to imagine her bargaining with her dad. Her expression was probably what it is now, stony-faced, unflinching.

'And your dad agreed to that?'

'Not straight away. Langdon Park's in the top one hundred in the league tables, but not high enough for him. And it was set up by Quakers, so it has this philosophy of helping others and not screwing up the world with personal ambition and all that stuff. That's not his style.'

'But what was the deal exactly?'

'What do you mean?'

'You said you made a deal. So far he's the one giving in to everything.'

She grimace-smiles. 'The deal is that I spend a bit more time with him, on holiday and stuff, and I'm supposed to be super-nice to his girlfriends.'

'He has more than one?'

'Well, no. Usually one at a time. But he's had three since I was eight, and his current one's the worst.'

'How so?'

My question irritates. She knows that's her style of asking questions.

'She's only about ten years older than me, but she acts like she's my age. A real airhead.'

'What does she do?'

'She's a university lecturer in New York.'

'And she's childish?'

'She's immature. She thinks my dad's *wonderful*, and *yummy* and she just *lurves* that English accent. She just can't get enough of it.'

She says this throwing her arms about, pretending to be the diva she hates. But then she notices that I've noticed.

'Trust me, she's not a nice person.'

'I'll bet she's not.'

She looks with some bitterness through the window at the sunny evening light.

'I'll miss you at Stonefield,' I say.

'You'll have Yasmin and David.'

'David won't stay on.'

'He says he will. He's counting on you to get him through History and probably his other subjects too.'

I cover my face with the pillow. 'This cannot be happening!'

She laughs at last, but now I'm not trying to be funny. I'm serious. Getting David through a single GCSE is going to be a nightmare, never mind A-levels.

'Yasmin's great,' she says, pathetically trying to make up for her own defection.

'But she never talks to anybody.'

'Yes, she does. Well, sometimes. But she's brilliant. You should sit next to her in maths.'

'I don't think she'd like that.'

'Sure she would. She thinks you're funny... when you're not being intense. And it would be good for your maths and physics. Sometimes I'm pretty sure she can see the multiverse.'

I'm not sure I like the direction of this conversation. 'Here's a question,' I say. 'How come you said you're not going to study English? Did you say that just to wind up the Hutch?'

'Partly. But I have to make a living. I won't be able to live off poetry.'

'But you could be a journalist, or a scriptwriter.'

'Seriously?' She looks at me as if I've offered her a large slug on a lettuce leaf. 'If I was a journalist I'd only want to be the investigative kind.

But I've met a lot of journos, thanks to my dad, and it's pretty clear I'd have to deal with a lot of creeps before I got to do what I really wanted. As for scriptwriting, I lack the gift for writing dialogue.'

Does this sort of thing come out of her own head, or is this stuff she picks up from adults?

'No,' she continues, 'I've decided to be a doctor. You can earn a decent living and you have to take the Hippocratic Oath. So you can't be a creep and pretend not to know it. I can read and write in my spare time. Then I can retire early and have even more time for writing. And I can take in my poverty-stricken mum.'

'What does she say about that?'

'She's got dibs on the garden shed so she can keep on potting till she drops.'

'But what if you get married and have kids and your husband doesn't like the idea?'

'Then I'll have proposed to the wrong person and would have to reconsider.' Her chin firms up and the laughter in her eyes stops dancing.

'You don't do self-depredation, do you?' I say.

The tiny creases between her eyebrows deepen. I reckon I've hit the mark.

'You should eat that while it's warm. It's not as tasty when cold.'

She's off down the stairs by the end of that sentence.

'And by the way,' she calls from the landing below. 'Yasmin fixed your tablet. It's downstairs. *If* you think you deserve it.'

What did I do? What did I say? *If* I deserve it? Why would she say that? Bel, I mean. Just because I point out something about her lack of self-depredation. Why can't people be honest about themselves?

And why would she do that? Yasmin, I mean. How can I thank her? If she's fixed my tablet. *If.* I bet she hasn't. Not really. I've never met a girl who can revive a dead computer without spending a ton of money. Or a bloke for that matter. Maybe I should get out more. Now my head hurts again.

'I forgot to tell you.' Bel's back in the doorway. 'Sonia came by while you were sleeping. She wants you back.'

'Back for what?'

'Tennis and weeding. She said Rawley promised to hit with her, but they both gave up on that idea. He's hopeless and hates getting beaten by her. And she can't find anyone who weeds as neatly as you do.'

'Does she know I can't do much just now?'

'We told her you'd have to recover from your drinking spree.'

'You told her that? Why?'

'Don't worry. She thought it was funny.'

'Why didn't you tell her I got injured?'

'We told her that ages ago.'

'She didn't come to the hospital.'

'Yeah, I know. She's such a selfish, over-privileged cow. Just like me and my mum.'

'I didn't mean ... '

'Anyway, we negotiated an extra pound an hour. And Sonia will offer you a free tennis lesson with her coach once a fortnight. Unless you prefer boozing with your new mates.'

She turns and goes, no doubt hoping her thick trail of sarcasm will do its work. But all this tells me is that I was being underpaid at Buckston Manor. Now Sonia has realised what she was missing and has had to up her bid for my services.

In any case, how does she know her coach is better than me? Maybe I should ask for the tennis lessons in cash. She must be getting some sort of deal. So why should I fall for that? Does she still think she can get me on the cheap?

We'll see. I'll have to examine the whole deal more thoroughly when my head doesn't hurt so much.

But Bel's back again, still not finished with me.

'And by the way,' she says with flashing eyes but in that cool tone she uses for haughtiness, 'the word is self-deprecation, which I do plenty of, if you could be bothered to notice. Self-*depredation* isn't really a word, but maybe it should be. It is pretty much what *you* do most of the time.'

I wanted to say, 'Yeah, well, remember that poem you wrote about rugby? Well, guess what? Garryowen isn't a person, it's a place. So not everybody can know everything, can they, clever clogs?!'

But I didn't. I don't know why. Maybe for the same reason I didn't point it out at the time. Whatever that was.

There was a young man from EnZed

There was a young man from EnZed
With a foolish idea in his head
To guzzle some beers
Confirm our worst fears
And lie sick as a dog on a bed.

Live chat
Hi Bel,
Nice limerick.
Do you think he's a loser boozer?

Hi Yasmin,
Hard to tell. My mum says it
could go either way.

What'll you do?

Wait. What else can I do?

Move on?

To what?

Something better?

Any ideas?

Lots more fish in the sea.

I don't want a fish.

Good point.

What's the answer to no 7?

$2x^3 - 2x^{-1} + 5x + c$
Stick to poetry, Bel.
You're crap at maths.

I'm crap at *your* maths.
Not everybody's brilliant.
Miss you. My dad's new squeeze
is a cow. (Not literally.) xx

Miss you, too. My dad's
dating again. Says it's
'for my sake'. LOL xx

Part Seven

If only

One year later

Choose a topic

Either
My Summer Holidays
Or
Rumour and Gossip

Belinda Wilde, 12A

The classic start-of-new-year topic is to write an account of one's holidays. It used to bore me beyond any desire to string three sentences together. But the topic of 'Gossip and Rumour' suddenly brings my summer holiday into focus in unexpected ways. It turns out there are different versions: the one I experienced, and the alternative created by rumour. The second sounds more exciting.

The background is that my best friend at my last school – let's call her Y – has been hearing some juicy gossip about me and my family ever since I left just over a year ago. We often meet online or in person to exchange news of ourselves that we may have missed.

> 'Open your ears; for which of you will stop
> The vent of hearing when loud Rumour speaks?'

To summarise the rumours:

My dad lives abroad because he's a 'tax dodger'. My mum is an artist and therefore a mistress of transgression. She can't possibly make a living, so she must be 'living on benefits'. Men are seen arriving and leaving at all hours. I always thought they were couriers, gas fitters, chimney sweeps, kiln maintenance technicians, photographers, piano tuners and other potters. Apparently not. All the stories point in another direction and it's about time the scales fell from my eyes.

It gets worse, for Mother has an 'assistant'. She is also tall and pretty. They work together, pretending to be potter and apprentice. In reality, it seems, they are 'swingers', 'escorts', 'sex workers' and, to add insult to those males they reject, almost certainly 'lesbians'.

Is that, I wonder, why Mother agreed to send me to a boarding school? Is she so devious that when I was at home for three weeks last autumn with tonsillitis, I noticed nothing at all except Mum and her assistant working all hours to make and sell pots while also looking after me?

There is a lesson in all of this and I am determined to learn it. I must pay more attention and notice things in my immediate environment that others comprehend at a distance, even those who have never come within half a mile of our doorstep.

This may not be easy. My mother made sure I ignored rumour as a child by quoting aphorisms. 'Birds peck at the best fruit'. 'Rumour travels at the speed of delight'. Was this a ruse, so that I would ignore her morally reprehensible lifestyle, blithely sailing through my childhood in ignorance?

Perhaps this has led to me living a life in denial, of being one of the least aware people on the planet. According to Y, there are girls at my old school who know why I left. I had been made pregnant by one of four teenage lovers. Two of these attended my old school. The third was seen walking a London street with me during an Easter holiday. (That would have been a cousin.) A fourth was seen dancing with me at a club in town during half term earlier this year. This, I should warn the reader, was a boy attending this school. He is famous within these walls as a star of school entertainments. He loves dressing up. Everybody knows who he is.

I recently heard someone say that celebrity gossip is useful and necessary. It diverts the majority of us away from spreading rumours about our neighbours and work colleagues. I asked my mother about this and she looked blank. Then I recalled that she is oblivious to rumour and gossip. She simply has no time for it.

So I asked my father instead. He scoffed. 'Rumour and gossip oil the machinery of work and social life. Without them, you don't know who to trust.'

I asked how that works.

'Simple. Don't trust anybody. Everybody is being positioned or manipulated. Just think of the way your mother spreads rumours about me.'

I was about to reply that my mother does no such thing, but realised he was probably fishing for information about whether or not she did. So I kept quiet.

I later realised this was a mistake. Keeping quiet probably confirmed his notion that she bad-mouths him on a regular basis. I know he talks rubbish about her, as I've been present and have had to set him straight, not that anyone would take my teenage views into account. But clearly there are times when you have to deny malign tittle-tattle, even if it's only for the record.

Is there a difference between gossip and rumour? Certainly my mother gossips about my dad. But I would call this useful information. It's important for me to know that he drank and took drugs in his youth. Why? Because it helps me understand him now. He's quite successful, thanks to his connections from Eton and Cambridge. But he could have done so much better without the uppers and downers. My mother's gossip helps me understand his moods and motives now. She only tells me what I need to know. It's not idle rumour: it's truth.

Which of them am I most like in this respect? I'd prefer to be like my mother and treat malicious gossip with the disdain it deserves. But I do enjoy my sessions with Y, as she brings me up to date with life at my old school.

The headlines in brief.

Teachers' pet did well in his GCSEs, but not well enough for his father. The headmaster applied pressure to certain teachers to increase their assessment scores and also made several phone calls to examining board adjudicators. Lo and behold, 10 GCSEs at A grade, 9 of them starred.

The school's bad boy scraped 5 GCSEs, thanks to help from a friend who, it is rumoured, did most of his coursework. It didn't help that 'bad boy' was suspended from school on three occasions. Once for calling a teacher a 'bitch' in front of the whole class. He denied this, saying he'd actually called her a 'betch'. No one understood the distinction. Suspended for one week.

On the second occasion he threw a boy's mobile phone out of a fifth floor window. It landed on an assistant head teacher's car and did some damage. Suspended for two weeks.

On the third occasion he threw the owner of the aforementioned mobile phone out of a window, though this time on the ground floor and onto grass just three feet below the window sill. Matters were made worse by the fact that a teacher was mid-class and described the victim being held through the window and 'body-slammed' onto the ground outside. 'Bad boy' claimed he did this in response to the spreading of an unpleasant rumour about my friend Y. Apparently she and I are in a lesbian relationship and we join my mother in learning the ropes of the world's oldest profession at weekends. The victim denied spreading tall tales while his assailant was suspended for three weeks and required to attend an anger-management course.

The victim's parents removed their son from school, sending him to a private establishment to spare him the company of violent riff-raff. This story suggests to me that wily rumour-mongers will always win out over angry truth-tellers.

If gossip is the passing of information about people we know, then I appreciate a lot of the news I get from Y. She tells me about a boy I liked, perhaps still like. It's important to have enough data to make the right decisions, as most of us will spend a lot of our lives in relationships. How many of these do we begin with adequate knowledge?

The boy I liked/like is on and off the rails like a toy train. He was suspended from school for truancy, though he claimed he was in the local library instead because he found it easier to work without distractions. After this vile slander against the school, he also was obliged to take a drugs test as a condition of his return.

He was sacked from his job as a gardener for pruning an old apple tree, then reinstated by the sacker's wife for correctly diagnosing fireblight and trying to save it. He was sacked again for 'arriving late', and reinstated again when it transpired he'd been out to buy plant bulbs for the sacker's wife and was arriving for a second time that morning. The cross he bears is being able to offer facts in response to every false accusation. At what point will he run out of facts and supporters?

'...covert enmity
Under the smile of safety, wounds the world'

His clothes are increasingly worn and he looks as if he's fallen on hard times, like a young *Tom Jones*. I sometimes see him biking down the lane in tops and trousers too big or too small, wearing battered workingmen's boots.

I wonder where he gets these clothes. There are numerous charity shops in our town and he'd have no trouble finding garments that fit. (Rumour has it that he steals from washing lines.) His pallor is mostly grey, with a labourer's tan in summer.

Y tells me he went through a period of barely speaking to anyone at school, except to her and his 'bad boy' friend. He fell behind with schoolwork, fell asleep in the library, appeared to be 'on' something, though Y thinks he's sleep-deprived and drowsy. He catches up with schoolwork during holidays, as if attending school interferes with his progress. He's now back to conversing with schoolmates, but with a grim, business-like smile. The contrast between this and the open-faced innocence of his first few days at that school are painful.

He is the son of my mum's 'lesbian', 'escort', 'sex working' pottery assistant. Like me, he is the victim of vicious rumour, innuendo, criticism and ridicule. I'd like to tell him that birds peck at the best fruit, but I fear I'd get a defensive, dismissive answer. After all, I have no idea what he's going through. I have two parents who care for and about me in different ways. In his family he's the one that has to do a lot of the caring, and I don't know how deprivation and stress will affect his character and personality. Sometimes I think he's like a young tree, being warped early on, and you wonder if it can ever grow straight again.

Moving from the particular to the general, spreading rumour is one method of shaping social or professional conformity.

'Rumour is a pipe
Blown by surmises, jealousies, conjectures,
And of so easy and so plain a stop
That the blunt monster with uncounted heads,
The still-discordant wav'ring multitude,
Can play upon it.'

It's designed to enforce certain social behaviours. If you fail to observe a clique's social norms, you will be the target of half-truths, malicious gossip or innuendo. If you succeed, a clique will draw you into the circle of rumour where your task is to listen to, agree with, and spread the latest smears about other people. The prime instrument is the fear of losing self-esteem and group approval.

My father tells me it's an excellent preparation for adult life. My mother says it's a waste of life and should not be countenanced at any price. On balance, I want to side with her, but I still find the whole business mesmerising, like staring into a crate of deadly snakes.

What does this have to do with my summer?

'Upon my tongues continual slanders ride,
The which in every language I pronounce,
Stuffing the ears of men with false reports.'

Apparently, I went to New York, Greece, Turkey and Italy. I was "deflowered" in three of these countries, in ways I don't want to mention here.

In Greece I was photographed lying drunk in the street with my skirt over my head. The evidence is on Facebook, not with a statement but a question: 'Are these Oxfam's knickers?'

The evidence from Italy is a headless, naked, sunbathing torso and the question: 'Are these Oxfam's knockers?'

From Istanbul comes the image of a nearly naked woman in a nightclub. 'Is this Oxfam doing a pole dance for wealthy Arabs?'

According to my theory, I could stop this bullying by sucking up to the blatherskites, by diluting their poison in offering entertaining tidbits about some other potential victim. But I know the slander would have to be about one of their current scapegoats. In other words, I'd have to lose a friend to gain some peace.

But do I need peace? Isn't the constant blether just a fear of silence suffered by the rumour-mongers. My silence, my inscrutability, my distance induces fear in them.

I've thoroughly enjoyed both of my holidays. I'm planning another. My lack of communication during this will no doubt kindle a further holiday of the imagination. To which I say: 'By all means, if I am the 'celebrity' that gives licence to your fantasies, who am I to deny you? The only thing you can't invent, so long as I'm still here, is my demise.'

After all that, here I am, just being me.

All quotations from William Shakespeare, Henry IVth Part 2.

15/20 That was entertaining, Bel, but you would have to approach it differently in an exam. To begin with, examiners tend to be strict, so don't try to be clever and answer both questions at the same time. It is also long. Try to condense your arguments. I'd like to see less description and more analysis, with categorisation of different kinds of rumour and gossip.

As my expectations of you are at least 18/20 this term, please rewrite and resubmit.

Part Eight

Same old same old

Another year later

Last chance saloon

I creep down the stairs trying not to wake Mum. The carpetless steps creak and squawk, but they don't interfere with Mum's steady breathing. She sleeps with her mouth open these days, wheezing and snortling, then wonders why she wakes with a sore throat.

'I do *not* wheeze.'

'Yeah, you do. And sometimes you snort and snuffle.'

'I may snuffle, but I'm pretty sure I don't snort. I'd just wake myself up.'

'You certainly wake *me* up.'

'Then you should close your door.'

If only. Nowadays I wake like clockwork a little after three and go downstairs to make sure everything's been turned off. No running water, no gas rings lit on the cooker, no boiler turned up to max for a bath that was planned then forgotten.

Grandad and I sometimes grumble that we shouldn't have bothered to put in a bathroom. It creates as much worry as convenience. Bath taps running and forgotten. Overflowing baths. Bathroom floods. Water seeping under the floorboards. Watermarks on the ceiling. Electricity and gas bills through the roof. If I shut my bedroom door I'd never get to sleep wondering what I couldn't hear that might end up in some mini or major disaster.

I know when it started. The Sunday morning I came home early from tennis practice, thanks to a torrential downpour. I found her dozing on the sofa, one arm dangling, the back of one hand resting on the carpet. The wristbands were off and I caught sight of the pale memory of a gash, a shallow ravine going against the grain, cutting across the delta of veins into the hand. I sat on an armchair opposite, dripping rainwater on the carpet, shivering, and waited for her to shift in her sleep so I could confirm a similar scar on the other wrist.

Then I had to go out again and ride through the rain.

I don't know if she woke as I left, if she sensed my presence and guessed that I knew, but we've never mentioned it. Would knowing that I knew make things worse for her? Would it tip her over the edge during one of her black periods? I don't want to talk about it. It's better this way, with me walking on eggshells instead of trampling all over her self-esteem.

She must have had another late night. Her bedroom door's wide open and a dressing gown lies on the landing.

I glance at the living room. Her armchair is the usual nest of blankets and glossy magazines that I liberate from skips. Glasses and teacups litter the low table. The TV screen announces the return of a shopping channel at 5pm.

I dig among the blankets and cushions, find the telephone and dial.

'Zelda? It's Bran. I don't think you should expect Mum today.'

I sometimes wonder how Zelda can be so understanding. You'd think she'd give up and find someone else. Even Grandad loses patience and utters the wasted, useless words. 'Can't you just snap out of it?'

But not Zelda.

'Give her a few more days.' 'I'll come by and keep her company. She needs a break.'

I catch sight of myself in the hall mirror as I put on my school blazer. It's at least a size too small. What to do? Hunch my shoulders? Droop? Put my hands in my pockets and slouch? Not a good start to my final year.

Archaeology's becoming my thing, so I search through the bottom of the hall cupboard. Buried at the back is a very large white plastic bag with green lettering. It brings back bad memories but could be my salvation. There's an old sleeveless puffer jacket and some worn shirts. The maroon pullovers are too small, but at the bottom is a dark blue blazer. It's musty and creased, made of a heavy material none of the Stonefield kids seem to be wearing these days. But it has the crucial thing: the badge.

This must have belonged to Nash senior, a boy so far ahead of me I never managed to identify him with any precision. Perhaps he left before I arrived. Judging from his blazer he was a bit shorter than me and broader, but not by enough to make much difference. I won't get high marks for style, but at least this jacket doesn't end halfway up my backside. Nash junior left last year, so there'll be no pointing and jeering. Maybe there's something to be said for Audrey after all.

I leave a note for Mum. 'Off to school. Will call at lunchtime.'

The air outside is cool but dry, with the thinnest veil of mist rising over the fields. Perfect for biking. I get off the main road as soon as possible and start taking the short cuts. My goal is a shiny cupola in the distance. It sits atop the new supermarket built on a playing field sold off by Stonefield Comp.

There was a fuss. Grandad signed a petition. Locals and parents banded together and demonstrated outside the school gates. Mr Edwards started a rumour that an important archaeological site lurked beneath the topsoil. Accusations of 'lining pockets' were bandied about, but nothing changed. The supermarket went up during the long holiday and Councillor Collier smiled for the cameras as the Mayor cut the inaugural ribbon.

It doesn't matter to me. I'm semi-detached. Not quite English, not quite southern hemisphere. The only connection I have to this matter is that somewhere just below the flooring in the 'Hot Drinks and Biscuits' aisle is where I smash-tackled Councillor Collier's son, and got off to a career-threatening start at Stonefield Comprehensive.

Matt Collier must have negotiated a parking space on the edge of the supermarket car park nearest the school. He's emerging from his starter Mercedes, an A-Class five-door sports model. Just the thing for the new Head Boy, especially as its dark-blue metallic finish is virtually the same colour as Matt's new blazer, which looks hand-tailored from selected lightweight cloth. The badge is embroidered into the pocket.

Stepping from the passenger seat is Carl Jenkins, Vice-Head of School. Emerging from the rear doors are Alison and Alys, our Head and Vice-Head Girls for this year. They're all immaculately tanned.

Yet there is one apple of discord. The Three As were broken up last term by the absence of a role for Alicia, who clearly believed she was Head Girl material or, at the very least, a candidate for Vice. Would she recover from this snub? Would the Three As reconcile? How many friendships would be sacrificed on the altar of these meaningless appointments?

Mr Edwards put my name forward for a prefect's tie at the end of Year 12. He should have asked.

'I can't afford to be a prefect.'

'It doesn't cost anything.'

You have to smile. Even the most well-intentioned teachers are clueless. Just look at the investment Matt's parents have made for the final year beauty parade.

Besides, Mr Edwards' vote wouldn't have been enough. I and 'that Jones boy' are linked like Siamese twins in the minds of most teachers. David may not be the walking, talking accident-waiting-to-happen that he used to be, but his younger brother is in the school and already making a name for himself.

'Are you related to David Jones in Year 12?'

'Yeah, he's me brother.'

The teacher rolled his eyes at the ceiling and sighed. 'Oh, no. Not *another* one.'

The story travelled around school like a breeze fanning a bonfire. Every time Mikey Jones walked through the school gates or entered a classroom some bright spark kicked off a mass chant, 'Oh, no! Not another one!'

Mr Carson tried to stamp it out with whole-class detentions but only made it worse. Parents complained that the words to 'Oh, no, not another one' had no punishable content. Why not put the teacher who started it in detention until it stopped?

Mr Carson is head of Year 13. After taking register, he embarks on a pep talk.

'You have two excellent Heads of School, and I strongly recommend that you all take your cue from them. This is an important year. Most of you will be applying to university later this term. You can still influence the references you receive from your teachers. If you are prefects, set an example and perform your duties. If you are chosen to represent the school in sport or anything else, turn up and do your best. It will be noticed and you will receive the credit you deserve. But don't take on too many out-of-school activities. Keep a good study-life balance, but when you work, work hard. For most of you, this year is a stepping-stone to your new careers. However… ,' he pauses for effect and glances around the room until his eyes rest on David and me, '… for a few of you, this year is the last chance saloon. It is yours to waste or make the most of. Are you paying attention, Jones and Kelleher?'

A buzz of amusement courses through the hall. I glance at David. His muscular neck flushes crimson. He's wearing a slim white plaster over one eyebrow, like a young man accustomed to street brawls.

'Well?' Mr Carson repeats the question.

Another buzz is cut short when it's clear that David is not only listening but judging what he's heard.

'Well, that's an improvement,' says Mr Carson. 'David Jones has nothing to say.'

Laughter.

'Excuse me, Mr Carson… '

It's a voice from the back.

'Yes?'

'Why are you citing David Jones and Bran Kelleher?'

Heads turn. The girl's tone is challenging, offended, and Mr Carson is suddenly caught on the back foot, though he recovers fairly well.

'Just making sure they're listening.'

He closes the register and leaves the room, but I sense that Mr Carson has a new name in his little black book: Yasmin Abbasi.

'Not responding to provocation?' I say to David as we head to the Year 13 computer room.

'That one's not worth it.'

I indicate the plaster. 'Clash of heads, was it?'

'Yeah, if the guy's brain was in his knee.'

'Australian?'

'Nah. One of your lot.'

'Did you win?'

'Don't be daft. They smashed us 46-9. Hard as nails them Kiwis.'

There was a time when David was proud to walk beside me down a school corridor, when everyone knew I was a budding rugby star. But now he's the one who catches the younger kids' attention. He's still shorter than me, but seems twice as wide. First-years hug the walls as we go past.

'Kelleher. Jones.'

We stop and turn. It's Carl Jenkins, our embryo Vice-Head of School, wearing his new experimental expression of 'deputy Marshal in this here town'. I've been wondering how Carl might position himself in his new role. Will he be a laid-back friend to us all? Or will he aspire to be his Master's yappy little terrier, doing the dirty work while the suave Matt keeps his hands clean and fingernails manicured? Judging by Carl's apparent offence at our height compared to his, he's going to take the second approach.

He waves a hand vaguely at David's neckline. 'Do your tie up properly, Jones.' He scans my jacket. 'Is that a genuine school blazer?'

'In what sense genuine?'

'Did you get it from the approved supplier?'

I watch David for signs of clenching fists followed by a punch to the throat. He must weigh somewhere in the region of sixteen stone and a casual slap could do serious damage.

We look down at Carl with his tight, determined lips, officious little frown and anxious eyes. Does he fear that David will repeat what he did to Greg Potts two years ago and body-slam him through a window?

David and I burst out laughing at the same moment.

'Nice one,' says David over one shoulder as we march off down the corridor. 'He could be an actor,' he says to me as we turn up a stairway.

'So could you,' I reply.

'I'll need to be. I haven't done a stroke of homework all summer.'

'But you read that book I lent you?'

'Which one?'

'Don't tell me you've lost it.'

' 'Course I haven't. But I might have mislaid it.'

'But you read the chapter on Henry and Becket, right?'

'Becket? He was a writer, right?'

'Not *that* Becket.'

'So which Becket?'

'Henry's Archbishop of Canterbury.'

'Which Henry?'

'Henry II.'

'As far back as that?'

'Yeah, we are studying Medieval History.'

'Maybe I should have done the Modern course.'

'If you don't read the books it doesn't matter what course you choose.'

He ignores this. 'Has there been a Henry after Henry VIII?'

'Yeah, lots. But none of them was a King of this country.'

'I wonder why. Maybe because Henry VIII did for all those wives. Created a bad karma around the name. What do you reckon?'

'I reckon you should ask Ted about that.'

'Yeah, reckon I will. Stop 'im banging on about your Becket bloke. At least till I gets up to speed.'

As we take our places at the computer keyboards and he scrabbles about in his bag for something to write on, he pauses as though struck by an idea. This happens a lot these days, but the idea is rarely a good one.

'I reckon we should call Matt Collier "Cnut", y'know, after that Viking king.'

'Is there a reason?'

'Yeah. First, 'cos I reckon it suits 'im. Second, 'cos he'll probably realise he can't stop the tide rushing in even if he orders it to. And third, 'cos I can call Carl "Halfacnut". Woddya reckon?'

'Why would you do that?'

''Cos the Anglo-Saxon Chronicle said he never did anything good during his reign.'

I want to say that we're picking up just where we left off last term. But, if David is making jokes about King Cnut and his successor Harthacnut, if he's organising his thoughts and numbering them from one to three, and if he's quoting the Anglo-Saxon Chronicle and almost getting it right, there's an outside chance he's read at least one paragraph of that book he borrowed. This represents a glimmer of hope.

Gardening this weekend

s.partington@memail.com

Hi Bran,

I'll be away for a few weeks from tomorrow, but I hope you can keep the Manor gardens in good shape. I'm planning a garden party for the weekend after I get back (weather permitting) so the lawn needs to look as neat as possible.

Could you keep brushing the dead leaves off the pool cover? Otherwise it looks a bit of a mess.

Those roses we talked about last month have finally died. I never really liked them and I'm sure we can do a lot better with that part of the garden. Could you dig over that area and rake it for neatness? Then we'll see what we want to do with it when I get back.

I'll leave your payment with Zelda. She'll disburse it weekly.

Best regards,

Sonia

By the way, Mr Partington has asked if you could leave your bicycle round the back of the stables when you visit.

Competition

Phil turns my racket this way and that. His expression rarely betrays a radical thought. Understatement is his style, both on and off court.

'You might want to replace a string or two.'

Considering that the frame is broken in two places and resembles more a piece of junk than an item of sports equipment, he may have a point.

'Don't worry about it. I'll get my guy to string up a couple of decent frames.'

'Not sure I can afford that.'

Phil smiles. 'We'll chalk it up, shall we? You can pay me back when you win your first tourney.'

Like that's going to happen. It's an act of charity and we both know it.

'I've seen the draw, by the way.'

'Who've I got?'

'Some kid called Brett Taylor.'

I groan.

'What?'

'He's a kid who's left school and trains in Spain. What's he doing playing a winter regional in the UK?'

'I forgot,' grins Phil. 'You read the tennis mags.'

'I read the LTA website. He's ranked number 2 in the under-18s.'

'Yeah, but that's the point, isn't it? You have to beat the top guys sometime if you want to progress. Anyway, you're in the under-18s now, so last chance saloon for you.'

'Why does everybody keep saying that? I've never been inside *any* kind of saloon.'

'I just mean it's time to win a big one.'

'Yeah, but I need a break in the first round. I don't want to meet a top-three player who spends most of his time playing tennis.'

'Oh, ye of little faith.'

'You think I can beat him?'

'Of course you can. Especially if he thinks you're first-round fodder.'

'Do you know anything about his game?'

Phil stops smiling and looks like a man who's never possessed a sense of humour.

'I'm your coach. I know everything about his game.'

'OK. Sorry. So?'

'So what?'

'So what *is* his game?'

'Biggish first serve and very solid from the back.'

'What's his weakness?'

'So-so second serve, which you should try to be all over like a ninja.'

'OK.'

'OK. You can have this racket for practice. Work on *your* second serve. My Auntie Mabel could have creamed that today. See you next Saturday, same time.' He's already halfway to his car. 'And don't be late again.'

'I had a reason.'

'There's always a reason afterwards. Just don't have one before.'

I know he's joking, but I still find it irritating. I'm supposed to beat Britain's second-best under-18 tennis player and I have to do it with a borrowed racket.

I bin my busted one behind the old stable block. I doubt the recycling police will fine someone of Sonia's standing for having 'inappropriate' items in a wheelie bin. There's a rumour that Rawley's about to be appointed an assistant to the Lord Lieutenant of the County.

The tools are just where I left them last weekend along with my battered jeans, moth-eaten pullover, battered jacket and well-worn working gloves. I like the smell of cool earthy sweat regenerated by my body heat, but not what it represents. Sonia appreciates my work, but Rawley just blanks me. Never a glance, never a wave, never a sign that I exist. I'm just a useful oik to him.

Same old same old. Not all the weeds have had time to grow back

- I keep on top of these things - but the dandelions in certain parts of the lawn just never give up. Luckily, these are just the sort of plants I can use. Dandelion leaves are full of vitamins and iron. I tell Mum it's spinach, otherwise she'd never eat it. If you dig up the roots, dry and grind them, you can make a coffee substitute. Mum thinks it's a newly discovered skin-rejuvenating cereal beverage from Guatemala, though she has her doubts.

I spend my last hour digging out a couple of old rose bushes Sonia managed to kill this year. I warned her not to prune them back so severely.

'They were here before I came. If they survive, good for them. If not, tough.'

Dig up the roses. I'll take a few roots home, just in case I can revive them in our garden at the Dabs. Dig out the soil. Never plant new roses where old ones have grown. Grandad taught me that bit of gardening lore.

Fetch some well-rotted horse manure from the compost bins. Dig out the holes even further so the whole area is renewed. Find some old rags and bits of plastic that make the digging awkward. A double-take as I turn up something small and shiny. The size of an old sixpence, but thicker and imperfectly round. Much heavier than a sixpence, and with unusual markings when you rub the soil away between finger and thumb.

I check for more, but turn up nothing better than bits of an old fountain pen.

Fill the holes with compost and fresh soil, then cover with a thin layer of wood chippings to hold in the moisture. Clean the tools and wheelbarrows, store them neatly in the storeroom. Change back into sports gear and stow the working clothes in my bag. A wash will do them no harm and make me smell less like a yokel. Put my swag in plastic bags: the dandelions, a handful of mushrooms and blackberries harvested before I cut back the brambles. Fill out my time sheet, then use the back of another to write a note to Sonia.

'I found the enclosed while digging in the rose garden. It looks like an unusual coin and very old. Even if it isn't, I'd like to know what it is. Bran.'

Make an origami envelope out of the note and drop the coin in. Post through the letter box along with the timesheet.

There's been no one home for a few weekends. It seems a waste for a house like this to have no one living here for weeks on end. Why is that? Do Rawley and Sonia have so many other *better* places to be? Lucky them.

I have to swing past Zelda's and bring her up to speed.

'Mum's back in hospital.'

'I'm sorry. Same place?'

'Yes.'

'I'll visit.'

'Don't be surprised if she doesn't recognise you. She's having ECT again.'

Zelda's usually a box of fireworks, but she gives me a long, serious look.

'Has she ever not recognised you?'

'Once.'

Her eyes go moist but she says nothing.

'I guess you might have to find someone else soon.'

She's startled. 'What do you mean?'

'In the pottery. To help out.'

'Why would I do that? But I could pay you to help out if you've got time.'

'What could I do?'

'Wedge and knead the clay.'

'I don't know what that means.'

'It's just mixing clay to the right consistency. It's heavy work, but you need some skill. Not everybody can do it. Your mum's brilliant at it.'

Sometimes I think my mother has a secret life. I only ever see her being clinically depressed. Maybe I'm the reason. Maybe my birth messed up the chemical equilibrium in her body. Maybe I'm just a millstone, a wet blanket. As soon as I leave the house she becomes another person. Maybe a spell in hospital and a dose of electro-convulsive therapy is like a welcome break from the dead weight that is me.

'Did you like the cake?' asks Zelda.

'The cake?'

'The cake I gave your mum for you.'

Cake? What cake? What do I say? That Mum sometimes eats a whole cake by herself while staring absent-mindedly through a window?

'Yes, thanks. Very tasty.'

'Hmm,' she says, as if my answer's somehow inadequate. 'We'll have some cake when Bel gets back. Should be here any minute. They're walking Oscar.'

'They?'

'Bel's brought a friend home for the weekend. An American. Exchange student. Come on. Let's see if you're as talented as your mum at wedging.'

In the end there's not a great deal of talent involved. It's heavy work if you try working lumps that are too large: otherwise it's a cinch.

'I thought you'd say that. But not everybody can do it. They don't have a feel for physical objects. I'll pay you £6 an hour.'

'Six? That's one pound fifty more than my hourly rate.'

'A new de-airing pugmill would cost me four thousand. If you can come twice a week for an hour it would be a real help.'

Maybe she interprets my hesitation as reluctance.

'There'll be cake,' she adds playfully, as if I were a child.

'Fine. If I can come on Saturdays after gardening and maybe on Sundays after tennis practice.'

'Perfect.'

I suddenly notice that the other colour in Zelda's hair is not a streak of porcelain left by strand-seeking fingers, but a swoosh of grey. Crowsfeet are the price her eyes pay for all the good-natured smiling. It suddenly strikes me that this is what Bel will look like when she's forty-five.

Nash always divided our mothers into NEVIDs and WOSANs. Not Even If Desperate and Wouldn't Say No. According to him, Zelda and my mum were WOSANs, and we were supposed to be flattered. Bel would respond with 'NACH!' which he thought meant natch as in 'Naturally'. What she meant was 'Not a Chance', and we all laughed at his ignorance.

And that's what I fear. Even if Zelda is overworked and underpaid, even if her daughter was left high and dry by her rich but selfish father, I'd still be NACH to them. I'm just an occasionally entertaining, marginally foreign sort of bloke who can do jobs around the garden and workshop. But I'm not Life Partner material, never will be. I'm just DESCO: Deserves Some Cake Occasionally.

As I'm being given a slice in the conservatory, there's a kerfuffle at the back door and Oscar comes bounding in. There's Bel's unmistakable laugh and a new voice, a very different voice. An American accent and… guess what? … unmistakably male.

Why did I assume the friend would be a girl? Why am I sitting here in clay-smudged sports gear, looking like a chav, when I'm being introduced to a suave New Yorker wearing red cord jeans, expensive heavy twill shirt and a cravat? (Seriously, a cravat!)

Why didn't I just suss the situation and push off homewards on my bike? Instead of having to make chit-chat with Zak Weidenbaum of New York, New York.

'So this is the famous Bran?'

'Famous?'

'Sure. The budding tennis champ, right? Wimbledon here we come.'

'Yeah, well, that's a long shot.'

'Why?'

'I doubt I'll be that good.'

'Yeah, but you gotta have ambition, right?'

'Do you play sports?'

'Me? No way. Not my thing.'

'What do you do?'

'I'm gonna be an artist.'

'What sort?'

'There are sorts?'

'Yeah, y'know, painter? Sculptor? Film maker?'

'Whatever media gets the job done.'

'You mean, you're skilled in all media?'

He looks puzzled for a moment. 'Oh, you think… I get it… No, I'm not going to be a *maker*. I wanna be more of a conceptual artist. I'll get others to make the stuff. I mean, you can't really monetize *making*. Concepts are the thing these days.'

I sense Bel and Zelda watching us, like spectators at a tennis match, waiting for the deciding stroke. I'm not sure anyone has won that point. Zelda smiles wryly and makes herself scarce. I suddenly wish she'd stay.

'C'mon,' says Bel, blowing past whatever the point was, 'we were going to listen to some music.'

This is where I should take my leave, but I follow them into the sitting room.

'What do we fancy?'

'We should let Bran have first pick.'

Brain-freeze. I plump for the first name that comes into my head. 'How about some Justin Bieber?'

They pause, blank-faced, until Bel gets it. It gives me time to rack my brains and think of a composer.

'He's joking,' she says in my defence.

'Oh, right! Good one. So, whaddya want?'

'Have you got Clara Haskil playing Schumann's *Scenes from Childhood*?' I know she has: she introduced me to it.

'Oh, no!' honks Zak like two middle notes on a bassoon and flops full-length onto a sofa. 'He likes the wrong Schu!'

'Shoe? What?'

'Y'know, who do you prefer? Schumann or Schubert?'

'So, Schumann's the wrong Schu?'

'I just think Schubert's the superior composer.' He waves his hands in the air above his head. 'Call me old-fashioned…'

This seems like an in-joke between him and Bel.

I recall one of Bill's tactics on these occasions. 'As soon as some wally starts waxing pretentious about music, ask 'em if they play an instrument. Most of 'em couldn't play a triangle. That's like a car designer who can't drive.'

I used to be impressed by Bill's homespun philosophy, but it seems crude to me now.

'Do you play an instrument?'

Zak's not even slightly embarrassed. 'I took violin classes when I was a kid. But, no, I just like good music.'

Bel's still watching us with that tiny lop-sided smile, like we're amusing animals in a zoo. But she's already located the CD and is placing it in the tray on the player.

'I heard Lang-Lang at Carnegie Hall at the end of last year,' says Zak.

'I know you did,' says Bel. 'I was there, remember?'

Zak grabs both sides of his head in a melodramatic gesture. 'Of course you were! How could I forget? But I *lurved* that *Kinderszenen*.'

Not only am I going to have to go home and research Schumann and Schubert, I'll have to learn German as well to keep up with this guy.

'Don't you love Lang Lang's playing?'

He's asking me. Brain-fade. What to say? That I've never heard Lang Lang on the radio, let alone heard him - or is it her? – live in New York?

'Yeah, not bad. Sounds a bit Clang Clang at times.'

A theatrical intake of breath and bulging eyes. Is this genuine outrage or fake indignation?

'Oh! I don't *believe* what I'm hearing!'

We listen to the CD while Zak comments on every piece. Divine! So tender! Magical! Such wonderfully fluid playing!

When it's over he pays me a compliment.

'Great choice.'

'Bel introduced me to that.'

'I did?'

'You did.'

'OK, my turn,' says Zak, taking over the CD player. 'Why don't we have…,' he slips a CD from its sleeve, '… some Horacio Ferrer and Astor Piazzolaaaah?'

Bel giggles. This is a worry: she's not usually a giggler. Unless it's just me and I have no skills in making girls feel a bit flighty. Or maybe not this girl.

The music begins.

'Shall we… ,' he's offering arms and hands, '… tango?'

She stands up with a laugh, head thrown back, eyes sparkling.

I can't detect much in the lyrics beyond the often repeated name 'Maria, Maria, Maria de Buenos Aires'.

Zak's a skilled dancer and Bel is clearly his pupil. They look as if they've done this before. Many times. He coaches her under his breath. 'Pause… and turn… and step… and lean back. Yeah!' She looks completely smitten by … by what? The music? The dance? By her partner?

I've never thought of Bel as athletic. She never showed any interest in sport at Stonefield, but she seems as strong and lithe as any of the girls who play hockey or do gymnastics.

Zelda comes into the room.

'A tango! Wonderful!'

'Join in,' exclaims Zak. 'Come on, Bran! Don't leave a lady standing.'

Zelda is clearly up for it, her expression a question mark. She's ready to tango in spite of dusty potting clothes and unruly hair.

'I don't dance.'

'Of course you do,' says Zak. 'It's easy. Just a few basic steps.'

'Really, I'll just mess it up.'

Zelda watches me for a second or two, then saves my blushes by passing by to do whatever she intended in the first place.

I get up and head for the door.

'Are you leaving?' asks Bel.

'Yep. Gotta write an essay.'

Zak refuses to let it lie. 'What's the topic?'

'Henry II's legal reforms.'

'Henry II? Sounds kinda medieval.'

'Not kinda. It is.' I almost stumble from the room. 'See ya. Thanks. Bye.'

Bel follows me out.

'Well, that was *kinda* rude.'

'What? Whad-I-say?'

Zelda's emerges from the house behind us and heads towards her workshop. She seems fully aware and mildly amused by this brewing spat.

'He was just trying to be friendly.'

'Wasn't I friendly?'

'Not everything's a contact sport, you know.'

'I don't know what you mean. Was I supposed to be especially polite or summat?'

Bad move. It opens a line of attack.

'No, normally polite would do. Zak's an exchange student. He's here because he's interested in how other people live. He doesn't have to be. His father's the founder of MapTech. He could do anything he likes. But he likes mixing with all sorts of people, not just the mega rich.'

I don't know what to do with this information. Zillionaire dad. Slumming it in the UK. Exploring how the 99.9% live. But I've got to go home and check out the expiry date on the bacon I'll be having with baked beans.

'OK, so just accept that *I'm* all sorts of people and I'm rude. But I've been working all day and I'm knackered. I need a meal and I've got work to do. Sorry I couldn't slouch on your sofa all evening.'

I don't really want to say any of this, but it pours out: emotions in need of linguistic structure. How does that work? Does Bel press a button and *bing!* get the worst out of me?

'Speaking of food, did you like that cake my mum gave you?'

The cake again!

'Yes, it was great. Thanks. I've told her already.'

'I doubt you even remember what kind of cake it was.'

'Fruity, spongy. Some chocolate? Very tasty.'

The tiny lop-sided smile straightens out and there's a little bit of hurt in the eyes, but also a firmness and decision. I'm busted.

'You don't actually care, do you?'

'About what?' Wrong words. 'Of course I care. But a cake? I mean, I've thanked your mum already. Ask her. She'll tell you.'

Bel turns away before I can apply toe to pedal. This is the same as having the last word. This may sound weird, but the back of her head looks furious. I don't know how heads manage that, but they do.

It's only when I'm halfway home I realise that maybe, just maybe, Bel baked that cake herself.

And maybe honesty is the best policy. My mother probably ate the cake before I could even lay eyes on it. I know zilch about classical music. I'm just a hick from Hicksville. I'm one of those jocks who'd need a scholarship in thwacking balls between white lines to stand any chance of going to university. Tonight I'll be leaning over a bath to wash clothes because the washing machine's bust. Audrey is willing to do it for me but not without a constant natter of criticism.

'Do you have to fall over when you play sport?'

No, I just fall over for the hell of it. I'm also guilty of sweating into my work clothes and tennis shirts.

Soak same in bath. Start my essay. Wash the clothes and hang them up before going to bed. Otherwise they may not be dry by Sunday night in time for ironing. But should I bother, just because Matt and Carl are on my case?

'Has the concept of the clothes iron entered your household, Kelleher?'

I should tackle the bedclothes, too. Soak overnight, wash tomorrow. Spend a second night in my sleeping bag while they dry. Bike out to the hospital to see Mum in the afternoon. Finish my essay and prepare for that wretched debate Ted is insisting I take part in.

Maybe I should become a gardener. I've got weeding skills and, if I play my cards right, a word of mouth recommendation from the wife of a future assistant to the Lord Lieutenant of Berkshire. Just don't ask *him*.

The wish

If envy is green
and jealousy black,
what colour is my wish
that grows from a lack,
like life removed
from a glimmering fish
silver on china slab,
fins without element,
eyes numbed and scales drab?

I sometimes wonder,
am I angler or fish?
The one who lowers or spies
that wriggling worm of deceit,
a soft, steel-concealing promise?
Many more fish in the sea, but
this one, caught by my conceit,
lured by my tongue-tied wish,
turns the colour of regret.

B. Wilde

The unimportance of being earnest

Mr Edwards waylays me in the corridor. He's rheumy-eyed but breezy as always, his fingers stained with the red, blue and black of non-permanent ink.

'I see you're already making a contribution to local history, Bran.'

'I am?'

'Yes, we're all very excited at the museum.'

'What about?'

'Your find, of course. I'm on the acquisitions committee. Mrs Partington brought in that coin you found in her garden. The museum's sending a team to look for more. They'll probably want to know exactly where you found it. Byzantine, we think. But we can't for the life of us imagine what a Byzantine coin would be doing in southern Britain. Of course, Mrs Partington hopes there's some massively valuable horde buried beneath her bushes. We'll see. Now, then, are you ready for this battle of wits?'

'I doubt it.'

He thinks I'm joking. 'Good, wait outside with the others.'

Matt, Carl and Alicia are there already. You couldn't cut the tension with a knife: you'd need a chainsaw.

'Don't you ever polish your shoes?' asks Carl with his usual tight smirk.

'Is that the point of this exercise? Some sort of fashion parade?'

'No, it's supposed to hone our skills for getting into university.' He turns away in apparent disgust and resumes his conversation with Matt. 'I read that one of the US President's daughters is applying to Oxford this year.'

'Yeah, I heard that.'

'Maybe you should apply to the same college.'

Matt responds with a mock-humble grin.

'Why not?' says Alicia. 'It's all good networking practice.'

'Summer holidays in Cape Cod,' continues Carl, not noticing Alicia's sarcasm.

I wonder if Matt takes any of this seriously. Apart from anything else, the idea that he's a shoo-in for Oxford. I've caught sight of books in his briefcase with titles like 'How to get in to Oxbridge' and 'The Real Rules for Oxbridge Admission'. If he's so confident, why waste time and money on those?

The Crease opens the door and calls us in. Ted is in a seat at the back, clearly looking forward to the thrust and parry of debate.

'Right, you know the rules. The aim is to sharpen your thinking skills and make you light on your intellectual feet.'

She holds out a small canvas bag. We take turns to dip in and pull out a slip of paper.

Mine reads:

Your role: supporting speaker. Propose the motion based on a quotation from Boris Pasternak: 'No one makes history, we do not see it, any more than we see the grass grow.'

Carl and I are set to propose the motion while Matt and Alicia oppose. The advantage is that I'll speak third, after Matt. The downer is that Carl will summarise both our positions. We have five minutes each.

Carl's line is that we all make history, but he manages to namecheck a few great figures who did great things. It's no surprise that Matt pounces.

'I'm sure all of us noticed Carl's concession that some people contribute more than others. The idea that great or powerful individuals don't affect outcomes is outdated. We see how American presidents make a difference. At the local government level I can see how my father has been able to get his own ideas put into practice. So we can all shape our future and change the course of history if we choose. Besides, the study of history is all about seeing the grass grow and understanding how it grew in that particular way.'

And more in the same style.

Then it's my turn.

'I'm not sure I've understood the quotation correctly…

(Hesitancy is rarely a smart move, but it's too late now.)

'... but I think I can see what Pasternak was saying. Sometimes there are powerful forces operating that nobody understands at the time or can do much about. At best we can only react and adapt. Climate change can have effects locally and around the world. Populations move from one part of the world to another for different reasons that we don't begin to understand until the process is well under way. This happened in the past following wars, famines and natural disasters – it happened in the Ice Age – and it seems to be happening again now on a pretty big scale. There are large populations in the Middle East and northern Africa under the age of eighteen. It's only natural that they look for food, water, employment, greater freedom and better prospects elsewhere if they can't find them at home. To a large extent better prospects elsewhere drove the British empire's expansion.

'Leaders don't always understand what's going on at the grass roots. They may eventually react, but sometimes too late. They're often behind the curve. They end up fighting old battles and not noticing new threats. Democracy is a slow process. You need to get consent. It takes time before one can react to what's happening. Sometimes the voters don't want to face difficult questions, so they look away and are then surprised by events.

'Politicians can let banks do pretty much as they like or build lots of new shopping centres because it's part of the zeitgeist and others are telling them it's a good idea. But in a few years' time it could turn out to be the wrong move. That's why the study of history is important. You can get a sense of how the grass grew, and ...'

'Time's up.'

The Crease is being strict, though I'm sure Matt got a few seconds longer.

Not that it matters. I'm clearly rubbish at this and Matt has a field day.

'Thankfully we've moved on from the Ice Age and the British empire. With twenty-twenty hindsight anything can be called the wrong move. But you'll never do anything if you take that approach. Luckily our leaders in the democracies have a better understanding of what's going on than Mr Kelleher…'

And so on.

The audience smile and snigger. I'm being pulped.

We lose the vote 24-6, which almost exactly mirrors the numbers taking Modern History and Medieval. David withholds his vote for my side until the very last second to keep me in suspense, but then slowly raises his hand with just the hint of a sly grin. Moron.

Amazingly we get an extra vote when Alicia raises her hand in our favour.

'You were a speaker against the motion. You don't get a vote,' says the Crease.

'Then I'd just like to say that I would have voted for the proposers.'

Carl is furious with me.

'We were supposed to be a team, but you hum and ha about what the motion means!'

'I thought the point was to explore the question from various angles.'

'The point is to win!'

He leaves the classroom with Matt, the bustling lieutenant, eager to please, beside the taller, long-striding Captain with his effortless superiority.

Mr Edwards comes breezing up. 'Well done, Bran.'

'But we lost.'

'Only the vote. You made some very good points. That's the important thing. Besides, who said two dozen pupils can never be wrong? But you might want to work on seeming more relaxed. Crack a joke or two. After all, we live in the age of stand-up comedy. Or slip in a thought-provoking paradox. Try not to be too earnest. As a great man once said, "History never looks like history when you're living through it." Or "There are no great men or women, just people standing on the shoulders of others and drawing attention to themselves." Or "History is what should never be allowed to happen again, if only we could guess what it was." You don't have to explain. Most people just blow past the meaning if it sounds cute.'

I think about this for a second or two. 'No, that's not really my style. I need to know what it means.'

He raises his eyebrows and watches me. 'Then stick with your style. Do what comes naturally.'

That must be his kindly way of giving up on a student.

I go along the corridor thinking I could have settled my side of the argument with a few choice sentences instead of doggedly gnawing at the subject like a toothless terrier. I'll never be a self-confident soundbite merchant. I'll just have to accept I'm a loser.

Conversations adults have about teenagers: Number 2

'I think we should encourage young Kelleher to apply for Oxford or Cambridge,' says Malcom Edwards.

'You can't be serious,' says Edith Creasey, truly startled. 'If we started putting candidates like that forward we'd lose all credibility.'

'Why do you say that?'

'For a start I don't see him making the right impression at interview.'

'In what sense?'

'In any sense. He's arrogant, competitive and coarse.'

'Is he? He's always struck me as a rather sensitive boy.'

'A sensitive boy wouldn't call others obscene names.'

'Does he?'

'Haven't you heard? The whole school is calling our Head Boy "Cnut" and, by association, our Vice Head is "Halfacnut".'

'I see. That's what all the graffiti's about.'

'Yes, costing the school a fortune to clean up, and started by Kelleher.'

'Are you sure? That sounds more like something cooked up by Jones.'

'Jones wouldn't have the wit.'

'On the contrary. That's the one thing Jones does have, apart from a rugby player's physique.'

'Jones is a thug and Kelleher is his half-brother and best friend. I rest my case. Hardly university material, let alone Oxbridge.'

'You can't always judge a boy by the company he keeps.'

'By the company he chooses to keep.'

'He's at least as sharp as Collier, and probably more thoughtful.'

'Collier is the best university candidate we've had in years. He deserves a place at Oxford. He got a superb set of GCSE results.'

'True, but a lot of that was based on teacher assessment. The new final exam format is a different ball game.'

'Matt Collier would excel in any format. I'm predicting four A-stars.'

'Has he been excused sports and extra-curricular activities?'

'His father requested it.'

'To guarantee success?'

'Giving his son the best possible opportunity.'

'Yes, but it's bound to cause resentment.'

'Boys like Kelleher and Jones don't even make themselves available for school sports.'

'Well, Jones plays elite rugby and I think Kelleher has a Saturday job.'

'That's the choice he makes. He earns money to spend on who-knows-what and Matt Collier spends his Saturdays and Sundays having extra tuition.'

'With you?'

'Among others, yes. He's really committed, and I'm quite happy to help out. The Colliers are a really nice family.'

'I suspect young Kelleher's family can't afford any of that.'

'From what I hear his father's a very dodgy customer with plenty of cash. It's what they decide to spend it on.'

'And, yet, Kelleher certainly got the better of Collier this morning.'

'Were we listening to the same debate? I thought Kelleher was arrogant and personal. Doubting what Matt's father has achieved. He can be quite nasty sometimes.'

'So you wouldn't support an application to Oxbridge?'

'Certainly not. I might support him to do a degree at the local FE college. But Oxbridge? Out of the question. I'm surprised he was allowed to do four A-Levels.'

'Perhaps four teachers had faith in him.'

'Sometimes faith is not enough. We also have to exercise sound judgement of ability and character.'

The tell-tale signs

The alarm goes. Five to seven. Switch to snooze. Another Monday. Do I have to get up?

The alarm goes. Twenty past seven. I've got to get up. Make tea for Mum. Make sure she's got what she needs. Find out if she's going in to work this week. It'll save me having to wedge and knead for Zelda.

The alarm doesn't go. It's ten to nine. I forgot to set it back on snooze. Something else is going. My phone.

'Orright?'

'Grandad?'

'I've been calling for an hour.'

'Sorry, I didn't hear.'

'Are you still in bed?'

'Yeah.'

'Anything wrong?'

'No, just… 'There's no way I can use the word 'tired' to Grandad. 'I overslept.'

'You're going to be late.'

'I am late.'

'Lucky for you I'm coming round. I'll give you a lift. How's your mother?'

'Don't know. I don't think she's up yet.'

'Why am I not surprised?' He sounds irritated, sarcastic. 'I'll be round in ten minutes.'

Can you inherit clinical depression? Maybe I'm going to be like my mum. Can't get up in the morning. Lie in bed till nine. Late for school. Can't raise any enthusiasm for what I do. Can't be bothered to plan for the future. Might as well join Grandad in his building and landscaping business. People will always need walls built and gardens re-designed. But not sure if Grandad would employ me. He probably thinks I'm lazy.

Mum's still asleep when Grandad arrives.

'Let her sleep. I brought some shopping.' He puts the bags on the table and starts loading up the fridge and cupboards. 'How'd it go yesterday?'

'Knocked out in the first round.'

'Tough opponent?'

'British number two.'

'What was the score?'

'Seven-six, seven-five.'

'Well, that's not too bad.'

'Phil says I should have won.'

'Phil always says that.'

'He was right. I'd worked him out, discovered his weakness. Should have finished him off.'

'Why didn't you?'

'Dunno.'

'No idea?'

'Phil says I lack the killer instinct.'

'Every coach says that when their player has chances and loses. Was there something else?'

'Dunno. I felt...'

'What?'

'I felt kinda... tired.'

'You probably were.'

'How could I be tired? We started playing at two o'clock. I'd been sitting down for hours. How could I be tired?'

Grandad ignores the question. 'This other kid who beat you? Did he get up at five in the morning to travel down to Portsmouth?'

'Dunno.'

Grandad grunts. 'Did you win a consolation match?'

'Yeah, I won both of *those*.'

'So you bounced back.'

'They weren't top ten. Well, one of them was number eleven and he messed up his first match, too.'

'So what will your rank be after this?'

'Dunno.'

'There seems to be a lot you don't know. What's going on with you?'

'Dunno.'

'C'mon, Bran. I can get tight-lipped out of your mother any day of the week. What's going on?'

He waits while I think.

'You take your time. I'll make a cup of tea. The world's been waiting half the morning, so it can wait a bit longer.'

He's like a dog with a bone. His stare demands an answer as he stirs two spoonfuls of sugar into his tea. Should I tell him its poison according to some recent research? Or would that just raise his blood pressure?

'I dunno. I just wonder if I'm gonna be depressed like Mum.'

'Why do you think that?'

'I'm not motivated enough for anything.'

'Such as?'

'Schoolwork.'

'You're not doing your homework?'

'No, I do it. But what's the point?'

'Work is its own reward.'

He always says that.

'There's a rumour going round. One of the teachers overheard Mrs Creasey saying she wouldn't give me a decent reference. Not even for an FE college. She said something about me coming from a crap family.'

Grandad closes his eyes and sighs. He looks weary. Why am I doing this to him? I know he has enough trouble with Mum and Audrey, but sometimes I can't help myself. I hear myself grinding on, but I can't stop till I've said it all.

'I've great teachers in all my subjects. I like them, and they seem to like me. But the people who matter don't like me at all.'

'What people?'

'The head, the assistant heads. The people who'll write my references. There's something about me they don't like.'

'Look, Bran. The exam system's been changed, hasn't it? Your teachers can't influence the results with course work assessments. The people who mark your exams won't know you from Adam, right?'

'True.'

'So, if you get good grades, it doesn't matter what this Mrs Creasey or any of them think. Your results will speak for themselves.'

'But the references are important.'

He loses patience. 'A lot of things are important, Bran. The important thing is to be in control of the things you can control and don't obsess about the things you can't.'

'That's what Phil says.'

'In that case, he's not a totally useless coach. And if I can stop you having the last word, for once, when's your last exam?'

'Thursday, June 3rd. Chemistry practical.'

'Provided you don't blow up the lab, are you free the Saturday after?'

'I'll have tennis practice and gardening.'

'I'll do your gardening, if you can fix it with Sonia Partington.'

'But I'll need the money.'

He shuts his eyes again. 'I'll do your gardening and give you the money.'

'But that's not fair...'

'Bran, will you lighten up? I'm asking you for a favour. Can you keep Saturday, June 5th free? It's important to me.'

'You said lunchtime.'

'Yes, just lunchtime.'

'It's not something involving Audrey, is it?'

'No, Bran, I would not foist my wife on you without asking you first.'

'So, what is it?'

'I can't say.'

His face turns puce. Not from anger, from stress.

'All right. I'll do it.'

'Thank you,' he murmurs. 'Thank you very much. Put it in your diary. And now you can get on your bike and push off to school. I need to talk to your mother.'

I love my Grandad, but he has no patience. And he's unreliable. Promises to take me to school one minute and changes his mind the next. *And* he avoided my question about being depressed. Why do adults insist on answers to trivial questions while dodging the big ones?

On arrival at school I run into two trainee adults practising the trivial stuff.

'Why are you late, Kelleher?'

'None of your business, Collier.'

'You're talking to your Head of School,' says Carl. 'Show some respect.'

'I respect people who respect others.'

'Right, I'm putting you on detention.'

Matt started this exchange and is observing progress.

'For what?' I demand.

'For being late and insubordinate.' Carl enjoys the long word.

'Whereas you are always on time and subordinate.'

'Yes, I am!'

'Good for you. I trust you enjoy your subordination. Perhaps it offers you a *frisson* from time to time?'

'That'll be double detention.'

'Again, for what?'

'Insinuendo.'

'I accept your double detention on condition that you write that particular reason beside it. Anyway, why are you wasting your time here instead of doing some work? The state is paying for your education and you're just hanging around in the lobby like a pair of not-so-bright security guards.'

Carl turns on his heel and marches off to the secretary's office, probably to record my double, if not triple, detention.

'Watch it, Kelleher,' says Matt with a grim little smile.

'You'll have to define "it",' I say, turning down the corridor.

He mutters at my back. 'With you, "it" is being late and uteless, as usual.'

David is at a computer in the study room, his notes littering the floor.

'Win your match?' he asks.

'Nope.'

'I always knew you were useless. Anyway, you're late. I need some help with this presentation on King Richard.'

'Which one?'

'There was more than one?'

'Richard I, II or III?'

'Lionheart.'

'That's Richard I. What about him?'

'About his wife, Eleanor.'

'His wife was Berengaria, his mother was Eleanor of Aquitaine.'

'Whatever. What's the deal with them?'

'Do you mean, why were they important?'

'Yeah.'

'He married Berengaria of Navarre to protect the southern border of his French possessions while he went off on crusade. She was there to cover his back…,' How to explain this? '… like a full back in rugby. His mother Eleanor acted like his regent in England, keeping an eye on everything, a bit like a scrum half or a number 10. Makes sense?'

'Yeah.'

'You can say that in your presentation, but don't write it in the exam.'

'Why not?'

' 'Cos they'll mark you down for using inappropriate register.'

'What's the register got to do with it?'

'Register means language style. You've gotta keep it academic.'

'God, this stuff's boring!'

'It isn't really. Eleanor was one of the most powerful women in Europe, and seriously hot. She married two kings, had loads of kids, ruled England and had a long line of lovers. Or maybe not. We can't be sure because they didn't have cameras with long-range lenses. Berengaria genuinely loved Richard, but he might have been gay or bisexual, which might be the reason she ended her life in a convent pining for love.'

He shoots me a sceptical frown. 'Are you bullshitting me, you?'

'That's what plenty of writers reckon.'

'Mm. Right, then.' He turns his attention more keenly to the screen and his notes.

Sometimes you have to dumb down to have any chance of braining up.

Getting personal

Mrs Creasey oversees Stonefield's applications to university.

'If you wish to apply for university or college this autumn, start writing your personal statements now. Don't leave it to the last minute. If you need help, bring your statements to me or Mr Carson. We'll do what we can to ensure you achieve your goals. You will, of course, require a reference from us.'

'I've been interested in politics from an early age. My father was a Councillor and twice Mayor while I was growing up. He is currently Leader of the Council. It's been a fascinating experience to listen and learn as policies are discussed, crafted and enacted, both at party and Council level. I feel that the skills observed in these environments have helped me in my role as Head Boy at Stonefield School. Above all, I have learned the humility and self-discipline involved in leading and being led.

The University of Oxford, particularly the Politics, Philosophy and Economics course, has a rich tradition in producing leaders, including many Prime Ministers of this country. I cannot think of a better training ground for people who wish to serve their communities...'

'I come from a large family. There are five ~~kids~~ children at home and at least ~~twenty-one~~ twenty-two half-brothers and sisters (that I know of) elsewhere. My ~~mam~~ mother is Welsh and provides a warm and loving home, but there are problems. Single parents don't have much money or time. It was easy for me as a ~~nipper~~ child to do ~~what~~ as I wanted. My ~~da~~ father is ~~a Jack the Lad~~ an irresponsible person, probably a criminal, who always seems to ~~get away with it~~ escape the consequences. He wants me to ~~hook up with him~~ join him in what he calls 'the family business'. ~~No surprise~~ Not surprisingly I was a ~~total loser~~ borderline delinquent for the first fourteen years of my life.

~~But~~ However, one day a new ~~kid~~ boy turned up at our school from the other side of the world. He didn't really want to be my friend, but I stuck to him like a ~~leech~~ burr. I didn't know why at first. He was just different. He cared about things. He thought it was important to do things as well as you can. He wasn't just interested in himself: he was interested in other people's abilities and talents. One day, he pointed out a talent I never knew I had. So I tried to copy his way of developing this and turning it into ability. I know I'll never be as smart as he is, but I've been incredibly lucky to have a ~~brother~~ friend who helps me and wants me to succeed ...'

'My life so far has been a catalogue of false starts. I once lived in New Zealand, but moved abruptly to England. I once imagined I'd be a top class rugby player, but suffered a serious injury and can no longer play the sport. I once thought I'd become an engineer, but then I turned up a rare coin while digging in a garden.

My first thoughts weren't about how much it was worth, but a rush of questions: 'Where did this come from, where was it made, what's it made of, who made it and when, who owned it? How did it get here and when, why did it end up here in a garden under a rose bush?' I passed it to the owner of the house, who passed it to the local museum. All we know so far is that it could be Byzantine. What I did know for certain at that moment was that I wanted to be an archaeologist ... '

Mrs Creasey likes to keep on top of things.

'Who has a personal statement I haven't yet seen? I got yours yesterday, Matt. Excellent, as usual. Just a few tweaks needed here and there.'

''Scuse me, Mrs Creasey. Can we see Matt's and use it as a template, like?'

'No, it's supposed to be personal.'

'Then why's *you* looking at 'em?'

'Do you mean, why *are* you looking at them?'

'Got it in one.'

'It's to help you maximise your chances, David Jones. I expect to see yours on my desk shortly.'

'Not necessary. I got someone else to look at it.'

'May I ask who?'

'Me mam. And someone else.'

'Good luck with that. And what about you, Bran Kelleher?'

'I'm not applying.'

'What do you mean?'

'Simple as that. I'm not applying.'

Part Nine

The Reckonings

Conversations adults have about teenagers: Number 3

He walks into the space behind the pub and glances at the three men sitting at the table. He swiftly takes in the stacked bottle crates, metal caskets and assorted cleaning gear. He does not approve of this venue.

'Which one's Reg?'

'That's me,' says the thin one in the middle with the overlong hair and sideburns. 'Frank?'

'Maybe.'

The three men at the table are surprised that 'Frank', if that is his name, would venture onto their territory alone. He's either foolhardy or very confident. But his clothes are expensive. Sharp suit, genuine Rolex and shoes none of them can afford.

'You alone?' asks one of the 'muscle' sitting beside Reg.

'No, *you're* alone,' says 'Frank'.

Reg senses that he needs to change the tone of this conversation.

'Have a drink.'

'Frank' looks at the surroundings once more. 'What, here?'

That is a very definite 'no' and somewhat insulting. But the three hosts know they'll have to ignore this calculated insult, just in case 'Frank' has a small army encamped inside the pub. These London boys don't fool around.

'The thing is, Reg, Mr Archibald isn't happy.'

'I guessed that.'

'You promised him deliveries, but the numbers are down. Well down.'

'It's not easy …'

'But you guaranteed results. You said you had access to kids to do the deliveries.'

'The recruitment process is slower than usual. You know what teenagers are like. Completely unreliable.'

'But we're not talking about paper rounds, Reg.'

'I know.'

'So get things moving, or we'll have to find another contractor.'

'I'll make things happen.'

'You've got thirty days. We want to see a twenty per cent increase by the end of March, then five per cent minimum month on month for a year. Otherwise, you know what.'

'Yeah, fine, but you should tell Mr Archibald …'

'No, Reg. I don't tell Mr Archibald anything. I just deliver messages like I'm told.'

Once more 'Frank' scans the so-called patio at The Broken Glass with a sceptical expression. His contempt is barely concealed. There is little doubt that if he were Mr Archibald he wouldn't have anything to do with chancers operating from such low-life premises.

'Have a glass anyway,' says Reg, desperate to improve his standing.

'Frank' looks mystified. 'No time,' he says. 'Mr Archibald runs a serious business. I don't have time to sit around drinking in the middle of the day. And let's face it, neither do you.'

Conversations adults have about teenagers: Number 4

Phil Baker spends his first hour at every tournament saying 'hello' to all the people he knows on the circuit.. It's a ritual that many coaches detest. They don't have time; they're worrying about the mental state of their latest charges; parents-from-Hell are on their case as to why their offspring are not getting the results that'll turn them into the next Roger Federer or Serena Williams. But Phil is popular because he hides all these cares beneath a light-hearted, generous demeanour.

'Hi, Mark. How's it going?'

'Oh hi, Phil. Not bad. I see I'm up against your boy in the first round.'

'Yes. Your lad's number four. That's a remarkable rise up the ranks.'

'Yeah, he works hard enough and he's had some luck.'

'You must be working your usual magic.'

'Well, you know how it is. You get a long way if a kid's got a biggish serve. How about your boy?'

'Lovely lad. Good all-round player. Works hard, but lacks the killer instinct.'

'Well, my kid's got that in buckets. He's a little shit, to tell you the truth.'

'Is he?'

'Yes, just like his father. He actually withheld twenty per cent of my fee last tournament because his boy lost in the semi.'

'That's not polite.'

'To put it mildly. In fact I'm thinking of dropping that family. You don't want 'em, do you?'

'No, I've got my hands full trying to get my lad to win a big one.'

'What's his problem?'

'Troubled home, no father, mother with mental health problems. Which means almost no money, of course.'

'That's a hard road.'

'Yeah. He loves the game, but spends all his time caring for other people. Doesn't know how to be ruthless when he needs to be.'

'Sounds like a decent lad.'

'Yes, far too nice.'

'Maybe I should have a word. I'm pretty good at encouraging a ruthless streak.'

'I believe you are acknowledged as the master, Mark.'

'Where is he?'

'Over there. The tall lad in the blue top.'

Phil watches Mark stroll over to the cluster of players, parents and coaches waiting for their turn on the warm-up courts. Although he's out of earshot, he pays close attention to Bran's expression as Mark strikes up a conversation.

'Hi, are you Bran Kelleher?'

'Yeah.'

'Playing Keith Rennie in the first round?'

'Yeah.'

'Just thought you ought to know. Keith has been spreading rumours about you. Says you and your family are trailer trash. Says your mum's a slapper and a nut-job.'

Mark notices the boy's friendly gaze harden as he listens.

'Don't take it out on me. Just thought you ought to know the kind of person you'll be playing in half an hour.' He puts his hand on the boy's shoulder and leans in close. 'Stay cool, but smash the little creep. You'll be doing us all a favour. He hates it if you keep taking pace off the ball. Gets frustrated and starts overhitting.'

Phil watches Mark saunter away, then wanders over himself.

'All right, Bran? Quick warm-up?'

Bran doesn't say a word, but somewhere just behind the eyes it's clear that he's hatching a sporting homicide.

Framed

Mum's still up when I get back.

'How did it go?'

'I lost.'

'Oh, no. I'm sorry, love. In the first round again?'

'No, in the final.'

'In the final? But that's great.'

'No, it isn't. I lost.'

'What was the score?'

'6-7, 7-6, 9-11.'

'But that was close.'

'Close, but no cigar.'

'Was it that boy that beat you last time? That Brett Somebody-or-Other?'

'No, beat him in the semi.'

'Who was it then?'

'A kid who's number one in the Under-18s.'

'He's probably a year older than you.'

'Maybe.'

'Didn't you get a cup or something?'

'Got a silver plate. A small one.' I point to my kitbag. 'It's in there somewhere.'

'Well, you sit down. I'll put a pizza in the oven.'

I shrug my assent and slump down on a chair in the kitchen. Mum moves between fridge and cooker. She used to glide, now she bustles. Her dressing gown is faded and worn, strands of hair have escaped their hairclips and the backs of her slippers are broken down. How will she cope when I'm gone? I'd need to be earning a small fortune to get us out of this downward spiral. But that'll never happen. I can't win tennis matches. I probably have the depression gene. We'll end up here together, barely surviving.

Mum sits down opposite.

'Bran, are you all right?'

'Yeah, 'course.'

'Zelda told me that you turned down at least two invitations to dances at Bel's school.'

'They're not my thing.'

'You have to enjoy yourself sometimes.'

'No, I don't.'

'All work and no play makes Jack a dull boy.'

'Who's Jack?'

'He's closely related to my son, the smart-Alec. He might even be the same person.'

'Sounds like a split poisonality.'

'Grandad said you're worried about being depressed like me.'

'Grandad yaks too much.'

'Your grandad cares.'

'Yeah, I suppose.'

'Oh, do cheer up, Bran. You won matches today. So you were runner-up. You know the saying. You think you're hard up if you have no trainers until you hear about the kid with no feet.'

'Yeah, so the kid with no feet monopolises the sympathy. It's just a rhetorical device for saying hardly anybody has reason to complain.'

'Well, now you're just being a misery.'

'That's me. Signor Miserabile, at your service.'

'Now who's playing word games? Listen, Bran.' She insists on looking me in the eye. 'There is no way you're depressed. Do you understand? Sometimes, you're despondent. It's not the same thing.'

'How can you be sure?'

'Trust me. I've spent a long time in hospital these past few years and I know who's depressed and who isn't.'

'Yeah, but maybe that's what you want to believe. It could be a case of wilful blindness.'

She gives me her very best arch look, head on one side, one eyebrow raised, lips pursed.

'No, Bran. The reason I know you're not depressed is because you're pretty much the opposite. You're a driven, pedantic, over-critical, perfectionist maniac.'

A ringing phone saves me from having to laugh at that. Otherwise it was definitely game, set and match to the famous trailer-trash slapper and nut-job.

'Bran?'

'Yeah. Why are you calling on the landline, David?'

'Don't have time. Listen to me. Go through all the bags you had at school on Friday and see if you can find a small packet that looks like sugar or salt.'

'What?'

'Anything that looks like white powder.'

'What?'

'If you find anything like that, get rid of it. Get it out of your house. Don't even flush it down the loo, 'cos it'll leave traces.'

'What are you talking about?'

'Just do it. You've been set up. They're coming to the house after the pubs close. If they find it first, you're stuffed.'

'Who?'

'My Dad and his mates. They got my brother to stitch us up. He put these sachets in our bags at school.'

'Which one?'

'What?'

'Which brother?'

'Mikey, of course. Who else?'

'I don't understand.'

'Just find the stuff and get it out of there. Do it now. I'll explain later.'

'What about you?'

'I'm gonna sort 'im out.'

'Careful, he's a lot smaller than you.'

'Not Mikey, you idiot, me Da.'

Before I can warn him about trying something that stupid, he hangs up.

'Who was that?' asks Mum.

'Never mind. I've gotta do something.'

'See? I told you. You're manic.'

I head for the stairs.

'I think your Grandad's here. Let him in, will you?'

I twitch the curtain. It's not Grandad's old banger, but a black American-style pick-up with tinted windows.

I sprint up the stairs.

'Bran?'

'Don't let them in.'

'What?'

'Don't let them in. Don't even open the door.'

I find my schoolbag and rifle through the contents. There it is, in a side pocket. The little creep must have slid it in while chatting to me on Friday. I thought it was weird. He never usually speaks to me.

A banging on the door. No time to go downstairs. What do I do? Open a top floor window. Slide down the roof over the outdoor loo. Hide in the garden till they're gone. But what about Mum? I've got to get them away from her.

I grab the bike from the back wall, sprint across the front garden, lift the bike and myself over the fence and set off down the main road. If I can reach the footpath first, they won't be able to follow.

I hear the shouting and slamming of doors. An engine starts, then the headlights pin my shadow to the road as the pick-up turns to follow. A hundred yards to the track. An idea. I overshoot and let the pick-up get to within twenty yards, then do a U-ie, head back to the track and turn off the road. The pick-up has to stop, wait for another car to pass, then do a three-point turn. Only then do they realise the track is too narrow to follow, but they know the area and head for a lane that will cut me off.

I know the path pretty well, but it's dark and some of the humps and dips take me by surprise. One fall pitches me head-first into a bed of nettles. By the time I get up I've lost any idea of where they are. Maybe they're staying on the parallel lane, or maybe they've gone through a gate and are headed across the fields. Either way, they could cut me off in the farm and wastelands, then hunt me down. I need to reach a maze of streets. Then I have to get lucky.

It seems easy enough as I lift the bike over a stile and set off into the streets of suburban Stonefield. Most people are indoors watching TV. There's a party in a house on a corner. Otherwise, it's quiet.

I know a copse with some undergrowth set back from the road where it curves round to follow the foot of a hillock. I could hide out there till morning. The only danger would be raising the suspicions of late-night dog walkers. Maybe I could just drop the sachet there. Rip it open, pour the contents into a shallow hole and fill it in. Mustn't get the stuff on my clothes. What is it, anyway? It might just be flour or salt. Would they plant genuine drugs on me?

Mr Edwards says there are certain times when musings are the stuff of inspiration. At other times, they're dangerous. I haven't noticed the vehicle creeping along without lights. Until it's too late.

Now there's only one place I can go. Sprint down the street. Leap off the bike. Leave it there. Jump a fence, then another – that'll be the crunch of the pick-up running over my bike – and run across the back gardens till I reach the border of the industrial estate. It's the way I used to come when skipping, except this time in reverse.

That house never had a big black dog. Well, it does now.

'Oi! Go on, get 'im, Max!'

Max is quick, heavy and has nasty, chomping, tearing gnashers. He pins my legs to the side of a trellis for a few seconds and tries to have a second dinner.

The climb over the high wire fence at the end leaves me exposed for several seconds, but I get a sight of headlights coming down the road into the industrial estate. Now I can only hope there's a security guard, or at the very least some good alarm systems.

Bend double and scoot along the row of skips. Climb the back of one and drop down.

I find myself face down on steel mesh. They've put cages over the skips to stop dumpster divers!

The vehicle by the fence is turning this way and that, its headlights sweeping the yards. Can I get low enough so they can't see me? I press myself to the mesh. The back of one thigh feels wet, the pain changing from sting to throb. At the same time, I've got to get rid of the stuff, so I reach into my pocket, pull out the sachet, split the top and pour the contents through the mesh. A tiny amount of white powder. What a ridiculous substance for building empires and ruining lives.

I've barely finished when a huge shadow falls across the yard. I scrunch my head round slowly to see what's happening.

On the far side of the fence, the pick-up with its headlights on full beam. On this side, a single security guard with a flashlight. It's his shadow being cast across the yard. He doesn't have the wattage, but they dip their headlights in deference to his uniform.

'What can I do for you gentlemen?'

'We're chasing a burglar. He just broke into my shed. Have you seen anybody run through here?'

'No. Which house was it?'

'One just down the road.'

'What's the address?'

'Does it matter?'

'Well, seems like a job for the police.'

The guard starts dialling and the pick-up backs away.

'Don't worry,' says the guard, 'I've got your number.'

He means the car registration.

The pick-up roars off down the road with some very angry acceleration.

The guard flips his torch round and lets the beam interrogate the skips. It's not long before it picks out my shape. It comes blindingly near.

'What's this about?'

'I was being chased by thugs.'

'I could see what they were. But what are you?'

'They trashed my bike. I don't know what they want.'

'Well, whatever you are, clear off and I don't want to see you here again.'

'I can't. I'm bleeding. Can you call my Grandad? He'll come and get me.'

He rolls his eyes. 'I should just hand you over to the cops.'

'Please.'

He pauses, grimaces and shakes his head.

'What's the number?'

David's ultimatum

David has mislaid his sense of humour.

'What?' he demands.

'I said, this is becoming a habit. You, visiting my sickbed.'

'Look, I'm really sorry.'

This is worrying. I've never seen David truly, deeply sorry for anything. It must be serious.

'I was more worried about you than myself,' I say.

'How's that?'

'When you said you were going to sort out your dad.'

'Yeah, well. Lucky for 'im, mind, somebody else got there first.'

'What? Who?'

'No idea. I went down to the pub and was gonna wait outside, but then an ambulance turned up and they brought 'im out of an alley round the back. On a stretcher. Then a cop car turned up and I cleared off.'

'Was he… y'know….?'

'Yeah, he was alive. Waving his arms about and making a racket. Somebody'd just beaten the crap out of him and one of his mates.'

'That was lucky for you.'

'I can take my dad, easy.'

There's no question about that. Given the size of David he can take most dads, easy.

'I meant you'd end up in court. A criminal conviction would ruin everything.'

'Not for me so much. But when I heard he was getting you stitched up, too, that was it. I'd 'ad enough.'

'How did you find out?'

'Mum started in on Mikey for being a little shit as usual, and he let the cat out of the bag. He's jealous, see. So he had to bring me down. Y'know, the favourite son and all that. He said I was running drugs for me da and so were you. Said he could prove it. So I got 'im on 'is own and he spilled the whole story. Poor kid's such a loser, he can't keep his mouth shut long enough to carry through a simple plan.'

'Do you run drugs for your dad?'

'I did. Haven't done for years now.'

'That's what he meant when he said stuff like shiny football boots don't come for free?'

'Yeah, summat like that.'

'Does Mikey work for him?'

'Yeah. I've tried to stop it, but he won't listen.'

'But why would he want to frame us?'

'He can't find enough kids to do the work. So he plants drugs on 'em, then blackmails 'em into delivering stuff to customers. At least, that's the plan.'

'Yeah, but how do they get away with it?'

'They find the stuff on you, then say you stole it or took it without paying. So they make you pay it back. 'Course, they set a high price that nobody can pay, so you have to pay it back by working for them. And they film you as they discover the stuff and threaten to put the clip on You Tube and stuff like that. The cops couldn't ignore that, could they? They say you can buy them off by making a few deliveries, but they keep blackmailing you as long as they can keep using you. The worst thing is they could blackmail your family too. So if they'd found it in your house, they'd have blackmailed your mam as well.'

'Scum.'

'Yeah, that's our so-called da.'

'But why use kids for deliveries?'

' 'Cos nobody suspects 'em. They're local kids, what they call "clean skins". No criminal records. Kids a cop wouldn't normally stop and search.'

'I s'pose not. Does your dad make a lot of money out of it?'

'Nah, he's small time. The big boys are in London. It's their idea to use schoolkids and teenagers.'

'Are they dangerous?'

'The London boys are.'

'But they'll come after us again.'

'Nah. It was me da and his mates chasing you. They don't want no publicity. Anyway, I've sent my father an ultimatum.'

This is a surprise. A grammatically and lexically conventional sentence ending with an impressive word.

'You mean, like Sir Edward Grey or Neville Chamberlain?'

'If they were people who told a bloke to fuck off and not come back, then, yeah, like thems.'

'You told him to get lost?'

'Yeah. I disowned 'im as well. Sent him a letter to the hospital. Said he was no longer me da and lucky I didn't get to him first.'

'But you can get done for threatening people.'

'Tell that to your Grandad. He threatened to shop me and my whole family to the newspapers.'

'He can get a bit fired up.'

'Fired up? He was in orbit. Blamed me for the whole thing. Frightened the life out of me mam.'

'Well, your dad and his mates scared my mother. He was bound to be furious. Did you explain it to him?'

'Do I look stupid?'

It's open to debate, but I say 'no'.

'Of course I didn't explain. I said it was a misunderstanding.'

'Good. 'Cos I blamed you.'

He tenses ever so slightly, like a massive wobbly spring that stops wobbling for two seconds.

'You did?'

'I told him you needed some study notes urgently and that a dog attacked me out of nowhere as I was taking a shortcut on my bike.'

He thinks about it. 'That's not a bad story.'

'Except he doesn't believe it.'

'Why not?'

'Because you told him something different.'

'Yeah… I s'pose I did. But what I told him was pretty vague, so we might have got away with it.'

'I doubt that somehow. Anyway, my point stands. You can get done for sending threatening letters.'

'Don't be a dick'ead, Bran. I didn't sign it. It was anonymous. I cut letters out of a newspaper and put it in a 'don't get well' card.'

My brain feels like it's being short-circuited. He sent a letter saying that he was disowning his father – whom he would also beat to a pulp – and that his father wasn't supposed to know who it was from… because he'd used cut-out letters from a newspaper. Is it worth exploring this further? Probably not. Instead I say:

'I've never seen a 'don't get well' card.'

'You just write 'don't' in front of 'get well'.

'Yeah, I see. That'll do it.'

'So, did you win your match then?'

'Won four matches and lost the final.'

'Not as rubbish as you were before then.'

'I s'pose not. And your ultimatum might turn out a lot better than Sir Edward Grey's or Neville Chamberlain's.'

'How's that?'

' 'Cos the blokes they sent their ultimatums to didn't actually fuck off.'

'Well, you 'ave to know 'ow to do it proper, like.'

Back on the bus

The yellow school bus slows and stops. The door opens with a satisfying, dinosaur hiss.

Callum smiles. ' 'Morning number two.'

'Number two?'

'I heard you only got beat by the number one.'

'Yeah, but it doesn't mean I'm number two. I might be five or six.'

I notice the bandages around his knuckles.

'What happened to your hands?'

He grins. 'What happened to your backside?'

I know when to take a hint. Callum gestures down the aisle.

'He's at the back.'

I look down the bus. Nobody sets up a taunting chant or even sniggers. I get nothing but respectful glances. Some kids are glued to their mobile phones or tablets. Others talk in hushed tones. Even Mikey Jones sits quietly, looking chastened and doing his best to avoid my gaze. It's like the quiet carriage on a train.

Sitting in the middle seat at the back is David, taking up three spaces, legs splayed, books piled on the seats either side. Just in front and next to the window is Yasmin, on her own and sitting beside David's holdall, which clearly has a seat of its own. Callum's bus has become David's fiefdom. He rules with a rod of iron. Instead of grinning inanely at me down the aisle and causing a ruckus, he's studying a textbook with a furrowed brow. That is why Callum's conveyance is the most civilised school bus on the planet: David Jones is swotting for his A-levels and requires no disturbance. Nobody quarrels with a sixteen-and-a-half-stone prop forward riding shotgun for a driver who may or may not be a karate black belt.

Party animal

In the past few months my mother's answer to everything is a shimmy, a pirouette, a waltz or a full blown heavy-metal head-mash. I suspect there's something else going on, something or someone that has lightened her mood and given her hope. But she's good at protecting her privacy.

'None of your business. And, anyway, I've always loved a party.'

Which is why she can't understand my reluctance to attend the school dance.

'But it's your last chance. You've worked so hard. You deserve it.'

'It's a leavers' prom. I don't do proms.'

'But why not? You only leave school once.'

'It'll be the second time for me and the first was pretty unceremonious.'

It's a mean comment. I know she feels responsible for my leaving the school I really liked, but it only keeps her quiet for about ten seconds.

'I washed your black jeans and I got you a present you can wear. I think you'll like it.'

'Mum, it's formal. The guys'll be wearing black tie and the girls will look like big meringues.'

'Honestly, Bran. You're so cynical.'

'I'm realistic. This is a teenage coming-of-age ceremony imported from America. A chance to show what kind of proto-adult you've become.'

'But you're a tennis star, and I'm sure you've done well in your exams. You don't have to play a role.'

'First of all, I'm not a tennis star. I'm a jobbing player without the job. And I doubt I did well in the exams.'

She gets up and heads to the stairs. 'Well, if you're going to sit around here being a wet blanket and watching telly you're showing everybody what kind of adult you're going to be.'

She's got a point, but she hasn't a clue what these things cost. The ticket is £30. Suit hire is at least £90. Your 'date', if you have one, expects to arrive in a limo, or at the very least a well valeted four-door saloon. Two-doors are permissible, but only if the vehicle is a sports cabriolet. The girls have been comparing notes all month about how their dresses are costing up to £500 a flounce. What with dropping various jobs to revise, I have precisely £4.75 in the world.

I can hear Mum on the phone upstairs. I hope she's not pulling some stunt. There is no way I'm going to humiliate myself at some low-rent, pretend Vegas-fest in the Berkshire 'burbs.

'There you are.'

She drops a soft package into my lap.

'What's this?'

'I got it for you. Just open it.'

I pull reluctantly at the strips of sellotape until the tissue paper unfolds.

'What do you think?'

It is the most amazing T-shirt. Black with subtle colours of forest green, ochre reds and silver threads of darting light around misty figures.

'Can you see what it is?'

'It looks like... Maoris... EnZedders doing a haka.'

'Do you like it?'

'It's fantastic. Where'd you get it?'

'From EnZed.'

'Who from?'

She pauses. 'I got it online.'

The pause is suspicious. She's generally fibbing when she does that. She also pulls her chin in before speaking. It's a twitch of indignation, as though somebody's forcing her to tell an untruth.

But the T-shirt is a work of art. It must have cost a bomb.

'You'd wear that to the prom, wouldn't you?'

'I might.'

'Well, don't think too hard. David's coming round to pick you up at seven. You've got time for a shower.'

'I can't anyway. Haven't got a ticket.'

'He's got tickets.'

She's looking tense, but still pretty pleased with herself.

'Did you set this up?'

'No, David made the arrangements.'

This is not information designed to make your heart sing. In fact it sinks as I come down the stairs in my black jeans and new T-shirt. David is standing in the hall wearing a weird tux.

'They didn't 'ave my size round here, so I 'ad to get it special. Mate of mine in Wales got it from a shop in the Rhondda. They supply suits for bouncers.'

The sleeves are a touch too long, the trousers a touch too short and showing a flash of pink (PINK!) socks. It looks as if his chest will come bursting through the white shirt at any moment. The bow tie looks like a propeller blade that's stopped at an angle of its own choosing. The shiny brass buckles on the slip-on shoes are the final touch.

My mother gives me a peck on the cheek. 'Have a lovely time.' I have an uncomfortable feeling of being 'the girl', of being picked up by my 'date'.

Outside is a classic, racing green 1960s Mark II Jaguar. In the driver's seat is a chauffeur wearing a peaked cap.

'I could've got a stretch limo, but I know you'd hate that.'

'I like the car, but won't we look a bit… y'know… climbing out of that together?'

'What? A bit gay?'

'Well, yeah.'

'There's a girl in the back, dimwit.'

It's Yasmin. She's wearing a long black kaftan with a gold zigzag pattern down one side. And her hair's sort of piled up on top and she's wearing long earrings. Don't ask me to describe this stuff: I'm wearing jeans and a black T-shirt.

'Hi.'

'Hi,' she says with a sweet smile.

'You look great.'

'Thanks. So do you.'

I'm not sure I should ask questions with a couple of witnesses present, but they're boring holes in my skull. On the other hand, Yasmin probably doesn't listen anyway unless there's an equation involved, and chauffeurs are supposed to be graveyards for secrets.

'How did you… y'know… afford all this?'

'I mentioned it to our coach in the Wales set-up, and a couple of the senior players had a whip-round.'

'They must think a lot of you.'

'They want me to sign for one of the professional clubs over there.'

'Will you?'

'If I get into uni in Cardiff or Swansea. Yeah, probably.'

If. It seems like a long shot.

'I can't pay you back for the ticket,' I say. 'Not for a while. I'm broke.'

'Forget it. Without you I'd never be sitting A-levels in the first place.'

From her seat between us, Yasmin turns her head and gives me a long, gorgeous smile.

What does that *mean*? Is this a set-up? Why is she even here? I'm really grateful she's here, which means I don't have to climb out of this car with a bloke. But I can't work out what's going on.

'Just one thing, though,' continues David. 'I'm going to ask you to do one thing tonight, and you have to agree. OK?'

'Is it legal?'

' 'Course it is.'

'Does it involve harming any person or object?'

'No.'

'Does it involve humiliation?'

'No.'

'Will it make me look stupid?'

Yasmin's giggling. First a smile, now a giggle. Where's that coming from?

'No. You just have to be yourself.'

'Promise?'

'Have I ever done anything... ?'

'Yes,' I leap in. 'Lots of times. Would you like a list?'

Yasmin squirms about between us, actually laughing. I think I catch the hint of a smile on the driver's face in his rearview mirror. We're clearly a comedy duo.

'So just answer the question. When I ask, will you do it?'

'Yeah, OK. What the hell.'

'Great. Just try to enjoy yourself.'

The driveway down to the front entrance is clogged with traffic.

Mr Carson is directing.

A barrage of phone photography. A crush of kids taking selfies with mates.

'It's a fairy tale,' says Yasmin. 'But you have to have the visual evidence.'

A Bentley garlanded with white carnations disgorges two girls wearing small mounds of silk and taffeta.

'It's the Two-As!'

Where they go the Head and Vice Head Boys will not be far behind.

David winds down his side window. 'Listen.'

A sound that could easily be mistaken for booing breaks briefly from the ruck around the entrance.

'Cnoooooot!'

Until Mr Carson puts a stop to it with a withering glance.

David rocks the car as he throws himself back in his seat in a paroxysm of sheer joy.

'I done that!' he crows.

'I *did* that,' corrects Yasmin. 'And you shouldn't have done that. It's cruel.'

'Lay off. You're as bad as 'im.'

He means me. I check Yasmin's expression. She may say it's cruel but her grin (yes, with teeth showing!) suggests she doesn't entirely disapprove.

There's a heartfelt cheer as we emerge from the Jag, but Carl Jenkins never misses an opportunity.

'It's supposed to be black tie, not Thai-dye.'

'It's Kiwi black tie.'

'What have you come as?' asks Alys. She's leaning into Carl as if they're a couple.

'As myself. What are you pretending to be?'

The hall's already rocking with Callum on lead vocals. I didn't know his repertoire extended beyond Irish ballads.

'Right, the champagne's alcohol-free, but we all want some, right?' says David.

'Is the Pope Catholic?' says Yasmin and they move off in opposite directions, leaving me feeling like a fish out of water.

I'm getting weird glances from the others. What am I doing here in jeans and T-shirt? It's like turning up to a wedding in work gear. I can tell that some kids sit comfortably in their ties and jackets. Others are ill at ease. But at least they've made the effort. Pretty much every girl has spent hours, if not days, on her appearance. I look like the beggar at the feast. Even Yasmin is stunningly elegant in her Persian kaftan.

And that's when I see her. A figure in the crowd, moving to the music. She's wearing a simple, short, blue-grey dress with a low-cut back and a sort of Hawaiian-style silk garland around the hem. (Don't ask me, I'm wearing jeans and T-shirt.)

Then I see him. Zak Weidenbaum of New York, New York. He's wearing a tux, a colourful cummerbund and a bolo tie. He's right there, opposite her. His dancing is much more elaborate than hers. He's doing a sort of mating stork dance, wings outspread, shielding her, but at the same time putting on a display. You wouldn't want to get too close if you valued your eyes or teeth.

I glance around. Who could I dance with? Who might want to dance with the guy who fails to understand the concept of a celebration? Because that is what we're supposed to be doing. I spot Alicia. She's with a guy who looks a good deal older. Both look as if they're going through the motions, humouring these other poor deluded souls. Maybe Alicia's a fellow cynic. But a cynic with a mature boyfriend. A good statement. No sooner is school over than she's out of our league.

'Here y'are.' David is back with a magnum in one fist and half a dozen glasses in the other.

He waves to summon Yasmin back from the heaving crowd. She re-emerges with Bel and Zak in tow.

'No... ,' I begin to say.

'What?' demands David.

'Nothing.'

'Hi!' Zak is all transatlantic bonhomie. 'Wow! I love your T-shirt. Man, what is that?'

Soon, they're all looking closely.

'It's a haka theme.'

'That is so cool! Where can I get one of those?'

'Well, a basic qualification is knowing how to do the haka.'

'Where can I learn?'

I want to say 'catch a plane to New Zealand', but David gets in first.

'He can teach you.'

'OK, let's do it.'

Bel is standing back looking... what exactly? ... if I didn't know all about her fierce intelligence, I'd say 'demure'. Is Zak Weidenbaum of New York, New York suppressing her individuality? Is she making a pact with a comfortable future in exchange for not being her bright, feisty, independent self? Before I can ask or say anything, a small crowd has formed.

'Oh, look, it's Belinda! What are you doing here?'

The Two-As have grown out of calling her Oxfam, though they can't resist the satire of small gestures and coded looks.

'Just thought I'd come by my old school and catch up.'

Zak doesn't wait to be introduced. 'Hi, I'm Zak Weidenbaum. Over here on an exchange program.'

He rattles off a series of questions to elicit everybody's condensed CV. He even starts pouring champagne like a host.

'So, what's next for you, Belinda?' asks Matt with his best proprietorial air.

'I've applied to Cambridge.'

'Ah, the *other* lot,' says Matt with a middle-aged chuckle.

'Which means you're hoping for Oxford, right?' demands Zak.

'Like Belinda, I've applied.'

'Because I have trouble with British understatement and all these subtle signals flying around.'

'Are we subtle?'

'Seems so to me. There's all this social class stuff going on and I can sense it, but I don't understand it.'

'Oh, I think there's less of that than you imagine.'

'So I'm *imagining* it?'

'We don't really do social class these days.'

'Coulda fooled me.'

'It doesn't really matter what social class you're from these days. We're all so affluent. We need to concentrate on people who are really deprived. In the developing world, for example.'

'But that's a cop-out, right? So you can ignore your deprived neighbour and make a career out of appearing to help others on the other side of the world.'

'You sound like a politician.'

'So do you.'

I don't want to, but I'm beginning to warm to Zak. Where did he get that instant animosity towards Matt?

'Right. Time to lighten up,' says David. 'Let's rock.'

'Fo sho, bro,' says Zak. They each take one of Yasmin's hands and dive back into the crowd.

I'm left facing Bel.

'Wanna dance?'

'Sure.'

Callum's doing a suite of old *Queen* numbers.

'You got mud on yo' face, you big disgrace!'

'Haven't seen you for ages,' says Bel.

'Been busy,' I reply.

'I heard you got to a final.'

'Yeah. I lost.'

We stamp our feet to the chorus. David's a few yards away. It feels as if he could put a shoe through the floor at any moment.

'I was speaking to Mr Edwards earlier.'

She indicates one corner of the room. I hadn't noticed the clusters of teachers till now. Mrs Creasey, Mr Carson, the Hutch and the Head are in one group. Perhaps they've been weighed down by years of responsibility, but they seem more vigilant than cheerful. Ted's in another group having a carefree laugh with all my favourite teachers. He must be at least thirty years older than them, but he fits right in.

'He said you didn't apply to university.'

'No, I'd have to get a scholarship, and I'll never get one of those.'

'You might.'

'I doubt it.'

'What'll you do?'

'Dunno. It depends on my results. What about you? Which college did you apply to?'

'Emmanuel.'

'Why that one?'

'My dad went there.'

'Does it help?'

'Not officially, but probably. I also tick their "student from single-parent, poor-household" background, even though my dad supports me and went to Eton.' She shrugs. 'That's how it works.'

'Yeah, I guess.'

As the song ends, David comes over.

'Right, this is it. Remember what you promised.'

'What?'

He points up at Callum and they exchange pre-arranged signals.

'OK, now you've got your stamping moves nicely warmed up. It's time for something unusual. Bran Kelleher's going to show us how it's done. We're going to the Southern Hemisphere. It's time for a haka. Just follow Bran's lead and join in.'

Callum thumps out a haka rhythm on a bongo drum, and I wonder if I can remember how it goes. But it's like riding a bike. Once you know, you never forget.

I take up the starting position with knees bent.

'All right!' Zak jumps in beside me.

Hold the hands in front of the face and shake the fingers. Begin to stamp the right foot, slowly at first, then more forcefully.

Callum has learned some words, so I don't have to worry about that.

'*Ringa pakia!*'

'*Uma tiraha!*'

'*Turi whatia?*'

'*Hope whai ake!*'

'*Warwae takahia kia kino!*'

The pace picks up and suddenly there are about fifty kids doing the haka behind me. David's shaking the floorboards again, and Yasmin's testing the tightness of her kaftan. Bel has kicked off her shoes and has joined in, though all the girls in high heels, including the Two-As, have decided to sit this one out. Alicia and her man are joining in. He seems to be in his element. But I catch sight of Matt and Carl watching us like a couple of school inspectors who'll be submitting a report.

I close my eyes and travel back, trying to find my roots. This dance is supposed to define me. Maybe it did once upon a time, but not any more, not quite. I'm doing a haka, but my EnZed passport expired more than a year ago. Yet this place, this school, still feels like a foreign country. It's not mine. Bel must feel the same but for different reasons. She's disconnected from here, but her roots are still in this country. Where are mine?

It's good of David to make this gesture. He's doing me a massive favour without knowing it, making me ask myself where I belong. The answer's nowhere. I can do the dance, but not the words. They sound hollow. The fact is I have to find a home of my own, and I don't know where that is. And I don't know where to start.

The dance ends and there's a massive round of applause.

'Man, that was awesome!' exclaims Zak.

There's a huddle, lots of hugging. Bel's in there somewhere, but she's mostly being hugged by Zak. David's lifting me off my feet.

'Right, let's quit this joint,' says David. 'The Golden Pheasant's just down the road. Then the Colliers are giving a late-night party at Gino's.'

'They'll never let us in.'

'No problem, the doorman's Welsh and a rugby fan. I've had a word already. We'll raid the Colliers' freebies. Then Yasmin's parents are putting on a spread at their place.'

'Fantabulous!' says Zak.

'Are you coming?' asks Bel.

'Yeah, I'll be back in a minute.'

I head to the loos, then turn towards the main entrance. I feel bad about cutting and running, but there's no way I can go to an after party. I'll have just enough money for the bus fare home, then out to my tennis class tomorrow.

So this is the end of my school prom. No date, no final 'boy gets girl', no rousing vindication, no 'friends forever', no rosy future beckoning just beyond tomorrow. Just sloping off up the school drive to catch a bus. If there is one at this hour. At least I won't be standing at the bus stop in a tux.

Up ahead I see Ted's narrow, slightly bowed back heading for his car.

'Mr Edwards!' I catch him up. 'Can you give me a lift?'

'Bran. Leaving already?'

'Got a tennis lesson first thing.'

'Where do you live?'

'Stonefield Road.'

'Right. That's easy enough. Hop in.'

He's got a new white Fiat 500.

'Stylish,' I say.

'Cheap to run,' he smiles. 'I was going to have a pint in my local. Do you have time to join me?'

'I guess.'
'Are you eighteen yet?'
'No.'
'Then it's orange juice for you.'

Edwardian values

Ted's local is a cosy little place down a lane I've never travelled.

'This country's full of these places,' he says. 'Small villages with one very large manor house and an impressive church endowed by at least one wealthy family down the centuries. They used to be on the main roads, till the canals and railways passed them by. Now hardly anyone knows they exist. We speed by on motorways and hardly guess at our hinterland.'

'But you live here and enjoy it.'

'I do. My son lives in London and wonders why I wouldn't prefer what he calls "the buzz". I was once a wannabe in the city. But now I like to understand the world, not just watch it pouring past.'

'That's why I want to be an archaeologist.'

'A good choice. It's one of the more exciting disciplines at present.'

'Have you heard any news about our Byzantine coin?'

'Ah.' He sips his beer. 'I have. But I have to swear you to secrecy. If anyone ever finds out I told you, I could lose more than my place on the acquisitions committee.'

'I'd never tell anyone. I'd just like to know.'

'That's what I thought. The fact is that your coin is almost worthless in monetary terms, but a goldmine in terms of what it can teach.'

'That sounds like a paradox.'

'It is. To start at the beginning, it's a modern copy of a Byzantine coin. It was probably struck in the mid-1980s.'

'But how did it end up in the Partingtons' garden?'

'Good question. And this is where your discretion is absolutely vital. You see, Mr Partington tried to fob the committee off with an explanation. But the Chairwoman and I had already made our own enquiries. What we discovered doesn't cast Mr Partington in the best possible light.'

'I promise I won't tell.'

'OK. That's good enough for me. What we already knew was that Rawley Partington was married before, but we didn't know that he had a lot of affairs. One of his lovers in the mid-Nineties was a Greek who lived in Athens. She gave him presents. One of those was the coin you found. When his first wife found out about the affair, she threw the presents out of the house. Pens, ties, shoes. They ended up being thrown into bushes or put on bonfires.'

'I see.'

'Nice gossip, but not very exciting, eh?'

'Not really.'

'Of course, Sonia Partington has no idea. She's no doubt fully aware of his first wife but, you know how it is, he probably cast her in a bad light to his new bride.'

I don't know how it is, but I can see how that would work.

'But the story doesn't end there.' Mr Edwards' eyes suddenly sparkle. 'Every artefact, however modest, has a history. So I began to look into it more closely. One question was, why did Rawley Partington's Greek lover give him a cheap knock-off? And where did she get it? What did it mean to her? These are the sorts of questions we need to ask. She was part of a wealthy family from Salonika. But they hadn't always been wealthy. In fact they'd been kicked out of their ancestral Black Sea home by the Turkish army in 1922. They lost almost everything and had to begin again as incomers in a distant Greek city. How did they do that? Can you guess?'

'I dunno. Business? Trading?'

'Yes, they did some of that, but it requires hard work and luck. They needed something else. A get-rich-quick scheme.'

'No. I've no idea.'

'The population of Salonika was about 40% Jewish in the 1920s and 30s. They'd been there since King Ferdinand and Queen Isabella kicked them out of Spain in 1492. They'd built up some of the most established businesses and owned some of the best land in Salonika, especially near the coastline. As you may know, seaside property in or near a city became a licence to print money in the twentieth century. When the Nazis invaded Greece in 1941, the family of Partington's lover became German collaborators. They helped the Nazis steal Jewish property before they packed their victims off to the death camps. Expensive fabrics from the Levant, gold and silver, precious stones, buildings, factories, land, cash, everything. They intimidated the owners into handing over the keys and signing away their property before they were put on cattle trucks heading for Central Europe.

'After the war, these collaborators were never brought to justice. They were too rich and well connected. Land is easy to appropriate. If you've got the signed documentation, the land is yours. But other kinds of property aren't so easy. Like artworks and artefacts. I strongly believe that the coin you found was melted down from silver stolen from Jewish families in Salonika. Rawley Partington's lover had a cousin who opened a jewellery store in Athens. I think they were recycling a horde of precious metals by melting them down and making look-alike ancient coins and so on. It's safer than keeping the silver in its original form which can be identified.'

'So it was stolen property. Looted. Plundered.'

'Exactly. So even a piece of silver worth about six dollars on ebay can have a fascinating story.'

'What'll happen to it?'

'The coin? We gave it back to Mr Partington.'

'It doesn't seem fair. Shouldn't it go to a Jewish charity or something?'

'Good point. But Rawley Partington doesn't see it that way. In fact, he sees himself as the injured party. The chairwoman of our committee happens to be a good friend of the Lord Lieutenant of the County. She doesn't approve of men who cheat on their wives. So Rawley Partington's hopes of becoming an assistant to the Lord Lieutenant have probably gone up in smoke. Thanks to your attentive digging.'

'Oh.'

'More like 'oops'. I have to warn you that you're not exactly flavour of the month with Mr Partington. Not that he can do much about it. But watch your back.'

'Thanks for the warning.'

'No problem. If you stick with history in any shape or form, you'll have to get used to being PNG.'

'What's that?'

'Persona non grata. Lots of people hate us for being interested in what really happened. Politicians for a start. Anyone trying to sell a false narrative, a pig in a poke, a wonky prospectus. A good rule of thumb is, find out who loathes historians and you'll find the dodgy characters. Probably a whole battalion of them. The ones who hate us with a vengeance are the tribalists on the one hand and conmen on the other. The tribalists are the ones who think life is one long football match. You're either for us or against us. Our side, right or wrong. Conmen hate us for obvious reasons.'

He sips his beer, frowning then brightening in quick succession as he contemplates his next point.

'So, the more hated you are, the better the job you're doing. Unless you happen to be a tribalist or conman-type historian. But that's another *very* long story.'

'You make it sound like a lonely life.'

'It doesn't have to be. Always beware of people who put their private needs before their stated values. Which is pretty much the same as saying beware of everybody. But what I mean is, if you trust no one, you'll never be disappointed, and will therefore have every chance of remaining optimistic.'

'Now *that's* a paradox.'

'It is. If you were another Shakespeare, you'd weave the human tapestry in fiction, plays, poetry. But I'm not, and I don't think you are either.'

I shake my head.

'No, there's only one William Shakespeare, as the football fans fail to chant. So you and I are left with true stories. As in the case of your coin, if you dig deep enough, you'll be able to document and more fully appreciate the human condition.' He draws an expansive semi-circle in the air with one hand, his fingers splayed. 'Mapping the full, glorious, catastrophic tragi-comedy.'

He knows he's being theatrical and ironic, but then turns serious.

'But what you shouldn't do is allow that knowledge to make you callous or cynical. However highly educated we become, most are still driven by their own needs and prejudices. But it doesn't mean we can't love or befriend each other. Obviously you need to avoid the really nasty pieces of work, but don't let other people's understandable failings interfere with your relationships. Don't judge people too harshly. We're only human, after all.'

He pauses to let that sink in.

'Am I making sense?'

'Yes. I think I get it.'

The side of his glass touches mine.

'Good. Drink up. Time to get you home.'

Who's your father?

Phil is also in an end-of-era mood, but for material reasons. Sonia's been paying him for my lessons, but it can't go on forever. She's not my mother, and I'll be officially an adult in a few months' time. Unless I can keep paying Phil, our partnership is at an end.

'What'll you do?'

'It depends on my exam results.'

'You should keep it up. You can always give lessons. It's better than stacking shelves in a supermarket.'

'How about you?'

'Oh, I might be coaching a certain former number 4 who's licking his wounds after being beaten by a former number 16.'

'You wouldn't do that, would you? I mean, not *him*.'

'Maybe not for long, but why not? He needs a coach and he's got the makings of a competitive animal. He might have what it takes.'

'Would you say that *I* have what it takes?'

'To be what? A tennis pro?' He stops smiling for a moment. 'I'm told that it looks great from the top of the pile. But the way up is brutal. You have to be totally focused, single-minded, ruthless. You have to want it, completely and utterly. Only you count. Everybody else comes second to your needs. Are you that person?'

'Maybe not.'

'I get the impression you're interested in lots of things. You like to go where your curiosity leads. You're an explorer. Your tennis talents can support you in that. You don't have to be ruthless, just canny. You don't have to be top 100. You don't even have to be a pro. Let tennis be whatever you want it to be. Does that make sense?'

'Yeah, it does. Thanks.'

'It's all part of the service.' He nods towards the lane. 'Is this your ride?'

A white Range Rover Vogue is crawling up the lane and comes to a halt on the grass verge. I'm about say 'I doubt it' when Grandad steps out on the passenger side.

Phil stands up. 'Right, I'm off for a game of golf.' He offers me his hand. 'Good luck, and keep in touch. You know my number.'

Grandad is wearing his job-that-has-to-be-done expression.

'There's somebody to see you. Go easy on him. And don't be late coming back to get me.'

I watch him waddle away towards the gates of Buckston Manor. His back still looks broad and strong but he has a slight limp as if one leg is shorter than the other.

There's no movement in the Range Rover, its tinted windows maintaining its secret. Apparently it's my choice to walk over and open the door, or walk away. Why is it up to me to make these decisions? Why doesn't whoever's in that car climb out and come to meet me? Why do adults make things so complicated?

I open the door.

'Hello, Bran.'

'Hi, Bill.'

'Hop in?'

'Sure.'

I've imagined this meeting over and over again. The conversation never begins or continues the same way, but the ending is always the same. I tell him where to get off. But it only works out that way because I supply his lines. In real life, you can't always tell what the other person will say.

'It's great to see you at last, Bran.'

'At last? You could have seen me any time.'

He frowns at this, but not in anger. He seems genuinely perplexed.

'I was told to stay away.'

'Who told you that?'

'Everybody.'

It turns out that the Reverend Love was right. Everybody's fighting their own private battle. Everybody has their own story. Understanding people is like archaeology. If you really want to know what's going on, you have to dig, peel back the surface and peer beneath. Then use your judgement to work out what's likely to be true and what isn't.

Bill was told to stay away for various reasons. He'd make Mum's condition worse. He'd unsettle my education. He wasn't needed. His financial help was unnecessary. He could get in touch when I'd done my GCSEs. This was delayed when Bill announced he'd married. The news had devastated my mother and would probably send me off the rails. He could get in touch when I reached eighteen or when I finished school, whichever came first.

While I thought he didn't care, there'd been emails, phone calls and text messages to Grandad and Audrey. After electronic communications had been cut off, there'd been letters and cards back and forth. He'd even got a solicitor involved, but was told he had no rights in the matter. I wasn't his natural son, so all he could do was butt out and wait till I was old enough to make my own decisions.

'I was really worried. I had no idea what was going on in your life. All I got were reports that you were doing fine at school and that the rugby was going great. Until your injury.'

'You sent me a card.'

'They let me do that.'

'Did you organise the cards from Greystone's as well?'

'Some of the staff always wanted to know how you were doing. But they'd never had replies.'

'I didn't know they sent me stuff.'

'Your mates sent emails and cards for a while, but they stopped when there were no replies.'

'I never got their cards.'

'They sent them to your grandfather's address.'

'He never told me.'

'I think he wanted to. But Audrey kept him up to the mark.'

'What did Audrey have to do with it?'

'Don't go there, Bran. Audrey never liked me.'

'I don't know what Grandad sees in her.'

'Neither do I. But don't be hard on him. He probably can't face too many more dramas at his time of life. And he did what he could for you. Just ask Audrey for your mail. She's probably kept it.'

'I sent you a card when I was in hospital.'

He smiles grimly. 'Yeah, that hurt.'

'I did mean it at the time.'

'I guessed that somebody had been talking a bucketload of shit about me.'

'No, they just left me to draw my own... confusions.'

'Yeah, that'll work as well.'

'So, you got married.'

'Yeah. And there's a brother and a sister you haven't met.'

'But I'm not your son.'

He suddenly looks as if this is the most hurtful thing I could say.

'I never stopped thinking of you as my son, Bran. I never thought your mum and I would break up. Even when that happened, I never thought I'd lose you. I don't know if this makes any sense, but you were still a baby when we first met. I promised your mother I'd be your father, and I meant it. Both of you were my responsibility. I still feel as if I'm your father. I want to be your dad. I've been putting cash into a fund for your education. It's your money. I want you to have it. It tore me up wondering how you were coping. I should have known you'd manage, 'cos at heart you're a proper Kiwi, a real battler. Not like these soft-centred Poms, eh?'

He's trying to cover up his emotions with a bad joke.

'But the best thing in the world for me, would be if you wanted to call me Dad again.'

I have to get out of the car and walk, but with no idea where to go. I just need to move and keep moving. Over the first stile, then along a path. Find another stile a few fields away and just sit there.

The thing I prayed would happen years ago has happened. He's come to find me. But now I don't know what to do. Why do adults say nothing for years, then dump it all on you? Their actions become your consequences. Suddenly you hold their wellbeing in your hands. Say the wrong thing and they'll be ruined forever. Or so they say. But I'm not a light switch. Lights off, go to sleep. They want you back in their lives: flick a switch, lights on. I feel like Hercules, told to clean out massive piles of emotional cow dung from the Augean stables. But I'm not a mythical hero. I don't have two rivers I can re-route through the stables and wash all that crap away. I've got a shovel, that's all.

Half an hour later, Grandad comes limping across the field. He looks red-eyed.

'Bloody hell, Bran. Don't sit here all day. I've just been sacked from your job and I've got a grown man blubbing in a car.'

We walk back together.

'What happened?'

'I tried to get into the tool shed, like you said, but it was locked. When I went over to the house, Rawley Partington said we were fired. Said he'd found somebody else.'

'Don't worry. I know about that. It's not your fault.'

'I hope not. Not that as well.'

'It's just life, Grandad.'

'Tell me about it.'

Betrayal

Disappointed!!
s.partington@memail.com
Bran,
I have reason to believe that you found more than one silver coin in the rose beds. I must say that I am extremely disappointed in you and feel thoroughly betrayed, especially after I paid for your tennis lessons. Mr Partington says I should never have expected more, but I did and do. Please return the other coins as soon as possible and I will not take this any further. At the very least let me know what you did with them.
Sonia Partington

Re: Disappointed!!
bran@brankelleher.com
Dear Sonia,
I am very sorry there is an untrue story circulating about the number of coins I found. I can confirm it was one. The person to contact will be the chairwoman of the museum acquisitions committee. I understand she is in possession of all the facts after an interview with Mr Partington. I know only that all the parties agree there was only ever one coin.
I am very grateful to you for my Saturday job and tennis lessons. I would never have done anything to let you down, whatever anybody else might say.
Best wishes,
Bran Kelleher

Re: Re: Disappointed!!
s.partington@memail.com
Dear Bran,
I'm really sorry there has been a misunderstanding. I spoke to the

Chairperson of the museum's Acquisitions Committee and she has provided me with a full account. My husband has confirmed that there was indeed only one coin of that type belonging to the family. I have also discovered how it came to be in the garden.

Please disregard my earlier email. I wish I had never written it, as I was working with misleading information.

I asked Mr Partington to let me reinstate you as gardener, but he insisted that your grandfather said something unpleasant to him, so I'm afraid that won't be possible.

Best of luck in your exams. Do keep me informed of your progress.

Warm regards,

Sonia

Brunettes get passes too, you know

Grandad drops me off at the top of the drive. We've got a job digging a French drain around a house with rising damp, so I'm wearing my work clothes.

The scene unfolds as I walk down the drive towards the main entrance. On the juniors' playground a photographer is directing half a dozen girls with varying shades of blond hair. He wants them in a straight line. The Two-As are prominent. They're holding single sheets of paper. On the snapper's instruction they leap into the air. It's a straight up and down, Maasai warrior kind of jump, so he asks them to do it again, but this time with manic grins – 'like they mean it' – arms and legs going in various directions. He's looking for blond delirium.

There's a scrum outside the main doors. Mr Carson is standing with another photographer when he spots me.

'Ah, here's one of our star students.'

They look me up and down and decide I'm not properly dressed. The scarred jeans and worn work boots wouldn't make quite the right impression in the local rag.

David's inside with his mother and Mr Edwards. He wraps me in a bear hug.

'I did it! I did it!'

'What did you do?'

'I got a B, a C and a D. I can't believe it.'

David's mother, Sian, is crying. 'I wish my mother was alive. To think her grandson is going to University College Cardiff. She'd be so proud.'

'Go on, Bran,' says Mr Edwards. 'Go and get your envelope.'

He looks confident, but I'm half-numb with hope and fear.

The secretary hands it over with a smile. 'There you are, dear.'

I decide to open it there and then, in front of a single witness. It's all very straightforward, but I have to look twice to make sure.

'Is it what you wanted?'

'Yes, that'll do,' I say.

'Well done. Best of luck.'

With those words I become part of another cohort out the door.

'Well, Bran?'

Mr Edwards knows already, but he wants to hear me say it.

'Three A-stars and an A.'

It'll soon become a mantra.

'Well done. You deserved it.' He offers me his hand. 'I hope you'll keep in touch. I've had pupils going off to universities all over the country, but you're the first of a kind. It was a pleasure teaching you. If you have time, send me a postcard. I don't do social media.'

'I promise.'

Sian Jones buries me in a well soaped, perfumed, hair-sprayed hug. 'He swears his B is down to you.'

'And Mr Edwards.'

'Yes, but you know what he's like. He never listens to grown-ups. Not properly, anyway.'

David's outside, demanding a photo. More and more cars pull into the driveway, the final school run. The tearing of envelopes and rustling of paper is accompanied by squeals and screams of excitement, and my mantra begins.

'What did you get?'

'Three A-stars and an A.'

'You don't seem very excited.'

'I'm dazed.'

'Yeah, I know what you mean.'

Yasmin is standing quietly by the noticeboard with her dad and new step-mum. I go across.

'Are you pleased?' she asks.

'Yes. Are you?'

'Yes.'

'What did you get?'

'Six A-stars.'

All three of them smile at my gobsmacked expression.

'I didn't know you were taking six subjects.'

'I did Arabic and Farsi privately.'

'You must be the school's ace pupil.'

'No question,' says Mr Abbasi. 'But can we get our photograph in the paper? I doubt it somehow.'

'Ask David to fix it. He's good at that.'

Mr Abbasi observes David's antics through the floor to ceiling window with some distaste. Yasmin doesn't say a word. If I hadn't sat just behind her in Physics, my A could easily have been a B, yet she seems to have day-dreamed her way to six top grades. Bel was right. She must be able to see the multiverse.

'I just got a text from Bel,' she says. 'She got into Cambridge to do Medicine.'

'What did she get?' demands Mr Abbasi.

'Two A-stars and two As.'

'Hm! She gets about half what you got, but she's going to Cambridge.'

'Dad, I don't want to go there.'

'I don't see why not.'

'Please, Dad. Not now.'

'Where are you going?' I ask.

'Imperial.' She smiles at the prospect. 'Right by Hyde Park and the Albert Hall.'

'You could have gone to Imperial for your second degree, *after* Cambridge.'

'Or the other way round,' says Yasmin firmly.

Mr Abbasi shakes his head. 'It's not the same thing,' he sniffs, but doesn't explain.

Carl Rogers is hovering outside the Head's office. He sidles over.

'How'd you do?'

'Three A-stars and an A.'

'Well done. I thought you'd do all right.'

'And you?'

'Two Bs and a D.'

'Is that what you needed?'

'Yeah, Economics at Bournemouth.'

'Are you going to be a captain of industry?' asks Mr Abbasi.

'Yes, well, banking, probably.'

'Good for you. It's up to your generation to sort it out, you know.'

Carl looks bemused for a moment, but switches to the manner of a man-in-the-know.

'Talking about sorting it out...' He nods towards the Head's office. 'Looks like Matt's dad is demanding a full investigation.'

Yasmin and I are happy to let his impulse to gossip twist in the wind, but Yasmin' step-mum can't let it hang.

'An investigation into what?'

'Why Matt blew it. He scraped a B, two Cs and a D. The head and his dad made phone calls, but there's no chance of getting into Oxford with that. He'll struggle to get through Clearing with those grades.'

Rather than sorrow for a friend, I sense Carl's not-so-secret satisfaction.

My first reaction is 'Yeah, take that'. The ambition, the arrogance, the sense of entitlement have all collapsed like mud walls in a monsoon. But my second reaction is sadness and compassion. Who wouldn't crumble under the pressure of an ambitious father, who thinks that climbing the greasy pole of local politics is the result of talent and intelligence, not pretence, self-promotion and bluster.

'But why an investigation?' asks Mr Abbasi.

'Councillor Collier says the school must have failed to adjust its teaching to the new curriculum.' He purses his lips. 'But Matt had plenty of private tuition on top of the same classes we all had. So it can't have been that, can it?'

The spectacle of Matt's failure being picked over by his supposedly best friend is sickening. One slip, one show of human frailty and the vultures descend. The lobby suddenly feels claustrophobic.

'Let's get that photo,' I say to the Abbasis.

We march outside, leaving Carl on his own, hovering and no doubt itching to spread 'the news'.

'We need a photo,' I say to David. 'Quick, 'cos I'm working today.'

I know we won't get in the local paper, but Mr Abbasi offers to pay the photographer for jpegs that Yasmin will send on as attachments. Yasmin in the middle. A boy mountain on one side, and a tall skinny builder's labourer on the other.

Mr Carson catches me before I can break free and make off up the drive.

'Bran. Well done. I take back everything I ever said about you.'

'What did you say?' demands David.

'Not now, Mr Jones.' Carson smiles indulgently. The Abbasis are still within earshot. 'You should come in one day and chat about applying to university. You can go to a Russell Group university with those grades. I'm sure the Head will give you an excellent reference.'

'No need, Mr Carson. These grades mean I've got a tennis scholarship to Princeton.'

'You're off to the USA?' says Mrs Abbasi, showing some interest.

'Yes.'

'And who supplied your references?' frowns Mr Carson.

'Oh, I believe all information about references is confidential. Sorry, got to run.'

I jog up the drive and climb into Grandad's old banger.

'Orright?'

'Yeah, fine.'

'America, is it?'

'Yep.'

'Good lad.'

Part Ten

Crossing the Pond

Alternative ending number 1
Trans-Pacific

Life is about the choices you make, even when you think you have few or none at all.

In the run-up to my first Spring Break I have far too many choices. The professor liked my presentation on the medieval castles of the Peloponnese and wonders if I'd like to sign up for some extra classes in Latin and Greek. There are several txts from David asking if I'd like to visit him in Wales and watch him play rugby. There's even a message from Yasmin to say that some friends are getting together to support David and 'do you want to join us?'.

A fellow tennis scholar wants me to travel home with him to California and celebrate Spring Break on the beach.

Mum hopes I'm working hard, eating properly and wonders if I'm coming home, but warns me that she and Zelda have a string of pottery fairs to attend, including one in Europe.

Finally, Dad suggests I visit him, my new family and old friends in New Zealand. He reckons I could pay for the trip by hustling middle-aged businessmen at the prestigious tennis club he's joined.

'In their dreams they could have been Roger Federer or Rafa Nadal, and they love to play for money, the suckers. Give 'em a game or two, then clean up.'

It sounds like fun, but there's also this girl I've met. It's nothing serious, but she comes from upstate New York and plays fourth-string tennis for Princeton. She's not that good to be honest and plays mainly for social reasons. But she does attend the coaching sessions run by the tennis scholars. It gives me coaching experience and a break from the intensity of team matches. I met her parents last week and they invited me to stay. They've got a big property with woods and fields and Lauren's mother is a fanatical horse rider. I've been promised horse riding lessons in exchange for tennis coaching. I guess this is what Phil meant when he said tennis can open doors and help you build a life without having to slog around the pro circuit. So far it's been great for my college experience and social life.

So what will I choose? The paper on the castles of the Peloponnese was fun and I appreciated the mark I got from the professor. But the idea of giving up Spring Break to take *extra* classes in two dead languages is a bit optimistic on his part. Those may have been his choices, but he knows I'm a tennis jock and need fresh air from time to time.

I'd love to see David play in a top-flight match – he is my half-brother after all and making fantastic progress – but rugby isn't a major interest these days. Besides, Spring Break is only a week. Two days flying back and forth. A day to travel into Wales and back, then a week recovering from all the sitting down in cramped seats, not to mention the jetlag and carbon footprint.

The same applies to visiting Mum. She might not be at home. Even if she is, it'll mean hanging out with Zelda. She might get me wedging and kneading clay: this time for nothing. While hearing about Bel and whichever Cambridge toff she's dating. I heard about how Bel was the only first year medical student at her college who needed a loan to pay the tuition fees. There'll be rich pickings and good luck to her.

At least she didn't get together with Zak Weidenbaum. I didn't believe David's theory, but he was right after all.

'The lad's gay.'

'Don't be daft. He's just American. They're more demonstrative than Brits.'

'Sometimes I think youse blind, man.'

'What about youse? Do you think Bel's blind too?'

'She knows he's gay. That's the point, dumbo.'

He was all right, Zak Weidenbaum. A pity I didn't get to know him better. I wish I'd been there to witness the famous scene at the Colliers' post-prom party hosted at *Gino's*. David and Zak crashing their 'do'. David being loud and objectionable. Zak singing 'La Donne e Mobile' badly for the benefit of Gino, only to discover that the place was run by Rumanians and staffed by Albanians. David stumbling against a table laden with food and crockery and sending it crashing to the floor. Councillor Collier losing his cool and threatening to summon the police. Zak writing a cheque for two thousand pounds to cover the whole gig.

'If it's a little over the top, give your staff a nice tip.'

He made out and handed the cheque to 'Gino', not Councillor Collier.

Yeah, I'm sorry I wasn't there to see that.

Taking cash off Dad's new tennis mates in Auckland sounds like fun, but that's a lot of travel in just one week. I'll postpone that until the long vacation. Who knows? I might be travelling with a girlfriend by then. Lauren's a huge fan of 'The Lord of the Rings' films, especially the scenes shot in New Zealand. She's been dropping huge hints about how she'd *lurve* to go there. And there's nothing ironic about her lurve. She's a straight-down-the-line sort of girl.

I know Dad wants me to join him in the car trade. Having someone he can trust setting up an electric car franchise in America would be a big boost for the business. And Lauren's a material girl. She wouldn't mind the prestige cars and the trans-Pacific lifestyle.

So, it looks like upper-state New York for Spring Break. I'd better message everybody and let them know. I'm sure they'll understand. Life moves on. People move on. You have to play the percentages in this world. Passions and dreams are all very well when you're a teenager, but we all have to grow up sometime.

Alternative ending number 2
Transatlantic

I consult my ticket. Principality Stadium. East Stand, middle tier. Row A, seat 18. I squeeze past a row of supporters singing 'Men of Harlech', then spot a familiar face alone in a small island of empty seats.

'Mr Edwards.'

'Bran! Lovely to see you. And many thanks for the postcards.'

'Don't mention it. It was fun choosing them. Thanks for organising this.'

He looks surprised. 'It wasn't me. It was Yasmin.'

'Yasmin?'

He gives me a quizzical look. 'They'll be here any minute. Tell me what you're up to, before we can no longer hear ourselves think.'

'I came over to meet an academic at Oxford. He's an expert on medieval castles in mainland Greece. I might study them as a special subject in my final year.'

'Good for you. Do you know Kevin Andrews's book?'

'I'm trying to get a copy, but they're rare and expensive.'

'I'll lend you mine. Fascinating man, Andrews. You know his father was the first celebrity archaeologist? The inspiration for Spielberg's "Indiana Jones".'

'I didn't know that.'

'A complex man. I've got one or two other books by him, if you're interested. What else?'

'I'll be taking an extra course in ceramic petrography next semester, and I'll begin courses in Latin and Ancient Greek in the semester after that. And I'm getting private instruction in using UAVs for finding and mapping archaeological sites.'

'UAVs?'

'Drones. Unmanned Aerial Vehicles.'

'VUTs. Very Useful Things. But expensive.'

'Bill Kelleher's paying for it. I refused the sports car he offered, so I'm getting drone flying lessons instead.'

'Good idea. Widening your options.'

'And I'm joining a Princeton dig in Cyprus this summer. For the practical experience.'

'Excellent. Make the most of it.' He glances over my shoulder. 'Here they are.'

Yasmin is edging down the row, followed by her parents, Amjad and Nashva Abbasi. Sian Jones brings up the rear, but slowly, stopping every few seats for a spot of banter with supporters. She barrels past the Abbasis to get to me.

'Look at you! Come and get a cwtch!'

Which is like being buried in perfumed sofa cushions during a minor earthquake.

'David's thrilled you came.'

'Wouldn't miss it for anything.'

'Your mam sends her love, and you're not to worry.' She leans in confidentially. 'Love 'er, she's doing just fine, what with all the pottery and stuff.'

This is reassuring, though the 'stuff' might be cause for concern.

'Sian, I think your seat is *that* one.'

Mr Abbasi wants to sit down.

'All right, Amjad. Don't get your knickers in a twist.'

She rolls her eyes, pulls a bored-girl face, but squeezes past to the seat beyond Mr Edwards.

Mr Abbasi starts to sit down next to me.

'No, baba, that's not your seat,' says Yasmin.

He pulls away, leaving an empty seat to my right.

'I got us some of these.' Sian passes song sheets down the row.

'But these are all religious songs,' says Mr Abbasi. 'Guide me, O Thou Great Redeemer. All Through the Night. Delilah.'

'That's the next one. You all have to sing, otherwise it's not an occasion.'

Amjad Abbasi looks at me despairingly. 'It took me years to be able to sing the British national anthem and mean it. Now I'm going to have to learn the Welsh one as well.'

He still doesn't get 'Delilah', even though he makes a good fist of singing along.

'That is the most peculiar song of devotion I've ever heard.'

Yasmin sits on the far side of her parents wearing an attentive but distant smile. Amjad and Nashva Abbasi look like dutiful attendees at an event they neither understand nor approve, though Mr Edwards is getting on like a house on fire with Sian Jones.

'My grandmother was Welsh, you know.'

'Well, why aren't you wearing the colours? I've got a spare hat in my bag.'

'I'm not sure a Welsh Ladies hat would suit me.'

'It's not one of those. It's a daffodil hat. See?'

'Are you going to wear one?'

' 'Course I am! Couldn't do without my daff now, could I?'

'Well, maybe I could borrow a scarf.'

'Go on, have the hat.'

'But if we get on TV, my wife might think we're a pair.'

'A right pair, you mean. Oh, come on, I'm sure she's got a sense of humour. Whoever saw a single daffodil all on its own?'

I'm about to ask Amjad who's supposed to be occupying the spare seat, when I see her squeezing down the row past the swaying supporters. A big hug for Yasmin, Nashva and Amjad.

She looks past me.

'Hello, Mr Edwards. Hello, Sian.'

'Oh, love 'er. Look at you, all growed up!'

She takes her seat and finally turns to me.

'Hello, Bran.'

'Hello, Bel.'

The same big blue eyes, the same kind but candid smile.

'How are you?' she asks.

'I'm fine. How are you? Didn't expect to see you here.'

'No, well, you have to support your friends. Yasmin asked me, so...'

So it was the most natural thing in the world to say yes.

The crowd's getting pumped up and it's hard to hear.

She leans in. 'What?'

'I said, how come Yasmin's organising tickets to watch David?'

She looks puzzled. 'Are you serious?'

'Yeah, I mean... '

She starts to laugh. 'You really are very unobservant sometimes.'

This again.

'Yasmin and David are together. Have been for years.'

My stunned expression makes her laugh even louder and she leans across the Abbasis towards Yasmin. I can't hear what she says, but Yasmin leans back towards me.

'Oh, yes,' she says in a matter-of-fact tone, 'it's always been David.'

Mr Abbasi raises his eyebrows at me. 'I'm with you. I've *never* understood it.'

I try re-running scenes on Callum's school bus, searching for evidence. Maybe. Maybe. But, surely, no *hard* evidence.

'You can't blame me,' I say to Bel. 'Yasmin's an enigma.'

'Only to certain people.'

Here we go again, unless I change the subject.

'How's Cambridge? How's it going with Medicine?'

'Cambridge is OK. Full of people who are far more privileged than they imagine, but aren't always as clever as they think. And I've given up Medicine.'

'You have? Too difficult?'

She's mildly offended by this. 'No. Just not my thing. I've switched to English.'

'You have to pursue your passion, right?'

'Pretty much.'

At last we have agreement.

'And how about you? How's the tennis?'

'Not bad. Won some, lost some. No draws, though.'

She gets the joke with an understated gesture.

'But I'm dropping the tennis. They've let me transfer to an archaeology scholarship.'

'Following your passion?'

'Yep.'

'It does feel right, doesn't it? I've told my mother I'll be too poor to keep her in luxury later on, but she says she doesn't mind. All she needs is an old caravan at the bottom of the garden.'

'Garden? Is she mad? Our generation can't afford houses with gardens.'

She laughs. 'I'm going to help her build a new kiln in your mum's garden this summer.'

'Is Zelda expanding the pottery?'

'No… well, yes… sort of. Didn't you know? Your mum's started to make pots. Raku fired. Mum's helping her get started.'

'You'd better make it foolproof or she'll set the garden ablaze and most likely the house as well.'

'Then maybe you should help out. Make sure we do it right.'

'Maybe I should.'

'And you can check out the potter guy my mum introduced her to. Y'know, make sure you approve.'

She's teasing now.

'Yeah, very important I do that.'

We both know my opinion would make no difference.

'Unless you've got other plans.'

'I'm walking the Peloponnese for a month looking at castles.'

'Walking?'

'Yeah, I'm still uteless. But you see more, meet more people, learn more Greek if you walk. Then I'm off to Cyprus on a dig.'

'Sounds great.'

There's something in her look and tone that lures me into asking a really stupid question.

'Wanna come?'

There's not a heartbeat's hesitation.

'I'd love to.'

There's no point carrying this conversation any further because the roar of the crowd behind almost knocks us forward in our seats. The Welsh boys are striding onto the pitch. I look for David but can't see him.

'Which one?'

Bel points.

'Number three!'

There's a 3 at the back of the line, but that mass of wavy hair almost halfway down his back and partially obscuring name and number surely can't belong to David Jones. He was a boy mountain a year ago. Now the mountain has become a man, and is probably still growing.

Bel leans towards me. 'Do you wish you were doing this?'

I look back at the pitch as the players turn to face the crowd for the anthems.

'Are you crazy? Look at the size of 'em!'

So, it's decided. I'll help Bel and our mothers – and maybe some dodgy potter bloke – to build a kiln in my mum's back garden. Then Bel will walk the Peloponnese with me, sleeping in a small tent under the olive trees, or wrapped in a shepherd's flokati on the beach. She might even come to Cyprus, if I don't mind her lounging around all day in the shade, reading novels and writing poetry.

I didn't know she still wrote poetry. I think we might have trouble making a living, let alone looking after our mothers. There's not much money in poetry or studies of medieval castles. Maybe David and Yasmin will let us live over their pool house when we get old.

Excavation

My boy, my man, my love
was stung on the heel
by a scorpion.

The others wanted to kill it,
but he said, poor thing,
it had no choice.

It's fighting a private battle
none of us will ever know.
So be kind.

They've been here longer than us,
generation after generation
on this barren hillside

guarding the old clay pots
they call home, defending
the little they know.

So the scorpion scuttled away
to sting another day
as I checked the colours

of arachnid and poisoned leg.
One alive and lucky
it had met my boy,

one swelling and rested
in the sky-sifting shade
of an ancient olive tree.

Both of us found and freed
from our hidden places,
side by side in sunlight.

Glossary

The list includes words and expressions used in context in this novel. They are common in New Zealand, Australia, the UK and the USA. Some words will have different meanings in other contexts.

A

a few sammies short of a picnic – not quite right in the head, not very bright (**sammie** – sandwich)
Albion – England
A-levels – Advanced Level exams usually taken at the end of Year 12 or 13 in the UK.
alkie – alcoholic
ankle-biter – young child, toddler
Anzac and Afghan cookies - popular biscuits in New Zealand

B

back row – players wearing numbers 6, 7 and 8 in rugby union.
bats – crazy
beanie – woollen hat
big ask – difficult task or job
blank someone – ignore someone, pretend they are not there
blatherskite – gossip (a person who gossips)
blether – gossip
bludge off someone – take money from someone without paying back
bonhomania – another of Bran's made up words. He means bonhomie – cheerful friendliness
bonzo – crazy person
boozer – heavy drinker (of alcohol)
bottle it – lack the courage to do something
box of budgies – a cheerful person
brill – short for brilliant
brunch – a meal between the usual times for breakfast and lunch

bunk off – leave school without permission

C

carks it – dies
chav – uneducated, unsophisticated person
cheeking – being cheeky to somebody
cheesy – sentimental, poor quality
chopper – helicopter
chuck a sickie – pretend to be sick to miss school or work
chugger – old car in poor condition
cinch – something that's easy
cost a bundle – cost a lot of money
crack someone up – make someone laugh
crack up – laugh uncontrollably
creed – belief system, religion
cwtch – the Welsh word for a cuddle, hug

D

dabbed on – added
daft as a two-bob watch – not making any sense (like a cheap watch that doesn't work properly)
dig – criticism
dimbo – dim, stupid person
doddle – something that's easy
dodgy – unreliable, badly made, dishonest, dangerous, borderline criminal
dolly – a weak shot in a ball game
dorm – dormitory, where a number of people sleep
dosh – money
drop kick – a half volley method of kicking a ball by letting it hit the ground before kicking
dumpster – skip
dumpster diver – a person who steals from skips

E

earwigging – listening to others' conversations

F

fishy – suspicious
flak – criticism
floordrobe – a pile of clothes on the floor instead of in a wardrobe
Friday night pizza – a pool of sick on the street
front five – rugby forwards in the first two rows of a rugby pack
full of himself – overconfident
fussed – angry

G

gabby – talkative, gossipy, indiscreet
Garryowen – a high kick in rugby, named after the club and town in Ireland where it was first used as a tactic. (Notice that Belinda thinks it is named after a person called Gary Owen).
GCSEs – General Certificate of Secondary Education exams usually taken at the end of Year 11 in UK schools.
gazump – get what you want by offering an amount of money that is higher than your rival's offer.
get uppity – become aggressive
give it heaps – try hard, make an effort
glottal stop – a 't' not pronounced in speech
granny flat – a small part of a house or property set aside for use by an elderly family member
grumpy – annoyed

H

H – the shape of rugby posts
haka – traditional Maori dance
hard yakka – difficult walking over a long distance
hoity-toity – posh, upper class

hooker – the rugby forward who hooks the ball back in a scrum

I

ICT – Information Communications Technology
IMHO – in my humble opinion
intimation – a hint, suggestion (another misuse of a word by Bran when he meant intuition – understanding)

J

jandal – a sandal (known as a thong in Australia); **give it some jandal** – make an effort to do something (UK expression: give it some wellie)
josh – joke

K

keep tabs on – be aware of, keep control over
kerfuffle – a fuss, disturbance
King's – King's College, a well-known independent school in New Zealand
knockers - people who criticise or sneer. Also slang for female breasts.

L

L&P – a soft drink made in New Zealand
Lindisfarne – Lindisfarne College, a well-known independent school in New Zealand
lit out – set off at speed

M

mo' – moment
moonball – a ball hit high and softly in tennis
multiverse – multiple universes which may exist alongside ours

N

necking – drinking
nifty – good, skilful
niggle – annoy, irritate
nobble – injure
nosh – food

O

oik – ignorant, unsophisticated person
once-over – a look or glance

P

pack – group of eight forwards in a rugby team
pack a sad - look or become sad or upset, sulk
pill – ball
Po Atarau – 'This is the hour', a famous song of farewell in New Zealand.
Polynesian Festival (Polyfest) – an annual festival of Polynesian culture
Pom – an English person (NZ and Australian slang)
Pommie – English
Pomsville – England
prezzie (also **pressie**) – present, gift
punt – a high kick (like one made by a goalkeeper in football)

Q

q-fest – a series of questions
quid – pound (money)

R

recon job – reconditioning to make a car almost like new
Richie McCaw – one of the most famous and successful New Zealand rugby players
Ridgeway – an ancient pathway on a high ridge west of London

riff raff – people of low social status
right pair – pair of fools
roll of bull's wool – a lot of nonsense
ropey – poor quality
ruck – a situation where rugby players compete for the ball
ruckers – rugby players involved in a ruck
Ruman Heights – Bran is drunk and means Human Rights

S

sammies – sandwiches
Second Six – second-string or B-team of six players
self-depredation – does not exist. Bran means self-deprecation or being humble. Depredation means an act of attacking, robbery or destruction.
shear – cut
Shear Delight – a play on words using shear and sheer.
sheer – pure, total
shtum – quiet
(sic) – from Latin meaning 'thus it was written'. Used to show that what is written is inaccurate, mistaken or spelled incorrectly.
skip – a very large metal container placed in the street for rubbish
skipper – person who steals from skips
skipping – stealing from skips
skive off – avoid work or school
slag off – criticise
smart-Alec – (adj) clever **A smart-Alec** – a person who tries to be clever
snitch – tell tales that can get others into trouble
souped up – (usually said of car engines) highly tuned for maximum performance
spat – argument
spits the dummy – gets really upset
sticks and stones – from the saying: "Sticks and stones can break my bones, but names can never hurt me."

stone – unit of weight (1 stone = 6.35 kilos)
stunner – something that is very surprising
suss – work out, understand
sustrans – countryside route for walkers and bikers
swot – study hard

T
tad – a little, a bit
take a flyer – make a guess
tat – cheap, low-quality items
throw – transform soft clay into a pot shape on a potter's wheel
tinnie – car made of poor, cheap materials
tinnie – tin or can of beer
togs – swimming costume
tramp – a long walk, hike, trek
trek – a long walk, hike
tux – tuxedo, formal suit for a man
twig – notice

U
uni – university
ute – utility vehicle, small truck with low sides

W
wally – fool
wangle – get (by persuading somebody else to give or help)
weekly boarder – a school pupil who boards at school from Monday morning to Friday afternoon but spends weekends at home.
What's his beef? – What's his problem?
wheels – car or other vehicle
whinge – a complaint, to complain
Woop Woop – a remote, distant, uncivilised place
wussed it – failed to finish a job

Y

yak – chat, gossip
yakker – person who likes to chat, gossip
yakking – talking, chatting, conversing informally, gossiping
yakka - work
yokel – peasant, uneducated person

Lightning Source UK Ltd.
Milton Keynes UK
UKHW012209280820
368997UK00004B/53/J

9 781916 084308